MOBY-DICK; OR, THE WHALE

SELECTIONS

MOBY-DICK; OR, THE WHALE

SELECTIONS

Herman Melville

a *Broadview Anthology of American Literature* edition

Contributing Editors, *Moby-Dick; or the Whale: Selections*:
Nora Ruddock and Maxwell Uphaus

General Editors, *The Broadview Anthology of American Literature*:

Derrick R. Spires, Cornell University
Rachel Greenwald Smith, Saint Louis University
Christina Roberts, Seattle University
Joseph Rezek, Boston University
Justine S. Murison, University of Illinois, Urbana-Champaign
Laura L. Mielke, University of Kansas
Christopher Looby, University of California, Los Angeles
Rodrigo Lazo, University of California, Irvine
Alisha Knight, Washington College
Hsuan L. Hsu, University of California, Davis
Michael Everton, Simon Fraser University
Christine Bold, University of Guelph

broadview press

BROADVIEW PRESS – www.broadviewpress.com
Peterborough, Ontario, Canada

Founded in 1985, Broadview Press remains a wholly independent publishing house. Broadview's focus is on academic publishing: our titles are accessible to university and college students as well as scholars and general readers. With over 800 titles in print, Broadview has become a leading international publisher in the humanities, with world-wide distribution. Broadview is committed to environmentally responsible publishing and fair business practices.

Library and Archives Canada Cataloguing in Publication

Title: Moby-Dick, or, The whale : selections / Herman Melville ; contributing editors, Moby-Dick, or, The whale: selections: Nora Ruddock and Maxwell Uphaus.
Other titles: Moby Dick. Selections (Broadview Press) | Whale
Names: Melville, Herman, 1819-1891, author. | Ruddock, Nora, 1978- editor. | Uphaus, Maxwell, editor.
Description: Series statement: A Broadview anthology of American literature edition. | Includes bibliographical references.
Identifiers: Canadiana (print) 20230449468 | Canadiana (ebook) 20230449646 | ISBN 9781554816323 (softcover) | ISBN 9781770489042 (PDF) | ISBN 9781460408360 (EPUB)
Subjects: LCSH: Melville, Herman, 1819-1891—Criticism and interpretation. | LCSH: American fiction—19th century—History and criticism. | LCGFT: Fiction.
Classification: LCC PS2384 .M62 2023 | DDC 813/.3—dc233

Broadview Press handles its own distribution in North America:
PO Box 1243, Peterborough, Ontario K9J 7H5, Canada
555 Riverwalk Parkway, Tonawanda, NY 14150, USA
Tel: (705) 743-8990; Fax: (705) 743-8353
email: customerservice@broadviewpress.com

For all territories outside of North America, distribution is handled by Eurospan Group.

Broadview Press acknowledges the financial support of the Government of Canada for our publishing activities.

Canada

Developmental Editors: Nora Ruddock, Max Uphaus
Cover Designer: Lisa Brawn
Typesetter: Alexandria Stuart

PRINTED IN CANADA

Contents

Introduction

Herman Melville
1819 – 1891

Herman Melville is widely acknowledged to be one of America's most significant literary figures, a formidable writer of the sea, and a strong voice for the quintessentially American ideals of democracy, freedom, and equality; he was also fierce in condemning the forces that impeded the fulfillment of those ideals. Though Melville died in relative obscurity, his novels and short fiction have become enduringly popular and highly acclaimed for their narrative power, philosophical depth, thematic richness, and stylistic innovation. One biographer wrote of *Moby-Dick* (1851) that it is "the most daring and prolonged aesthetic adventure that had ever been conducted in the hemisphere in the English language." A persistent and eloquent defender of those who suffer within hierarchical, patriarchal, and racist power structures, Melville wrote about the lives of sailors, enslaved people, office clerks, and factory workers, defying dominant ideologies of masculinity, capitalism, "whiteness," and colonialism.

Herman Melvill was born in 1819 to Allan Melvill and Maria Gansevoort Melvill (the "e" was added later). He was descended on both sides from prominent families: his paternal grandfather played a part in the Boston Tea Party, and his maternal grandfather, General Peter Gansevoort, was a Revolutionary War hero. The Melvill children were raised in Maria's Dutch Reformed Calvinist faith, with its emphasis on original sin, damnation, and predestination; while Melville came to reject this interpretation of Christianity, it had a profound effect on his imagination. Melville began his education in New York City, but when Allan Melvill's importing business failed, the family moved to Albany, where Herman was enrolled at Albany Academy. He was educated there only for a year, before he was withdrawn for financial reasons. When Herman was twelve, his father died after descending into madness, leaving the family in debt, and in 1832 the twelve-year-old Herman began work as a clerk in the New York State Bank. It was at this time that Maria added the "e" to the family name, perhaps in an effort to distance themselves from Allan Melvill's bankruptcy.

Over the next five years, Melville worked at his brother Gansevoort's fur store and attended the Albany Academy again. In 1837, he took up a teaching post near Pittsfield, and in 1838 enrolled at the Lansingburgh Academy to study engineering, but in the following year he changed course dramatically by signing up as a cabin boy on the merchant ship *St. Lawrence*, which sailed from New York to Liverpool and back. On his return, Melville took up teaching, first in Greenbush and then in Brunswick, New York. In 1840 he decided to go to sea again, this time aboard a whaling ship, the *Acushnet*, which sailed from New Bedford to the South Seas on 3 January 1841. After sailing for over a year, Melville jumped ship on 9 July 1842 with his friend Richard Tobias Greene at the Marquesas Islands, where he lived with the islanders of the Taipi Valley for four weeks before joining an Australian whaling crew aboard the *Lucy Ann*. He shortly afterwards went to shore in Tahiti, where he was imprisoned as a mutineer; after escaping in October 1842, he signed on with a Nantucket whaling ship, the *Charles and Henry*. Upon completing the cruise in 1843, Melville spent time in the Hawaiian Islands, where he worked various jobs, including as a pin setter in a bowling alley. Later that year, Melville enlisted in the United States Navy and sailed on a frigate, the *United States*, until 1844, when he landed in Boston and was discharged.

In 1846, Melville published *Typee*, an account of his time among the Marquesas islanders; the book was first printed in London and then in New York. This travel narrative, and its sequel, *Omoo*, which recounts Melville's adventures in Tahiti, were very popular in America and Britain, establishing the young Melville as a literary celebrity known for sultry, action-packed adventure stories. While successes, *Typee* and *Omoo* were also controversial: in both books, Melville attacked the Christian missionaries who sought to "civilize" the Indigenous peoples of the islands. While Melville's depiction of the islanders partook of the racial stereotypes of his day, he asserted very clearly that the barbarism of white people far exceeded any that could be found among the islanders: "the fiend-like skill we display in the invention of all manner of death-dealing engines, the vindictiveness with which we carry on our wars, and the misery and desolation that follow in their train, are enough of themselves to distinguish the white civilized man as the most ferocious animal on the face of the earth." Such statements proved provocative enough that the publishers of *Typee* chose to soften the book's comments on missionaries in the second printing.

Typee was dedicated to Lemuel Shaw, Chief Justice of the Massachusetts Supreme Court and father of Elizabeth Shaw, whom Melville married in 1847; the couple would in time have four children. Melville and Elizabeth settled first in New York City, and most of Melville's family moved in with them: his mother Maria, his four sisters, and his brother and sister-in-law. Melville's early fame brought him into the literary circle of the Duyckinck brothers in New York, from whose libraries Melville borrowed many books. He entered on a course of intense reading, which in turn exerted a profound influence over his future writing; in addition to the Old Testament prophets, he read Shakespeare with increasing wonderment, as well as Defoe, Milton, Rabelais, Swift, Mary Shelley, Byron, Montaigne, and Sir Thomas Browne.

In 1849, Melville turned from writing semi-autobiographical travel narratives to more inventive forms of fiction, as he felt an "invincible distaste" for facts and "a longing to plume my pinions for flight." Looking to engage a more sophisticated audience in addition to the "superficial skimmer of pages" whom he believed had enjoyed his earlier works, Melville's first fully fictional novel, *Mardi* (1849), shifted away from the realist mode to engage in a philosophical allegory that emphasizes the supreme importance of freedom and equality. The book sold poorly and was rejected by critics, and Melville responded by writing two more books in quick succession: *Redburn* in 1849 and *White-Jacket* in 1850. In a letter to his father-in-law, Melville wrote of these books that "they are two jobs, which I have done for money—being forced to it, as other men are to sawing wood." These two novels, which were in many ways a return to his earlier style, found a wide readership. After members of Congress read Melville's scathing denunciation of flogging in *White-Jacket*, as well as his depiction of the authoritarian, unequal conditions of naval life, they banned flogging on all American ships. *Redburn*, which delves into themes of sexuality, nationalism, and the place of refugees in antebellum society, has been receiving increased critical attention, with one scholar deeming it "one of the great nineteenth-century works about race and emigration."

In September 1850, Melville and his growing family moved out of New York City to Arrowhead, a farm in Pittsville, Massachusetts, which Melville bought with money borrowed from his father-in-law. While in the area earlier in the summer, Melville had met Nathaniel Hawthorne, and the two quickly became friends. In late August 1850, Melville published "Hawthorne and His Mosses" in the *Literary World* magazine, in which he praises Hawthorne's genius, as well as his originality, darkness, and Americanness: "the smell of your beeches and hemlocks is upon him; your own prairies are in his soul ... you will hear the far roar of his Niagara." Viewed as an early expression of the Young America movement, the essay argues for the excellence and potential of American writers, with Hawthorne as an exemplary figure "who breathe[s] that unshackled, democratic spirit of Christianity in all things."

Melville's friendship with Hawthorne, and Hawthorne's literary influence on Melville, came at a time of great creativity—he was in the process of writing *Moby-Dick*. His passionate letters to Hawthorne, as well as the frequent expression of homoerotic desire in his work, have led many to suppose the friendship between the two writers was a romantic one. If so, evidence for it is one-sided: while Melville was clearly passionately attached to Hawthorne, and while Hawthorne very much admired Melville and his work, only one letter from Hawthorne to Melville exists, and it is a request for Melville to pick up some mail. Though there is no clear biographical proof that Melville had sexual relationships with men, his work certainly celebrates homoerotic desire, linking it with, among other things, creativity and resistance to conventional power structures based on heterosexual norms. For this reason, Melville is frequently hailed as a trailblazer, one of the most significant early writers in the queer American literary tradition.

At Arrowhead during the winter of 1850–51, Melville worked on *Moby-Dick* from early in the morning through to the afternoon.

His sister Augusta would every day copy out the work from the day before, and she wrote in a letter that she found the book "very fine." After finishing the manuscript, Melville wrote to Hawthorne that "I have written a wicked book, and feel spotless as a lamb." Unfortunately, though British reviews contained favorable impressions of the novel, American critics at the time were unappreciative and overwhelmed, complaining that the book was too long, too mystical, and overwrought. A reviewer for *The New York Evangelist* wrote in 1851 that "oddity is the governing character [of *Moby-Dick*]" and that Melville "has reached the very limbo of eccentricity." In the wake of the public dismissal of both *Mardi* and *Moby-Dick*, Melville grew increasingly embittered with his readers and reviewers, but continued writing fiction, publishing the novel *Pierre; or, the Ambiguities* in 1852. Critics were even more bewildered by this novel, calling it "morbid and unhealthy...[like] a horrid fit of the night-mare." *Pierre* did not increase Melville's income or reputation, and neither did his final novel, *The Confidence-Man* (1857). Now considered a masterly, metafictional tour-de-force, *The Confidence-Man* confused Melville's contemporary readership, confirming critics in their opinion that Melville had not developed his potential. He himself knew he had; in a letter to Hawthorne he wrote: "Though I wrote the Gospels in this century, I should die in the gutter."

Between 1853 and 1855, Melville turned to a form of fiction that was, at that time, often more lucrative than novels by contributing short stories to *Putnam's Monthly*. Melville was a keen reader of periodicals, and he created works for *Putnam's* that reflected the influence of contemporary writers of short fiction, including Hawthorne, Edgar Allan Poe, and Charles Dickens. Melville continued, in these stories, to explore themes from his novels—the dehumanizing effects of capitalist, patriarchal social structures, the inhumanity of white supremacist attitudes, the mystery of the sea, and the draw of travel. He collected six of his stories and published them as *The Piazza Tales* (1856), including the now well-known tales *Benito Cereno*, "Bartleby, the Scrivener," and "The Encantadas." Reviews for the volume were quite positive, but sales were not, and this disappointment, when paired with the discouraging reception of *Mardi*, *Moby-Dick*, and *Pierre*, contributed to Melville's decision to stop writing fiction for the foreseeable future.

The ensuing decade in Melville's life was a dark one, and one that coincided with the national crisis of the Civil War. In 1856–57, he took a trip to Europe and the Middle East in an attempt to regain his spirits, but things did not improve, and he struggled to support his family on his return. In 1866 he took a job at the New York Custom House, a position he worked for nineteen years, earning four dollars a day. Melville's mental state deteriorated to a point where his wife Elizabeth nearly left him in 1867; that same year Melville's eldest son, Malcolm, died by suicide at the age of eighteen.

Melville did not stop writing, however; instead of fiction, he turned to poetry. *Battle-Pieces*, a collection of poems reflecting on the Civil War, was published in 1866; in an appendix, Melville urged the North to treat the South with mercy. His next work, *Clarel* (1876), was a seven-thousand-line poem inspired by his spiritual crisis and by his trip to the Middle East. *Clarel* was Melville's last publication during his lifetime. Two more books of poetry, *John Marr and Other Sailors* (1888) and *Timoleon* (1891), were printed in runs of twenty-five copies each and circulated privately. Melville's poetry has, until recently, been largely absent from accounts of American literary history, which long held Walt Whitman and Emily Dickinson to be the only great post-bellum nineteenth-century poets. The formal innovations of Melville's poems are being increasingly recognized, including their shift away from Romantic subjectivity, and scholars are integrating Melville's three decades of poetic output into a more nuanced history of nineteenth-century American poetry. In addition to another book of poems, *Weeds and Wildings Chiefly*, an unfinished novella, *Billy Budd*, was found in manuscript after Melville's death in 1891; it was not published until 1924. At once hailed as a masterpiece by Thomas Mann, among others, the story of the execution of the beautiful young sailor has taken its place alongside *Moby-Dick* as one of Melville's most critically acclaimed and often adapted works.

When Melville died, the *North American Review* printed a notice, which said that he "wrote out of his heart ... [but] his books are now but little read. When he died the other day ... men who could give you the names of fifty living poets and perhaps a hundred living American novelists owned that they had never heard of Herman Melville." The *New York Times* encapsulated Melville's obscurity when it printed a brief article in honor of his life entitled "The

Late Hiram Melville." It was not until the height of the Modernist movement in the 1920s that the so-called "Melville Revival" brought Melville's work, particularly *Moby-Dick*, into prominence. Raymond Weaver's *Herman Melville: Mariner and Mystic* (1921) launched the revival, and writers such as Virginia Woolf, D.H. Lawrence, and Lewis Mumford wrote essays highlighting Melville's formal and linguistic innovations. His influence on these writers, and on many writers that followed in the twentieth and twenty-first centuries, has been profound; poets such as W.H. Auden and Hart Crane have commemorated Melville in verse, and Ralph Ellison's groundbreaking novel *Invisible Man* (1952) creatively interprets aspects of *The Confidence-Man* and bears an epigraph drawn from *Benito Cereno*. Melville's reputation among readers and critics has only increased in the century that followed the Revival, but for a long time his fame was based almost solely on *Moby-Dick*, and to a lesser extent *Billy Budd*; it was not until the 1960s that critics and readers began engaging with the short fiction, and not until even more recently that his poetry has found an appreciative audience.

Twenty-first-century scholars have continued to explore the aesthetic, generic, and formal dimensions of Melville's work, and his fiction and poetry are essential to discourses in American literary studies on sexuality, transatlanticism, ecocriticism, and race, as well as to conversations around settler colonialism, imperialism, and the excesses of capitalism—his story "Bartleby, the Scrivener," for example, was an inspirational text for the Occupy Wall Street movement. As American literary studies move away from a nationalist approach and towards a more hemispheric one, Melville has taken on a more global identity—one anticipated, in the 1950s, by the Trinidadian anticolonial activist C.L.R. James's enthusiastic admiration for him. Melville's "ruthless democracy," as he himself called it, made him a voice for the displaced and oppressed; his unwavering commitment to depict the "meanest mariners, and renegades, and castaways" and "weave around them tragic graces" continues to forge connections with new generations of readers, who come to his allusive, complex texts again and again for their sheer linguistic power, but also for their unique ability to bring the reader to the outer edges of perception, where change becomes possible.

Moby-Dick; or, the Whale

During the Melville Revival of the 1920s, when critics and writers began to appreciate the depth and extent of Melville's literary contributions, the British poet and novelist D.H. Lawrence called him "the greatest seer and poet of the sea." That power is most acutely exemplified in *Moby-Dick*. This multifarious novel is, at its core, a tumultuous dramatic tragedy, a revenge narrative in which Captain Ahab, his crew, and the white whale, Moby Dick, fight to the death among the most sublime elements of nature: the sea, the sky, the human mind and heart, and the massive bodies of whales. Yet the novel contains far more than a story of passionate vengeance. The narrator, Ishmael, sets the revenge tragedy within the structure of his own quest narrative, and his friendship with the harpooner Queequeg, along with his philosophical musings, constitute vital threads of the novel; the stories and characters of the ship's crew—ranging from the high-ranking officers Starbuck, Flask, and Stubb to the humble black cabin boy Pip—constitute others; and interwoven through it all is the massive presence of the sperm whale: its physiology, habits, tendernesses, violences, and mystery. The central drama of the *Pequod* and the white whale is also set within the larger overarching drama of nineteenth-century whaling, and within the pages of the novel we find an unflinching depiction of its violence—of the bravery of the hunters, but also of their greed and cruelty. *Moby-Dick* contains not only a compelling plot told in the fieriest and most beautiful prose: it is a story fully embedded in its historical and scientific contexts, as well as a literary experiment of the most daring kind.

As literature courses across North America continue to be taught on the semester model, and as they typically aim to teach many texts in such a short time frame, a book as long and complex as *Moby-Dick* has often fallen off introductory course syllabi, despite its central place in the history of American literature. This edition aims to offer a judicious selection of chapters that will allow students to get caught up in the story, and also to get a fair sense of the range of Melville's thematic and stylistic innovations; readers will find herein the gripping action and interpersonal drama of *Moby-Dick*'s core plot, together with many examples of the scientific, philosophical, and metaphysical disquisitions and audacious literary experiments that this wide-ranging novel builds into itself. The intention of this edition is to offer a reliable, annotated teaching text to those instructors who do not have time to teach *Moby-Dick* in its entirety, but who want to introduce this essential novel to their students. As editors, we can only say that we sincerely hope that students encountering this selected edition will be inspired to read the full novel—and our conviction is that, once they are swept into the magic of this novel, for many students that will happen. In the meantime, a carefully chosen robust selection of *Moby-Dick* in the classroom is surely better than very little, or none at all.

Note on the Text

The text of *Moby-Dick* has been prepared while consulting the first American edition of *Moby-Dick*, the first British edition (*The Whale*), and the authoritative Northwestern-Newberry edition (1998). The *Broadview Anthology of American Literature*'s usual practices of modernization have not been followed in the case of *Moby-Dick*; spelling and punctuation from the original printings have been retained.

from *Moby-Dick, or The Whale*

Chapter 1. Loomings[1]

Call me Ishmael.[2] Some years ago—never mind how long precisely—having little or no money in my purse, and nothing particular to interest me on shore, I thought I would sail about a little and see the watery part of the world. It is a way I have of driving off the spleen,[3] and regulating the circulation. Whenever I find myself growing grim about the mouth; whenever it is a damp, drizzly November in my soul; whenever I find myself involuntarily pausing before coffin warehouses, and bringing up the rear of every funeral I meet; and especially whenever my hypos[4] get such an upper hand of me, that it requires a strong moral principle to prevent me from deliberately stepping into the street, and methodically knocking people's hats off—then, I account it high time to get to sea as soon as I can. This is my substitute for pistol and ball.[5] With a philosophical flourish Cato throws himself upon his sword;[6] I quietly take to the ship. There is nothing surprising in this. If they but knew it, almost all men in their degree, some time or other, cherish very nearly the same feelings towards the ocean with me.

---

1 *Loomings* Things that are coming into, or just lingering out of, sight.

2 *Ishmael* In the Book of Genesis, Ishmael is the first son of Abraham, born to his wife Sarah's handmaiden Hagar; when Hagar is pregnant, an angel comes to her and says: "Behold, thou art with child and shalt bear a son, and shalt call his name Ishmael … / And he will be a wild man; his hand will be against every man, and every man's hand against him; and he shall dwell in the presence of all his brethren" (Genesis 16.11–12). God promises Abraham that he would establish a "great nation" through Ishmael, even though his "covenant" would be established through Abraham and Sarah's son, Isaac. The biblical figure of Ishmael is also associated with exile, because Hagar and Ishmael were banished to the wilderness: "And God was with the lad; and he grew, and dwelt in the wilderness, and became an archer" (Genesis 21.20). Ishmael is traditionally considered the patriarch of the Arabic peoples and a forefather of Muhammad.

3 *spleen* Bad mood, ill temper; anger.

4 *hypos* Depression, anxiety; hypochondria.

5 *ball* Bullet.

6 *With a philosophical … sword* The Roman senator Marcus Porcius Cato, also known as Cato the Younger (95–46 BCE), a Stoic philosopher and opponent of Julius Caesar, died by suicide rather than live in a state under Caesar's domination.

There now is your insular city of the Manhattoes,[1] belted round by wharves as Indian isles by coral reefs—commerce surrounds it with her surf. Right and left, the streets take you waterward. Its extreme down-town is the Battery, where that noble mole[2] is washed by waves, and cooled by breezes, which a few hours previous were out of sight of land. Look at the crowds of water-gazers there.

Circumambulate the city of a dreamy Sabbath afternoon. Go from Corlears Hook to Coenties Slip, and from thence, by Whitehall,[3] northward. What do you see?—Posted like silent sentinels all around the town, stand thousands upon thousands of mortal men fixed in ocean reveries. Some leaning against the spiles;[4] some seated upon the pier-heads; some looking over the bulwarks[5] of ships from China; some high aloft in the rigging, as if striving to get a still better seaward peep. But these are all landsmen; of week days pent up in lath[6] and plaster—tied to counters, nailed to benches, clinched to desks. How then is this? Are the green fields gone? What do they here?

But look! here come more crowds, pacing straight for the water, and seemingly bound for a dive. Strange! Nothing will content them but the extremest limit of the land; loitering under the shady lee of yonder warehouses will not suffice. No. They must get just as nigh the water as they possibly can without falling in. And there they stand—miles of them—leagues. Inlanders all, they come from lanes and alleys, streets and avenues—north, east, south, and west. Yet here they all unite. Tell me, does the magnetic virtue of the needles of the compasses of all those ships attract them thither?

Once more. Say you are in the country; in some high land of lakes. Take almost any path you please, and ten to one it carries you down in a dale, and leaves you there by a pool in the stream. There

---

1 *Manhattoes* Name given by the Dutch colony of New Amsterdam to the southern tip of Manhattan island; the term came to be applied to the Wecquaesgeek people who used the island as a hunting ground.

2 *Battery* Park at the southern tip of Manhattan facing New York harbor and the Hudson river; *mole* Pier.

3 *Corlears Hook* Land that juts out into the East River in the Lower East Side of Manhattan; *Coenties Slip* Inlet in the East River in Lower Manhattan that was filled in 1835 and turned into a street; *Whitehall* Street in Lower Manhattan leading to the Battery; the area was named by British governor Peter Stuyvesant, who built a mansion at the southern tip.

4 *spiles* Large pieces of timber used to secure a foundation.

5 *bulwarks* Woodwork that, rising above the decks, surrounds the ship on all sides.

6 *lath* Thin strips of wood used to hold plaster.

is magic in it. Let the most absent-minded of men be plunged in his deepest reveries—stand that man on his legs, set his feet a-going, and he will infallibly lead you to water, if water there be in all that region. Should you ever be athirst in the great American desert,[1] try this experiment, if your caravan happen to be supplied with a metaphysical professor.[2] Yes, as every one knows, meditation and water are wedded for ever.

But here is an artist. He desires to paint you the dreamiest, shadiest, quietest, most enchanting bit of romantic landscape in all the valley of the Saco.[3] What is the chief element he employs? There stand his trees, each with a hollow trunk, as if a hermit and a crucifix were within; and here sleeps his meadow, and there sleep his cattle; and up from yonder cottage goes a sleepy smoke. Deep into distant woodlands winds a mazy way, reaching to overlapping spurs of mountains bathed in their hill-side blue. But though the picture lies thus tranced, and though this pine-tree shakes down its sighs like leaves upon this shepherd's head, yet all were vain, unless the shepherd's eye were fixed upon the magic stream before him. Go visit the Prairies in June, when for scores on scores of miles you wade knee-deep among Tiger-lilies—what is the one charm wanting?—Water—there is not a drop of water there! Were Niagara but a cataract of sand, would you travel your thousand miles to see it? Why did the poor poet of Tennessee, upon suddenly receiving two handfuls of silver, deliberate whether to buy him a coat, which he sadly needed, or invest his money in a pedestrian trip to Rockaway Beach?[4] Why is almost every robust healthy boy with a robust healthy soul in him, at some time or other crazy to go to sea? Why upon your first voyage as a passenger, did you yourself feel such a mystical vibration, when first told that you and

1 *great American desert* I.e., the Great Plains.

2 *metaphysical professor* One who is interested in and discusses transcendental ideas—phenomena lying outside the physical senses.

3 *Saco* River that flows from the White Mountains in New Hampshire to Saco Bay, Maine, where it joins the Atlantic ocean. In the 1850s the White Mountains, and the Saco river valley, were quintessential landscapes for the White Mountain artists of the early nineteenth century, including Benjamin Champney (1817–1907), who wrote that "the banks of the Saco were dotted all about with white umbrellas [sheltering painters] in great numbers." Melville goes on to describe some of the romanticized clichés common in nineteenth-century American landscape painting.

4 *poor poet of Tennessee* Unclear to whom this refers (likely not a historical reference); *Rockaway Beach* Beach and neighborhood in Queens, New York City.

your ship were now out of sight of land? Why did the old Persians hold the sea holy? Why did the Greeks give it a separate deity, and own brother of Jove?[1] Surely all this is not without meaning. And still deeper the meaning of that story of Narcissus, who because he could not grasp the tormenting, mild image he saw in the fountain, plunged into it and was drowned.[2] But that same image, we ourselves see in all rivers and oceans. It is the image of the ungraspable phantom of life; and this is the key to it all.

Now, when I say that I am in the habit of going to sea whenever I begin to grow hazy about the eyes, and begin to be over conscious of my lungs, I do not mean to have it inferred that I ever go to sea as a passenger. For to go as a passenger you must needs have a purse, and a purse is but a rag unless you have something in it. Besides, passengers get sea-sick—grow quarrelsome—don't sleep of nights—do not enjoy themselves much, as a general thing;—no, I never go as a passenger; nor, though I am something of a salt, do I ever go to sea as a Commodore,[3] or a Captain, or a Cook. I abandon the glory and distinction of such offices to those who like them. For my part, I abominate all honorable respectable toils, trials, and tribulations of every kind whatsoever. It is quite as much as I can do to take care of myself, without taking care of ships, barques, brigs, schooners,[4] and what not. And as for going as cook,—though I confess there is considerable glory in that, a cook being a sort of officer on ship-board—yet, somehow, I never fancied broiling fowls;—though once broiled, judiciously buttered, and judgmatically salted and peppered, there is no one who will speak more respectfully, not to say reverentially, of a broiled fowl than I will. It is out of the idolatrous dotings of the old Egyptians upon broiled ibis and roasted river horse,[5] that you see the mummies of those creatures in their huge bake-houses the pyramids.

---

1 *Greeks ... brother of Jove* In Greek mythology, Poseidon is god of the sea and brother to the sky-god Zeus (Jove to the Romans).

2 *Narcissus ... drowned* In Greek mythology, a beautiful young man named Narcissus fell in love with his own image reflected in a pool; unable to grasp the image, Narcissus (depending on the version of the myth) either wastes away from passion or falls into the image and drowns, turning into a flower (the narcissus, or daffodil).

3 *salt* Seasoned, experienced sailor; *Commodore* Naval officer ranking above a ship captain.

4 *barques* Small ships; *brigs* Square-rigged ships with two masts; *schooners* Small ship with three or four masts.

5 *river horse* Hippopotamus.

No, when I go to sea, I go as a simple sailor, right before the mast, plumb down into the forecastle, aloft there to the royal mast-head.[1] True, they rather order me about some, and make me jump from spar to spar, like a grasshopper in a May meadow. And at first, this sort of thing is unpleasant enough. It touches one's sense of honor, particularly if you come of an old established family in the land, the Van Rensselaers, or Randolphs, or Hardicanutes.[2] And more than all, if just previous to putting your hand into the tar-pot,[3] you have been lording it as a country schoolmaster, making the tallest boys stand in awe of you. The transition is a keen one, I assure you, from a schoolmaster to a sailor, and requires a strong decoction of Seneca and the Stoics[4] to enable you to grin and bear it. But even this wears off in time.

What of it, if some old hunks of a sea-captain orders me to get a broom and sweep down the decks? What does that indignity amount to—weighed, I mean, in the scales of the New Testament? Do you think the archangel Gabriel thinks anything the less of me, because I promptly and respectfully obey that old hunks in that particular instance? Who aint a slave? Tell me that. Well, then, however the old sea-captains may order me about—however they may thump and punch me about, I have the satisfaction of knowing that it is all right; that everybody else is one way or other served in much the same way—either in a physical or metaphysical point of view, that is; and so the universal thump is passed round, and all hands should rub each other's shoulder-blades, and be content.

Again, I always go to sea as a sailor, because they make a point of paying me for my trouble, whereas they never pay passengers a single penny that I ever heard of. On the contrary, passengers themselves

---

1 *forecastle* Front of the vessel. Ordinary sailors slept under the forecastle deck; *mast-head* Highest part of the mast, often supplied with a small platform for observation.

2 *Van Rensselaers* Prominent family among the earliest Dutch colonists in New York state; *Randolphs* Wealthy and influential political family that first settled in colonial Virginia in 1643; *Hardicanutes* Harthacnut was King of Denmark from 1035 to 1042 and King of England from 1040 to 1042.

3 *tar-pot* Tar was used on ships to preserve ropes, seal wood, and waterproof clothing; applying tar was a task that would fall to the lot of ordinary sailors.

4 *Seneca and the Stoics* Roman Stoic philosophers argued that the wise person would not succumb to negative emotions such as fear, envy, and excessive desire, and that only virtue would lead to sustained happiness. Seneca (c. 4 BCE–65 CE) was a Stoic philosopher and playwright.

must pay. And there is all the difference in the world between paying and being paid. The act of paying is perhaps the most uncomfortable infliction that the two orchard thieves entailed upon us.[1] But *being paid*,—what will compare with it? The urbane activity with which a man receives money is really marvellous, considering that we so earnestly believe money to be the root of all earthly ills, and that on no account can a monied man enter heaven.[2] Ah! how cheerfully we consign ourselves to perdition!

Finally, I always go to sea as a sailor, because of the wholesome exercise and pure air of the forecastle deck. For as in this world, head winds are far more prevalent than winds from astern (that is, if you never violate the Pythagorean maxim[3]), so for the most part the Commodore on the quarter-deck[4] gets his atmosphere at second hand from the sailors on the forecastle. He thinks he breathes it first; but not so. In much the same way do the commonalty lead their leaders in many other things, at the same time that the leaders little suspect it. But wherefore it was that after having repeatedly smelt the sea as a merchant sailor, I should now take it into my head to go on a whaling voyage; this the invisible police officer of the Fates,[5] who has the constant surveillance of me, and secretly dogs me, and influences me in some unaccountable way—he can better answer than any one else. And, doubtless, my going on this whaling voyage, formed part of the grand programme of Providence that was drawn up a long time ago. It came in as a sort of brief interlude and solo between more extensive performances. I take it that this part of the bill[6] must have run something like this:

---

1 *act of paying … upon us* The "two orchard thieves" were Adam and Eve, and the payment their theft entailed on humankind was sin and death. See Genesis 1–3.

2 *on no account … heaven* See Matthew 19.24, when Christ says, "And again I say unto you, It is easier for a camel to go through the eye of a needle, than for a rich man to enter into the kingdom of God."

3 *Pythagorean maxim* Greek philosopher Pythagoras (c. 570–495 BCE) and his followers did not eat beans.

4 *quarter-deck* Upper deck behind the mainmast, traditionally reserved for the captain or commodore.

5 *Fates* In Greek mythology, the fates were three sister-goddesses who wove the fortunes of each mortal life.

6 *bill* List of events in a theater program.

"*Grand Contested Election for the Presidency of the United States.*

"WHALING VOYAGE BY ONE ISHMAEL.

"BLOODY BATTLE IN AFFGHANISTAN."[1]

Though I cannot tell why it was exactly that those stage managers, the Fates, put me down for this shabby part of a whaling voyage, when others were set down for magnificent parts in high tragedies, and short and easy parts in genteel comedies, and jolly parts in farces—though I cannot tell why this was exactly; yet, now that I recall all the circumstances, I think I can see a little into the springs and motives which being cunningly presented to me under various disguises, induced me to set about performing the part I did, besides cajoling me into the delusion that it was a choice resulting from my own unbiased freewill and discriminating judgment.

Chief among these motives was the overwhelming idea of the great whale himself. Such a portentous and mysterious monster roused all my curiosity. Then the wild and distant seas where he rolled his island bulk; the undeliverable, nameless perils of the whale; these, with all the attending marvels of a thousand Patagonian[2] sights and sounds, helped to sway me to my wish. With other men, perhaps, such things would not have been inducements; but as for me, I am tormented with an everlasting itch for things remote. I love to sail forbidden seas, and land on barbarous coasts. Not ignoring what is good, I am quick to perceive a horror, and could still be social with it—would they let me—since it is but well to be on friendly terms with all the inmates of the place one lodges in.

By reason of these things, then, the whaling voyage was welcome; the great flood-gates of the wonder-world swung open, and in the wild conceits[3] that swayed me to my purpose, two and two there

---

1 *Contested Election ... United States* Likely a reference to the 1840 presidential election, which saw Whig candidate William Henry Harrison (1773–1841) defeat the incumbent Democratic President Martin Van Buren (1782–1862) by creating a wide coalition of support using innovative campaigning techniques; *BLOODY BATTLE IN AFFGHANISTAN* The first Anglo-Afghan War was fought between 1839 and 1842. The battle mentioned here might refer to the 1842 retreat from Kabul (also called the Massacre of Elphinstone's army), in which the British lost 4,500 soldiers and 12,000 civilians.

2 *Patagonian* Wild and remote—Patagonia is located on the southernmost tip of South America.

3 *conceits* Ideas, notions.

floated into my inmost soul, endless processions of the whale, and, midmost of them all, one grand hooded phantom, like a snow hill in the air.

[The narrator packs a bag and arrives at the Spouter-Inn, in New Bedford, Massachusetts, on his way to Nantucket.]

Chapter 3. The Spouter-Inn

Entering that gable-ended Spouter-Inn, you found yourself in a wide, low, straggling entry with old-fashioned wainscots,[1] reminding one of the bulwarks of some condemned old craft. On one side hung a very large oil-painting so thoroughly besmoked, and every way defaced, that in the unequal cross-lights by which you viewed it, it was only by diligent study and a series of systematic visits to it, and careful inquiry of the neighbors, that you could any way arrive at an understanding of its purpose. Such unaccountable masses of shades and shadows, that at first you almost thought some ambitious young artist, in the time of the New England hags,[2] had endeavored to delineate chaos bewitched. But by dint of much and earnest contemplation, and oft repeated ponderings, and especially by throwing open the little window towards the back of the entry, you at last come to the conclusion that such an idea, however wild, might not be altogether unwarranted.

But what most puzzled and confounded you was a long, limber, portentous, black mass of something hovering in the centre of the picture over three blue, dim, perpendicular lines floating in a nameless yeast. A boggy, soggy, squitchy picture truly, enough to drive a nervous man distracted. Yet was there a sort of indefinite, half-attained, unimaginable sublimity about it that fairly froze you to it, till you involuntarily took an oath with yourself to find out what that marvellous painting meant. Ever and anon a bright, but, alas, deceptive idea would dart you through.—It's the Black Sea in a midnight gale.—It's

---

1 *gable-ended* Both sides of a gable-ended building include triangular sections that extend from the eaves to the roof's ridge; *wainscots* Wood paneling covering the lower half of rooms.

2 *time of the New England hags* Period of the witch trials in Salem, Massachusetts (1692–93).

the unnatural combat of the four primal elements.—It's a blasted heath.[1]—It's a Hyperborean[2] winter scene.—It's the breaking-up of the icebound stream of Time. But at last all these fancies yielded to that one portentous something in the picture's midst. *That* once found out, and all the rest were plain. But stop; does it not bear a faint resemblance to a gigantic fish? even the great leviathan himself?

In fact, the artist's design seemed this: a final theory of my own, partly based upon the aggregated opinions of many aged persons with whom I conversed upon the subject. The picture represents a Cape-Horner[3] in a great hurricane; the half-foundered ship weltering there with its three dismantled masts alone visible; and an exasperated whale, purposing to spring clean over the craft, is in the enormous act of impaling himself upon the three mast-heads.

The opposite wall of this entry was hung all over with a heathenish array of monstrous clubs and spears. Some were thickly set with glittering teeth resembling ivory saws; others were tufted with knots of human hair; and one was sickle-shaped, with a vast handle sweeping round like the segment made in the new-mown grass by a long-armed mower. You shuddered as you gazed, and wondered what monstrous cannibal and savage could ever have gone a death-harvesting with such a hacking, horrifying implement. Mixed with these were rusty old whaling lances and harpoons, all broken and deformed. Some were storied weapons. With this once long lance, now wildly elbowed, fifty years ago did Nathan Swain[4] kill fifteen whales between a sunrise and a sunset. And that harpoon—so like a corkscrew now—was flung in Javan seas, and run away with by a whale, years afterwards slain off the Cape of Blanco.[5] The original iron entered nigh the tail, and, like a restless needle sojourning in the body of a man, travelled full forty feet, and at last was found imbedded in the hump.

---

1 *blasted heath* In Shakespeare's *Macbeth*, the three witches meet and confront Macbeth for the first time on a "blasted heath" (1.3.79).

2 *Hyperborean* Far-north, arctic.

3 *Cape-Horner* Large ship capable of navigating the rough and dangerous seas around Cape Horn, the southern-most tip of South America.

4 *elbowed* Bent at right angles; *Nathan Swain* Nathaniel Swain (1727–81) was from a well-known whaling family from Nantucket.

5 *Cape of Blanco* Cape Blanco is a headland in southwestern Oregon that juts out into the Pacific. Winds and reefs in the area make it perilous for ships.

Crossing this dusky entry, and on through yon low-arched way—cut through what in old times must have been a great central chimney with fireplaces all round—you enter the public room. A still duskier place is this, with such low ponderous beams above, and such old wrinkled planks beneath, that you would almost fancy you trod some old craft's cockpits,[1] especially of such a howling night, when this corner-anchored old ark rocked so furiously. On one side stood a long, low, shelf-like table covered with cracked glass cases, filled with dusty rarities gathered from this wide world's remotest nooks. Projecting from the further angle of the room stands a dark-looking den—the bar—a rude attempt at a right whale's head. Be that how it may, there stands the vast arched bone of the whale's jaw, so wide, a coach might almost drive beneath it. Within are shabby shelves, ranged round with old decanters, bottles, flasks; and in those jaws of swift destruction, like another cursed Jonah[2] (by which name indeed they called him), bustles a little withered old man, who, for their money, dearly sells the sailors deliriums and death.

Abominable are the tumblers into which he pours his poison. Though true cylinders without—within, the villanous green goggling glasses deceitfully tapered downwards to a cheating bottom.[3] Parallel meridians rudely pecked into the glass, surround these footpads'[4] goblets. Fill to *this* mark, and your charge is but a penny; to *this* a penny more; and so on to the full glass—the Cape Horn measure, which you may gulp down for a shilling.[5]

Upon entering the place I found a number of young seamen gathered about a table, examining by a dim light divers specimens of *skrimshander*.[6] I sought the landlord, and telling him I desired to be accommodated with a room, received for answer that his house

1 *cockpits* Sunken spaces where a ship's helm is placed; in war ships, the cockpit was an area where junior officers were quartered—including the ship's doctor—and where the wounded were tended.

2 *Jonah* Old Testament prophet who sought to run away from God by taking ship. He was swallowed by a whale, and, upon humbling himself to God and accepting his calling, was spat back up. See the Book of Jonah.

3 *cheating bottom* False bottomed—the glasses are designed to look bigger than they are.

4 *meridians* Lines; *footpads* Robbers who steal while on foot (rather than on horseback).

5 *measure* Drink (of a certain size); *shilling* British coin that continued in circulation in America into the nineteenth century; it was worth about twenty-four cents.

6 *divers* Various; *skrimshander* Small carvings made by sailors while on a journey, usually made out of ivory or bone (often whale teeth or bone).

was full—not a bed unoccupied. "But avast," he added, tapping his forehead, "you haint no objections to sharing a harpooneer's[1] blanket, have ye? I s'pose you are goin' a-whalin', so you'd better get used to that sort of thing."

I told him that I never liked to sleep two in a bed; that if I should ever do so, it would depend upon who the harpooneer might be, and that if he (the landlord) really had no other place for me, and the harpooneer was not decidedly objectionable, why rather than wander further about a strange town on so bitter a night, I would put up with the half of any decent man's blanket.

"I thought so. All right; take a seat. Supper?—you want supper? Supper'll be ready directly."

I sat down on an old wooden settle, carved all over like a bench on the Battery. At one end a ruminating tar[2] was still further adorning it with his jack-knife, stooping over and diligently working away at the space between his legs. He was trying his hand at a ship under full sail, but he didn't make much headway, I thought.

At last some four or five of us were summoned to our meal in an adjoining room. It was cold as Iceland—no fire at all—the landlord said he couldn't afford it. Nothing but two dismal tallow candles, each in a winding sheet.[3] We were fain to button up our monkey jackets,[4] and hold to our lips cups of scalding tea with our half frozen fingers. But the fare was of the most substantial kind—not only meat and potatoes, but dumplings; good heavens! dumplings for supper! One young fellow in a green box coat, addressed himself to[5] these dumplings in a most direful manner.

"My boy," said the landlord, "you'll have the nightmare to a dead sartainty."

---

1 *harpooneer* In whale boats, the harpooner was the one designated to throw the harpoon and initially spear the whale; successful harpooners were highly skilled and well-paid.

2 *tar* Sailor. See note 3, page 21.

3 *tallow candles ... in a winding sheet* Candles made of animal fat that have collected a mass of drippings, which have hardened along the side. These drippings, creased so they resemble a sheet, were considered an omen of disaster and death (the term "winding sheets" also refers to shrouds for wrapping the dead).

4 *monkey jackets* Coats that taper in the back and fit closely; they were commonly worn by sailors.

5 *box coat* Heavy coat traditionally worn by coachmen; *addressed himself to* I.e., started eating.

"Landlord," I whispered, "that aint the harpooneer, is it?"

"Oh, no," said he, looking a sort of diabolically funny, "the harpooneer is a dark complexioned chap. He never eats dumplings, he don't—he eats nothing but steaks, and likes 'em rare."

"The devil he does," says I. "Where is that harpooneer? Is he here?"

"He'll be here afore long," was the answer.

I could not help it, but I began to feel suspicious of this "dark complexioned" harpooneer. At any rate, I made up my mind that if it so turned out that we should sleep together, he must undress and get into bed before I did.

Supper over, the company went back to the bar-room, when, knowing not what else to do with myself, I resolved to spend the rest of the evening as a looker on.

Presently a rioting noise was heard without. Starting up, the landlord cried, "That's the Grampus's crew. I seed her reported in the offing[1] this morning; a four years' voyage, and a full ship. Hurrah, boys; now we'll have the latest news from the Feegees."

A tramping of sea boots was heard in the entry; the door was flung open, and in rolled a wild set of mariners enough. Enveloped in their shaggy watch coats, and with their heads muffled in woollen comforters, all bedarned[2] and ragged, and their beards stiff with icicles, they seemed an eruption of bears from Labrador. They had just landed from their boat, and this was the first house they entered. No wonder, then, that they made a straight wake[3] for the whale's mouth—the bar—when the wrinkled little old Jonah, there officiating, soon poured them out brimmers[4] all round. One complained of a bad cold in his head, upon which Jonah mixed him a pitch-like potion of gin and molasses, which he swore was a sovereign cure for all colds and catarrhs[5] whatsoever, never mind of how long standing, or whether caught off the coast of Labrador, or on the weather side[6] of an ice-island.

---

1 *offing* At a certain visible distance from shore (ships in the offing are approaching land but still outside of inshore hazards).

2 *watch coats* Heavy coats worn by sailors while on deck during their shifts of duty (called "watches"); *bedarned* Mended.

3 *wake* Track or path (usually refers to the track a ship leaves on the surface of the water).

4 *brimmers* Glasses full to the brim.

5 *catarrhs* Nasal congestions and watery eyes.

6 *weather side* Side receiving the wind and waves (the windward side).

The liquor soon mounted into their heads, as it generally does even with the arrantest topers[1] newly landed from sea, and they began capering about most obstreperously.

I observed, however, that one of them held somewhat aloof, and though he seemed desirous not to spoil the hilarity of his shipmates by his own sober face, yet upon the whole he refrained from making as much noise as the rest. This man interested me at once; and since the sea-gods had ordained that he should soon become my shipmate (though but a sleeping-partner[2] one, so far as this narrative is concerned), I will here venture upon a little description of him.

He stood full six feet in height, with noble shoulders, and a chest like a coffer-dam.[3] I have seldom seen such brawn in a man. His face was deeply brown and burnt, making his white teeth dazzling by the contrast; while in the deep shadows of his eyes floated some reminiscences that did not seem to give him much joy. His voice at once announced that he was a Southerner, and from his fine stature, I thought he must be one of those tall mountaineers from the Alleghanian Ridge in Virginia. When the revelry of his companions had mounted to its height, this man slipped away unobserved, and I saw no more of him till he became my comrade on the sea. In a few minutes, however, he was missed by his shipmates, and being, it seems, for some reason a huge favorite with them, they raised a cry of "Bulkington! Bulkington! where's Bulkington?" and darted out of the house in pursuit of him.

It was now about nine o'clock, and the room seeming almost supernaturally quiet after these orgies,[4] I began to congratulate myself upon a little plan that had occurred to me just previous to the entrance of the seamen.

No man prefers to sleep two in a bed. In fact, you would a good deal rather not sleep with your own brother. I don't know how it is, but people like to be private when they are sleeping. And when it comes to sleeping with an unknown stranger, in a strange inn, in a strange town, and that stranger a harpooneer, then your objections indefinitely multiply. Nor was there any earthly reason why I as a

---

1 *arrantest topers* Most notorious heavy drinkers.

2 *sleeping-partner* Silent business partner.

3 *coffer-dam* Watertight structure attached to a ship's side to allow for repairs underwater.

4 *orgies* In this context, loud singing, talking, excessive drinking.

sailor should sleep two in a bed, more than anybody else; for sailors no more sleep two in a bed at sea, than bachelor Kings do ashore. To be sure they all sleep together in one apartment, but you have your own hammock, and cover yourself with your own blanket, and sleep in your own skin.

The more I pondered over this harpooneer, the more I abominated the thought of sleeping with him. It was fair to presume that being a harpooneer, his linen or woollen, as the case might be, would not be of the tidiest, certainly none of the finest. I began to twitch all over. Besides, it was getting late, and any decent harpooneer ought to be home and going bedwards. Suppose now, he should tumble in upon me at midnight—how could I tell from what vile hole he had been coming?

"Landlord! I've changed my mind about that harpooneer.—I shan't sleep with him. I'll try the bench here."

"Just as you please; I'm sorry I can't spare ye a tablecloth for a mattress, and it's a plaguy rough board here"—feeling of the knots and notches. "But wait a bit, Skrimshander;[1] I've got a carpenter's plane there in the bar—wait, I say, and I'll make ye snug enough." So saying he procured the plane; and with his old silk handkerchief first dusting the bench, vigorously set to planing away at my bed, the while grinning like an ape. The shavings flew right and left; till at last the plane-iron came bump against an indestructible knot. The landlord was near spraining his wrist, and I told him for heaven's sake to quit—the bed was soft enough to suit me, and I did not know how all the planing in the world could make eider down of a pine plank. So gathering up the shavings with another grin, and throwing them into the great stove in the middle of the room, he went about his business, and left me in a brown study.[2]

I now took the measure of the bench, and found that it was a foot too short; but that could be mended with a chair. But it was a foot too narrow, and the other bench in the room was about four inches higher than the planed one—so there was no yoking them. I then placed the first bench lengthwise along the only clear space against the wall, leaving a little interval between, for my back to settle down

1 *Skrimshander* Someone who whittles small sculptures out of bone; a sailor (see note 6, page 26).

2 *brown study* State of gloomy thoughtfulness.

in. But I soon found that there came such a draught of cold air over me from under the sill of the window, that this plan would never do at all, especially as another current from the rickety door met the one from the window, and both together formed a series of small whirlwinds in the immediate vicinity of the spot where I had thought to spend the night.

The devil fetch that harpooneer, thought I, but stop, couldn't I steal a march on him—bolt his door inside, and jump into his bed, not to be wakened by the most violent knockings? It seemed no bad idea; but upon second thoughts I dismissed it. For who could tell but what the next morning, so soon as I popped out of the room, the harpooneer might be standing in the entry, all ready to knock me down!

Still, looking round me again, and seeing no possible chance of spending a sufferable night unless in some other person's bed, I began to think that after all I might be cherishing unwarrantable prejudices against this unknown harpooneer. Thinks I, I'll wait awhile; he must be dropping in before long. I'll have a good look at him then, and perhaps we may become jolly good bedfellows after all—there's no telling.

But though the other boarders kept coming in by ones, twos, and threes, and going to bed, yet no sign of my harpooneer.

"Landlord!" said I, "what sort of a chap is he—does he always keep such late hours?" It was now hard upon twelve o'clock.

The landlord chuckled again with his lean chuckle, and seemed to be mightily tickled at something beyond my comprehension. "No," he answered, "generally he's an airley bird—airley to bed and airley to rise—yes, he's the bird what catches the worm.—But to-night he went out a peddling, you see, and I don't see what on airth keeps him so late, unless, may be, he can't sell his head."

"Can't sell his head?—What sort of a bamboozingly story is this you are telling me?" getting into a towering rage. "Do you pretend to say, landlord, that this harpooneer is actually engaged this blessed Saturday night, or rather Sunday morning, in peddling his head around this town?"

"That's precisely it," said the landlord, "and I told him he couldn't sell it here, the market's overstocked."

"With what?" shouted I.

"With heads to be sure; ain't there too many heads in the world?"

"I tell you what it is, landlord," said I, quite calmly, "you'd better stop spinning that yarn to me—I'm not green."[1]

"May be not," taking out a stick and whittling a toothpick, "but I rayther guess you'll be done *brown*[2] if that ere harpooneer hears you a slanderin' his head."

"I'll break it for him," said I, now flying into a passion again at this unaccountable farrago[3] of the landlord's.

"It's broke a'ready," said he.

"Broke," said I—"*broke*, do you mean?"

"Sartain, and that's the very reason he can't sell it, I guess."

"Landlord," said I, going up to him as cool as Mt. Hecla[4] in a snow-storm—"landlord, stop whittling. You and I must understand one another, and that too without delay. I come to your house and want a bed; you tell me you can only give me half a one; that the other half belongs to a certain harpooneer. And about this harpooneer, whom I have not yet seen, you persist in telling me the most mystifying and exasperating stories, tending to beget in me an uncomfortable feeling towards the man whom you design for my bedfellow—a sort of connexion, landlord, which is an intimate and confidential one in the highest degree. I now demand of you to speak out and tell me who and what this harpooneer is, and whether I shall be in all respects safe to spend the night with him. And in the first place, you will be so good as to unsay that story about selling his head, which if true I take to be good evidence that this harpooneer is stark mad, and I've no idea of sleeping with a madman; and you, sir, *you* I mean, landlord, *you*, sir, by trying to induce me to do so knowingly, would thereby render yourself liable to a criminal prosecution."

"Wall," said the landlord, fetching a long breath, "that's a purty long sarmon for a chap that rips[5] a little now and then. But be easy, be easy, this here harpooneer I have been tellin' you of has just arrived from the south seas, where he bought up a lot of 'balmed[6] New Zea-

---

1 *green* Inexperienced, gullible.

2 *done brown* Roasted, but also taken in or fooled.

3 *farrago* Confusion.

4 *Mt. Hecla* Active volcano located in southern Iceland—it had erupted in 1845–46, several years before the publication of *Moby-Dick*.

5 *rips* Speaks strongly or angrily.

6 *'balmed* Embalmed, preserved from decay.

land heads (great curios, you know), and he's sold all on 'em but one, and that one he's trying to sell to-night, cause to-morrow's Sunday, and it would not do to be sellin' human heads about the streets when folks is goin' to churches. He wanted to, last Sunday, but I stopped him just as he was goin' out of the door with four heads strung on a string, for all the airth like a string of inions."

This account cleared up the otherwise unaccountable mystery, and showed that the landlord, after all, had had no idea of fooling me—but at the same time what could I think of a harpooneer who stayed out of a Saturday night clean into the holy Sabbath, engaged in such a cannibal business as selling the heads of dead idolators?

"Depend upon it, landlord, that harpooneer is a dangerous man."

"He pays reg'lar," was the rejoinder. "But come, it's getting dreadful late, you had better be turning flukes[1]—it's a nice bed: Sal and me slept in that ere bed the night we were spliced.[2] There's plenty of room for two to kick about in that bed; it's an almighty big bed that. Why, afore we give it up, Sal used to put our Sam and little Johnny in the foot of it. But I got a dreaming and sprawling about one night, and somehow, Sam got pitched on the floor, and came near breaking his arm. Arter that, Sal said it wouldn't do. Come along here, I'll give ye a glim[3] in a jiffy"; and so saying he lighted a candle and held it towards me, offering to lead the way. But I stood irresolute; when looking at a clock in the corner, he exclaimed "I vum[4] it's Sunday—you won't see that harpooneer to-night; he's come to anchor somewhere—come along then; *do* come; *won't* ye come?"

I considered the matter a moment, and then up stairs we went, and I was ushered into a small room, cold as a clam, and furnished, sure enough, with a prodigious bed, almost big enough indeed for any four harpooneers to sleep abreast.

"There," said the landlord, placing the candle on a crazy old sea chest that did double duty as a wash-stand and centre table; "there, make yourself comfortable now, and good night to ye." I turned round from eyeing the bed, but he had disappeared.

---

1 *turning flukes* Turn in, go to bed (flukes are the two halves of the whale's tail; when a whale "turns flukes," it heads down into the sea, with the tail being the last part of its body visible).

2 *spliced* Married.

3 *glim* Light.

4 *vum* Vow.

Folding back the counterpane,[1] I stooped over the bed. Though none of the most elegant, it yet stood the scrutiny tolerably well. I then glanced round the room; and besides the bedstead and centre table, could see no other furniture belonging to the place, but a rude shelf, the four walls, and a papered fireboard[2] representing a man striking a whale. Of things not properly belonging to the room, there was a hammock lashed up, and thrown upon the floor in one corner; also a large seaman's bag, containing the harpooneer's wardrobe, no doubt in lieu of a land trunk. Likewise, there was a parcel of outlandish bone fish hooks on the shelf over the fire-place, and a tall harpoon standing at the head of the bed.

But what is this on the chest? I took it up, and held it close to the light, and felt it, and smelt it, and tried every way possible to arrive at some satisfactory conclusion concerning it. I can compare it to nothing but a large door mat, ornamented at the edges with little tinkling tags something like the stained porcupine quills round an Indian moccasin. There was a hole or slit in the middle of this mat, the same as in South American ponchos. But could it be possible that any sober harpooneer would get into a door mat, and parade the streets of any Christian town in that sort of guise? I put it on, to try it, and it weighed me down like a hamper,[3] being uncommonly shaggy and thick, and I thought a little damp, as though this mysterious harpooneer had been wearing it of a rainy day. I went up in it to a bit of glass[4] stuck against the wall, and I never saw such a sight in my life. I tore myself out of it in such a hurry that I gave myself a kink in the neck.

I sat down on the side of the bed, and commenced thinking about this head-peddling harpooneer, and his door mat. After thinking some time on the bed-side, I got up and took off my monkey jacket, and then stood in the middle of the room thinking. I then took off my coat, and thought a little more in my shirt sleeves. But beginning to feel very cold now, half undressed as I was, and remembering what the landlord said about the harpooneer's not coming home at all that

---

1 *counterpane* Quilt.

2 *fireboard* Decorated board used to screen or cover a fireplace.

3 *hamper* Weight located in the upper regions of a ship, particularly the weight of the sails and rigging.

4 *glass* Mirror.

night, it being so very late, I made no more ado, but jumped out of my pantaloons and boots, and then blowing out the light tumbled into bed, and commended myself to the care of heaven.

Whether that mattress was stuffed with corn-cobs or broken crockery, there is no telling, but I rolled about a good deal, and could not sleep for a long time. At last I slid off into a light doze, and had pretty nearly made a good offing towards the land of Nod,[1] when I heard a heavy footfall in the passage, and saw a glimmer of light come into the room from under the door.

Lord save me, thinks I, that must be the harpooneer, the infernal head-peddler. But I lay perfectly still, and resolved not to say a word till spoken to. Holding a light in one hand, and that identical New Zealand head in the other, the stranger entered the room, and without looking towards the bed, placed his candle a good way off from me on the floor in one corner, and then began working away at the knotted cords of the large bag I before spoke of as being in the room. I was all eagerness to see his face, but he kept it averted for some time while employed in unlacing the bag's mouth. This accomplished, however, he turned round—when, good heavens! what a sight! Such a face! It was of a dark, purplish, yellow colour, here and there stuck over with large blackish looking squares. Yes, it's just as I thought, he's a terrible bedfellow; he's been in a fight, got dreadfully cut, and here he is, just from the surgeon. But at that moment he chanced to turn his face so towards the light, that I plainly saw they could not be sticking-plasters[2] at all, those black squares on his cheeks. They were stains of some sort or other. At first I knew not what to make of this; but soon an inkling of the truth occurred to me. I remembered a story of a white man—a whaleman too—who, falling among the cannibals, had been tattooed by them. I concluded that this harpooneer, in the course of his distant voyages, must have met with a similar adventure. And what is it, thought I, after all! It's only his outside; a man can be honest in any sort of skin. But then, what to make of his unearthly complexion, that part of it, I mean, lying round about, and completely independent of the squares of tattooing. To be sure, it might

1 *land of Nod* Sleep, land of dreams. It is also a biblical place-name in Genesis 4.16, where it is a land on the borderlands of the civilized world: "And Cain went out from the presence of the Lord, and dwelt in the land of Nod, on the east of Eden."

2 *sticking-plasters* Adhesive strips or squares of fabric used to dress superficial wounds.

be nothing but a good coat of tropical tanning; but I never heard of a hot sun's tanning a white man into a purplish yellow one. However, I had never been in the South Seas; and perhaps the sun there produced these extraordinary effects upon the skin. Now, while all these ideas were passing through me like lightning, this harpooneer never noticed me at all. But, after some difficulty having opened his bag, he commenced fumbling in it, and presently pulled out a sort of tomahawk, and a seal-skin wallet[1] with the hair on. Placing these on the old chest in the middle of the room, he then took the New Zealand head—a ghastly thing enough—and crammed it down into the bag. He now took off his hat—a new beaver hat—when I came nigh singing out with fresh surprise. There was no hair on his head—none to speak of at least—nothing but a small scalp-knot twisted up on his forehead. His bald purplish head now looked for all the world like a mildewed skull. Had not the stranger stood between me and the door, I would have bolted out of it quicker than ever I bolted a dinner.

Even as it was, I thought something of slipping out of the window, but it was the second floor back. I am no coward, but what to make of this head-peddling purple rascal altogether passed my comprehension. Ignorance is the parent of fear, and being completely nonplussed and confounded about the stranger, I confess I was now as much afraid of him as if it was the devil himself who had thus broken into my room at the dead of night. In fact, I was so afraid of him that I was not game enough just then to address him, and demand a satisfactory answer concerning what seemed inexplicable in him.

Meanwhile, he continued the business of undressing, and at last showed his chest and arms. As I live, these covered parts of him were checkered with the same squares as his face; his back, too, was all over the same dark squares; he seemed to have been in a Thirty Years' War,[2] and just escaped from it with a sticking-plaster shirt. Still more, his very legs were marked, as if a parcel of dark green frogs were running up the trunks of young palms. It was now quite plain that he must be some abominable savage or other shipped aboard of a whaleman in the South Seas, and so landed in this Christian country. I quaked to think of it. A peddler of heads too—perhaps the

---

1 *wallet* Travel bag.

2 *Thirty Years' War* Refers to the destructive war fought in Europe between 1618 and 1648.

heads of his own brothers. He might take a fancy to mine—heavens! look at that tomahawk!

But there was no time for shuddering, for now the savage went about something that completely fascinated my attention, and convinced me that he must indeed be a heathen. Going to his heavy grego, or wrapall, or dreadnaught,[1] which he had previously hung on a chair, he fumbled in the pockets, and produced at length a curious little deformed image with a hunch on its back, and exactly the colour of a three days' old Congo baby. Remembering the embalmed head, at first I almost thought that this black manikin was a real baby preserved in some similar manner. But seeing that it was not at all limber, and that it glistened a good deal like polished ebony, I concluded that it must be nothing but a wooden idol, which indeed it proved to be. For now the savage goes up to the empty fire-place, and removing the papered fire-board, sets up this little hunchbacked image, like a tenpin, between the andirons.[2] The chimney jambs and all the bricks inside were very sooty, so that I thought this fire-place made a very appropriate little shrine or chapel for his Congo idol.

I now screwed my eyes hard towards the half hidden image, feeling but ill at ease meantime—to see what was next to follow. First he takes about a double handful of shavings out of his grego pocket, and places them carefully before the idol; then laying a bit of ship biscuit on top and applying the flame from the lamp, he kindled the shavings into a sacrificial blaze. Presently, after many hasty snatches into the fire, and still hastier withdrawals of his fingers (whereby he seemed to be scorching them badly), he at last succeeded in drawing out the biscuit; then blowing off the heat and ashes a little, he made a polite offer of it to the little negro. But the little devil did not seem to fancy such dry sort of fare at all; he never moved his lips. All these strange antics were accompanied by still stranger guttural noises from the devotee, who seemed to be praying in a sing-song or else singing some pagan psalmody[3] or other, during which his face twitched about in the most unnatural manner. At last extinguishing the fire, he took the idol up very unceremoniously, and bagged it

1 *grego … wrapall … dreadnaught* These are all names for heavy, rugged overcoats worn by sailors.

2 *andirons* Pair of utensils used to support wood burning in the fireplace.

3 *psalmody* Arranged sequence of hymns.

again in his grego pocket as carelessly as if he were a sportsman bagging a dead woodcock.

All these queer proceedings increased my uncomfortableness, and seeing him now exhibiting strong symptoms of concluding his business operations, and jumping into bed with me, I thought it was high time, now or never, before the light was put out, to break the spell in which I had so long been bound.

But the interval I spent in deliberating what to say, was a fatal one. Taking up his tomahawk from the table, he examined the head of it for an instant, and then holding it to the light, with his mouth at the handle, he puffed out great clouds of tobacco smoke. The next moment the light was extinguished, and this wild cannibal, tomahawk between his teeth, sprang into bed with me. I sang out, I could not help it now; and giving a sudden grunt of astonishment he began feeling me.

Stammering out something, I knew not what, I rolled away from him against the wall, and then conjured him, whoever or whatever he might be, to keep quiet, and let me get up and light the lamp again. But his guttural responses satisfied me at once that he but ill comprehended my meaning.

"Who-e debel you?"—he at last said—"you no speak-e, dam-me, I kill-e." And so saying the lighted tomahawk began flourishing about me in the dark.

"Landlord, for God's sake, Peter Coffin!"[1] shouted I. "Landlord! Watch![2] Coffin! Angels! save me!"

"Speak-e! tell-ee me who-ee be, or dam-me, I kill-e!" again growled the cannibal, while his horrid flourishings of the tomahawk scattered the hot tobacco ashes about me till I thought my linen would get on fire. But thank heaven, at that moment the landlord came into the room light in hand, and leaping from the bed I ran up to him.

"Don't be afraid now," said he, grinning again, "Queequeg here wouldn't harm a hair of your head."

"Stop your grinning," shouted I, "and why didn't you tell me that that infernal harpooneer was a cannibal?"

"I thought ye know'd it;—didn't I tell ye, he was a peddlin' heads around town?—but turn flukes again and go to sleep. Queequeg,

---

1 *Peter Coffin* Landlord of the Spouter-Inn.

2 *Watch* Police officer on night patrol (night-watch).

look here—you sabbee me, I sabbee—you this man sleepe you—you sabbee?"

"Me sabbee plenty"—grunted Queequeg, puffing away at his pipe and sitting up in bed.

"You gettee in," he added, motioning to me with his tomahawk, and throwing the clothes to one side. He really did this in not only a civil but a really kind and charitable way. I stood looking at him a moment. For all his tattooings he was on the whole a clean, comely looking cannibal. What's all this fuss I have been making about, thought I to myself—the man's a human being just as I am: he has just as much reason to fear me, as I have to be afraid of him. Better sleep with a sober cannibal than a drunken Christian.

"Landlord," said I, "tell him to stash his tomahawk there, or pipe, or whatever you call it; tell him to stop smoking, in short, and I will turn in with him. But I don't fancy having a man smoking in bed with me. It's dangerous. Besides, I aint insured."

This being told to Queequeg, he at once complied, and again politely motioned me to get into bed—rolling over to one side as much as to say—I won't touch a leg of ye.

"Good night, landlord," said I, "you may go."

I turned in, and never slept better in my life.

Chapter 4. The Counterpane

Upon waking next morning about daylight, I found Queequeg's arm thrown over me in the most loving and affectionate manner. You had almost thought I had been his wife. The counterpane was of patchwork, full of odd little parti-colored squares and triangles; and this arm of his tattooed all over with an interminable Cretan labyrinth[1] of a figure, no two parts of which were of one precise shade—owing I suppose to his keeping his arm at sea unmethodically in sun and shade, his shirt sleeves irregularly rolled up at various times—this same arm of his, I say, looked for all the world like a strip of that same patchwork quilt. Indeed, partly lying on it as the arm did when I first

1 *parti-colored* Variously colored; *Cretan labyrinth* In Greek mythology, the confusing maze built by the artist Daedalus for King Minos of Crete. It was designed to hold the Minotaur, a monster that was half-bull, half-human.

awoke, I could hardly tell it from the quilt, they so blended their hues together; and it was only by the sense of weight and pressure that I could tell that Queequeg was hugging me.

My sensations were strange. Let me try to explain them. When I was a child, I well remember a somewhat similar circumstance that befell me; whether it was a reality or a dream, I never could entirely settle. The circumstance was this. I had been cutting up some caper or other—I think it was trying to crawl up the chimney, as I had seen a little sweep[1] do a few days previous; and my stepmother who, somehow or other, was all the time whipping me, or sending me to bed supperless,—my mother dragged me by the legs out of the chimney and packed me off to bed, though it was only two o'clock in the afternoon of the 21st June, the longest day in the year in our hemisphere. I felt dreadfully. But there was no help for it, so up stairs I went to my little room in the third floor, undressed myself as slowly as possible so as to kill time, and with a bitter sigh got between the sheets.

I lay there dismally calculating that sixteen entire hours must elapse before I could hope for a resurrection. Sixteen hours in bed! the small of my back ached to think of it. And it was so light too; the sun shining in at the window, and a great rattling of coaches in the streets, and the sound of gay voices all over the house. I felt worse and worse—at last I got up, dressed, and softly going down in my stockinged feet, sought out my stepmother, and suddenly threw myself at her feet, beseeching her as a particular favour to give me a good slippering[2] for my misbehaviour; anything indeed but condemning me to lie abed such an unendurable length of time. But she was the best and most conscientious of stepmothers, and back I had to go to my room. For several hours I lay there broad awake, feeling a great deal worse than I have ever done since, even from the greatest subsequent misfortunes. At last I must have fallen into a troubled nightmare of a doze; and slowly waking from it—half steeped in dreams—I opened my eyes, and the before sun-lit room was now wrapped in outer darkness. Instantly I felt a shock running through all my frame; nothing was to be seen, and nothing was to be heard; but a supernatural hand

---

1 *sweep* Chimney-sweep. Before the practice was regulated in the late nineteenth century, small children were put to the dangerous work of climbing up and down chimneys to clean them.

2 *slippering* Beating (using a slipper to administer the blows).

seemed placed in mine. My arm hung over the counterpane, and the nameless, unimaginable, silent form or phantom, to which the hand belonged, seemed closely seated by my bed-side. For what seemed ages piled on ages, I lay there, frozen with the most awful fears, not daring to drag away my hand; yet ever thinking that, if I could but stir it one single inch, the horrid spell would be broken. I knew not how this consciousness at last glided away from me; but waking in the morning, I shudderingly remembered it all, and for days and weeks and months afterwards I lost myself in confounding attempts to explain the mystery. Nay, to this very hour, I often puzzle myself with it.

Now, take away the awful fear, and my sensations at feeling the supernatural hand in mine were very similar, in their strangeness, to those which I experienced on waking up and seeing Queequeg's pagan arm thrown round me. But at length all the past night's events soberly recurred, one by one, in fixed reality, and then I lay only alive to the comical predicament. For though I tried to move his arm—unlock his bridegroom clasp—yet, sleeping as he was, he still hugged me tightly, as though naught but death should part us twain.[1] I now strove to rouse him—"Queequeg!"—but his only answer was a snore. I then rolled over, my neck feeling as if it were in a horse-collar;[2] and suddenly felt a slight scratch. Throwing aside the counterpane, there lay the tomahawk sleeping by the savage's side, as if it were a hatchet-faced baby. A pretty pickle, truly, thought I; abed here in a strange house in the broad day, with a cannibal and a tomahawk! "Queequeg!—in the name of goodness, Queequeg, wake!" At length, by dint of much wriggling, and loud and incessant expostulations upon the unbecomingness of his hugging a fellow male in that matrimonial sort of style, I succeeded in extracting a grunt; and presently, he drew back his arm, shook himself all over like a Newfoundland dog just from the water, and sat up in bed, stiff as a pike-staff,[3] looking at me, and rubbing his eyes as if he did not altogether remember how I came to be there, though a dim consciousness of knowing something about me seemed slowly dawning over him. Meanwhile, I lay quietly eyeing him, having no serious misgivings now, and bent upon narrowly observing so curious a creature. When, at last, his mind seemed

---

1 *twain* Two.

2 *horse-collar* Curved collar used to harness a plow-horse.

3 *stiff as a pike-staff* Proverbial phrase meaning "straight up"—pikestaffs are walking-sticks.

made up touching the character of his bedfellow, and he became, as it were, reconciled to the fact; he jumped out upon the floor, and by certain signs and sounds gave me to understand that, if it pleased me, he would dress first and then leave me to dress afterwards, leaving the whole apartment to myself. Thinks I, Queequeg, under the circumstances, this is a very civilized overture; but, the truth is, these savages have an innate sense of delicacy, say what you will; it is marvellous how essentially polite they are. I pay this particular compliment to Queequeg, because he treated me with so much civility and consideration, while I was guilty of great rudeness; staring at him from the bed, and watching all his toilette[1] motions; for the time my curiosity getting the better of my breeding. Nevertheless, a man like Queequeg you don't see every day—he and his ways were well worth unusual regarding.

He commenced dressing at top by donning his beaver hat, a very tall one, by the by, and then—still minus his trowsers—he hunted up his boots. What under the heavens he did it for, I cannot tell, but his next movement was to crush himself—boots in hand, and hat on—under the bed; when, from sundry violent gaspings and strainings, I inferred he was hard at work booting himself; though by no law of propriety that I ever heard of, is any man required to be private when putting on his boots. But Queequeg, do you see, was a creature in the transition stage—neither caterpillar nor butterfly. He was just enough civilized to show off his outlandishness in the strangest possible manner. His education was not yet completed. He was an undergraduate. If he had not been a small degree civilized, he very probably would not have troubled himself with boots at all; but then, if he had not been still a savage, he never would have dreamt of getting under the bed to put them on. At last, he emerged with his hat very much dented and crushed down over his eyes, and began creaking and limping about the room, as if, not being much accustomed to boots, his pair of damp, wrinkled cowhide ones—probably not made to order either—rather pinched and tormented him at the first go off of a bitter cold morning.

Seeing, now, that there were no curtains to the window, and that the street being very narrow, the house opposite commanded a plain

---

1 *toilette* Process of dressing and washing.

view into the room, and observing more and more the indecorous figure that Queequeg made, staving about[1] with little else but his hat and boots on; I begged him as well as I could, to accelerate his toilet somewhat, and particularly to get into his pantaloons as soon as possible. He complied, and then proceeded to wash himself. At that time in the morning any Christian would have washed his face; but Queequeg, to my amazement, contented himself with restricting his ablutions[2] to his chest, arms, and hands. He then donned his waistcoat, and taking up a piece of hard soap on the wash-stand centre-table, dipped it into water and commenced lathering his face. I was watching to see where he kept his razor, when lo and behold, he takes the harpoon from the bed corner, slips out the long wooden stock, unsheathes the head, whets it a little on his boot, and striding up to the bit of mirror against the wall, begins a vigorous scraping, or rather harpooning of his cheeks. Thinks I, Queequeg, this is using Rogers's best cutlery[3] with a vengeance. Afterwards I wondered the less at this operation when I came to know of what fine steel the head of a harpoon is made, and how exceedingly sharp the long straight edges are always kept.

The rest of his toilet was soon achieved, and he proudly marched out of the room, wrapped up in his great pilot monkey jacket, and sporting his harpoon like a marshal's baton.

[Ishmael and Queequeg eat breakfast, and Ishmael then goes for a walk in New Bedford, making his way to the Whaleman's Chapel, where he attends a sermon by Father Mapple on the subject of the story of the prophet Jonah and the vital importance of obedience to God.]

Chapter 10. A Bosom Friend

Returning to the Spouter-Inn from the Chapel, I found Queequeg there quite alone; he having left the Chapel before the benediction[4] some time. He was sitting on a bench before the fire, with his feet on

1 *staving about* Pacing intensely around.

2 *ablutions* Ritual washings.

3 *Rogers's best cutlery* Silver-plated cutlery made by the company started by American silversmith and entrepreneur William Hazen Rogers (1801–73).

4 *benediction* Blessing that closes the service.

the stove hearth, and in one hand was holding close up to his face that little negro idol of his; peering hard into its face, and with a jack-knife gently whittling away at its nose, meanwhile humming to himself in his heathenish way.

But being now interrupted, he put up the image; and pretty soon, going to the table, took up a large book there, and placing it on his lap began counting the pages with deliberate regularity; at every fiftieth page—as I fancied—stopping a moment, looking vacantly around him, and giving utterance to a long-drawn gurgling whistle of astonishment. He would then begin again at the next fifty; seeming to commence at number one each time, as though he could not count more than fifty, and it was only by such a large number of fifties being found together, that his astonishment at the multitude of pages was excited.

With much interest I sat watching him. Savage though he was, and hideously marred about the face—at least to my taste—his countenance yet had a something in it which was by no means disagreeable. You cannot hide the soul. Through all his unearthly tattooings, I thought I saw the traces of a simple honest heart; and in his large, deep eyes, fiery black and bold, there seemed tokens of a spirit that would dare a thousand devils. And besides all this, there was a certain lofty bearing about the Pagan, which even his uncouthness could not altogether maim. He looked like a man who had never cringed and never had had a creditor. Whether it was, too, that his head being shaved, his forehead was drawn out in freer and brighter relief, and looked more expansive than it otherwise would, this I will not venture to decide; but certain it was his head was phrenologically an excellent one.[1] It may seem ridiculous, but it reminded me of General Washington's head, as seen in the popular busts of him. It had the same long regularly graded retreating slope from above the brows, which were likewise very projecting, like two long promontories thickly wooded on top. Queequeg was George Washington cannibalistically developed.

1 *phrenologically … one* I.e., according to the dictates of the pseudoscience phrenology, which purported to trace the character of a person by the shape of the skull and structure of the face, Queequeg has an excellent head and hence an excellent character.

Whilst I was thus closely scanning him, half-pretending meanwhile to be looking out at the storm from the casement,[1] he never heeded my presence, never troubled himself with so much as a single glance; but appeared wholly occupied with counting the pages of the marvellous book. Considering how sociably we had been sleeping together the night previous, and especially considering the affectionate arm I had found thrown over me upon waking in the morning, I thought this indifference of his very strange. But savages are strange beings; at times you do not know exactly how to take them. At first they are overawing; their calm self-collectedness of simplicity seems a Socratic wisdom.[2] I had noticed also that Queequeg never consorted at all, or but very little, with the other seamen in the inn. He made no advances whatever; appeared to have no desire to enlarge the circle of his acquaintances. All this struck me as mighty singular; yet, upon second thoughts, there was something almost sublime in it. Here was a man some twenty thousand miles from home, by the way of Cape Horn, that is—which was the only way he could get there—thrown among people as strange to him as though he were in the planet Jupiter; and yet he seemed entirely at his ease; preserving the utmost serenity; content with his own companionship; always equal to himself. Surely this was a touch of fine philosophy; though no doubt he had never heard there was such a thing as that. But, perhaps, to be true philosophers, we mortals should not be conscious of so living or so striving. So soon as I hear that such or such a man gives himself out for a philosopher, I conclude that, like the dyspeptic[3] old woman, he must have "broken his digester."

As I sat there in that now lonely room; the fire burning low, in that mild stage when, after its first intensity has warmed the air, it then only glows to be looked at; the evening shades and phantoms gathering round the casements, and peering in upon us silent, solitary twain; the storm booming without in solemn swells; I began to be sensible of strange feelings. I felt a melting in me. No more my splintered heart and maddened hand were turned against the wolfish world. This soothing savage had redeemed it. There he sat, his

---

1 *casement* Window.

2 *simplicity … Socratic wisdom* Socrates (c. 470–399 BCE) was a Greek philosopher who began all of his investigations by first claiming to know nothing.

3 *dyspeptic* Suffering from dyspepsia, i.e., difficulty digesting; morbid, gloomy.

very indifference speaking a nature in which there lurked no civilized hypocrisies and bland deceits. Wild he was; a very sight of sights to see; yet I began to feel myself mysteriously drawn towards him. And those same things that would have repelled most others, they were the very magnets that thus drew me. I'll try a pagan friend, thought I, since Christian kindness has proved but hollow courtesy. I drew my bench near him, and made some friendly signs and hints, doing my best to talk with him meanwhile. At first he little noticed these advances; but presently, upon my referring to his last night's hospitalities, he made out to ask me whether we were again to be bedfellows. I told him yes; whereat I thought he looked pleased, perhaps a little complimented.

We then turned over the book together, and I endeavored to explain to him the purpose of the printing, and the meaning of the few pictures that were in it. Thus I soon engaged his interest; and from that we went to jabbering the best we could about the various outer sights to be seen in this famous town. Soon I proposed a social smoke; and, producing his pouch and tomahawk, he quietly offered me a puff. And then we sat exchanging puffs from that wild pipe of his, and keeping it regularly passing between us.

If there yet lurked any ice of indifference towards me in the Pagan's breast, this pleasant, genial smoke we had, soon thawed it out, and left us cronies. He seemed to take to me quite as naturally and unbiddenly as I to him; and when our smoke was over, he pressed his forehead against mine, clasped me round the waist, and said that henceforth we were married; meaning, in his country's phrase, that we were bosom friends; he would gladly die for me, if need should be. In a countryman, this sudden flame of friendship would have seemed far too premature, a thing to be much distrusted; but in this simple savage those old rules would not apply.

After supper, and another social chat and smoke, we went to our room together. He made me a present of his embalmed head; took out his enormous tobacco wallet, and groping under the tobacco, drew out some thirty dollars in silver; then spreading them on the table, and mechanically dividing them into two equal portions, pushed one of them towards me, and said it was mine. I was going to remonstrate; but he silenced me by pouring them into my trowsers' pockets. I let them stay. He then went about his evening prayers, took out his idol, and removed the paper fireboard. By certain signs and symptoms, I thought he seemed anxious for me to join him; but well knowing what was to follow, I deliberated a moment whether, in case he invited me, I would comply or otherwise.

I was a good Christian; born and bred in the bosom of the infallible Presbyterian Church.[1] How then could I unite with this wild idolator in worshipping his piece of wood? But what is worship? thought I. Do you suppose now, Ishmael, that the magnanimous God of heaven and earth—pagans and all included—can possibly be jealous of an insignificant bit of black wood? Impossible! But what is worship?—to do the will of God—*that* is worship. And what is the will of God?—to do to my fellow man what I would have my fellow man to do to me—*that* is the will of God.[2] Now, Queequeg is my fellow man. And what do I wish that this Queequeg would do to me? Why, unite with me in my particular Presbyterian form of worship. Consequently, I must then unite with him in his; ergo, I must turn idolator. So I kindled the shavings; helped prop up the innocent little idol; offered him burnt biscuit with Queequeg; salamed[3] before him twice or thrice; kissed his nose; and that done, we undressed and went to bed, at peace with our own consciences and all the world. But we did not go to sleep without some little chat.

How it is I know not; but there is no place like a bed for confidential disclosures between friends. Man and wife, they say, there open the very bottom of their souls to each other; and some old couples often lie and chat over old times till nearly morning. Thus, then, in our hearts' honeymoon, lay I and Queequeg—a cosy, loving pair.

Chapter 11. Nightgown

We had lain thus in bed, chatting and napping at short intervals, and Queequeg now and then affectionately throwing his brown tattooed legs over mine, and then drawing them back; so entirely sociable and free and easy were we; when, at last, by reason of our confabulations,

1 *Presbyterian Church* Protestant church founded by the Scottish dissenter John Knox (1514–72).

2 *to do ... will of God* See Matthew 7.12: "Therefore all things whatsoever ye would that men should do to you, do ye even so to them: for this is the law and the prophets."

3 *salamed* Low bow with the right hand placed on the forehead.

what little nappishness remained in us altogether departed, and we felt like getting up again, though day-break was yet some way down the future.

Yes, we became very wakeful; so much so that our recumbent position began to grow wearisome, and by little and little we found ourselves sitting up; the clothes well tucked around us, leaning against the head-board with our four knees drawn up close together, and our two noses bending over them, as if our knee-pans were warming-pans. We felt very nice and snug, the more so since it was so chilly out of doors; indeed out of bed-clothes too, seeing that there was no fire in the room. The more so, I say, because truly to enjoy bodily warmth, some small part of you must be cold, for there is no quality in this world that is not what it is merely by contrast. Nothing exists in itself. If you flatter yourself that you are all over comfortable, and have been so a long time, then you cannot be said to be comfortable any more. But if, like Queequeg and me in the bed, the tip of your nose or the crown of your head be slightly chilled, why then, indeed, in the general consciousness you feel most delightfully and unmistakably warm. For this reason a sleeping apartment should never be furnished with a fire, which is one of the luxurious discomforts of the rich. For the height of this sort of deliciousness is to have nothing but the blanket between you and your snugness and the cold of the outer air. Then, there you lie like the one warm spark in the heart of an arctic crystal.

We had been sitting in this crouching manner for some time, when all at once I thought I would open my eyes; for when between sheets, whether by day or by night, and whether asleep or awake, I have a way of always keeping my eyes shut, in order the more to concentrate the snugness of being in bed. Because no man can ever feel his own identity aright except his eyes be closed; as if darkness were indeed the proper element of our essences, though light be more congenial to our clayey part.[1] Upon opening my eyes then, and coming out of my own pleasant and self-created darkness into the imposed and coarse outer gloom of the unilluminated twelve-o'clock-at-night, I experienced a disagreeable revulsion. Nor did I at all object to the hint from Queequeg that perhaps it were best to strike a light, seeing that

1 *clayey part* Physical, rather than spiritual, body.

we were so wide awake; and besides he felt a strong desire to have a few quiet puffs from his Tomahawk. Be it said, that though I had felt such a strong repugnance to his smoking in the bed the night before, yet see how elastic our stiff prejudices grow when love once comes to bend them. For now I liked nothing better than to have Queequeg smoking by me, even in bed, because he seemed to be full of such serene household joy then. I no more felt unduly concerned for the landlord's policy of insurance. I was only alive to the condensed confidential comfortableness of sharing a pipe and a blanket with a real friend. With our shaggy jackets drawn about our shoulders, we now passed the Tomahawk from one to the other, till slowly there grew over us a blue hanging tester[1] of smoke, illuminated by the flame of the new-lit lamp.

Whether it was that this undulating tester rolled the savage away to far distant scenes, I know not, but he now spoke of his native island; and, eager to hear his history, I begged him to go on and tell it. He gladly complied. Though at the time I but ill comprehended not a few of his words, yet subsequent disclosures, when I had become more familiar with his broken phraseology, now enable me to present the whole story such as it may prove in the mere skeleton I give.

Chapter 12. Biographical

Queequeg was a native of Kokovoko, an island far away to the West and South. It is not down in any map; true places never are.

While yet a new-hatched savage running wild about his native woodlands in a grass clout,[2] followed by the nibbling goats, as if he were a green sapling; even then, in Queequeg's ambitious soul, lurked a strong desire to see something more of Christendom than a specimen whaler or two. His father was a High Chief, a King; his uncle a High Priest; and on the maternal side he boasted aunts who were the wives of unconquerable warriors. There was excellent blood in his veins—royal stuff; though sadly vitiated, I fear, by the cannibal propensity he nourished in his untutored youth.

1 *tester* Bed canopy.

2 *clout* Small piece of clothing, or one that is not worth much money.

A Sag Harbor[1] ship visited his father's bay, and Queequeg sought a passage to Christian lands. But the ship, having her full complement of seamen, spurned his suit; and not all the King his father's influence could prevail. But Queequeg vowed a vow. Alone in his canoe, he paddled off to a distant strait, which he knew the ship must pass through when she quitted the island. On one side was a coral reef; on the other a low tongue of land, covered with mangrove thickets that grew out into the water. Hiding his canoe, still afloat, among these thickets, with its prow seaward, he sat down in the stern, paddle low in hand; and when the ship was gliding by, like a flash he darted out; gained her side; with one backward dash of his foot capsized and sank his canoe; climbed up the chains; and throwing himself at full length upon the deck, grappled a ring-bolt there, and swore not to let it go, though hacked in pieces.

In vain the captain threatened to throw him overboard; suspended a cutlass over his naked wrists; Queequeg was the son of a King, and Queequeg budged not. Struck by his desperate dauntlessness, and his wild desire to visit Christendom, the captain at last relented, and told him he might make himself at home.[2] But this fine young savage—this sea Prince of Wales,[3] never saw the Captain's cabin. They put him down among the sailors, and made a whaleman of him. But like Czar Peter content to toil in the shipyards of foreign cities,[4] Queequeg disdained no seeming ignominy, if thereby he might happily gain the power of enlightening his untutored countrymen. For at bottom—so he told me—he was actuated by a profound desire to learn among the Christians, the arts whereby to make his people still happier than they were; and more than that, still better than they were. But, alas! the practices of whalemen soon convinced him that even Christians could be both miserable and wicked; infinitely more so, than all his father's heathens. Arrived at last in old Sag Harbor; and seeing what the sailors did there; and then going on to Nantucket, and seeing how

---

1 *Sag Harbor* Town on eastern Long Island, New York.

2 *desperate ... at home* In his book *The Sign of the Cannibal* (1998), Geoffrey Sanborn shows that Melville based Queequeg's story on that of Tupai Cupa, a Maori chief who went to similarly great lengths to go to England.

3 *Prince of Wales* In Britain, the son of the king or queen and heir to the throne.

4 *Czar Peter ... foreign cities* In 1697, Peter the Great of Russia traveled to England so he could learn shipbuilding.

they spent their wages in *that* place also, poor Queequeg gave it up for lost. Thought he, it's a wicked world in all meridians;[1] I'll die a pagan.

And thus an old idolator at heart, he yet lived among these Christians, wore their clothes, and tried to talk their gibberish. Hence the queer ways about him, though now some time from home.

By hints, I asked him whether he did not propose going back, and having a coronation; since he might now consider his father dead and gone, he being very old and feeble at the last accounts. He answered no, not yet; and added that he was fearful Christianity, or rather Christians, had unfitted him for ascending the pure and undefiled throne of thirty pagan Kings before him. But by and by, he said, he would return,—as soon as he felt himself baptized again. For the nonce, however, he proposed to sail about, and sow his wild oats in all four oceans. They had made a harpooneer of him, and that barbed iron was in lieu of a sceptre now.

I asked him what might be his immediate purpose, touching his future movements. He answered, to go to sea again, in his old vocation. Upon this, I told him that whaling was my own design, and informed him of my intention to sail out of Nantucket, as being the most promising port for an adventurous whaleman to embark from. He at once resolved to accompany me to that island, ship aboard the same vessel, get into the same watch, the same boat, the same mess with me, in short to share my every hap;[2] with both my hands in his, boldly dip into the Potluck of both worlds. To all this I joyously assented; for besides the affection I now felt for Queequeg, he was an experienced harpooneer, and as such, could not fail to be of great usefulness to one, who, like me, was wholly ignorant of the mysteries of whaling, though well acquainted with the sea, as known to merchant seamen.

His story being ended with his pipe's last dying puff, Queequeg embraced me, pressed his forehead against mine, and blowing out the light, we rolled over from each other, this way and that, and very soon were sleeping.

---

1 *meridians* Localities.

2 *hap* Chance.

[Ishmael and Queequeg go to Nantucket and sign articles to become part of the crew of the *Pequod*, under captain Ahab.[1] A stranger named Elijah warns them against sailing with Ahab and hints that the captain is of unsound mind after losing his leg to a whale on a previous journey. The craft is stocked and the call is made to go aboard; Ishmael notices some shadowy figures boarding the ship at dawn, which he can't account for when they get on board. The *Pequod* is brought to sea by the pilot ship and takes off into the Atlantic.]

Chapter 23. The Lee Shore

Some chapters back, one Bulkington was spoken of, a tall, newlanded mariner, encountered in New Bedford at the inn.

When on that shivering winter's night, the Pequod thrust her vindictive bows into the cold malicious waves, who should I see standing at her helm but Bulkington! I looked with sympathetic awe and fearfulness upon the man, who in mid-winter just landed from a four years' dangerous voyage, could so unrestingly push off again for still another tempestuous term. The land seemed scorching to his feet. Wonderfullest things are ever the unmentionable; deep memories yield no epitaphs; this six-inch chapter is the stoneless grave of Bulkington. Let me only say that it fared with him as with the storm-tossed ship, that miserably drives along the leeward[2] land. The port would fain give succor; the port is pitiful; in the port is safety, comfort, hearthstone, supper, warm blankets, friends, all that's kind to our mortalities. But in that gale, the port, the land, is that ship's direst jeopardy; she must fly all hospitality; one touch of land, though it but graze the keel, would make her shudder through and through. With all her might she crowds all sail off shore; in so doing, fights 'gainst the very winds that fain would blow her homeward; seeks all the lashed sea's landlessness again; for refuge's sake forlornly rushing into peril; her only friend her bitterest foe!

Know ye, now, Bulkington? Glimpses do ye seem to see of that mortally intolerable truth; that all deep, earnest thinking is but the intrepid effort of the soul to keep the open independence of her sea;

1 *Ahab* Ahab is described in the Old Testament as a wicked king who did "evil in the sight of the Lord above all that were before him" (1 Kings 16.30). Ahab worshipped the god Baal and married Jezebel, a pagan princess, both of which actions were subsequently denounced by the prophet Elijah.

2 *leeward* The side of a ship facing away from the wind.

while the wildest winds of heaven and earth conspire to cast her on the treacherous, slavish shore?

But as in landlessness alone resides highest truth, shoreless, indefinite as God—so, better is it to perish in that howling infinite, than be ingloriously dashed upon the lee, even if that were safety! For wormlike, then, oh! who would craven crawl to land! Terrors of the terrible! is all this agony so vain? Take heart, take heart, O Bulkington! Bear thee grimly, demigod! Up from the spray of thy ocean-perishing—straight up, leaps thy apotheosis![1]

Chapter 24. The Advocate

As Queequeg and I are now fairly embarked in this business of whaling; and as this business of whaling has somehow come to be regarded among landsmen as a rather unpoetical and disreputable pursuit; therefore, I am all anxiety to convince ye, ye landsmen, of the injustice hereby done to us hunters of whales.

In the first place, it may be deemed almost superfluous to establish the fact, that among people at large, the business of whaling is not accounted on a level with what are called the liberal professions. If a stranger were introduced into any miscellaneous metropolitan society, it would but slightly advance the general opinion of his merits, were he presented to the company as a harpooneer, say; and if in emulation of the naval officers he should append the initials S.W.F. (Sperm Whale Fishery) to his visiting card,[2] such a procedure would be deemed pre-eminently presuming and ridiculous.

Doubtless one leading reason why the world declines honoring us whalemen, is this: they think that, at best, our vocation amounts to a butchering sort of business; and that when actively engaged therein, we are surrounded by all manner of defilements. Butchers we are, that is true. But butchers, also, and butchers of the bloodiest badge have been all Martial Commanders whom the world invariably delights to honor. And as for the matter of the alleged uncleanliness of our business, ye shall soon be initiated into certain facts hitherto pretty generally

---

1 *apotheosis* Transformation into a god, resurrection.

2 *visiting card* Cards people in society would leave with each other to conduct rounds of social calls (somewhat like business cards today). Cards belonging to officers of the U.S. Navy would have the letters U.S.N. after their names.

unknown, and which, upon the whole, will triumphantly plant the sperm whale-ship at least among the cleanliest things of this tidy earth. But even granting the charge in question to be true; what disordered slippery decks of a whale-ship are comparable to the unspeakable carrion of those battle-fields from which so many soldiers return to drink in all ladies' plaudits?[1] And if the idea of peril so much enhances the popular conceit of the soldier's profession; let me assure ye that many a veteran who has freely marched up to a battery,[2] would quickly recoil at the apparition of the sperm whale's vast tail, fanning into eddies the air over his head. For what are the comprehensible terrors of man compared with the interlinked terrors and wonders of God!

But, though the world scouts[3] at us whale hunters, yet does it unwittingly pay us the profoundest homage; yea, an all-abounding adoration! for almost all the tapers, lamps, and candles that burn round the globe, burn, as before so many shrines, to our glory![4]

But look at this matter in other lights; weigh it in all sorts of scales; see what we whalemen are, and have been.

Why did the Dutch in De Witt's[5] time have admirals of their whaling fleets? Why did Louis XVI. of France, at his own personal expense, fit out whaling ships from Dunkirk,[6] and politely invite to that town some score or two of families from our own island of Nantucket? Why did Britain between the years 1750 and 1788 pay to her whalemen in bounties upwards of £1,000,000? And lastly, how comes it that we whalemen of America now outnumber all the rest of the banded whalemen in the world; sail a navy of upwards of seven hundred vessels; manned by eighteen thousand men; yearly consuming 4,000,000 of dollars; the ships' worth, at the time of sailing, $20,000,000; and every year importing into our harbors a well reaped harvest of $7,000,000. How comes all this, if there be not something puissant[7] in whaling?

1 *plaudits* Praisings, applause.

2 *battery* Enemy's artillery.

3 *scouts* Scorns.

4 *tapers* Candles; *burn … to our glory* Ishmael is referring to the fact that whale oil was one of the fuels used for lighting in the nineteenth century.

5 *De Witt* Johan de Witt (1625–72) was a prominent politician in the Dutch Republic.

6 *Louis XVI* King of France from 1774 to 1792; *Dunkirk* City on the coast of northern France, where in 1786 the American William Rotch Sr. set up a colony of Nantucket whalers, so they could avoid high French taxes on whale oil.

7 *puissant* Mighty.

But this is not the half; look again.

I freely assert, that the cosmopolite philosopher cannot, for his life, point out one single peaceful influence, which within the last sixty years has operated more potentially[1] upon the whole broad world, taken in one aggregate, than the high and mighty business of whaling. One way and another, it has begotten events so remarkable in themselves, and so continuously momentous in their sequential issues, that whaling may well be regarded as that Egyptian mother, who bore offspring themselves pregnant from her womb.[2] It would be a hopeless, endless task to catalogue all these things. Let a handful suffice. For many years past the whale-ship has been the pioneer in ferreting out the remotest and least known parts of the earth. She has explored seas and archipelagoes which had no chart, where no Cook or Vancouver[3] had ever sailed. If American and European men-of-war[4] now peacefully ride in once savage harbors, let them fire salutes to the honor and glory of the whale-ship, which originally showed them the way, and first interpreted between them and the savages. They may celebrate as they will the heroes of Exploring Expeditions, your Cooks, your Krusensterns;[5] but I say that scores of anonymous Captains have sailed out of Nantucket, that were as great, and greater than your Cook and your Krusenstern. For in their succorless empty-handedness, they, in the heathenish sharked waters, and by the beaches of unrecorded, javelin islands,[6] battled with virgin wonders and terrors that Cook with all his marines and muskets would not willingly have dared. All that is made such a flourish of in the old South Sea Voyages,[7] those things were but the life-time commonplaces of our

---

1 *potentially* Powerfully.

2 *Egyptian mother … womb* In Egyptian mythology, Osiris impregnates his twin sister Isis while still in their mother Nut's womb.

3 *Cook or Vancouver* James Cook (1728–79) and George Vancouver (1757–98) were legendary British explorers who both made significant expeditions in the Pacific.

4 *men-of-war* Warships.

5 *Exploring Expeditions* Five-volume authoritative work on the Pacific called the *Narrative of the United States Exploring Expedition* (1844). It reports on the American expedition to the Pacific and Antarctic led by Charles Wilkes (1798–1877); *Krusensterns* Adam Johann von Krusenstern (1770–1846) was a Baltic German explorer who commanded the first Russian global circumnavigation.

6 *javelin islands* I.e., islands where the Indigenous populations were armed with spears.

7 *South Sea Voyages* Dramatic accounts of travels to the Southern hemisphere, such as Edward Cooke's *A Voyage to the South Sea, and Round the World* (1712).

heroic Nantucketers. Often, adventures which Vancouver dedicates three chapters to, these men accounted unworthy of being set down in the ship's common log. Ah, the world! Oh, the world!

Until the whale fishery rounded Cape Horn, no commerce but colonial, scarcely any intercourse but colonial, was carried on between Europe and the long line of the opulent Spanish provinces on the Pacific coast. It was the whaleman who first broke through the jealous policy of the Spanish crown, touching those colonies; and, if space permitted, it might be distinctly shown how from those whalemen at last eventuated the liberation of Peru, Chili, and Bolivia from the yoke of Old Spain, and the establishment of the eternal democracy in those parts.

That great America on the other side of the sphere, Australia, was given to the enlightened world by the whaleman. After its first blunder-born discovery by a Dutchman,[1] all other ships long shunned those shores as pestiferously barbarous; but the whale-ship touched there. The whale-ship is the true mother of that now mighty colony.[2] Moreover, in the infancy of the first Australian settlement, the emigrants were several times saved from starvation by the benevolent biscuit of the whale-ship luckily dropping an anchor in their waters. The uncounted isles of all Polynesia confess the same truth, and do commercial homage to the whale-ship, that cleared the way for the missionary and the merchant, and in many cases carried the primitive missionaries to their first destinations. If that double-bolted land, Japan, is ever to become hospitable, it is the whale-ship alone to whom the credit will be due; for already she is on the threshold.[3]

But if, in the face of all this, you still declare that whaling has no aesthetically noble associations connected with it, then am I ready

---

1 *discovery by a Dutchman* The first European that landed in Australia was Willem Janszoon, a Dutch explorer who went there in 1606.

2 *mighty colony* The British colony of New South Wales, established as a penal colony on the southeastern Australian coast in 1788, grew to include most of what is now Australia as well as New Zealand. By the time *Moby-Dick* was published, several other Australian colonies and the colony of New Zealand had been separated out from it.

3 *If that ... threshold* At the time *Moby-Dick* was published, the Japanese state had severely restricted contact and trade between Japan and other countries for over two centuries. A U.S. naval expedition forced Japan to begin opening to the outside world three years after Melville's novel appeared.

to shiver[1] fifty lances with you there, and unhorse you with a split helmet every time.

The whale has no famous author, and whaling no famous chronicler, you will say.

The whale no famous author, and whaling no famous chronicler? Who wrote the first account of our Leviathan? Who but mighty Job![2] And who composed the first narrative of a whaling-voyage? Who, but no less a prince than Alfred the Great, who, with his own royal pen, took down the words from Other, the Norwegian whale-hunter[3] of those times! And who pronounced our glowing eulogy in Parliament? Who, but Edmund Burke![4]

True enough, but then whalemen themselves are poor devils; they have no good blood in their veins.

No good blood in their veins? They have something better than royal blood there. The grandmother of Benjamin Franklin was Mary Morrel; afterwards, by marriage, Mary Folger, one of the old settlers of Nantucket, and the ancestress to a long line of Folgers and harpooneers—all kith[5] and kin to noble Benjamin—this day darting the barbed iron from one side of the world to the other.

Good again; but then all confess that somehow whaling is not respectable.

Whaling not respectable? Whaling is imperial! By old English statutory law, the whale is declared "a royal fish."*

Oh, that's only nominal![6] The whale himself has never figured in any grand imposing way.

The whale never figured in any grand imposing way? In one of the mighty triumphs given to a Roman general upon his entering the world's capital, the bones of a whale, brought all the way from the

---

1 *shiver* Break, splinter (in a fight).

2 *Job* Main character of the Bible's Book of Job. A famous passage (not in Job's voice) near the end of the book describes the leviathan; see Job 41.1–34.

3 *Alfred the Great* (c. 848–99) was king of Wessex in England; *Other … whale-hunter* King Alfred gives an account of a Viking whaler named Ohthere of Hålogaland, who, with a team of five men, famously killed sixty whales in two days.

4 *Edmund Burke* Anglo-Irish orator, philosopher, and politician, who in 1775 gave a speech in Parliament that praised American intrepidity and success in whaling.

5 *kith* Friends and acquaintances.

* [Melville's note] See subsequent chapters for something more on this head. [See Chapter 90: Heads or Tails, not included in this selection.]

6 *nominal* In name only.

Syrian coast, were the most conspicuous object in the cymballed procession.*

Grant it, since you cite it; but, say what you will, there is no real dignity in whaling.

No dignity in whaling? The dignity of our calling the very heavens attest. Cetus[1] is a constellation in the South! No more! Drive down your hat in presence of the Czar, and take it off to Queequeg! No more! I know a man that, in his lifetime, has taken three hundred and fifty whales. I account that man more honorable than that great captain of antiquity who boasted of taking as many walled towns.

And, as for me, if, by any possibility, there be any as yet undiscovered prime thing in me; if I shall ever deserve any real repute in that small but high hushed world which I might not be unreasonably ambitious of; if hereafter I shall do anything that, upon the whole, a man might rather have done than to have left undone; if, at my death, my executors, or more properly my creditors, find any precious MSS.[2] in my desk, then here I prospectively ascribe all the honor and the glory to whaling; for a whale-ship was my Yale College and my Harvard.

Chapter 25. Postscript[3]

In behalf of the dignity of whaling, I would fain advance naught but substantiated facts. But after embattling[4] his facts, an advocate who should wholly suppress a not unreasonable surmise,[5] which might tell eloquently upon his cause—such an advocate, would he not be blameworthy?

It is well known that at the coronation of kings and queens, even modern ones, a certain curious process of seasoning them for their functions is gone through.

---

* [Melville's note] See subsequent chapters for something more on this head. [See Chapter 82: The Honor and Glory of Whaling, not included in this selection.]

1 *Cetus* Classical name for a large sea monster or whale; it is also the modern scientific term for "whale."

2 *MSS.* Manuscripts.

3 *Postscript* This chapter was not included in the 1851 British edition of *Moby-Dick* (which was entitled *The Whale).*

4 *embattling* Forming up in position; fortifying.

5 *surmise* Conjecture.

There is a saltcellar of state, so called, and there may be a caster[1] of state. How they use the salt, precisely—who knows? Certain I am, however, that a king's head is solemnly oiled at his coronation, even as a head of salad. Can it be, though, that they anoint it with a view of making its interior run well, as they anoint machinery? Much might be ruminated here, concerning the essential dignity of this regal process, because in common life we esteem but meanly and contemptibly a fellow who anoints his hair, and palpably smells of that anointing. In truth, a mature man who uses hair-oil, unless medicinally, that man has probably got a quoggy[2] spot in him somewhere. As a general rule, he can't amount to much in his totality.

But the only thing to be considered here, is this—what kind of oil is used at coronations? Certainly it cannot be olive oil, nor macassar oil,[3] nor castor oil, nor bear's oil, nor train oil, nor cod-liver oil. What then can it possibly be, but sperm oil in its unmanufactured, unpolluted state, the sweetest of all oils?

Think of that, ye loyal Britons! we whalemen supply your kings and queens with coronation stuff!

Chapter 26. Knights and Squires

The chief mate of the Pequod was Starbuck, a native of Nantucket, and a Quaker[4] by descent. He was a long, earnest man, and though born on an icy coast, seemed well adapted to endure hot latitudes, his flesh being hard as twice-baked biscuit. Transported to the Indies, his live blood would not spoil like bottled ale. He must have been born in some time of general drought and famine, or upon one of those fast days for which his state is famous.[5] Only some thirty arid summers had he seen; those summers had dried up all his physical

---

1 *caster* Implement used to dispense pepper, sugar, or other condiments; shaker.

2 *quoggy* Boggy, squishy.

3 *macassar oil* Hair oil that was popular in the nineteenth century.

4 *Quaker* The Quakers (formally known as the Society of Friends) are a Protestant sect that was and is committed to pacifism, equality of the sexes, and social reform. They typically sought to avoid worldly vanities, adhering to customs of plain dress, and using an old-fashioned diction (employing the pronouns *thee* and *thou*, for example).

5 *fast days … famous* The Puritans that settled in Massachusetts would hold community days of fasting and repentance periodically, particularly if outside events convinced them that God was displeased with the sins of the community.

superfluousness. But this, his thinness, so to speak, seemed no more the token of wasting anxieties and cares, than it seemed the indication of any bodily blight. It was merely the condensation of the man. He was by no means ill-looking; quite the contrary. His pure tight skin was an excellent fit; and closely wrapped up in it, and embalmed with inner health and strength, like a revivified Egyptian, this Starbuck seemed prepared to endure for long ages to come, and to endure always, as now; for be it Polar snow or torrid sun, like a patent chronometer, his interior vitality was warranted to do well in all climates. Looking into his eyes, you seemed to see there the yet lingering images of those thousand-fold perils he had calmly confronted through life. A staid, steadfast man, whose life for the most part was a telling pantomime of action, and not a tame chapter of sounds. Yet, for all his hardy sobriety and fortitude, there were certain qualities in him which at times affected, and in some cases seemed well nigh to overbalance all the rest. Uncommonly conscientious for a seaman, and endued with a deep natural reverence, the wild watery loneliness of his life did therefore strongly incline him to superstition; but to that sort of superstition, which in some organizations seems rather to spring, somehow, from intelligence than from ignorance. Outward portents and inward presentiments were his. And if at times these things bent the welded iron of his soul, much more did his far-away domestic memories of his young Cape[1] wife and child, tend to bend him still more from the original ruggedness of his nature, and open him still further to those latent influences which, in some honest-hearted men, restrain the gush of dare-devil daring, so often evinced by others in the more perilous vicissitudes of the fishery. "I will have no man in my boat," said Starbuck, "who is not afraid of a whale." By this, he seemed to mean, not only that the most reliable and useful courage was that which arises from the fair estimation of the encountered peril, but that an utterly fearless man is a far more dangerous comrade than a coward.

"Aye, aye," said Stubb, the second mate, "Starbuck, there, is as careful a man as you'll find anywhere in this fishery." But we shall ere long see what that word "careful" precisely means when used by a man like Stubb, or almost any other whale hunter.

---

1 *Cape* I.e., Cape Cod, Massachusetts.

Starbuck was no crusader after perils; in him courage was not a sentiment; but a thing simply useful to him, and always at hand upon all mortally practical occasions. Besides, he thought, perhaps, that in this business of whaling, courage was one of the great staple outfits of the ship, like her beef and her bread, and not to be foolishly wasted. Wherefore he had no fancy for lowering for whales after sun-down; nor for persisting in fighting a fish that too much persisted in fighting him. For, thought Starbuck, I am here in this critical ocean to kill whales for my living, and not to be killed by them for theirs; and that hundreds of men had been so killed Starbuck well knew. What doom was his own father's? Where, in the bottomless deeps, could he find the torn limbs of his brother?

With memories like these in him, and, moreover, given to a certain superstitiousness, as has been said; the courage of this Starbuck which could, nevertheless, still flourish, must indeed have been extreme. But it was not in reasonable nature that a man so organized, and with such terrible experiences and remembrances as he had; it was not in nature that these things should fail in latently engendering an element in him, which, under suitable circumstances, would break out from its confinement, and burn all his courage up. And brave as he might be, it was that sort of bravery chiefly, visible in some intrepid men, which, while generally abiding firm in the conflict with seas, or winds, or whales, or any of the ordinary irrational horrors of the world, yet cannot withstand those more terrific, because more spiritual terrors, which sometimes menace you from the concentrating brow of an enraged and mighty man.

But were the coming narrative to reveal in any instance, the complete abasement of poor Starbuck's fortitude, scarce might I have the heart to write it; for it is a thing most sorrowful, nay shocking, to expose the fall of valor in the soul. Men may seem detestable as joint stock-companies and nations; knaves, fools, and murderers there may be; men may have mean and meagre faces; but man, in the ideal, is so noble and so sparkling, such a grand and glowing creature, that over any ignominious blemish in him all his fellows should run to throw their costliest robes. That immaculate manliness we feel within ourselves, so far within us, that it remains intact though all the outer character seem gone; bleeds with keenest anguish at the undraped spectacle of a valor-ruined man. Nor can piety itself, at such a shameful sight, completely stifle her upbraidings against the permitting stars. But this august dignity I treat of, is not the dignity of kings and robes, but that abounding dignity which has no robed investiture. Thou shalt see it shining in the arm that wields a pick or drives a spike; that democratic dignity which, on all hands, radiates without end from God; Himself! The great God absolute! The centre and circumference of all democracy! His omnipresence, our divine equality!

If, then, to meanest mariners, and renegades and castaways, I shall hereafter ascribe high qualities, though dark; weave round them tragic graces; if even the most mournful, perchance the most abased, among them all, shall at times lift himself to the exalted mounts; if I shall touch that workman's arm with some ethereal light; if I shall spread a rainbow over his disastrous set of sun;[1] then against all mortal critics bear me out in it, thou just Spirit of Equality, which hast spread one royal mantle of humanity over all my kind! Bear me out in it, thou great democratic God! who didst not refuse to the swart convict, Bunyan, the pale, poetic pearl;[2] Thou who didst clothe with doubly hammered leaves of finest gold, the stumped and paupered arm of old Cervantes;[3] Thou who didst pick up Andrew Jackson from the pebbles; who didst hurl him upon a war-horse; who didst thunder him higher than a throne![4] Thou who, in all Thy mighty, earthly marchings, ever cullest Thy selectest champions from the kingly commons; bear me out in it, O God!

---

1 *set of sun* Sunset; see Shakespeare's *Macbeth* (1606), when one of the witches on the heath predicts a battle will be over "ere the set of sun" (1.1.5).

2 *swart convict ... pearl* John Bunyan was a poet and Puritan preacher who wrote *The Pilgrim's Progress* (1678), a Christian allegorical text that has been highly influential on English and American literature and culture. Bunyan was twice imprisoned under the Conventicle Act, which prohibited the holding of church services outside the Church of England.

3 *clothe ... old Cervantes* Miguel de Cervantes was a Spanish writer best known for his novel *Don Quixote* (1605–15). He lived in poverty most of his life. A wound incurred by Cervantes when he served in the military injured his left arm permanently (though it wasn't a "stump" as Melville suggests). The description of Cervantes here is drawn from Laurence Sterne's novel *Tristram Shandy* (1760–65).

4 *Andrew Jackson ... throne* Andrew Jackson grew up in a Scots-Irish immigrant family in the Carolinas. His father's early death meant that the family had little money. He was raised "higher than a throne," however, when he became President of the United States between 1829 and 1837. Jackson was widely seen, in Melville's time, as an advocate for democracy and for common people.

[Stubb, the second mate, is introduced, and Flask, the third mate. Together with Starbuck, they lead the three boats that take off from the *Pequod* and hunt the whales. Each boat has a harpooner: Queequeg is chosen by Starbuck for his crew; Tashtego, an Indigenous man from Martha's Vineyard, is chosen by Stubb; Daggoo, from the African coast, is the harpooner in Flask's boat.]

Chapter 28. Ahab

For several days after leaving Nantucket, nothing above hatches was seen of Captain Ahab. The mates regularly relieved each other at the watches,[1] and for aught that could be seen to the contrary, they seemed to be the only commanders of the ship; only they sometimes issued from the cabin with orders so sudden and peremptory, that after all it was plain they but commanded vicariously. Yes, their supreme lord and dictator was there, though hitherto unseen by any eyes not permitted to penetrate into the now sacred retreat of the cabin.

Every time I ascended to the deck from my watches below, I instantly gazed aft to mark if any strange face were visible; for my first vague disquietude touching the unknown captain, now in the seclusion of the sea, became almost a perturbation. This was strangely heightened at times by the ragged Elijah's diabolical incoherences uninvitedly recurring to me, with a subtle energy I could not have before conceived of. But poorly could I withstand them, much as in other moods I was almost ready to smile at the solemn whimsicalities of that outlandish prophet of the wharves. But whatever it was of apprehensiveness or uneasiness—to call it so—which I felt, yet whenever I came to look about me in the ship, it seemed against all warrantry to cherish such emotions. For though the harpooneers, with the great body of the crew, were a far more barbaric, heathenish, and motley set than any of the tame merchant-ship companies which my previous experiences had made me acquainted with, still I ascribed this—and rightly ascribed it—to the fierce uniqueness of the very nature of that wild Scandinavian vocation[2] in which I had so abandonedly embarked. But it was especially the aspect of the three chief officers of the ship, the mates, which was most forcibly calculated to

1 *watches* Scheduled times when sailors were on duty working the ship (usually four-hour stretches of time).

2 *Scandinavian vocation* I.e., whaling.

allay these colorless misgivings, and induce confidence and cheerfulness in every presentment of the voyage. Three better, more likely[1] sea-officers and men, each in his own different way, could not readily be found, and they were every one of them Americans; a Nantucketer, a Vineyarder, a Cape man. Now, it being Christmas when the ship shot from out her harbor, for a space we had biting Polar weather, though all the time running away from it to the southward; and by every degree and minute of latitude which we sailed, gradually leaving that merciless winter, and all its intolerable weather behind us. It was one of those less lowering, but still grey and gloomy enough mornings of the transition, when with a fair wind the ship was rushing through the water with a vindictive sort of leaping and melancholy rapidity, that as I mounted to the deck at the call of the forenoon watch, so soon as I levelled my glance towards the taffrail,[2] foreboding shivers ran over me. Reality outran apprehension; Captain Ahab stood upon his quarter-deck.

There seemed no sign of common bodily illness about him, nor of the recovery from any. He looked like a man cut away from the stake, when the fire has overrunningly wasted all the limbs without consuming them, or taking away one particle from their compacted aged robustness. His whole high, broad form, seemed made of solid bronze, and shaped in an unalterable mould, like Cellini's cast Perseus.[3] Threading its way out from among his grey hairs, and continuing right down one side of his tawny scorched face and neck, till it disappeared in his clothing, you saw a slender rod-like mark, lividly whitish. It resembled that perpendicular seam sometimes made in the straight, lofty trunk of a great tree, when the upper lightning tearingly darts down it, and without wrenching a single twig, peels and grooves out the bark from top to bottom, ere running off into the soil, leaving the tree still greenly alive, but branded. Whether that mark was born with him, or whether it was the scar left by some desperate wound, no one could certainly say. By some tacit consent, throughout the voyage little or no allusion was made to it, especially by the mates. But once Tashtego's senior, an old Gay-Head Indian among the crew,

---

1 *likely* Having the appearance of being capable and well-qualified; good-looking.

2 *taffrail* The rail going around the stern of the ship.

3 *Cellini's cast Perseus* Famous sculpture of Perseus holding the severed head of the Medusa by Benevenuto Cellini (1500–71).

superstitiously asserted that not till he was full forty years old did Ahab become that way branded, and then it came upon him, not in the fury of any mortal fray, but in an elemental strife at sea. Yet, this wild hint seemed inferentially negatived, by what a grey Manxman[1] insinuated, an old sepulchral man, who, having never before sailed out of Nantucket, had never ere this laid eye upon wild Ahab. Nevertheless, the old sea-traditions, the immemorial credulities, popularly invested this old Manxman with preternatural powers of discernment. So that no white sailor seriously contradicted him when he said that if ever Captain Ahab should be tranquilly laid out—which might hardly come to pass, so he muttered—then, whoever should do that last office for the dead, would find a birth-mark on him from crown to sole.

So powerfully did the whole grim aspect of Ahab affect me, and the livid brand which streaked it, that for the first few moments I hardly noted that not a little of this overbearing grimness was owing to the barbaric white leg upon which he partly stood. It had previously come to me that this ivory leg had at sea been fashioned from the polished bone of the sperm whale's jaw. "Aye, he was dismasted off Japan," said the old Gay-Head Indian once; "but like his dismasted craft, he shipped another mast without coming home for it. He has a quiver[2] of 'em."

I was struck with the singular posture he maintained. Upon each side of the Pequod's quarter deck, and pretty close to the mizzen shrouds,[3] there was an auger hole, bored about half an inch or so, into the plank. His bone leg steadied in that hole; one arm elevated, and holding by a shroud; Captain Ahab stood erect, looking straight out beyond the ship's ever-pitching prow. There was an infinity of firmest fortitude, a determinate, unsurrenderable wilfulness, in the fixed and fearless, forward dedication of that glance. Not a word he spoke; nor did his officers say aught to him; though by all their minutest gestures and expressions, they plainly showed the uneasy, if not painful, consciousness of being under a troubled master-eye. And not only that, but moody stricken Ahab stood before them with

---

1 *Manxman* Person from the Isle of Man.

2 *quiver* Container for holding arrows.

3 *mizzen shrouds* Set of ropes (shrouds) used to work the mizzen-sail (attached to the mizzen-mast, which is located to the rear of the main mast).

a crucifixion in his face; in all the nameless regal overbearing dignity of some mighty woe.

Ere long, from his first visit in the air, he withdrew into his cabin. But after that morning, he was every day visible to the crew; either standing in his pivot-hole, or seated upon an ivory stool he had; or heavily walking the deck. As the sky grew less gloomy; indeed, began to grow a little genial, he became still less and less a recluse; as if, when the ship had sailed from home, nothing but the dead wintry bleakness of the sea had then kept him so secluded. And, by and by, it came to pass, that he was almost continually in the air; but, as yet, for all that he said, or perceptibly did, on the at last sunny deck, he seemed as unnecessary there as another mast. But the Pequod was only making a passage now; not regularly cruising; nearly all whaling preparatives needing supervision the mates were fully competent to, so that there was little or nothing, out of himself, to employ or excite Ahab, now; and thus chase away, for that one interval, the clouds that layer upon layer were piled upon his brow, as ever all clouds choose the loftiest peaks to pile themselves upon.

Nevertheless, ere long, the warm, warbling persuasiveness of the pleasant, holiday weather we came to, seemed gradually to charm him from his mood. For, as when the red-cheeked, dancing girls, April and May, trip home to the wintry, misanthropic woods; even the barest, ruggedest, most thunder-cloven old oak will at least send forth some few green sprouts, to welcome such glad-hearted visitants; so Ahab did, in the end, a little respond to the playful allurings of that girlish air. More than once did he put forth the faint blossom of a look, which, in any other man, would have soon flowered out in a smile.

Chapter 32. Cetology[1]

Already we are boldly launched upon the deep; but soon we shall be lost in its unshored, harbourless immensities. Ere that come to pass; ere the Pequod's weedy hull rolls side by side with the barnacled hulls of the leviathan; at the outset it is but well to attend to a matter almost indispensable to a thorough appreciative understanding of the

1 *Cetology* Division of zoology that concerns whales.

more special leviathanic revelations and allusions of all sorts which are to follow.

It is some systematized exhibition of the whale in his broad genera,[1] that I would now fain put before you. Yet is it no easy task. The classification of the constituents of a chaos, nothing less is here essayed. Listen to what the best and latest authorities have laid down.

"No branch of Zoology is so much involved as that which is entitled Cetology," says Captain Scoresby,[2] A.D. 1820.

"It is not my intention, were it in my power, to enter into the inquiry as to the true method of dividing the cetacea into groups and families. * * * Utter confusion exists among the historians of this animal" (sperm whale), says Surgeon Beale,[3] A.D. 1839.

"Unfitness to pursue our research in the unfathomable waters." "Impenetrable veil covering our knowledge of the cetacea." "A field strewn with thorns." "All these incomplete indications but serve to torture us naturalists."

Thus speak of the whale, the great Cuvier, and John Hunter, and Lesson,[4] those lights of zoology and anatomy. Nevertheless, though of real knowledge there be little, yet of books there are a plenty; and so in some small degree, with cetology, or the science of whales. Many are the men, small and great, old and new, landsmen and seamen, who have at large or in little, written of the whale. Run over a few:—The Authors of the Bible; Aristotle; Pliny; Aldrovandi; Sir Thomas Browne; Gesner; Ray; Linnæus; Rondeletius; Willoughby; Green; Artedi; Sibbald; Brisson; Marten; Lacépède; Bonneterre; Desmarest; Baron Cuvier; Frederick Cuvier; John Hunter; Owen; Scoresby; Beale; Bennett; J. Ross Browne; the Author of Miriam Coffin;[5] Olmstead;

---

1 *genera* Kinds, classes.

2 *Captain Scoresby* English explorer and scientist William Scoresby. His books *An Account of the Arctic Regions and Northern Whale Fishery* (1820) and *Journal of a Voyage to the Northern Whale Fishery, including Researches and Discoveries on the Eastern Coast of Greenland* (1823) were important sources for Melville.

3 *Surgeon Beale* Thomas Beale, who worked on British whalers as a surgeon, wrote *The Natural History of the Sperm Whale* (1835; expanded and revised edition 1839).

4 The quotations in the paragraph above are taken from the works of William Scoresby; Baron Georges Cuvier (1769–1832); John Hunter (1728–93); and René-Primavère Lesson (1794–1849).

5 *Author of Miriam Coffin* Joseph C. Hart (1798–1855) was the author of the novel *Miriam Coffin, or, The Whale-Fishermen* (1834).

and the Rev. T. Cheever.[1] But to what ultimate generalizing purpose all these have written, the above cited extracts will show.

Of the names in this list of whale authors, only those following Owen ever saw living whales; and but one of them was a real professional harpooneer and whaleman. I mean Captain Scoresby. On the separate subject of the Greenland or right-whale, he is the best existing authority. But Scoresby knew nothing and says nothing of the great sperm whale, compared with which the Greenland whale is almost unworthy mentioning. And here be it said, that the Greenland whale is an usurper upon the throne of the seas. He is not even by any means the largest of the whales. Yet, owing to the long priority of his claims, and the profound ignorance which, till some seventy years back, invested the then fabulous or utterly unknown sperm-whale, and which ignorance to this present day still reigns in all but some few scientific retreats and whale-ports; this usurpation has been every way complete. Reference to nearly all the leviathanic allusions in the great poets of past days, will satisfy you that the Greenland whale, without one rival, was to them the monarch of the seas. But the time has at last come for a new proclamation. This is Charing Cross;[2] hear ye! good people all,—the Greenland whale is deposed,—the great sperm whale now reigneth!

There are only two books in being which at all pretend to put the living sperm whale before you, and at the same time, in the remotest degree succeed in the attempt. Those books are Beale's and Bennett's;[3] both in their time surgeons to English South-Sea whale-ships, and both exact and reliable men. The original matter touching the sperm whale to be found in their volumes is necessarily small; but so far as it goes, it is of excellent quality, though mostly confined to scientific description. As yet, however, the sperm whale, scientific or poetic, lives not complete in any literature. Far above all other hunted whales, his is an unwritten life.

---

1 *Authors of the Bible ... Cheever* This list of writers and natural philosophers, up until Linnaeus, is taken from the article on whales from *The Penny Cyclopedia* (1843), though Melville added Sir Thomas Browne (1605–82).

2 *Charing Cross* London outdoor gathering place where six roads meet, and where public proclamations were often made.

3 *Bennett* Frederick Debell Bennett (1806–59) was a ship surgeon and scientist who wrote *Narrative of a Whaling Voyage Round the Globe* (1840).

Now the various species of whales need some sort of popular comprehensive classification, if only an easy outline one for the present, hereafter to be filled in all its departments by subsequent laborers. As no better man advances to take this matter in hand, I hereupon offer my own poor endeavors. I promise nothing complete; because any human thing supposed to be complete, must for that very reason infallibly be faulty. I shall not pretend to a minute anatomical description of the various species, or—in this place at least—to much of any description. My object here is simply to project the draught[1] of a systematization of cetology. I am the architect, not the builder.

But it is a ponderous task; no ordinary letter-sorter in the Post-Office is equal to it. To grope down into the bottom of the sea after them; to have one's hands among the unspeakable foundations, ribs, and very pelvis of the world; this is a fearful thing. What am I that I should essay to hook the nose of this leviathan! The awful tauntings in Job[2] might well appal me. "Will he (the leviathan) make a covenant with thee? Behold the hope of him is vain!"[3] But I have swam through libraries and sailed through oceans; I have had to do with whales with these visible hands; I am in earnest; and I will try. There are some preliminaries to settle.

First: The uncertain, unsettled condition of this science of Cetology is in the very vestibule attested by the fact, that in some quarters it still remains a moot[4] point whether a whale be a fish. In his System of Nature, A.D. 1776, Linnæus[5] declares, "I hereby separate the whales from the fish." But of my own knowledge, I know that down to the year 1850, sharks and shad, alewives and herring, against Linnæus's express edict, were still found dividing the possession of the same seas with the Leviathan.

---

1 *draught* Draft.

2 *awful tauntings in Job* See Job 41, where the power of the leviathan reveals the power of God, and the uselessness of fighting the leviathan is compared to the uselessness of fighting God (for example, Job 41.1–3: "Canst thou draw out leviathan with an hook? Or his tongue with a cord which thou lettest down? / Canst thou put an hook into his nose? Or bore his jaw through with a thorn? / Will he make many supplications unto thee? Will he speak soft words unto thee?").

3 *Will he ... is vain* See Job 41, verses 4 and 9.

4 *moot* Debatable.

5 *Linnæus* Carl Linnaeus (1707–78) was a Swedish zoologist and botanist who created the modern system for categorizing and naming organisms.

The grounds upon which Linnæus would fain have banished the whales from the waters, he states as follows: "On account of their warm bilocular[1] heart, their lungs, their movable eyelids, their hollow ears, penem intrantem feminam mammis lactantem,"[2] and finally, "ex lege naturæ jure meritoque."[3] I submitted all this to my friends Simeon Macey and Charley Coffin, of Nantucket, both messmates of mine in a certain voyage, and they united in the opinion that the reasons set forth were altogether insufficient. Charley profanely hinted they were humbug.

Be it known that, waiving all argument, I take the good old fashioned ground that the whale is a fish, and call upon holy Jonah to back me. This fundamental thing settled, the next point is, in what internal respect does the whale differ from other fish. Above, Linnæus has given you those items. But in brief, they are these: lungs and warm blood; whereas, all other fish are lungless and cold blooded.

Next: how shall we define the whale, by his obvious externals, so as conspicuously to label him for all time to come? To be short, then, a whale is *a spouting fish with a horizontal tail.* There you have him. However contracted, that definition is the result of expanded meditation. A walrus spouts much like a whale, but the walrus is not a fish, because he is amphibious. But the last term of the definition is still more cogent, as coupled with the first. Almost any one must have noticed that all the fish familiar to landsmen have not a flat, but a vertical, or up-and-down tail. Whereas, among spouting fish the tail, though it may be similarly shaped, invariably assumes a horizontal position.

By the above definition of what a whale is, I do by no means exclude from the leviathanic brotherhood any sea creature hitherto identified with the whale by the best informed Nantucketers; nor, on the other hand, link with it any fish hitherto authoritatively regarded as alien.[4] Hence, all the smaller, spouting, and horizontal tailed fish

---

1 *bilocular* Consisting of two chambers.

2 *penem ... lactantem* Latin: [their] penis that enters the female, who offers milk from the breasts.

3 *ex lege ... meritoque* Latin: from the law of nature, justly and deservedly.

4 [Melville's note] I am aware that down to the present time, the fish styled Lamatins and Dugongs (Pig-fish and Sow-fish of the Coffins of Nantucket) are included by many naturalists among the whales. But as these pig-fish are a noisy, contemptible set, mostly lurking in the mouths of rivers, and feeding on wet hay, and especially as they do not spout, I

must be included in this ground-plan of Cetology. Now, then, come the grand divisions of the entire whale host.

First: According to magnitude I divide the whales into three primary BOOKS (subdivisible into CHAPTERS), and these shall comprehend them all, both small and large.

I. The FOLIO WHALE; II. the OCTAVO WHALE; III. the DUODECIMO[1] WHALE.

As the type of the FOLIO I present the *Sperm Whale*; of the OCTAVO, the *Grampus*;[2] of the DUODECIMO, the *Porpoise*.

FOLIOS. Among these I here include the following chapters:—I. The *Sperm Whale*; II. the *Right Whale*; III. the *Fin-Back Whale*; IV. the *Hump-backed Whale*; V. the *Razor Back Whale*; VI. the *Sulphur Bottom Whale*.[3]

BOOK I. (*Folio*), CHAPTER I. (Sperm Whale).—This whale, among the English of old vaguely known as the Trumpa whale, and the Physeter whale, and the Anvil Headed whale, is the present Cachalot of the French, and the Pottsfich of the Germans, and the Macrocephalus of the Long Words.[4] He is, without doubt, the largest inhabitant of the globe; the most formidable of all whales to encounter; the most majestic in aspect; and lastly, by far the most valuable in commerce; he being the only creature from which that valuable substance, spermaceti,[5] is obtained. All his peculiarities will, in many other places, be enlarged upon. It is chiefly with his name that I now have to do. Philologically considered, it is absurd. Some centuries ago, when the Sperm whale was almost wholly unknown in his own

---

deny their credentials as whales; and have presented them with their passports to quit the Kingdom of Cetology. [Melville is referring here to the aquatic mammals now known as manatees.]

1 *FOLIO … OCTAVO … DUODECIMO* These are terms used by printers to indicate the size of publications; folios are large books comprised of full-sized sheets of paper folded only once; octavos are smaller books comprised of full-sized sheets folded three times, forming sections of eight pages; duodecimo books are smaller still, with each page comprising one-twelfth of the full sheet of paper, forming sections of twenty-four pages.

2 *Grampus* Now known as the orca whale.

3 *Sulphur Bottom Whale* Now known as the blue whale.

4 *of the Long Words* I.e., those who use long words (writers who refer to animals and plants by their Latin names).

5 *spermaceti* Fragrant, waxy substance found in the head of sperm whales. The word means "sperm of whales," though spermaceti is not sperm, but in fact a liquid that helps the whale use echolocation and maintain buoyancy at great depths.

proper individuality, and when his oil was only accidentally obtained from the stranded fish; in those days spermaceti, it would seem, was popularly supposed to be derived from a creature identical with the one then known in England as the Greenland or Right Whale. It was the idea also, that this same spermaceti was that quickening humor[1] of the Greenland Whale which the first syllable of the word literally expresses. In those times, also, spermaceti was exceedingly scarce, not being used for light, but only as an ointment and medicament. It was only to be had from the druggists as you nowadays buy an ounce of rhubarb.[2] When, as I opine, in the course of time, the true nature of spermaceti became known, its original name was still retained by the dealers; no doubt to enhance its value by a notion so strangely significant of its scarcity. And so the appellation must at last have come to be bestowed upon the whale from which this spermaceti was really derived.

BOOK I. (*Folio*), CHAPTER II. (Right Whale).—In one respect this is the most venerable of the leviathans, being the one first regularly hunted by man. It yields the article commonly known as whalebone or baleen; and the oil specially known as "whale oil," an inferior article in commerce. Among the fishermen, he is indiscriminately designated by all the following titles: The Whale; the Greenland Whale; the Black Whale; the Great Whale; the True Whale; the Right Whale. There is a deal of obscurity concerning the identity of the species thus multitudinously baptised. What then is the whale, which I include in the second species of my Folios? It is the Great Mysticetus of the English naturalists; the Greenland Whale of the English whalemen; the Baleine Ordinaire of the French whalemen; the Growlands Walfish of the Swedes. It is the whale which for more than two centuries past has been hunted by the Dutch and English in the Arctic seas; it is the whale which the American fishermen have long pursued in the Indian ocean, on the Brazil Banks, on the Nor' West Coast,[3] and various other parts of the world, designated by them Right Whale Cruising Grounds.

Some pretend to see a difference between the Greenland whale of the English and the right whale of the Americans. But they precisely

1 *quickening humor* Life-giving substance, i.e., sperm.

2 *rhubarb* Preparations of the leaves and roots of rhubarb were once sold as laxatives.

3 *Nor' West Coast* Northern coasts of North America, both east and west.

agree in all their grand features; nor has there yet been presented a single determinate fact upon which to ground a radical distinction. It is by endless subdivisions based upon the most inconclusive differences, that some departments of natural history become so repellingly intricate. The right whale will be elsewhere treated of at some length, with reference to elucidating the sperm whale.

BOOK I. (*Folio*), CHAPTER III. (*Fin-Back*).—Under this head I reckon a monster which, by the various names of Fin-Back, Tall-Spout, and Long-John, has been seen almost in every sea and is commonly the whale whose distant jet is so often descried by passengers crossing the Atlantic, in the New York packet-tracks.[1] In the length he attains, and in his baleen, the Fin-back resembles the right whale, but is of a less portly girth, and a lighter color, approaching to olive. His great lips present a cable-like aspect, formed by the intertwisting, slanting folds of large wrinkles. His grand distinguishing feature, the fin, from which he derives his name, is often a conspicuous object. This fin is some three or four feet long, growing vertically from the hinder part of the back, of an angular shape, and with a very sharp pointed end. Even if not the slightest other part of the creature be visible, this isolated fin will, at times, be seen plainly projecting from the surface. When the sea is moderately calm, and slightly marked with spherical ripples, and this gnomon-like[2] fin stands up and casts shadows upon the wrinkled surface, it may well be supposed that the watery circle surrounding it somewhat resembles a dial, with its style and wavy hour-lines graved on it. On that Ahaz-dial the shadow often goes back.[3] The Fin-Back is not gregarious. He seems a whale-hater, as some men are man-haters. Very shy; always going solitary; unexpectedly rising to the surface in the remotest and most sullen waters; his straight and single lofty jet rising like a tall misanthropic spear upon a barren plain; gifted with such wondrous power and velocity

---

1 *New York packet-tracks* I.e., the wake of packet ships, ships that sailed on a regular schedule between America and Britain.

2 *gnomon-like* Similar to the rod or pillar that casts the shadow in a sun-dial.

3 *Ahaz-dial … back* The Dial of Ahaz is a sundial named after the king of Judah who was said to have invented it. In 2 Kings 20 and Isaiah 38, it is prophesied that King Hezekiah is to die; God hears his prayer to live and grants him fifteen more years; the prophet Isaiah is the one that relays God's message to Hezekiah, and the sign given of this favor is that God retraces the steps of the sundial by ten degrees. Ishmael is saying that the fin of the finback whale, unlike most sundials, moves backwards and forwards unpredictably.

in swimming, as to defy all present pursuit from man; this leviathan seems the banished and unconquerable Cain of his race, bearing for his mark that style[1] upon his back. From having the baleen in his mouth, the Fin-Back is sometimes included with the right whale, among a theoretic species denominated *Whalebone whales*, that is, whales with baleen. Of these so-called Whalebone whales, there would seem to be several varieties, most of which, however, are little known. Broad-nosed whales and beaked whales; pike-headed whales; bunched whales; under-jawed whales and rostrated[2] whales, are the fishermen's names for a few sorts.

In connection with this appellative of "Whalebone whales," it is of great importance to mention, that however such a nomenclature may be convenient in facilitating allusions to some kind of whales, yet it is in vain to attempt a clear classification of the Leviathan, founded upon either his baleen, or hump, or fin, or teeth; notwithstanding that those marked parts or features very obviously seem better adapted to afford the basis for a regular system of Cetology than any other detached bodily distinctions, which the whale, in his kinds, presents. How then? The baleen, hump, back-fin, and teeth; these are things whose peculiarities are indiscriminately dispersed among all sorts of whales, without any regard to what may be the nature of their structure in other and more essential particulars. Thus, the sperm whale and the humpbacked whale, each has a hump; but there the similitude ceases. Then, this same humpbacked whale and the Greenland whale, each of these has baleen; but there again the similitude ceases. And it is just the same with the other parts above mentioned. In various sorts of whales, they form such irregular combinations; or, in the case of any one of them detached, such an irregular isolation; as utterly to defy all general methodization formed upon such a basis. On this rock every one of the whale-naturalists has split.

But it may possibly be conceived that, in the internal parts of the whale, in his anatomy—there, at least, we shall be able to hit the right

1 *Cain* First son of Adam and Eve, who kills his brother, Abel. God condemns Cain to be "a fugitive and a vagabond" and sets a mark on him to prevent him from being murdered: "And the Lord said unto him, Therefore whosoever slayeth Cain, vengeance shall be taken on him sevenfold. And the Lord set a mark upon Cain, lest any finding him should kill him" (Genesis 4.15); *style* Sharp instrument used for engraving.

2 *rostrated* Beaked.

classification. Nay; what thing, for example, is there in the Greenland whale's anatomy more striking than his baleen? Yet we have seen that by his baleen it is impossible correctly to classify the Greenland whale. And if you descend into the bowels of the various leviathans, why there you will not find distinctions a fiftieth part as available to the systematizer as those external ones already enumerated. What then remains? nothing but to take hold of the whales bodily, in their entire liberal volume, and boldly sort them that way. And this is the Bibliographical system here adopted; and it is the only one that can possibly succeed, for it alone is practicable. To proceed.

BOOK I. (*Folio*), CHAPTER IV. (*Hump Back*).—This whale is often seen on the northern American coast. He has been frequently captured there, and towed into harbor. He has a great pack on him like a peddler; or you might call him the Elephant and Castle[1] whale. At any rate, the popular name for him does not sufficiently distinguish him, since the sperm whale also has a hump though a smaller one. His oil is not very valuable. He has baleen. He is the most gamesome and light-hearted of all the whales, making more gay foam and white water generally than any other of them.

BOOK I. (*Folio*), CHAPTER V. (*Razor Back*).—Of this whale little is known but his name. I have seen him at a distance off Cape Horn. Of a retiring nature, he eludes both hunters and philosophers. Though no coward, he has never yet shown any part of him but his back, which rises in a long sharp ridge. Let him go. I know little more of him, nor does anybody else.

BOOK I. (*Folio*), CHAPTER VI. (*Sulphur Bottom*).—Another retiring gentleman, with a brimstone belly, doubtless got by scraping along the Tartarian[2] tiles in some of his profounder divings. He is seldom seen; at least I have never seen him except in the remoter southern seas, and then always at too great a distance to study his countenance. He is never chased; he would run away with rope-walks of line. Prodigies are told of him. Adieu, Sulphur Bottom! I can say nothing more that is true of ye, nor can the oldest Nantucketer.

---

1 *Elephant and Castle* Popular name for inns and pubs, based on the medieval image of an elephant carrying a castle-like structure called a howdah—used for carrying people, often during warfare—on its back.

2 *Tartarian* In Greek mythology, Tartarus is the deepest part of the underworld, where those who have done evil are punished.

Thus ends BOOK I. (*Folio*), and now begins BOOK II. (*Octavo*).

OCTAVOES.[1]—These embrace the whales of middling magnitude, among which present may be numbered:—I., the *Grampus*; II., the *Black Fish*; III., the *Narwhale*; IV., the *Thrasher*; V., the *Killer*.

BOOK II. (*Octavo*), CHAPTER I. (*Grampus*).—Though this fish, whose loud sonorous breathing, or rather blowing, has furnished a proverb to landsmen,[2] is so well known a denizen of the deep, yet is he not popularly classed among whales. But possessing all the grand distinctive features of the leviathan, most naturalists have recognised him for one. He is of moderate octavo size, varying from fifteen to twenty-five feet in length, and of corresponding dimensions round the waist. He swims in herds; he is never regularly hunted, though his oil is considerable in quantity, and pretty good for light. By some fishermen his approach is regarded as premonitory of the advance of the great sperm whale.

BOOK II. (*Octavo*), CHAPTER II. (*Black Fish*).[3]—I give the popular fishermen's names for all these fish, for generally they are the best. Where any name happens to be vague or inexpressive, I shall say so, and suggest another. I do so now, touching the Black Fish, so-called, because blackness is the rule among almost all whales. So, call him the Hyena Whale, if you please. His voracity is well known, and from the circumstance that the inner angles of his lips are curved upwards, he carries an everlasting Mephistophelean grin[4] on his face. This whale averages some sixteen or eighteen feet in length. He is found in almost all latitudes. He has a peculiar way of showing his dorsal hooked fin in swimming, which looks something like a Roman nose.[5] When not more profitably employed, the sperm whale hunters sometimes capture the Hyena whale, to keep up the supply of cheap oil for domestic employment—as some frugal housekeepers, in the absence of company, and quite alone by themselves, burn unsavory

1 [Melville's note] Why this book of whales is not denominated the Quarto [size of book between the folio and octavo] is very plain. Because, while the whales of this order, though smaller than those of the former order, nevertheless retain a proportionate likeness to them in figure, yet the bookbinder's Quarto volume in its dimensioned form does not preserve the shape of the Folio volume, but the Octavo volume does.

2 *proverb to landsmen* I.e., "snoring or puffing like a grampus."

3 *Black Fish* Now known as the pilot whale.

4 *Mephistophelean grin* Devilish smile.

5 *Roman nose* Hooked, "eagle-like" nose.

tallow instead of odorous wax. Though their blubber is very thin, some of these whales will yield you upwards of thirty gallons of oil.

BOOK II. (*Octavo*), CHAPTER III. (*Narwhale*), that is, *Nostril whale*.—Another instance of a curiously named whale, so named I suppose from his peculiar horn being originally mistaken for a peaked nose. The creature is some sixteen feet in length, while its horn averages five feet, though some exceed ten, and even attain to fifteen feet. Strictly speaking, this horn is but a lengthened tusk, growing out from the jaw in a line a little depressed from the horizontal. But it is only found on the sinister side,[1] which has an ill effect, giving its owner something analogous to the aspect of a clumsy left-handed man. What precise purpose this ivory horn or lance answers, it would be hard to say. It does not seem to be used like the blade of the sword-fish and bill-fish; though some sailors tell me that the Narwhale employs it for a rake in turning over the bottom of the sea for food. Charley Coffin said it was used for an ice-piercer; for the Narwhale, rising to the surface of the Polar Sea, and finding it sheeted with ice, thrusts his horn up, and so breaks through. But you cannot prove either of these surmises to be correct. My own opinion is, that however this one-sided horn may really be used by the Narwhale—however that may be—it would certainly be very convenient to him for a folder in reading pamphlets.[2] The Narwhale I have heard called the Tusked whale, the Horned whale, and the Unicorn whale. He is certainly a curious example of the Unicornism to be found in almost every kingdom of animated nature. From certain cloistered old authors I have gathered that this same sea-unicorn's horn was in ancient days regarded as the great antidote against poison, and as such, preparations of it brought immense prices. It was also distilled to a volatile salts for fainting ladies, the same way that the horns of the male deer are manufactured into hartshorn. Originally it was in itself accounted an object of great curiosity. Black Letter[3] tells me that Sir Martin Frobisher on his return from that voyage, when Queen Bess[4] did

1 *sinister side* Left side.

2 *folder in reading pamphlets* I.e., a page turner.

3 *Black Letter* An invented author.

4 *Sir Martin Frobisher* English explorer who sailed to northeastern Canada in search of the Northwest Passage (c. 1535–94); *Queen Bess* Queen Elizabeth I, who ruled England and Ireland from 1553 until 1603.

gallantly wave her jewelled hand to him from a window of Greenwich Palace, as his bold ship sailed down the Thames; "when Sir Martin returned from that voyage," saith Black Letter, "on bended knees he presented to her highness a prodigious long horn of the Narwhale, which for a long period after hung in the castle at Windsor." An Irish author avers that the Earl of Leicester,[1] on bended knees, did likewise present to her highness another horn, pertaining to a land beast of the unicorn nature.

The Narwhale has a very picturesque, leopard-like look, being of a milk-white ground[2] color, dotted with round and oblong spots of black. His oil is very superior, clear and fine; but there is little of it, and he is seldom hunted. He is mostly found in the circumpolar seas.

BOOK II. (*Octavo*), CHAPTER IV. (*Killer*).—Of this whale little is precisely known to the Nantucketer, and nothing at all to the professed naturalist. From what I have seen of him at a distance, I should say that he was about the bigness of a grampus. He is very savage—a sort of Feegee fish.[3] He sometimes takes the great Folio whales by the lip, and hangs there like a leech, till the mighty brute is worried[4] to death. The Killer is never hunted. I never heard what sort of oil he has. Exception might be taken to the name bestowed upon this whale, on the ground of its indistinctness. For we are all killers, on land and on sea; Bonapartes and Sharks included.

BOOK II. (*Octavo*), CHAPTER V. (*Thrasher*).[5]—This gentleman is famous for his tail, which he uses for a ferule[6] in thrashing his foes. He mounts the Folio whale's back, and as he swims, he works his passage by flogging him; as some schoolmasters get along in the world by a similar process. Still less is known of the Thrasher than of the Killer. Both are outlaws, even in the lawless seas.

---

1 *Earl of Leicester* Robert Dudley, 1st Earl of Leicester (1532–88) was a suitor to Queen Elizabeth and one of her favorite courtiers. The story told here hints that the "horn" Leicester offers the queen is in fact his own sexual favors.

2 *ground* Background.

3 *Feegee fish* The Indigenous people of Fiji, known as Figians or iTaukei, were considered by colonial powers to be "savage" on account of their ritualistic practice of cannibalism, and European ships avoided landing on the islands.

4 *worried* Torn with the teeth, bit.

5 *Thrasher* This is likely also the orca.

6 *ferule* Rod or cane used for corporal punishment.

Thus ends BOOK II. (*Octavo*), and begins BOOK III. (*Duodecimo*).

DUODECIMOES.—These include the smaller whales. I. The Huzza Porpoise.[1] II. The Algerine Porpoise.[2] III. The Mealy-mouthed Porpoise.[3]

To those who have not chanced specially to study the subject, it may possibly seem strange, that fishes not commonly exceeding four or five feet should be marshalled among WHALES—a word, which, in the popular sense, always conveys an idea of hugeness. But the creatures set down above as Duodecimoes are infallibly whales, by the terms of my definition of what a whale is—i.e. a spouting fish, with a horizontal tail.

BOOK III. (*Duodecimo*), CHAPTER I. (*Huzza Porpoise*).—This is the common porpoise found almost all over the globe. The name is of my own bestowal; for there are more than one sort of porpoises, and something must be done to distinguish them. I call him thus, because he always swims in hilarious[4] shoals, which upon the broad sea keep tossing themselves to heaven like caps in a Fourth-of-July crowd. Their appearance is generally hailed with delight by the mariner. Full of fine spirits, they invariably come from the breezy billows to windward. They are the lads that always live before the wind. They are accounted a lucky omen. If you yourself can withstand three cheers at beholding these vivacious fish, then heaven help ye; the spirit of godly gamesomeness is not in ye. A well-fed, plump Huzza Porpoise will yield you one good gallon of good oil. But the fine and delicate fluid extracted from his jaws is exceedingly valuable. It is in request among jewellers and watchmakers. Sailors put it on their hones.[5] Porpoise meat is good eating, you know. It may never have occurred to you that a porpoise spouts. Indeed, his spout is so small that it is not very readily discernible. But the next time you have a chance, watch him; and you will then see the great Sperm whale himself in miniature.

BOOK III. (*Duodecimo*), CHAPTER II. (*Algerine Porpoise*).—A pirate. Very savage. He is only found, I think, in the Pacific. He is

---

1 *Huzza Porpoise* Now known as the harbor porpoise.

2 *Algerine Porpoise* Unclear which species Melville had in mind here.

3 *Mealy-mouthed Porpoise* Now known as the southern right whale dolphin.

4 *hilarious* Boisterous.

5 *hones* Whetstones, used for sharpening razors.

somewhat larger than the Huzza Porpoise, but much of the same general make. Provoke him, and he will buckle to a shark.[1] I have lowered for him many times, but never yet saw him captured.

BOOK III. (*Duodecimo*), CHAPTER III. (*Mealy-mouthed Porpoise*).—The largest kind of Porpoise; and only found in the Pacific, so far as it is known. The only English name, by which he has hitherto been designated, is that of the fishers—Right-Whale Porpoise, from the circumstance that he is chiefly found in the vicinity of that Folio. In shape, he differs in some degree from the Huzza Porpoise, being of a less rotund and jolly girth; indeed, he is of quite a neat and gentleman-like figure. He has no fins on his back (most other porpoises have), he has a lovely tail, and sentimental Indian eyes of a hazel hue. But his mealy-mouth spoils all. Though his entire back down to his side fins is of a deep sable, yet a boundary line, distinct as the mark in a ship's hull, called the "bright waist," that line streaks him from stem to stern, with two separate colors, black above and white below. The white comprises part of his head, and the whole of his mouth, which makes him look as if he had just escaped from a felonious visit to a meal-bag. A most mean and mealy aspect! His oil is much like that of the common porpoise.

* * * * * *

Beyond the DUODECIMO, this system does not proceed, inasmuch as the Porpoise is the smallest of the whales. Above, you have all the Leviathans of note. But there are a rabble of uncertain, fugitive, half-fabulous[2] whales, which, as an American whaleman, I know by reputation, but not personally. I shall enumerate them by their forecastle appellations; for possibly such a list may be valuable to future investigators, who may complete what I have here but begun. If any of the following whales, shall hereafter be caught and marked, then he can readily be incorporated into this System, according to his Folio, Octavo, or Duodecimo magnitude:—The Bottle-Nose Whale; the Junk Whale; the Pudding-Headed Whale; the Cape Whale; the Leading Whale; the Cannon Whale; the Scragg Whale; the Coppered Whale; the Elephant Whale; the Iceberg Whale; the Quog Whale; the Blue Whale; etc. From Icelandic, Dutch, and old English authorities,

---

1 *buckle to a shark* Fight like a shark.

2 *half-fabulous* Half-mythical.

there might be quoted other lists of uncertain whales, blessed with all manner of uncouth names. But I omit them as altogether obsolete; and can hardly help suspecting them for mere sounds, full of Leviathanism, but signifying nothing.[1]

Finally: It was stated at the outset, that this system would not be here, and at once, perfected. You cannot but plainly see that I have kept my word. But I now leave my cetological System standing thus unfinished, even as the great Cathedral of Cologne was left, with the crane still standing upon the top of the uncompleted tower.[2] For small erections may be finished by their first architects; grand ones, true ones, ever leave the copestone[3] to posterity. God keep me from ever completing anything. This whole book is but a draught—nay, but the draught of a draught. Oh, Time, Strength, Cash, and Patience!

Chapter 36. The Quarter-Deck

(*Enter Ahab: Then, all.*)

It was not a great while after the affair of the pipe,[4] that one morning shortly after breakfast, Ahab, as was his wont, ascended the cabin-gangway to the deck. There most sea-captains usually walk at that hour, as country gentlemen, after the same meal, take a few turns in the garden.

Soon his steady, ivory stride was heard, as to and fro he paced his old rounds, upon planks so familiar to his tread, that they were all over dented, like geological stones, with the peculiar mark of his walk. Did you fixedly gaze, too, upon that ribbed and dented brow; there also, you would see still stranger foot-prints—the foot-prints of his one unsleeping, ever-pacing thought.

---

1 *sounds … nothing* See *Macbeth*, 5.5.26–28, where life is described as "a tale / Told by an idiot, full of sound and fury, / Signifying nothing."

2 *Cathedral of Cologne … tower* Construction of the cathedral in Cologne, Germany, was begun in 1248 but paused in 1473, when a large crane was left on the unfinished south tower for 400 years, until work was recommenced in 1842 and was finally completed in 1880.

3 *copestone* Top stone—the finishing touch on a building.

4 *affair of the pipe* In Chapter 30, omitted in these selections, Ahab throws his lit pipe into the sea, quitting smoking, as it is "meant for sereneness," for men with "mild white hairs," not "torn iron-grey locks like mine."

But on the occasion in question, those dents looked deeper, even as his nervous step that morning left a deeper mark. And, so full of his thought was Ahab, that at every uniform turn that he made, now at the main-mast and now at the binnacle,[1] you could almost see that thought turn in him as he turned, and pace in him as he paced; so completely possessing him, indeed, that it all but seemed the inward mould of every outer movement.

"D'ye mark him, Flask?" whispered Stubb; "the chick that's in him pecks the shell. T'will soon be out."

The hours wore on;—Ahab now shut up within his cabin; anon, pacing the deck, with the same intense bigotry[2] of purpose in his aspect.

It drew near the close of day. Suddenly he came to a halt by the bulwarks, and inserting his bone leg into the auger-hole there, and with one hand grasping a shroud, he ordered Starbuck to send everybody aft.

"Sir!" said the mate, astonished at an order seldom or never given on ship-board except in some extraordinary case.

"Send everybody aft," repeated Ahab. "Mast-heads,[3] there! come down!"

When the entire ship's company were assembled, and with curious and not wholly unapprehensive faces, were eyeing him, for he looked not unlike the weather horizon when a storm is coming up, Ahab, after rapidly glancing over the bulwarks, and then darting his eyes among the crew, started from his standpoint; and as though not a soul were nigh him resumed his heavy turns upon the deck. With bent head and half-slouched hat he continued to pace, unmindful of the wondering whispering among the men; till Stubb cautiously whispered to Flask, that Ahab must have summoned them there for the purpose of witnessing a pedestrian feat. But this did not last long. Vehemently pausing, he cried:—

"What do ye do when ye see a whale, men?"

"Sing out for him!" was the impulsive rejoinder from a score of clubbed voices.

1 *binnacle* Box near the helm of a boat where the compass is kept.

2 *bigotry* Stubborn and irrational adherence to an idea or belief.

3 *Mast-heads* Sailors stationed high in the mast-heads of the ship as look-outs.

"Good!" cried Ahab, with a wild approval in his tones; observing the hearty animation into which his unexpected question had so magnetically thrown them.

"And what do ye next, men?"

"Lower away, and after him!"

"And what tune is it ye pull to, men?"

"A dead whale or a stove boat!"[1]

More and more strangely and fiercely glad and approving, grew the countenance of the old man at every shout; while the mariners began to gaze curiously at each other, as if marvelling how it was that they themselves became so excited at such seemingly purposeless questions.

But, they were all eagerness again, as Ahab, now half-revolving in his pivot-hole, with one hand reaching high up a shroud, and tightly, almost convulsively grasping it, addressed them thus:—

"All ye mast-headers have before now heard me give orders about a white whale. Look ye! d'ye see this Spanish ounce of gold?"—holding up a broad bright coin to the sun—"it is a sixteen dollar piece, men. D'ye see it? Mr. Starbuck, hand me yon top-maul."[2]

While the mate was getting the hammer, Ahab, without speaking, was slowly rubbing the gold piece against the skirts of his jacket, as if to heighten its lustre, and without using any words was meanwhile lowly humming to himself, producing a sound so strangely muffled and inarticulate that it seemed the mechanical humming of the wheels of his vitality in him.

Receiving the top-maul from Starbuck, he advanced towards the main-mast with the hammer uplifted in one hand, exhibiting the gold with the other, and with a high raised voice exclaiming: "Whosoever of ye raises me a white-headed whale with a wrinkled brow and a crooked jaw; whosoever of ye raises me that white-headed whale, with three holes punctured in his starboard fluke—look ye, whosoever of ye raises me that same white whale, he shall have this gold ounce, my boys!"

"Huzza! huzza!" cried the seamen, as with swinging tarpaulins[3] they hailed the act of nailing the gold to the mast.

---

1 *stove boat* Boat that has been destroyed by being bashed in.

2 *top-maul* Heavy hammer used on ships to set up the topmast rigging.

3 *tarpaulins* Hats that have been waterproofed with tar.

"It's a white whale, I say," resumed Ahab, as he threw down the topmaul: "a white whale. Skin your eyes for him, men; look sharp for white water; if ye see but a bubble, sing out."

All this while Tashtego, Daggoo, and Queequeg had looked on with even more intense interest and surprise than the rest, and at the mention of the wrinkled brow and crooked jaw they had started as if each was separately touched by some specific recollection.

"Captain Ahab," said Tashtego, "that white whale must be the same that some call Moby Dick."

"Moby Dick?" shouted Ahab. "Do ye know the white whale then, Tash?"

"Does he fan-tail a little curious, sir, before he goes down?" said the Gay-Header deliberately.

"And has he a curious spout, too," said Daggoo, "very bushy, even for a parmacetty, and mighty quick, Captain Ahab?"

"And he have one, two, three—oh! good many iron in him hide, too, Captain," cried Queequeg disjointedly, "all twiske-tee be-twisk, like him—him—" faltering hard for a word, and screwing his hand round and round as though uncorking a bottle—"like him—him—"

"Corkscrew!" cried Ahab, "aye, Queequeg, the harpoons lie all twisted and wrenched in him; aye, Daggoo, his spout is a big one, like a whole shock of wheat, and white as a pile of our Nantucket wool after the great annual sheep-shearing; aye, Tashtego, and he fan-tails like a split jib[1] in a squall. Death and devils! men, it is Moby Dick ye have seen—Moby Dick—Moby Dick!"

"Captain Ahab," said Starbuck, who, with Stubb and Flask, had thus far been eyeing his superior with increasing surprise, but at last seemed struck with a thought which somewhat explained all the wonder. "Captain Ahab, I have heard of Moby Dick—but it was not Moby Dick that took off thy leg?"

"Who told thee that?" cried Ahab; then pausing, "Aye, Starbuck; aye, my hearties all round; it was Moby Dick that dismasted me; Moby Dick that brought me to this dead stump I stand on now. Aye, aye," he shouted with a terrific, loud, animal sob, like that of a heart-stricken moose; "Aye, aye! it was that accursed white whale that

---

1 *jib* Triangular sail stretched from the jib-boom to the foremast.

razeed[1] me; made a poor pegging lubber[2] of me for ever and a day!" Then tossing both arms, with measureless imprecations he shouted out: "Aye, aye! and I'll chase him round Good Hope, and round the Horn, and round the Norway Maelstrom,[3] and round perdition's flames before I give him up. And this is what ye have shipped for, men! to chase that white whale on both sides of land, and over all sides of earth, till he spouts black blood and rolls fin out. What say ye, men, will ye splice[4] hands on it, now? I think ye do look brave."

"Aye, aye!" shouted the harpooneers and seamen, running closer to the excited old man: "A sharp eye for the white whale; a sharp lance for Moby Dick!"

"God bless ye," he seemed to half sob and half shout. "God bless ye, men. Steward! go draw the great measure of grog. But what's this long face about, Mr. Starbuck; wilt thou not chase the white whale? art not game for Moby Dick?"

"I am game for his crooked jaw, and for the jaws of Death too, Captain Ahab, if it fairly comes in the way of the business we follow; but I came here to hunt whales, not my commander's vengeance. How many barrels will thy vengeance yield thee even if thou gettest it, Captain Ahab? it will not fetch thee much in our Nantucket market."

"Nantucket market! Hoot! But come closer, Starbuck; thou requirest a little lower layer. If money's to be the measurer, man, and the accountants have computed their great counting-house the globe, by girdling it with guineas,[5] one to every three parts of an inch; then, let me tell thee, that my vengeance will fetch a great premium *here*!"

"He smites his chest," whispered Stubb, "what's that for? methinks it rings most vast, but hollow."

"Vengeance on a dumb brute!" cried Starbuck, "that simply smote thee from blindest instinct! Madness! To be enraged with a dumb thing, Captain Ahab, seems blasphemous."

---

1 *razeed* Cut a ship down in height by removing the upper deck.

2 *lubber* Clumsy person, not sailor-like.

3 *Good Hope ... the Horn ... Norway Maelstrom* Distant and dangerous seas: the Cape of Good Hope, Cape Horn, and the infamous whirlpool near Norway.

4 *splice* Join.

5 *guineas* Gold coins valued at twenty-one shillings, equivalent to just over one pound sterling.

"Hark ye yet again—the little lower layer. All visible objects, man, are but as pasteboard masks. But in each event—in the living act, the undoubted deed—there, some unknown but still reasoning thing puts forth the mouldings of its features from behind the unreasoning mask. If man will strike, strike through the mask! How can the prisoner reach outside except by thrusting through the wall? To me, the white whale is that wall, shoved near to me. Sometimes I think there's naught beyond. But 'tis enough. He tasks me; he heaps me; I see in him outrageous strength, with an inscrutable malice sinewing[1] it. That inscrutable thing is chiefly what I hate; and be the white whale agent, or be the white whale principal, I will wreak that hate upon him. Talk not to me of blasphemy, man; I'd strike the sun if it insulted me. For could the sun do that, then could I do the other; since there is ever a sort of fair play herein, jealousy presiding over all creations. But not my master, man, is even that fair play. Who's over me? Truth hath no confines. Take off thine eye! more intolerable than fiends' glarings is a doltish stare! So, so; thou reddenest and palest; my heat has melted thee to anger-glow. But look ye, Starbuck, what is said in heat, that thing unsays itself. There are men from whom warm words are small indignity. I meant not to incense thee. Let it go. Look! see yonder Turkish cheeks of spotted tawn[2]—living, breathing pictures painted by the sun. The Pagan leopards—the unrecking and unworshipping things, that live; and seek, and give no reasons for the torrid life they feel! The crew, man, the crew! Are they not one and all with Ahab, in this matter of the whale? See Stubb! he laughs! See yonder Chilian! he snorts to think of it. Stand up amid the general hurricane, thy one tost[3] sapling cannot, Starbuck! And what is it? Reckon it. 'Tis but to help strike a fin; no wondrous feat for Starbuck. What is it more? From this one poor hunt, then, the best lance out of all Nantucket, surely he will not hang back, when every foremast-hand has clutched a whetstone? Ah! constrainings seize thee; I see! the billow lifts thee! Speak, but speak!—Aye, aye! thy silence, then, that voices thee. (*Aside*) Something shot from my dilated nostrils, he has inhaled it in his lungs. Starbuck now is mine; cannot oppose me now, without rebellion."

---

1 *sinewing* Strengthening.

2 *tawn* I.e., tawny—golden-brown or bronze-colored.

3 *tost* Tossed.

"God keep me!—keep us all!" murmured Starbuck, lowly.

But in his joy at the enchanted, tacit acquiescence of the mate, Ahab did not hear his foreboding invocation; nor yet the low laugh from the hold; nor yet the presaging vibrations of the winds in the cordage; nor yet the hollow flap of the sails against the masts, as for a moment their hearts sank in. For again Starbuck's downcast eyes lighted up with the stubbornness of life; the subterranean laugh died away; the winds blew on; the sails filled out; the ship heaved and rolled as before. Ah, ye admonitions and warnings! why stay ye not when ye come? But rather are ye predictions than warnings, ye shadows! Yet not so much predictions from without, as verifications of the foregoing things within. For with little external to constrain us, the innermost necessities in our being, these still drive us on.

"The measure! the measure!" cried Ahab.

Receiving the brimming pewter, and turning to the harpooneers, he ordered them to produce their weapons. Then ranging them before him near the capstan,[1] with their harpoons in their hands, while his three mates stood at his side with their lances, and the rest of the ship's company formed a circle round the group; he stood for an instant searchingly eyeing every man of his crew. But those wild eyes met his, as the bloodshot eyes of the prairie wolves meet the eye of their leader, ere he rushes on at their head in the trail of the bison; but, alas! only to fall into the hidden snare of the Indian.

"Drink and pass!" he cried, handing the heavy charged flagon to the nearest seaman. "The crew alone now drink. Round with it, round! Short draughts—long swallows, men; 'tis hot as Satan's hoof. So, so; it goes round excellently. It spiralizes in ye; forks out at the serpent-snapping eye. Well done; almost drained. That way it went, this way it comes. Hand it me—here's a hollow! Men, ye seem the years; so brimming life is gulped and gone. Steward, refill!

"Attend now, my braves. I have mustered ye all round this capstan; and ye mates, flank me with your lances; and ye harpooneers, stand there with your irons; and ye, stout mariners, ring me in, that I may in some sort revive a noble custom of my fisherman fathers before me. O men, you will yet see that—Ha! boy, come back? bad pennies come

---

1 *capstan* Machine powered by hand and used to weigh anchor and hoist sails.

not sooner.[1] Hand it me. Why, now, this pewter had run brimming again, wer't not thou St. Vitus' imp—away, thou ague![2]

"Advance, ye mates! Cross your lances full before me. Well done! Let me touch the axis." So saying, with extended arm, he grasped the three level, radiating lances at their crossed centre; while so doing, suddenly and nervously twitched them; meanwhile, glancing intently from Starbuck to Stubb; from Stubb to Flask. It seemed as though, by some nameless, interior volition, he would fain have shocked into them the same fiery emotion accumulated within the Leyden jar[3] of his own magnetic life. The three mates quailed before his strong, sustained, and mystic aspect. Stubb and Flask looked sideways from him; the honest eye of Starbuck fell downright.

"In vain!" cried Ahab; "but, maybe, 'tis well. For did ye three but once take the full-forced shock, then mine own electric thing, *that* had perhaps expired from out me. Perchance, too, it would have dropped ye dead. Perchance ye need it not. Down lances! And now, ye mates, I do appoint ye three cupbearers to my three pagan kinsmen there—yon three most honorable gentlemen and noblemen, my valiant harpooneers. Disdain the task? What, when the great Pope washes the feet of beggars, using his tiara for ewer?[4] Oh, my sweet cardinals! your own condescension, *that* shall bend ye to it. I do not order ye; ye will it. Cut your seizings[5] and draw the poles, ye harpooneers!"

---

1 *bad pennies … sooner* Variant on the proverb "a bad penny always turns up," i.e., a disreputable person is quick to come back.

2 *St. Vitus' imp* St. Vitus (c. 290–303) was a Christian martyr from Sicily who is the patron saint of dancers and entertainers; people sought his help for epilepsy and chorea (diseases that cause people to twitch and move uncontrollably). Ahab calls the steward "St. Vitus' imp" because he has twitched or trembled while carrying the drink, causing him to spill some of it; *ague* Shaking or shivering fever.

3 *Leyden jar* A Leyden jar is made of glass and can store a significant charge of electricity between its conductors, one on the inside and one on the outside of the jar. It is still used today to show students the principles of electrostatics.

4 *great Pope … for ewer* Ahab enacts the rituals of Holy Thursday (or Maundy Thursday), the day Christians commemorate Christ's washing of his disciples' feet during the Last Supper (see John 13). On Holy Thursday the priest conducting mass—including the Pope—takes on Christ's role by washing the feet of twelve parishioners. Holy Thursday is also the day on which the Chrism Mass is celebrated, which is when priests reaffirm their vows, and when the holy oils used in ceremonies throughout the year are blessed.

5 *seizings* Cords that tie the iron points of the harpoons to their wooden shafts.

Silently obeying the order, the three harpooneers now stood with the detached iron part of their harpoons, some three feet long, held, barbs up, before him.

"Stab me not with that keen steel! Cant[1] them; cant them over! know ye not the goblet end? Turn up the socket! So, so; now, ye cup-bearers, advance. The irons! take them; hold them while I fill!" Forthwith, slowly going from one officer to the other, he brimmed the harpoon sockets with the fiery waters from the pewter.

"Now, three to three, ye stand. Commend the murderous chalices! Bestow them, ye who are now made parties to this indissoluble league. Ha! Starbuck! but the deed is done! Yon ratifying sun now waits to sit upon it. Drink, ye harpooneers! drink and swear, ye men that man the deathful whaleboat's bow—Death to Moby Dick! God hunt us all, if we do not hunt Moby Dick to his death!" The long, barbed steel goblets were lifted; and to cries and maledictions against the white whale, the spirits were simultaneously quaffed down with a hiss. Starbuck paled, and turned, and shivered. Once more, and finally, the replenished pewter went the rounds among the frantic crew; when, waving his free hand to them, they all dispersed; and Ahab retired within his cabin.

Chapter 38. Dusk

(*By the Mainmast; Starbuck leaning against it.*)

My soul is more than matched; she's overmanned; and by a madman! Insufferable sting, that sanity should ground arms[2] on such a field! But he drilled deep down, and blasted all my reason out of me! I think I see his impious end; but feel that I must help him to it. Will I, nill I, the ineffable thing has tied me to him; tows me with a cable I have no knife to cut. Horrible old man! Who's over him, he cries;—aye, he would be a democrat to all above; look, how he lords it over all below! Oh! I plainly see my miserable office,—to obey, rebelling; and worse yet, to hate with touch of pity! For in his eyes I read some lurid woe would shrivel me up, had I it. Yet is there hope. Time and tide flow wide. The hated whale has the round watery world to swim in, as

1 *Cant* Turn.

2 *ground arms* Lay down arms, i.e., surrender.

the small gold-fish has its glassy globe. His heaven-insulting purpose, God may wedge aside. I would up heart, were it not like lead. But my whole clock's run down; my heart the all-controlling weight, I have no key to lift again.[1]

(*A burst of revelry from the forecastle.*)

Oh, God! to sail with such a heathen crew that have small touch of human mothers in them! Whelped somewhere by the sharkish sea. The white whale is their demogorgon.[2] Hark! the infernal orgies! that revelry is forward![3] mark the unfaltering silence aft! Methinks it pictures life. Foremost through the sparkling sea shoots on the gay, embattled, bantering bow, but only to drag dark Ahab after it, where he broods within his sternward cabin, builded over the dead water of the wake, and further on, hunted by its wolfish gurglings. The long howl thrills me through! Peace! ye revelers, and set the watch! Oh, life! 'tis in an hour like this, with soul beat down and held to knowledge,—as wild, untutored things are forced to feed—Oh, life! 'tis now that I do feel the latent horror in thee! but 'tis not me! that horror's out of me! and with the soft feeling of the human in me, yet will I try to fight ye, ye grim, phantom futures! Stand by me, hold me, bind me, O ye blessed influences!

Chapter 41. Moby Dick

I, Ishmael, was one of that crew; my shouts had gone up with the rest; my oath had been welded with theirs; and stronger I shouted, and more did I hammer and clinch my oath, because of the dread in my soul. A wild, mystical, sympathetical feeling was in me; Ahab's quenchless feud seemed mine. With greedy ears I learned the history of that murderous monster against whom I and all the others had taken our oaths of violence and revenge.

---

1 *whole clock's ... lift again* Starbuck pictures himself as a weight-powered clock that requires winding with a key; in this metaphor, his heart is the weight and he has no key to raise its spirits.

2 *demogorgon* Powerful demon from hell.

3 *forward* I.e., in the forecastle.

For some time past, though at intervals only, the unaccompanied, secluded White Whale had haunted those uncivilized seas mostly frequented by the Sperm Whale fishermen. But not all of them knew of his existence; only a few of them, comparatively, had knowingly seen him; while the number who as yet had actually and knowingly given battle to him, was small indeed. For, owing to the large number of whale-cruisers; the disorderly way they were sprinkled over the entire watery circumference, many of them adventurously pushing their quest along solitary latitudes, so as seldom or never for a whole twelvemonth or more on a stretch, to encounter a single news-telling sail of any sort; the inordinate length of each separate voyage; the irregularity of the times of sailing from home; all these, with other circumstances, direct and indirect, long obstructed the spread through the whole world-wide whaling-fleet of the special individualizing tidings concerning Moby Dick. It was hardly to be doubted, that several vessels reported to have encountered, at such or such a time, or on such or such a meridian, a Sperm Whale of uncommon magnitude and malignity, which whale, after doing great mischief to his assailants, had completely escaped them; to some minds it was not an unfair presumption, I say, that the whale in question must have been no other than Moby Dick. Yet as of late the Sperm Whale fishery had been marked by various and not unfrequent instances of great ferocity, cunning, and malice in the monster attacked; therefore it was, that those who by accident ignorantly gave battle to Moby Dick; such hunters, perhaps, for the most part, were content to ascribe the peculiar terror he bred, more, as it were, to the perils of the Sperm Whale fishery at large, than to the individual cause. In that way, mostly, the disastrous encounter between Ahab and the whale had hitherto been popularly regarded.

And as for those who, previously hearing of the White Whale, by chance caught sight of him; in the beginning of the thing they had every one of them, almost, as boldly and fearlessly lowered for him, as for any other whale of that species. But at length, such calamities did ensue in these assaults—not restricted to sprained wrists and ankles, broken limbs, or devouring amputations—but fatal to the last degree of fatality; those repeated disastrous repulses, all accumulating and piling their terrors upon Moby Dick; those things had gone far to shake the fortitude of many brave hunters, to whom the story of the White Whale had eventually come.

Nor did wild rumors of all sorts fail to exaggerate, and still the more horrify the true histories of these deadly encounters. For not only do fabulous rumors naturally grow out of the very body of all surprising terrible events,—as the smitten tree gives birth to its fungi; but, in maritime life, far more than in that of terra firma, wild rumors abound, wherever there is any adequate reality for them to cling to. And as the sea surpasses the land in this matter, so the whale fishery surpasses every other sort of maritime life, in the wonderfulness and fearfulness of the rumors which sometimes circulate there. For not only are whalemen as a body unexempt from that ignorance and superstitiousness hereditary to all sailors; but of all sailors, they are by all odds the most directly brought into contact with whatever is appallingly astonishing in the sea; face to face they not only eye its greatest marvels, but, hand to jaw, give battle to them. Alone, in such remotest waters, that though you sailed a thousand miles, and passed a thousand shores, you would not come to any chiseled hearthstone, or aught hospitable beneath that part of the sun; in such latitudes and longitudes, pursuing too such a calling as he does, the whaleman is wrapped by influences all tending to make his fancy pregnant with many a mighty birth.

No wonder, then, that ever gathering volume from the mere transit over the widest watery spaces, the outblown rumors of the White Whale did in the end incorporate with themselves all manner of morbid hints, and half-formed fœtal[1] suggestions of supernatural agencies, which eventually invested Moby Dick with new terrors unborrowed from anything that visibly appears. So that in many cases such a panic did he finally strike, that few who by those rumors, at least, had heard of the White Whale, few of those hunters were willing to encounter the perils of his jaw.

But there were still other and more vital practical influences at work. Not even at the present day has the original prestige of the Sperm Whale, as fearfully distinguished from all other species of the leviathan, died out of the minds of the whalemen as a body. There are those this day among them, who, though intelligent and courageous enough in offering battle to the Greenland or Right whale, would perhaps—either from professional inexperience, or incompetency, or

1 *fœtal* I.e., fetal, embryonic.

timidity, decline a contest with the Sperm Whale; at any rate, there are plenty of whalemen, especially among those whaling nations not sailing under the American flag, who have never hostilely encountered the Sperm Whale, but whose sole knowledge of the leviathan is restricted to the ignoble monster primitively pursued in the North; seated on their hatches, these men will hearken with a childish fireside interest and awe, to the wild, strange tales of Southern whaling. Nor is the pre-eminent tremendousness of the great Sperm Whale anywhere more feelingly comprehended, than on board of those prows which stem[1] him.

And as if the now tested reality of his might had in former legendary times thrown its shadow before it; we find some book naturalists—Olassen and Povelson[2]—declaring the Sperm Whale not only to be a consternation to every other creature in the sea, but also to be so incredibly ferocious as continually to be athirst for human blood. Nor even down to so late a time as Cuvier's, were these or almost similar impressions effaced. For in his Natural History, the Baron himself affirms that at sight of the Sperm Whale, all fish (sharks included) are "struck with the most lively terrors," and "often in the precipitancy of their flight dash themselves against the rocks with such violence as to cause instantaneous death." And however the general experiences in the fishery may amend such reports as these; yet in their full terribleness, even to the bloodthirsty item of Povelson, the superstitious belief in them is, in some vicissitudes of their vocation, revived in the minds of the hunters.

So that overawed by the rumors and portents concerning him, not a few of the fishermen recalled, in reference to Moby Dick, the earlier days of the Sperm Whale fishery, when it was oftentimes hard to induce long practised Right whalemen to embark in the perils of this new and daring warfare; such men protesting that although other leviathans might be hopefully pursued, yet to chase and point lance at such an apparition as the Sperm Whale was not for mortal man. That to attempt it, would be inevitably to be torn into a quick eternity. On this head, there are some remarkable documents that may be consulted.

---

1 *stem* Defy.

2 *Olassen and Povelson* Eggart Ólafsson (1726–68) and Bjarni Pálsson (1719–79), authors of *Travels in Iceland* (1805).

Nevertheless, some there were, who even in the face of these things were ready to give chase to Moby Dick; and a still greater number who, chancing only to hear of him distantly and vaguely, without the specific details of any certain calamity, and without superstitious accompaniments, were sufficiently hardy not to flee from the battle if offered.

One of the wild suggestions referred to, as at last coming to be linked with the White Whale in the minds of the superstitiously inclined, was the unearthly conceit that Moby Dick was ubiquitous; that he had actually been encountered in opposite latitudes at one and the same instant of time.

Nor, credulous as such minds must have been, was this conceit altogether without some faint show of superstitious probability. For as the secrets of the currents in the seas have never yet been divulged, even to the most erudite research; so the hidden ways of the Sperm Whale when beneath the surface remain, in great part, unaccountable to his pursuers; and from time to time have originated the most curious and contradictory speculations regarding them, especially concerning the mystic modes whereby, after sounding to a great depth, he transports himself with such vast swiftness to the most widely distant points.

It is a thing well known to both American and English whale-ships, and as well a thing placed upon authoritative record years ago by Scoresby, that some whales have been captured far north in the Pacific, in whose bodies have been found the barbs of harpoons darted in the Greenland seas. Nor is it to be gainsaid, that in some of these instances it has been declared that the interval of time between the two assaults could not have exceeded very many days. Hence, by inference, it has been believed by some whalemen, that the Nor' West Passage,[1] so long a problem to man, was never a problem to the whale. So that here, in the real living experience of living men, the prodigies related in old times of the inland Strello mountain in Portugal[2] (near whose top there was said to be a lake in which the wrecks of ships floated up to the surface); and that still more wonderful story

1 *Nor' West Passage* Sea route through the Canadian Arctic that connects the Atlantic and Pacific oceans. For centuries ships sought safe passage through these seas in vain; in 1903–06 the Passage was successfully navigated for the first time.

2 *Strello mountain in Portugal* The Serra de Estrela mountain range.

of the Arethusa fountain near Syracuse (whose waters were believed to have come from the Holy Land by an underground passage); these fabulous narrations are almost fully equalled by the realities of the whalemen.

Forced into familiarity, then, with such prodigies as these; and knowing that after repeated, intrepid assaults, the White Whale had escaped alive; it cannot be much matter of surprise that some whalemen should go still further in their superstitions; declaring Moby Dick not only ubiquitous, but immortal (for immortality is but ubiquity in time); that though groves of spears should be planted in his flanks, he would still swim away unharmed; or if indeed he should ever be made to spout thick blood, such a sight would be but a ghastly deception; for again in unensanguined[1] billows hundreds of leagues away, his unsullied jet would once more be seen.

But even stripped of these supernatural surmisings, there was enough in the earthly make and incontestable character of the monster to strike the imagination with unwonted power. For, it was not so much his uncommon bulk that so much distinguished him from other sperm whales, but, as was elsewhere thrown out—a peculiar snow-white wrinkled forehead, and a high, pyramidical white hump. These were his prominent features; the tokens whereby, even in the limitless, uncharted seas, he revealed his identity, at a long distance, to those who knew him.

The rest of his body was so streaked, and spotted, and marbled with the same shrouded hue, that, in the end, he had gained his distinctive appellation of the White Whale; a name, indeed, literally justified by his vivid aspect, when seen gliding at high noon through a dark blue sea, leaving a milky-way wake of creamy foam, all spangled with golden gleamings.

Nor was it his unwonted magnitude, nor his remarkable hue, nor yet his deformed lower jaw, that so much invested the whale with natural terror, as that unexampled,[2] intelligent malignity which, according to specific accounts, he had over and over again evinced in his assaults. More than all, his treacherous retreats struck more of dismay than perhaps aught else. For, when swimming before his

1 *unensanguined* Unbloodied.
2 *unexampled* Unparalleled.

exulting pursuers, with every apparent symptom of alarm, he had several times been known to turn round suddenly, and, bearing down upon them, either stave their boats to splinters, or drive them back in consternation to their ship.

Already several fatalities had attended his chase. But though similar disasters, however little bruited ashore, were by no means unusual in the fishery; yet, in most instances, such seemed the White Whale's infernal aforethought of ferocity, that every dismembering or death that he caused, was not wholly regarded as having been inflicted by an unintelligent agent.

Judge, then, to what pitches of inflamed, distracted fury the minds of his more desperate hunters were impelled, when amid the chips of chewed boats, and the sinking limbs of torn comrades, they swam out of the white curds of the whale's direful wrath into the serene, exasperating sunlight, that smiled on, as if at a birth or a bridal.

His three boats stove around him, and oars and men both whirling in the eddies; one captain, seizing the line-knife from his broken prow, had dashed at the whale, as an Arkansas duellist[1] at his foe, blindly seeking with a six inch blade to reach the fathom-deep life of the whale. That captain was Ahab. And then it was, that suddenly sweeping his sickle-shaped lower jaw beneath him, Moby Dick had reaped away Ahab's leg, as a mower a blade of grass in the field. No turbaned Turk, no hired Venetian or Malay,[2] could have smote him with more seeming malice. Small reason was there to doubt, then, that ever since that almost fatal encounter, Ahab had cherished a wild vindictiveness against the whale, all the more fell for that in his frantic morbidness he at last came to identify with him, not only all his bodily woes, but all his intellectual and spiritual exasperations. The White Whale swam before him as the monomaniac incarnation of all those malicious agencies which some deep men feel eating in them, till they are left living on with half a heart and half a lung. That intangible malignity which has been from the beginning; to whose dominion even the modern Christians ascribe one-half of the

1 *Arkansas duellist* The Arkansas frontier was notorious for its duels.

2 *Turk ... hired Venetian or Malay* Soldiers from these countries and states were often hired as mercenaries and were considered particularly deadly.

worlds; which the ancient Ophites[1] of the east reverenced in their statue devil;—Ahab did not fall down and worship it like them; but deliriously transferring its idea to the abhorred white whale, he pitted himself, all mutilated, against it. All that most maddens and torments; all that stirs up the lees of things; all truth with malice in it; all that cracks the sinews and cakes the brain; all the subtle demonisms of life and thought; all evil, to crazy Ahab, were visibly personified, and made practically assailable in Moby Dick. He piled upon the whale's white hump the sum of all the general rage and hate felt by his whole race from Adam down; and then, as if his chest had been a mortar, he burst his hot heart's shell upon it.

It is not probable that this monomania in him took its instant rise at the precise time of his bodily dismemberment. Then, in darting at the monster, knife in hand, he had but given loose to a sudden, passionate, corporal animosity; and when he received the stroke that tore him, he probably but felt the agonizing bodily laceration, but nothing more. Yet, when by this collision forced to turn towards home, and for long months of days and weeks, Ahab and anguish lay stretched together in one hammock, rounding in mid winter that dreary, howling Patagonian Cape; then it was, that his torn body and gashed soul bled into one another; and so interfusing, made him mad. That it was only then, on the homeward voyage, after the encounter, that the final monomania seized him, seems all but certain from the fact that, at intervals during the passage, he was a raving lunatic; and, though unlimbed of a leg, yet such vital strength yet lurked in his Egyptian chest,[2] and was moreover intensified by his delirium, that his mates were forced to lace him fast, even there, as he sailed, raving in his hammock. In a strait-jacket, he swung to the mad rockings of the gales. And, when running into more sufferable latitudes, the ship, with mild stun'sails[3] spread, floated across the tranquil tropics, and, to all appearances, the old man's delirium seemed left behind him with the Cape Horn swells, and he came forth from his dark

---

1 *Ophites* Religious sect active in the first few centuries CE that worshipped the serpent in Genesis, believing it to be a god that freed mankind from ignorance.

2 *Egyptian chest* In Ancient Egypt, the internal (vital) organs of bodies that were to be mummified were taken out and placed in ornate chests, so that the dead person would have them in the afterlife.

3 *stun'sails* Extra sails set to increase a ship's speed in a favorable wind.

den into the blessed light and air; even then, when he bore that firm, collected front, however pale, and issued his calm orders once again; and his mates thanked God the direful madness was now gone; even then, Ahab, in his hidden self, raved on. Human madness is oftentimes a cunning and most feline thing. When you think it fled, it may have but become transfigured into some still subtler form. Ahab's full lunacy subsided not, but deepeningly contracted; like the unabated Hudson, when that noble Northman flows narrowly, but unfathomably through the Highland gorge.[1] But, as in his narrow-flowing monomania, not one jot of Ahab's broad madness had been left behind; so in that broad madness, not one jot of his great natural intellect had perished. That before living agent, now became the living instrument. If such a furious trope may stand, his special lunacy stormed his general sanity, and carried it, and turned all its concentred cannon upon its own mad mark; so that far from having lost his strength, Ahab, to that one end, did now possess a thousand fold more potency than ever he had sanely brought to bear upon any one reasonable object.

This is much; yet Ahab's larger, darker, deeper part remains unhinted. But vain to popularize profundities, and all truth is profound. Winding far down from within the very heart of this spiked Hotel de Cluny where we here stand—however grand and wonderful, now quit it;—and take your way, ye nobler, sadder souls, to those vast Roman halls of Thermes;[2] where far beneath the fantastic towers of man's upper earth, his root of grandeur, his whole awful essence sits in bearded state; an antique buried beneath antiquities, and throned on torsoes! So with a broken throne, the great gods mock that captive king; so like a Caryatid, he patient sits, upholding on his frozen brow the piled entablatures[3] of ages. Wind ye down there, ye prouder,

---

1 *Hudson ... Highland gorge* The Hudson Highlands, between Putnam and Orange counties, is where the Hudson River narrows and flows between Storm King, Bear, and Breakneck Ridge mountains.

2 *Hotel de Cluny ... Roman halls of Thermes* The Hotel de Cluny, now the Musée de Cluny, is a building in Paris that was built between 1485 and 1510, and that once housed the abbots of Cluny; it was built on top of Roman baths known as the Thermes de Cluny, the ruins of which are still accessible within the museum.

3 *Caryatid ... entablatures* A caryatid is a column shaped into a sculpture of a female figure, used to support other sculptural and structural elements known as entablatures—friezes and cornices, for example.

sadder souls! question that proud, sad king! A family likeness! aye, he did beget ye, ye young exiled royalties; and from your grim sire only will the old State-secret come.

Now, in his heart, Ahab had some glimpse of this, namely: all my means are sane, my motive and my object mad. Yet without power to kill, or change, or shun the fact; he likewise knew that to mankind he did long dissemble; in some sort, did still. But that thing of his dissembling was only subject to his perceptibility, not to his will determinate. Nevertheless, so well did he succeed in that dissembling, that when with ivory leg he stepped ashore at last, no Nantucketer thought him otherwise than but naturally grieved, and that to the quick, with the terrible casualty which had overtaken him.

The report of his undeniable delirium at sea was likewise popularly ascribed to a kindred cause. And so too, all the added moodiness which always afterwards, to the very day of sailing in the Pequod on the present voyage, sat brooding on his brow. Nor is it so very unlikely, that far from distrusting his fitness for another whaling voyage, on account of such dark symptoms, the calculating people of that prudent isle were inclined to harbor the conceit, that for those very reasons he was all the better qualified and set on edge, for a pursuit so full of rage and wildness as the bloody hunt of whales. Gnawed within and scorched without, with the infixed, unrelenting fangs of some incurable idea; such an one, could he be found, would seem the very man to dart his iron and lift his lance against the most appalling of all brutes. Or, if for any reason thought to be corporeally incapacitated for that, yet such an one would seem superlatively competent to cheer and howl on his underlings to the attack. But be all this as it may, certain it is, that with the mad secret of his unabated rage bolted up and keyed in him, Ahab had purposely sailed upon the present voyage with the one only and all-engrossing object of hunting the White Whale. Had any one of his old acquaintances on shore but half dreamed of what was lurking in him then, how soon would their aghast and righteous souls have wrenched the ship from such a fiendish man! They were bent on profitable cruises, the profit to be counted down in dollars from the mint. He was intent on an audacious, immitigable, and supernatural revenge.

Here, then, was this grey-headed, ungodly old man, chasing with curses a Job's whale round the world, at the head of a crew, too, chiefly made up of mongrel renegades, and castaways, and cannibals—morally enfeebled also, by the incompetence of mere unaided virtue or right-mindedness in Starbuck, the invulnerable jollity of indifference and recklessness in Stubb, and the pervading mediocrity in Flask. Such a crew, so officered, seemed specially picked and packed by some infernal fatality to help him to his monomaniac revenge. How it was that they so aboundingly responded to the old man's ire—by what evil magic their souls were possessed, that at times his hate seemed almost theirs; the White Whale as much their insufferable foe as his; how all this came to be—what the White Whale was to them, or how to their unconscious understandings, also, in some dim, unsuspected way, he might have seemed the gliding great demon of the seas of life,—all this to explain, would be to dive deeper than Ishmael can go. The subterranean miner that works in us all, how can one tell whither leads his shaft by the ever shifting, muffled sound of his pick? Who does not feel the irresistible arm drag? What skiff in tow of a seventy-four[1] can stand still? For one, I gave myself up to the abandonment of the time and the place; but while yet all a-rush to encounter the whale, could see naught in that brute but the deadliest ill.

Chapter 42. The Whiteness of the Whale

What the white whale was to Ahab, has been hinted; what, at times, he was to me, as yet remains unsaid.

Aside from those more obvious considerations touching Moby Dick, which could not but occasionally awaken in any man's soul some alarm, there was another thought, or rather vague, nameless horror concerning him, which at times by its intensity completely overpowered all the rest; and yet so mystical and well nigh ineffable was it, that I almost despair of putting it in a comprehensible form. It was the whiteness of the whale that above all things appalled me. But how can I hope to explain myself here; and yet, in some dim, random way, explain myself I must, else all these chapters might be naught.

Though in many natural objects, whiteness refiningly enhances beauty, as if imparting some special virtue of its own, as in marbles,

1 *skiff* Small, light, open boat; *seventy-four* Large heavy warship carrying seventy-four guns.

japonicas,[1] and pearls; and though various nations have in some way recognised a certain royal preeminence in this hue; even the barbaric, grand old kings of Pegu[2] placing the title "Lord of the White Elephants" above all their other magniloquent ascriptions of dominion; and the modern kings of Siam[3] unfurling the same snow-white quadruped in the royal standard; and the Hanoverian flag[4] bearing the one figure of a snow-white charger; and the great Austrian Empire, Cæsarian heir to overlording Rome,[5] having for the imperial colour the same imperial hue; and though this pre-eminence in it applies to the human race itself, giving the white man ideal mastership over every dusky tribe; and though, besides all this, whiteness has been even made significant of gladness, for among the Romans a white stone marked a joyful day; and though in other mortal sympathies and symbolizings, this same hue is made the emblem of many touching, noble things—the innocence of brides, the benignity of age; though among the Red Men of America the giving of the white belt of wampum[6] was the deepest pledge of honor; though in many climes, whiteness typifies the majesty of Justice in the ermine of the Judge, and contributes to the daily state of kings and queens drawn by milk-white steeds; though even in the higher mysteries of the most august religions it has been made the symbol of the divine spotlessness and power; by the Persian fire worshippers,[7] the white forked flame being held the holiest on the altar; and in the Greek mythologies, Great Jove himself being made incarnate in a snow-white bull; and though to the noble Iroquois, the midwinter sacrifice of the sacred White Dog was by far the holiest festival of their theology, that spotless, faithful creature being held the purest envoy they could send to the Great Spirit with the annual tidings of their own fidelity; and though directly from the

---

1 *japonicas* Flowering camellia plants from Japan.

2 *Pegu* Region that is located in what is now south-central Myanmar.

3 *Siam* Thailand.

4 *Hanoverian flag* Flag of the Electorate (later Kingdom) of Hanover, a German state from 1692 to 1807 and again from 1814 to 1837.

5 *Austrian Empire … overlording Rome* The Austrian Empire (1804–1918) evolved from the Holy Roman Empire, the emperor of which claimed his legitimacy from the ancient Roman emperors or "Caesars."

6 *wampum* Shell beads used by various Indigenous peoples of North America for purposes including gifts, record-keeping, and trade.

7 *Persian fire worshippers* Zoroastrians. Members of this faith pray in the presence of fire due to its association with wisdom and spiritual insight.

Latin word for white, all Christian priests derive the name of one part of their sacred vesture, the alb or tunic, worn beneath the cassock; and though among the holy pomps of the Romish faith, white is specially employed in the celebration of the Passion of our Lord; though in the Vision of St. John, white robes are given to the redeemed, and the four-and-twenty elders stand clothed in white before the great white throne, and the Holy One that sitteth there white like wool;[1] yet for all these accumulated associations, with whatever is sweet, and honorable, and sublime, there yet lurks an elusive something in the innermost idea of this hue, which strikes more of panic to the soul than that redness which affrights in blood.

This elusive quality it is, which causes the thought of whiteness, when divorced from more kindly associations, and coupled with any object terrible in itself, to heighten that terror to the furthest bounds. Witness the white bear of the poles, and the white shark of the tropics; what but their smooth, flaky whiteness makes them the transcendent horrors they are? That ghastly whiteness it is which imparts such an abhorrent mildness, even more loathsome than terrific, to the dumb gloating of their aspect. So that not the fierce-fanged tiger in his heraldic coat can so stagger courage as the white-shrouded bear or shark.[2]

Bethink thee of the albatross, whence come those clouds of spiritual wonderment and pale dread, in which that white phantom sails

---

1 *Vision of St. John ... wool* See the Book of Revelation (traditionally believed to have been written by St. John), especially 7.9–14, 4.4, and 1.14.

2 [Melville's note] With reference to the Polar bear, it may possibly be urged by him who would fain go still deeper into this matter, that it is not the whiteness, separately regarded, which heightens the intolerable hideousness of that brute; for, analysed, that heightened hideousness, it might be said, only rises from the circumstance, that the irresponsible ferociousness of the creature stands invested in the fleece of celestial innocence and love; and hence, by bringing together two such opposite emotions in our minds, the Polar bear frightens us with so unnatural a contrast. But even assuming all this to be true; yet, were it not for the whiteness, you would not have that intensified terror.

As for the white shark, the white gliding ghostliness of repose in that creature, when beheld in his ordinary moods, strangely tallies with the same quality in the Polar quadruped. This peculiarity is most vividly hit by the French in the name they bestow upon that fish. The Romish mass for the dead begins with "Requiem eternam" (eternal rest), whence Requiem denominating the mass itself, and any other funeral music. Now, in allusion to the white, silent stillness of death in this shark, and the mild deadliness of his habits, the French call him *Requin*.

in all imaginations? Not Coleridge first threw that spell;[1] but God's great, unflattering laureate, Nature.[2]

Most famous in our Western annals and Indian traditions is that of the White Steed of the Prairies; a magnificent milk-white charger, large-eyed, small-headed, bluff-chested, and with the dignity of a thousand monarchs in his lofty, overscorning carriage. He was the elected Xerxes[3] of vast herds of wild horses, whose pastures in those days were only fenced by the Rocky Mountains and the Alleghanies. At their flaming head he westward trooped it like that chosen star which every evening leads on the hosts of light. The flashing cascade of his mane, the curving comet of his tail, invested him with housings[4]

---

1 *Coleridge ... spell* Melville is referring to Samuel Taylor Coleridge's famous poem featuring an albatross, *The Rime of the Ancient Mariner* (1798).

2 [Melville's note] I remember the first albatross I ever saw. It was during a prolonged gale, in waters hard upon the Antarctic seas. From my forenoon watch below, I ascended to the overclouded deck; and there, dashed upon the main hatches, I saw a regal, feathery thing of unspotted whiteness, and with a hooked, Roman bill sublime. At intervals, it arched forth its vast archangel wings, as if to embrace some holy ark. Wondrous flutterings and throbbings shook it. Though bodily unharmed, it uttered cries, as some king's ghost in supernatural distress. Through its inexpressible, strange eyes, methought I peeped to secrets which took hold of God. As Abraham before the angels, I bowed myself [see Genesis 18.2]; the white thing was so white, its wings so wide, and in those for ever exiled waters, I had lost the miserable warping memories of traditions and of towns. Long I gazed at that prodigy of plumage. I cannot tell, can only hint, the things that darted through me then. But at last I awoke; and turning, asked a sailor what bird was this. A goney, he replied. Goney! I never had heard that name before; is it conceivable that this glorious thing is utterly unknown to men ashore! never! But some time after, I learned that goney was some seaman's name for albatross. So that by no possibility could Coleridge's wild Rhyme have had aught to do with those mystical impressions which were mine, when I saw that bird upon our deck. For neither had I then read the Rhyme, nor knew the bird to be an albatross. Yet, in saying this, I do but indirectly burnish a little brighter the noble merit of the poem and the poet.

I assert, then, that in the wondrous bodily whiteness of the bird chiefly lurks the secret of the spell; a truth the more evinced in this, that by a solecism of terms there are birds called grey albatrosses; and these I have frequently seen, but never with such emotions as when I beheld the Antarctic fowl.

But how had the mystic thing been caught? Whisper it not, and I will tell; with a treacherous hook and line, as the fowl floated on the sea. At last the Captain made a postman of it; tying a lettered, leathern tally [stick with carved messages] round its neck, with the ship's time and place; and then letting it escape. But I doubt not, that leathern tally, meant for man, was taken off in Heaven, when the white fowl flew to join the wing-folding, the invoking, and adoring cherubim!

3 *Xerxes* King of Persia (c. 518–465 BCE) who gained inherited, not elected, power.

4 *housings* Trappings or ornaments that extend from the horse's saddle over its back and sides.

more resplendent than gold and silver-beaters could have furnished him. A most imperial and archangelical apparition of that unfallen, western world,[1] which to the eyes of the old trappers and hunters revived the glories of those primeval times when Adam walked majestic as a god, bluff-browed and fearless as this mighty steed. Whether marching amid his aides and marshals in the van[2] of countless cohorts that endlessly streamed it over the plains, like an Ohio; or whether with his circumambient subjects browsing all around at the horizon, the White Steed gallopingly reviewed them with warm nostrils reddening through his cool milkiness; in whatever aspect he presented himself, always to the bravest Indians he was the object of trembling reverence and awe. Nor can it be questioned from what stands on legendary record of this noble horse, that it was his spiritual whiteness chiefly, which so clothed him with divineness; and that this divineness had that in it which, though commanding worship, at the same time enforced a certain nameless terror.

But there are other instances where this whiteness loses all that accessory and strange glory which invests it in the White Steed and Albatross.

What is it that in the Albino man so peculiarly repels and often shocks the eye, as that sometimes he is loathed by his own kith and kin! It is that whiteness which invests him, a thing expressed by the name he bears.[3] The Albino is as well made as other men—has no substantive deformity—and yet this mere aspect of all-pervading whiteness makes him more strangely hideous than the ugliest abortion.[4] Why should this be so?

Nor, in quite other aspects, does Nature in her least palpable but not the less malicious agencies, fail to enlist among her forces this crowning attribute of the terrible. From its snowy aspect, the gauntleted ghost of the Southern Seas has been denominated the White Squall. Nor, in some historic instances, has the art of human malice omitted so potent an auxiliary. How wildly it heightens the effect of that passage in Froissart, when, masked in the snowy symbol of their

1 *unfallen, western world* North America before European colonial encroachment.

2 *van* Forefront.

3 *Albino … name he bears* "Albino" is a borrowing from Portuguese, referring to a person lacking the pigment melanin; the term is based on the Latin "albus," meaning "white."

4 *abortion* In this context, a person imperfectly made, a monstrosity.

faction, the desperate White Hoods of Ghent murder their bailiff in the market-place![1]

Nor, in some things, does the common, hereditary experience of all mankind fail to bear witness to the supernaturalism of this hue. It cannot well be doubted, that the one visible quality in the aspect of the dead which most appals the gazer, is the marble pallor lingering there; as if indeed that pallor were as much like the badge of consternation in the other world, as of mortal trepidation here. And from that pallor of the dead, we borrow the expressive hue of the shroud in which we wrap them. Nor even in our superstitions do we fail to throw the same snowy mantle round our phantoms; all ghosts rising in a milk-white fog—Yea, while these terrors seize us, let us add, that even the king of terrors, when personified by the evangelist, rides on his pallid horse.[2]

Therefore, in his other moods, symbolize whatever grand or gracious thing he will by whiteness, no man can deny that in its profoundest idealized significance it calls up a peculiar apparition to the soul.

But though without dissent this point be fixed, how is mortal man to account for it? To analyse it, would seem impossible. Can we, then, by the citation of some of those instances wherein this thing of whiteness—though for the time either wholly or in great part stripped of all direct associations calculated to impart to it aught fearful, but nevertheless, is found to exert over us the same sorcery, however modified;—can we thus hope to light upon some chance clue to conduct us to the hidden cause we seek?

Let us try. But in a matter like this, subtlety appeals to subtlety, and without imagination no man can follow another into these halls. And though, doubtless, some at least of the imaginative impressions about to be presented may have been shared by most men, yet few perhaps were entirely conscious of them at the time, and therefore may not be able to recall them now.

Why to the man of untutored ideality,[3] who happens to be but loosely acquainted with the peculiar character of the day, does the

---

1 *Froissart … market-place* This description is from the *Chronicles* (written c. 1379–c. 1405) of the medieval French historian Jean Froissart.

2 *king of terrors … pallid horse* See Revelation 6.8, attributed to St. John the Evangelist: "And I looked, and behold a pale horse: and his name that sat on him was Death, and Hell followed with him."

3 *ideality* Imaginativeness.

bare mention of Whitsuntide[1] marshal in the fancy such long, dreary, speechless processions of slow-pacing pilgrims, down-cast and hooded with new-fallen snow? Or, to the unread, unsophisticated Protestant of the Middle American States, why does the passing mention of a White Friar or a White Nun,[2] evoke such an eyeless statue in the soul?

Or what is there apart from the traditions of dungeoned warriors and kings (which will not wholly account for it) that makes the White Tower of London tell so much more strongly on the imagination of an untravelled American, than those other storied structures, its neighbors—the Byward Tower, or even the Bloody?[3] And those sublimer towers, the White Mountains of New Hampshire, whence, in peculiar moods, comes that gigantic ghostliness over the soul at the bare mention of that name, while the thought of Virginia's Blue Ridge is full of a soft, dewy, distant dreaminess? Or why, irrespective of all latitudes and longitudes, does the name of the White Sea exert such a spectralness over the fancy, while that of the Yellow Sea[4] lulls us with mortal thoughts of long lacquered mild afternoons on the waves, followed by the gaudiest and yet sleepiest of sunsets? Or, to choose a wholly unsubstantial instance, purely addressed to the fancy, why, in reading the old fairy tales of Central Europe, does "the tall pale man" of the Hartz forests, whose changeless pallor unrustlingly glides through the green of the groves—why is this phantom more terrible than all the whooping imps of the Blocksburg?[5]

---

1 *Whitsuntide* Church season of Pentecost, beginning on Whitsunday (a contraction of "White Sunday"), that celebrated the descent of the Holy Spirit upon the Apostles. Confirmation and baptismal ceremonies are frequently held on Pentecost, for which white robes are traditionally worn.

2 *White Friar ... White Nun* Ghostly nuns and friars are common motifs in Gothic fiction.

3 *White Tower ... Byward Tower ... Bloody* Individual towers in the fortress known as the Tower of London. The White Tower, built between 1078 and 1097, is the keep of the castle and housed soldiers and acted as a prison. It was whitewashed inside and out in 1240 on the orders of Henry III. The Bloody Tower was built between 1238 and 1272 and was thought to be the site of the murder of the two "Princes in the Tower"—Edward V and his brother the Duke of York—as well as the site of the death of Henry VI. Byward Tower, also built between 1238 as 1272, was the gatehouse to the Outer Ward of the fortress.

4 *White Sea* Inlet of the Barents Sea off the northwest Russian coast; *Yellow Sea* Inlet off the Pacific Ocean between China and the Korean peninsula.

5 *tall pale man ... Hartz forests* Der Grossman, or the "Tall Man" or "Slenderman" is a medieval folktale figure who lives in the Black Forest, luring children to the woods; *imps of the Blocksburg* Blocksberg is the highest mountain in the Harz range in Germany; the mountain has long been thought to be peopled with devils and witches.

Nor is it, altogether, the remembrance of her cathedral-toppling earthquakes; nor the stampedoes of her frantic seas; nor the tearlessness of arid skies that never rain; nor the sight of her wide field of leaning spires, wrenched cope-stones, and crosses all adroop (like canted yards of anchored fleets); and her suburban avenues of house-walls lying over upon each other, as a tossed pack of cards;[1]—it is not these things alone which make tearless Lima, the strangest, saddest city thou can'st see. For Lima has taken the white veil;[2] and there is a higher horror in this whiteness of her woe. Old as Pizarro,[3] this whiteness keeps her ruins for ever new; admits not the cheerful greenness of complete decay; spreads over her broken ramparts the rigid pallor of an apoplexy[4] that fixes its own distortions.

I know that, to the common apprehension, this phenomenon of whiteness is not confessed to be the prime agent in exaggerating the terror of objects otherwise terrible; nor to the unimaginative mind is there aught of terror in those appearances whose awfulness to another mind almost solely consists in this one phenomenon, especially when exhibited under any form at all approaching to muteness or universality. What I mean by these two statements may perhaps be respectively elucidated by the following examples.

First: The mariner, when drawing nigh the coasts of foreign lands, if by night he hear the roar of breakers, starts to vigilance, and feels just enough of trepidation to sharpen all his faculties; but under precisely similar circumstances, let him be called from his hammock to view his ship sailing through a midnight sea of milky whiteness—as if from encircling headlands shoals of combed white bears were swimming round him, then he feels a silent, superstitious dread; the shrouded phantom of the whitened waters is horrible to him as a real ghost; in

---

1 *arid skies … never rain* Lima, Peru, receives less than two inches or rain per year; *canted yards* Supports for the sails that are tilted while a vessel is at anchor; *wrenched cope-stones … tossed pack of cards* An earthquake in 1746 caused extensive damage to Lima, which was still evident when Melville visited in 1844.

2 *Lima … white veil* Some of the most prominent architecture in Lima at this time was made with white stone (the Presidential Palace, the Cathedral of Lima, the Archbishop's Palace, and Aliaga House, for example).

3 *Pizarro* Francisco Pizarro (c. 1470–1541) founded Lima in 1535.

4 *apoplexy* Sudden loss of consciousness, a stroke.

vain the lead assures him he is still off soundings;[1] heart and helm they both go down; he never rests till blue water is under him again. Yet where is the mariner who will tell thee, "Sir, it was not so much the fear of striking hidden rocks, as the fear of that hideous whiteness that so stirred me?"

Second: To the native Indian of Peru, the continual sight of the snow-howdahed[2] Andes conveys naught of dread, except, perhaps, in the mere fancying of the eternal frosted desolateness reigning at such vast altitudes, and the natural conceit of what a fearfulness it would be to lose oneself in such inhuman solitudes. Much the same is it with the backwoodsman of the West, who with comparative indifference views an unbounded prairie sheeted with driven snow, no shadow of tree or twig to break the fixed trance of whiteness. Not so the sailor, beholding the scenery of the Antarctic seas; where at times, by some infernal trick of legerdemain[3] in the powers of frost and air, he, shivering and half shipwrecked, instead of rainbows speaking hope and solace to his misery, views what seems a boundless church-yard grinning upon him with its lean ice monuments and splintered crosses.

But thou sayest, methinks that white-lead[4] chapter about whiteness is but a white flag hung out from a craven soul; thou surrenderest to a hypo, Ishmael.

Tell me, why this strong young colt, foaled in some peaceful valley of Vermont, far removed from all beasts of prey—why is it that upon the sunniest day, if you but shake a fresh buffalo robe behind him, so that he cannot even see it, but only smells its wild animal muskiness—why will he start, snort, and with bursting eyes paw the ground in phrensies[5] of affright? There is no remembrance in him of any gorings of wild creatures in his green northern home, so that the strange muskiness he smells cannot recall to him anything associated with the experience of former perils; for what knows he, this New England colt, of the black bisons of distant Oregon?

---

1 *off soundings* In water deep enough that the soundings—the lines and weights used to test the depth of surrounding water—do not hit bottom.

2 *snow-howdahed* Snow-topped (a howdah is the structure placed on top of an elephant's back to seat riders).

3 *legerdemain* Sleight of hand.

4 *white-lead* Carbonate of lead used to make white pigments.

5 *phrensies* I.e., frenzies.

No: but here thou beholdest even in a dumb brute, the instinct of the knowledge of the demonism in the world. Though thousands of miles from Oregon, still when he smells that savage musk, the rending, goring bison herds are as present as to the deserted wild foal of the prairies, which this instant they may be trampling into dust.

Thus, then, the muffled rollings of a milky sea; the bleak rustlings of the festooned frosts of mountains; the desolate shiftings of the windrowed[1] snows of prairies; all these, to Ishmael, are as the shaking of that buffalo robe to the frightened colt!

Though neither knows where lie the nameless things of which the mystic sign gives forth such hints; yet with me, as with the colt, somewhere those things must exist. Though in many of its aspects this visible world seems formed in love, the invisible spheres were formed in fright.

But not yet have we solved the incantation of this whiteness, and learned why it appeals with such power to the soul; and more strange and far more portentous—why, as we have seen, it is at once the most meaning symbol of spiritual things, nay, the very veil of the Christian's Deity; and yet should be as it is, the intensifying agent in things the most appalling to mankind.

Is it that by its indefiniteness it shadows forth the heartless voids and immensities of the universe, and thus stabs us from behind with the thought of annihilation, when beholding the white depths of the milky way? Or is it, that as in essence whiteness is not so much a color as the visible absence of color; and at the same time the concrete of all colors; is it for these reasons that there is such a dumb blankness, full of meaning, in a wide landscape of snows—a colorless, all-color of atheism from which we shrink? And when we consider that other theory of the natural philosophers,[2] that all other earthly hues—every stately or lovely emblazoning—the sweet tinges of sunset skies and woods; yea, and the gilded velvets of butterflies, and the butterfly cheeks of young girls; all these are but subtile deceits, not actually inherent in substances, but only laid on from without; so that all

---

1 *windrowed* Blown into rows by the wind.

2 *natural philosophers* Those studying the physical and natural world, precursors to today's scientists. Some, such as John Locke (1628–1704), believed that "secondary" qualities in physical objects (like color) are painted on by the mind and are not inherent in the object itself.

deified Nature absolutely paints like the harlot, whose allurements cover nothing but the charnel-house within;[1] and when we proceed further, and consider that the mystical cosmetic which produces every one of her hues, the great principle of light, for ever remains white or colorless in itself, and if operating without medium upon matter, would touch all objects, even tulips and roses, with its own blank tinge—pondering all this, the palsied universe lies before us a leper; and like wilful travellers in Lapland, who refuse to wear colored and coloring glasses[2] upon their eyes, so the wretched infidel gazes himself blind at the monumental white shroud that wraps all the prospect around him. And of all these things the Albino whale was the symbol. Wonder ye then at the fiery hunt?

[In the chapters omitted here, a sailor named Archy on the night-watch hears sounds in the after-hold that suggest there are people sleeping there (where no people were thought to be). Ahab decides that to keep the crew happy they should hunt whales on their way to finding Moby Dick; whales are sighted, and Ahab appears on deck with "five dusky phantoms"—a crew for his own boat that he had secretly stowed on board.]

Chapter 48. The First Lowering

The phantoms, for so they then seemed, were flitting on the other side of the deck, and, with a noiseless celerity, were casting loose the tackles and bands of the boat which swung there. This boat had always been deemed one of the spare boats, though technically called the captain's, on account of its hanging from the starboard quarter. The figure that now stood by its bows was tall and swart,[3] with one white tooth evilly protruding from its steel-like lips. A rumpled Chinese jacket of black cotton funereally invested him, with wide black trowsers of the same dark stuff. But strangely crowning this ebonness was a glistening white plaited turban, the living hair braided and coiled round and round upon his head. Less swart in aspect, the

1 *allurements ... within* See Matthew 23.27: "Woe unto you, scribes and Pharisees, hypocrites! for ye are like unto whited sepulchres, which indeed appear beautiful outward, but are within full of dead men's bones, and of all uncleanness."

2 *colored and coloring glasses* I.e., sunglasses.

3 *swart* I.e., swarthy, dark.

companions of this figure were of that vivid, tiger-yellow complexion peculiar to some of the aboriginal natives of the Manillas;[1]—a race notorious for a certain diabolism of subtilty, and by some honest white mariners supposed to be the paid spies and secret confidential agents on the water of the devil, their lord, whose counting-room they suppose to be elsewhere.

While yet the wondering ship's company were gazing upon these strangers, Ahab cried out to the white-turbaned old man at their head, "All ready there, Fedallah?"

"Ready," was the half-hissed reply.

"Lower away then; d'ye hear?" shouting across the deck. "Lower away there, I say."

Such was the thunder of his voice, that spite of their amazement the men sprang over the rail; the sheaves whirled round in the blocks;[2] with a wallow, the three boats dropped into the sea; while, with a dexterous, off-handed daring, unknown in any other vocation, the sailors, goat-like, leaped down the rolling ship's side into the tossed boats below.

Hardly had they pulled out from under the ship's lee, when a fourth keel, coming from the windward side, pulled round under the stern, and showed the five strangers rowing Ahab, who, standing erect in the stern, loudly hailed Starbuck, Stubb, and Flask, to spread themselves widely, so as to cover a large expanse of water. But with all their eyes again riveted upon the swart Fedallah and his crew, the inmates of the other boats obeyed not the command.

"Captain Ahab?—" said Starbuck.

"Spread yourselves," cried Ahab; "give way, all four boats. Thou, Flask, pull out more to leeward!"

"Aye, aye, sir," cheerily cried little King-Post, sweeping round his great steering oar. "Lay back!" addressing his crew. "There!—there!—there again! There she blows right ahead, boys!—lay back!"

"Never heed yonder yellow boys, Archy."

"Oh, I don't mind 'em, sir," said Archy; "I knew it all before now. Didn't I hear 'em in the hold? And didn't I tell Cabaco here of it? What say ye, Cabaco? They are stowaways, Mr. Flask."

---

1 *Manillas* Philippines.

2 *sheaves … blocks* I.e., the ropes whirled in the pulleys.

"Pull, pull, my fine hearts-alive; pull, my children; pull, my little ones," drawlingly and soothingly sighed Stubb to his crew, some of whom still showed signs of uneasiness. "Why don't you break your backbones, my boys? What is it you stare at? Those chaps in yonder boat? Tut! They are only five more hands come to help us—never mind from where—the more the merrier. Pull, then, do pull; never mind the brimstone—devils are good fellows enough. So, so; there you are now; that's the stroke for a thousand pounds; that's the stroke to sweep the stakes![1] Hurrah for the gold cup of sperm oil, my heroes! Three cheers, men—all hearts alive! Easy, easy; don't be in a hurry—don't be in a hurry. Why don't you snap your oars, you rascals? Bite something, you dogs! So, so, so, then:—softly, softly! That's it—that's it! long and strong. Give way[2] there, give way! The devil fetch ye, ye ragamuffin rapscallions; ye are all asleep. Stop snoring, ye sleepers, and pull. Pull, will ye? pull, can't ye? pull, won't ye? Why in the name of gudgeons[3] and ginger-cakes don't ye pull?—pull and break something! pull, and start your eyes out! Here!" whipping out the sharp knife from his girdle; "every mother's son of ye draw his knife, and pull with the blade between his teeth. That's it—that's it. Now ye do something; that looks like it, my steel-bits. Start her—start her, my silver-spoons! Start her, marling-spikes!"[4]

Stubb's exordium to his crew is given here at large, because he had rather a peculiar way of talking to them in general, and especially in inculcating the religion of rowing. But you must not suppose from this specimen of his sermonizings that he ever flew into downright passions with his congregation. Not at all; and therein consisted his chief peculiarity. He would say the most terrific things to his crew, in a tone so strangely compounded of fun and fury, and the fury seemed so calculated merely as a spice to the fun, that no oarsman could hear such queer invocations without pulling for dear life, and yet pulling for the mere joke of the thing. Besides he all the time looked so easy and indolent himself, so loungingly managed his steering-oar, and so broadly gaped—open-mouthed at times—that the mere sight of

1 *sweep the stakes* I.e., win the jackpot.

2 *Give way* Pull harder.

3 *gudgeons* Small bait-fish (can also refer to gullible people).

4 *marling-spikes* Sharp tools used by sailors to splice rope; also a common name for sea-birds with tail streamers, such as jaegers.

such a yawning commander, by sheer force of contrast, acted like a charm upon the crew. Then again, Stubb was one of those odd sort of humorists, whose jollity is sometimes so curiously ambiguous, as to put all inferiors on their guard in the matter of obeying them.

In obedience to a sign from Ahab, Starbuck was now pulling obliquely across Stubb's bow; and when for a minute or so the two boats were pretty near to each other, Stubb hailed the mate.

"Mr. Starbuck! larboard boat there, ahoy! a word with ye, sir, if ye please!"

"Halloa!" returned Starbuck, turning round not a single inch as he spoke; still earnestly but whisperingly urging his crew; his face set like a flint[1] from Stubb's.

"What think ye of those yellow boys, sir!"

"Smuggled on board, somehow, before the ship sailed. (Strong, strong, boys!)" in a whisper to his crew, then speaking out loud again: "A sad business, Mr. Stubb! (seethe her,[2] seethe her, my lads!) but never mind, Mr. Stubb, all for the best. Let all your crew pull strong, come what will. (Spring, my men, spring!) There's hogsheads[3] of sperm ahead, Mr. Stubb, and that's what ye came for. (Pull, my boys!) Sperm, sperm's the play! This at least is duty; duty and profit hand in hand."

"Aye, aye, I thought as much," soliloquized Stubb, when the boats diverged, "as soon as I clapt eye on 'em, I thought so. Aye, and that's what he went into the after hold for, so often, as Dough-Boy[4] long suspected. They were hidden down there. The White Whale's at the bottom of it. Well, well, so be it! Can't be helped! All right! Give way, men! It ain't the White Whale to-day! Give way!"

Now the advent of these outlandish strangers at such a critical instant as the lowering of the boats from the deck, this had not unreasonably awakened a sort of superstitious amazement in some of the ship's company; but Archy's fancied discovery having some time

---

1 *set like a flint* See Isaiah 50.7: "For the Lord God will help me; therefore shall I not be confounded: therefore have I set my face like a flint, and I know that I shall not be ashamed."

2 *seethe her* Possibly a command to the crew to work their oars so strongly that the seawater seems to boil or "seethe."

3 *hogsheads* Large barrels.

4 *Dough-Boy* Ahab's steward, who in Chapter 29 tells Stubb that Ahab made nightly trips to the after-hold.

previous got abroad among them, though indeed not credited then, this had in some small measure prepared them for the event. It took off the extreme edge of their wonder; and so what with all this and Stubb's confident way of accounting for their appearance, they were for the time freed from superstitious surmisings; though the affair still left abundant room for all manner of wild conjectures as to dark Ahab's precise agency in the matter from the beginning. For me, I silently recalled the mysterious shadows I had seen creeping on board the Pequod during the dim Nantucket dawn, as well as the enigmatical hintings of the unaccountable Elijah.

Meantime, Ahab, out of hearing of his officers, having sided the furthest to windward, was still ranging ahead of the other boats; a circumstance bespeaking how potent a crew was pulling him. Those tiger yellow creatures of his seemed all steel and whalebone; like five trip-hammers[1] they rose and fell with regular strokes of strength, which periodically started the boat along the water like a horizontal burst boiler out of a Mississippi steamer.[2] As for Fedallah, who was seen pulling the harpooneer oar, he had thrown aside his black jacket, and displayed his naked chest with the whole part of his body above the gunwale, clearly cut against the alternating depressions of the watery horizon; while at the other end of the boat Ahab, with one arm, like a fencer's, thrown half backward into the air, as if to counterbalance any tendency to trip; Ahab was seen steadily managing his steering oar as in a thousand boat lowerings ere the White Whale had torn him. All at once the outstretched arm gave a peculiar motion and then remained fixed, while the boat's five oars were seen simultaneously peaked. Boat and crew sat motionless on the sea. Instantly the three spread boats in the rear paused on their way. The whales had irregularly settled bodily down into the blue, thus giving no distantly discernible token of the movement, though from his closer vicinity Ahab had observed it.

"Every man look out along his oars!" cried Starbuck. "Thou, Queequeg, stand up!"

---

1 *trip-hammers* Huge hammers powered by wheels.

2 *a horizontal … steamer* I.e., Ahab's crew propel his boat explosively fast. Trying to achieve too much speed in a steamboat—a common mode of transportation on American waterways, including the Mississippi, by the time *Moby-Dick* was written—could cause a buildup of heat and pressure in the boiler that would lead to a boiler explosion.

Nimbly springing up on the triangular raised box in the bow, the savage stood erect there, and with intensely eager eyes gazed off towards the spot where the chase had last been descried. Likewise upon the extreme stern of the boat where it was also triangularly platformed level with the gunwale, Starbuck himself was seen coolly and adroitly balancing himself to the jerking tossings of his chip of a craft, and silently eyeing the vast blue eye of the sea.

Not very far distant Flask's boat was also lying breathlessly still; its commander recklessly standing upon the top of the loggerhead, a stout sort of post rooted in the keel, and rising some two feet above the level of the stern platform. It is used for catching turns with the whale line. Its top is not more spacious than the palm of a man's hand, and standing upon such a base as that, Flask seemed perched at the mast-head of some ship which had sunk to all but her trucks.[1] But little King-Post was small and short, and at the same time little King-Post was full of a large and tall ambition, so that this loggerhead stand-point of his did by no means satisfy King-Post.

"I can't see three seas off; tip us up an oar there, and let me on to that."

Upon this, Daggoo, with either hand upon the gunwale to steady his way, swiftly slid aft, and then erecting himself volunteered his lofty shoulders for a pedestal.

"Good a mast-head as any, sir. Will you mount?"

"That I will, and thank ye very much, my fine fellow; only I wish you fifty feet taller."

Whereupon planting his feet firmly against two opposite planks of the boat, the gigantic negro, stooping a little, presented his flat palm to Flask's foot, and then putting Flask's hand on his hearse-plumed head and bidding him spring as he himself should toss, with one dexterous fling landed the little man high and dry on his shoulders. And here was Flask now standing, Daggoo with one lifted arm furnishing him with a breastband to lean against and steady himself by.

At any time it is a strange sight to the tyro[2] to see with what wondrous habitude of unconscious skill the whaleman will maintain an erect posture in his boat, even when pitched about by the most

---

1 *trucks* Square wooden caps placed on top of a ship's mast-heads.

2 *tyro* Novice, beginner.

riotously perverse and cross-running seas. Still more strange to see him giddily perched upon the loggerhead itself, under such circumstances. But the sight of little Flask mounted upon gigantic Daggoo was yet more curious; for sustaining himself with a cool, indifferent, easy, unthought of, barbaric majesty, the noble negro to every roll of the sea harmoniously rolled his fine form. On his broad back, flaxen-haired Flask seemed a snow-flake. The bearer looked nobler than the rider. Though truly vivacious, tumultuous, ostentatious little Flask would now and then stamp with impatience; but not one added heave did he thereby give to the negro's lordly chest. So have I seen Passion and Vanity stamping the living magnanimous earth, but the earth did not alter her tides and her seasons for that.

Meanwhile Stubb, the third[1] mate, betrayed no such far-gazing solicitudes. The whales might have made one of their regular soundings, not a temporary dive from mere fright; and if that were the case, Stubb, as his wont in such cases, it seems, was resolved to solace the languishing interval with his pipe. He withdrew it from his hatband, where he always wore it aslant like a feather. He loaded it, and rammed home the loading with his thumb-end; but hardly had he ignited his match across the rough sandpaper of his hand, when Tashtego, his harpooneer, whose eyes had been setting to windward like two fixed stars, suddenly dropped like light from his erect attitude to his seat, crying out in a quick phrensy of hurry, "Down, down all, and give way!—there they are!"

To a landsman, no whale, nor any sign of a herring, would have been visible at that moment; nothing but a troubled bit of greenish white water, and thin scattered puffs of vapor hovering over it, and suffusingly blowing off to leeward, like the confused scud[2] from white rolling billows. The air around suddenly vibrated and tingled, as it were, like the air over intensely heated plates of iron. Beneath this atmospheric waving and curling, and partially beneath a thin layer of water, also, the whales were swimming. Seen in advance of all the other indications, the puffs of vapor they spouted, seemed their forerunning couriers and detached flying outriders.

1 *third* Stubb is actually the second mate, ranking below Starbuck and above Flask.
2 *scud* Rain or spray driven fast by the wind.

All four boats were now in keen pursuit of that one spot of troubled water and air. But it bade fair to outstrip them; it flew on and on, as a mass of interblending bubbles borne down a rapid stream from the hills.

"Pull, pull, my good boys," said Starbuck, in the lowest possible but intensest concentrated whisper to his men; while the sharp fixed glance from his eyes darted straight ahead of the bow, almost seemed as two visible needles in two unerring binnacle compasses. He did not say much to his crew, though, nor did his crew say anything to him. Only the silence of the boat was at intervals startlingly pierced by one of his peculiar whispers, now harsh with command, now soft with entreaty.

How different the loud little King-Post. "Sing out and say something, my hearties. Roar and pull, my thunderbolts! Beach me, beach me on their black backs, boys; only do that for me, and I'll sign over to you my Martha's Vineyard plantation, boys; including wife and children, boys. Lay me on—lay me on! O Lord, Lord! but I shall go stark, staring mad: See! see that white water!" And so shouting, he pulled his hat from his head, and stamped up and down on it; then picking it up, flirted it far off upon the sea; and finally fell to rearing and plunging in the boat's stern like a crazed colt from the prairie.

"Look at that chap now," philosophically drawled Stubb, who, with his unlighted short pipe, mechanically retained between his teeth, at a short distance, followed after—"He's got fits, that Flask has. Fits? yes, give him fits—that's the very word—pitch fits into 'em. Merrily, merrily, hearts-alive. Pudding for supper, you know;—merry's the word. Pull, babes—pull, sucklings—pull, all. But what the devil are you hurrying about? Softly, softly, and steadily, my men. Only pull, and keep pulling; nothing more. Crack all your backbones, and bite your knives in two—that's all. Take it easy—why don't ye take it easy, I say, and burst all your livers and lungs!"

But what it was that inscrutable Ahab said to that tiger-yellow crew of his—these were words best omitted here; for you live under the blessed light of the evangelical land.[1] Only the infidel sharks in the audacious seas may give ear to such words, when, with tornado brow, and eyes of red murder, and foam-glued lips, Ahab leaped after his prey.

1 *evangelical land* I.e., Christian countries.

Meanwhile, all the boats tore on. The repeated specific allusions of Flask to "that whale," as he called the fictitious monster which he declared to be incessantly tantalizing his boat's bow with its tail—these allusions of his were at times so vivid and life-like, that they would cause some one or two of his men to snatch a fearful look over the shoulder. But this was against all rule; for the oarsmen must put out their eyes, and ram a skewer through their necks; usage pronouncing that they must have no organs but ears, and no limbs but arms, in these critical moments.

It was a sight full of quick wonder and awe! The vast swells of the omnipotent sea; the surging, hollow roar they made, as they rolled along the eight gunwales, like gigantic bowls in a boundless bowling-green; the brief suspended agony of the boat, as it would tip for an instant on the knife-like edge of the sharper waves, that almost seemed threatening to cut it in two; the sudden profound dip into the watery glens and hollows; the keen spurrings and goadings to gain the top of the opposite hill; the headlong, sled-like slide down its other side;—all these, with the cries of the headsmen and harpooneers, and the shuddering gasps of the oarsmen, with the wondrous sight of the ivory Pequod bearing down upon her boats with outstretched sails, like a wild hen after her screaming brood;—all this was thrilling. Not the raw recruit, marching from the bosom of his wife into the fever heat of his first battle; not the dead man's ghost encountering the first unknown phantom in the other world;—neither of these can feel stranger and stronger emotions than that man does, who for the first time finds himself pulling into the charmed, churned circle of the hunted sperm whale.

The dancing white water made by the chase was now becoming more and more visible, owing to the increasing darkness of the dun cloud-shadows flung upon the sea. The jets of vapor no longer blended, but tilted everywhere to right and left; the whales seemed separating their wakes. The boats were pulled more apart; Starbuck giving chase to three whales running dead to leeward. Our sail was now set, and, with the still rising wind, we rushed along; the boat going with such madness through the water, that the lee oars could scarcely be worked rapidly enough to escape being torn from the row-locks.

Soon we were running through a suffusing wide veil of mist; neither ship nor boat to be seen.

"Give way, men," whispered Starbuck, drawing still further aft the sheet of his sail; "there is time to kill a fish yet before the squall comes. There's white water again!—close to! Spring!"

Soon after, two cries in quick succession on each side of us denoted that the other boats had got fast; but hardly were they overheard, when with a lightning-like hurtling whisper Starbuck said: "Stand up!" and Queequeg, harpoon in hand, sprang to his feet.

Though not one of the oarsmen was then facing the life and death peril so close to them ahead, yet with their eyes on the intense countenance of the mate in the stern of the boat, they knew that the imminent instant had come; they heard, too, an enormous wallowing sound as of fifty elephants stirring in their litter. Meanwhile the boat was still booming through the mist, the waves curling and hissing around us like the erected crests of enraged serpents.

"That's his hump. *There, there*, give it to him!" whispered Starbuck.

A short rushing sound leaped out of the boat; it was the darted iron of Queequeg. Then all in one welded commotion came an invisible push from astern, while forward the boat seemed striking on a ledge; the sail collapsed and exploded; a gush of scalding vapor shot up near by; something rolled and tumbled like an earthquake beneath us. The whole crew were half suffocated as they were tossed helter-skelter into the white curdling cream of the squall. Squall, whale, and harpoon had all blended together; and the whale, merely grazed by the iron, escaped.

Though completely swamped, the boat was nearly unharmed. Swimming round it we picked up the floating oars, and lashing them across the gunwale, tumbled back to our places. There we sat up to our knees in the sea, the water covering every rib and plank, so that to our downward gazing eyes the suspended craft seemed a coral boat grown up to us from the bottom of the ocean.

The wind increased to a howl; the waves dashed their bucklers together; the whole squall roared, forked, and crackled around us like a white fire upon the prairie, in which, unconsumed, we were burning; immortal in these jaws of death! In vain we hailed the other boats; as well roar to the live coals down the chimney of a flaming furnace as hail those boats in that storm. Meanwhile the driving scud, rack, and mist, grew darker with the shadows of night; no sign of the ship could be seen. The rising sea forbade all attempts to bale out the boat. The oars were useless as propellers, performing now the office of life-preservers. So, cutting the lashing of the waterproof match keg, after many failures Starbuck contrived to ignite the lamp in the lantern; then stretching it on a waif pole, handed it to Queequeg as the standard-bearer of this forlorn hope. There, then, he sat, holding up that imbecile candle in the heart of that almighty forlornness. There, then, he sat, the sign and symbol of a man without faith, hopelessly holding up hope in the midst of despair.

Wet, drenched through, and shivering cold, despairing of ship or boat, we lifted up our eyes as the dawn came on. The mist still spread over the sea, the empty lantern lay crushed in the bottom of the boat. Suddenly Queequeg started to his feet, hollowing his hand to his ear. We all heard a faint creaking, as of ropes and yards hitherto muffled by the storm. The sound came nearer and nearer; the thick mists were dimly parted by a huge, vague form. Affrighted, we all sprang into the sea as the ship at last loomed into view, bearing right down upon us within a distance of not much more than its length.

Floating on the waves we saw the abandoned boat, as for one instant it tossed and gaped beneath the ship's bows like a chip at the base of a cataract; and then the vast hull rolled over it, and it was seen no more till it came up weltering astern. Again we swam for it, were dashed against it by the seas, and were at last taken up and safely landed on board. Ere the squall came close to, the other boats had cut loose from their fish and returned to the ship in good time. The ship had given us up, but was still cruising, if haply it might light upon some token of our perishing,—an oar or a lance pole.

Chapter 49. The Hyena

There are certain queer times and occasions in this strange mixed affair we call life when a man takes this whole universe for a vast practical joke, though the wit thereof he but dimly discerns, and more than suspects that the joke is at nobody's expense but his own. However, nothing dispirits, and nothing seems worth while disputing. He bolts down all events, all creeds, and beliefs, and persuasions, all hard things visible and invisible, never mind how knobby; as an ostrich of potent digestion gobbles down bullets and gun flints. And as for small difficulties and worryings, prospects of sudden disaster, peril of life and limb; all these, and death itself, seem to him only sly, good-natured hits, and jolly punches in the side bestowed by the unseen and unaccountable old joker. That odd sort of wayward mood I am speaking of, comes over a man only in some time of extreme tribulation; it comes in the very midst of his earnestness, so that what just before might have seemed to him a thing most momentous, now seems but a part of the general joke. There is nothing like the perils of whaling to breed this free and easy sort of genial, desperado philosophy; and with it I now regarded this whole voyage of the Pequod, and the great White Whale its object.

"Queequeg," said I, when they had dragged me, the last man, to the deck, and I was still shaking myself in my jacket to fling off the water; "Queequeg, my fine friend, does this sort of thing often happen?" Without much emotion, though soaked through just like me, he gave me to understand that such things did often happen.

"Mr. Stubb," said I, turning to that worthy, who, buttoned up in his oil-jacket, was now calmly smoking his pipe in the rain; "Mr. Stubb, I think I have heard you say that of all whalemen you ever met, our chief mate, Mr. Starbuck, is by far the most careful and prudent. I suppose then, that going plump on a flying whale with your sail set in a foggy squall is the height of a whaleman's discretion?"

"Certain. I've lowered for whales from a leaking ship in a gale off Cape Horn."

"Mr. Flask," said I, turning to little King-Post, who was standing close by; "you are experienced in these things, and I am not. Will you tell me whether it is an unalterable law in this fishery, Mr. Flask, for an oarsman to break his own back pulling himself back-foremost into death's jaws?"

"Can't you twist that smaller?" said Flask. "Yes, that's the law. I should like to see a boat's crew backing water up to a whale face foremost. Ha, ha! the whale would give them squint for squint, mind that!"

Here then, from three impartial witnesses, I had a deliberate statement of the entire case. Considering, therefore, that squalls and capsizings in the water and consequent bivouacks on the deep, were matters of common occurrence in this kind of life; considering that at the superlatively critical instant of going on to the whale I must resign my life into the hands of him who steered the boat—oftentimes a fellow who at that very moment is in his impetuousness upon the point of scuttling the craft with his own frantic stampings; considering that the particular disaster to our own particular boat was chiefly to be imputed to Starbuck's driving on to his whale almost in the teeth of a squall, and considering that Starbuck, notwithstanding, was famous for his great heedfulness in the fishery; considering that I belonged to this uncommonly prudent Starbuck's boat; and finally considering in what a devil's chase I was implicated, touching the White Whale: taking all things together, I say, I thought I might as well go below and make a rough draft of my will. "Queequeg," said I, "come along, you shall be my lawyer, executor, and legatee."

It may seem strange that of all men sailors should be tinkering at their last wills and testaments, but there are no people in the world more fond of that diversion. This was the fourth time in my nautical life that I had done the same thing. After the ceremony was concluded upon the present occasion, I felt all the easier; a stone was rolled away from my heart.[1] Besides, all the days I should now live would be as good as the days that Lazarus lived after his resurrection;[2] a supplementary clean gain of so many months or weeks as the case might be. I survived myself; my death and burial were locked up in my chest. I looked round me tranquilly and contentedly, like a quiet ghost with a clean conscience sitting inside the bars of a snug family vault.

Now then, thought I, unconsciously rolling up the sleeves of my frock, here goes for a cool, collected dive at death and destruction, and the devil fetch the hindmost.

[In chapters omitted here, the *Pequod* encounters some other whaling ships, including the *Town-Ho*, from which they hear grim news of Moby Dick, who drowned the *Town-Ho*'s first mate, Radney. Stubb and his crew kill a sperm whale.]

---

1 *stone … heart* After Christ's crucifixion and burial, his followers came to the grave, "And they found the stone rolled away from the sepulchre" (Luke 24.2).

2 *Lazarus … resurrection* One of Christ's miracles was to raise Lazarus from the dead. See John 11.1–45.

Chapter 64. Stubb's Supper

Stubb's whale had been killed some distance from the ship. It was a calm; so, forming a tandem of three boats, we commenced the slow business of towing the trophy to the Pequod. And now, as we eighteen men with our thirty-six arms, and one hundred and eighty thumbs and fingers, slowly toiled hour after hour upon that inert, sluggish corpse in the sea; and it seemed hardly to budge at all, except at long intervals; good evidence was hereby furnished of the enormousness of the mass we moved. For, upon the great canal of Hang-Ho, or whatever they call it, in China, four or five laborers on the foot-path will draw a bulky freighted junk[1] at the rate of a mile an hour; but this grand argosy we towed heavily forged along, as if laden with pig-lead[2] in bulk.

Darkness came on; but three lights up and down in the Pequod's main-rigging dimly guided our way; till drawing nearer we saw Ahab dropping one of several more lanterns over the bulwarks. Vacantly eyeing the heaving whale for a moment, he issued the usual orders for securing it for the night, and then handing his lantern to a seaman, went his way into the cabin, and did not come forward again until morning.

Though, in overseeing the pursuit of this whale, Captain Ahab had evinced his customary activity, to call it so; yet now that the creature was dead, some vague dissatisfaction, or impatience, or despair, seemed working in him; as if the sight of that dead body reminded him that Moby Dick was yet to be slain; and though a thousand other whales were brought to his ship, all that would not one jot advance his grand, monomaniac object. Very soon you would have thought from the sound on the Pequod's decks, that all hands were preparing to cast anchor in the deep; for heavy chains are being dragged along the deck, and thrust rattling out of the port-holes. But by those clanking links, the vast corpse itself, not the ship, is to be moored. Tied by the head to the stern, and by the tail to the bows, the whale now lies with its black hull close to the vessel's, and seen through the darkness of the night, which obscured the spars and rigging aloft, the

---

1 *Hang-Ho* Yün-Ho, China's Grand Canal; *junk* Sailing ship frequently found in East Asia.

2 *argosy* The largest type of merchant ship; *pig-lead* Unrefined lead.

two—ship and whale, seemed yoked together like colossal bullocks, whereof one reclines while the other remains standing.[1]

If moody Ahab was now all quiescence, at least so far as could be known on deck, Stubb, his second mate, flushed with conquest, betrayed an unusual but still good-natured excitement. Such an unwonted bustle was he in that the staid Starbuck, his official superior, quietly resigned to him for the time the sole management of affairs. One small, helping cause of all this liveliness in Stubb, was soon made strangely manifest. Stubb was a high liver; he was somewhat intemperately fond of the whale as a flavorish thing to his palate.

"A steak, a steak, ere I sleep! You, Daggoo! overboard you go, and cut me one from his small!"

Here be it known, that though these wild fishermen do not, as a general thing, and according to the great military maxim, make the enemy defray the current expenses of the war (at least before realizing the proceeds of the voyage), yet now and then you find some of these Nantucketers who have a genuine relish for that particular part of the Sperm Whale designated by Stubb; comprising the tapering extremity of the body.

About midnight that steak was cut and cooked; and lighted by two lanterns of sperm oil, Stubb stoutly stood up to his spermaceti supper at the capstan-head, as if that capstan were a sideboard. Nor was Stubb the only banqueter on whale's flesh that night. Mingling their mumblings with his own mastications, thousands on thousands of sharks, swarming round the dead leviathan, smackingly feasted on its fatness. The few sleepers below in their bunks were often startled by the sharp slapping of their tails against the hull, within a few inches of the sleepers' hearts. Peering over the side you could just see them

1 [Melville's note] A little item may as well be related here. The strongest and most reliable hold which the ship has upon the whale when moored alongside, is by the flukes or tail; and as from its greater density that part is relatively heavier than any other (excepting the side-fins), its flexibility even in death, causes it to sink low beneath the surface; so that with the hand you cannot get at it from the boat, in order to put the chain round it. But this difficulty is ingeniously overcome: a small, strong line is prepared with a wooden float at its outer end, and a weight in its middle, while the other end is secured to the ship. By adroit management the wooden float is made to rise on the other side of the mass, so that now having girdled the whale, the chain is readily made to follow suit; and being slipped along the body, is at last locked fast round the smallest part of the tail, at the point of junction with its broad flukes or lobes.

(as before you heard them) wallowing in the sullen, black waters, and turning over on their backs as they scooped out huge globular pieces of the whale of the bigness of a human head. This particular feat of the shark seems all but miraculous. How at such an apparently unassailable surface, they contrive to gouge out such symmetrical mouthfuls, remains a part of the universal problem of all things. The mark they thus leave on the whale, may best be likened to the hollow made by a carpenter in countersinking for a screw.

Though amid all the smoking horror and diabolism of a sea-fight, sharks will be seen longingly gazing up to the ship's decks, like hungry dogs round a table where red meat is being carved, ready to bolt down every killed man that is tossed to them; and though, while the valiant butchers over the deck-table are thus cannibally carving each other's live meat with carving-knives all gilded and tasselled, the sharks, also, with their jewel-hilted mouths, are quarrelsomely carving away under the table at the dead meat; and though, were you to turn the whole affair upside down, it would still be pretty much the same thing, that is to say, a shocking sharkish business enough for all parties; and though sharks also are the invariable outriders of all slave ships crossing the Atlantic, systematically trotting alongside, to be handy in case a parcel is to be carried anywhere, or a dead slave to be decently buried; and though one or two other like instances might be set down, touching the set terms, places, and occasions, when sharks do most socially congregate, and most hilariously feast; yet is there no conceivable time or occasion when you will find them in such countless numbers, and in gayer or more jovial spirits, than around a dead sperm whale, moored by night to a whaleship at sea. If you have never seen that sight, then suspend your decision about the propriety of devil-worship, and the expediency of conciliating the devil.

But, as yet, Stubb heeded not the mumblings of the banquet that was going on so nigh him, no more than the sharks heeded the smacking of his own epicurean[1] lips.

"Cook, cook!—where's that old Fleece?" he cried at length, widening his legs still further, as if to form a more secure base for his supper;

1 *epicurean* Decadent. The Greek philosopher Epicurus (341–270 BCE) was a materialist who placed primary value on pleasure (which he defined as the absence of pain and fear).

and, at the same time darting his fork into the dish, as if stabbing with his lance; "cook, you cook!—sail this way, cook!"

The old black, not in any very high glee at having been previously roused from his warm hammock at a most unseasonable hour, came shambling along from his galley, for, like many old blacks, there was something the matter with his knee-pans,[1] which he did not keep well scoured like his other pans; this old Fleece, as they called him, came shuffling and limping along, assisting his step with his tongs, which, after a clumsy fashion, were made of straightened iron hoops; this old Ebony floundered along, and in obedience to the word of command, came to a dead stop on the opposite side of Stubb's sideboard; when, with both hands folded before him, and resting on his two-legged cane, he bowed his arched back still further over, at the same time sideways inclining his head, so as to bring his best ear into play.

"Cook," said Stubb, rapidly lifting a rather reddish morsel to his mouth, "don't you think this steak is rather overdone? You've been beating this steak too much, cook; it's too tender. Don't I always say that to be good, a whale-steak must be tough? There are those sharks now over the side, don't you see they prefer it tough and rare? What a shindy they are kicking up! Cook, go and talk to 'em; tell 'em they are welcome to help themselves civilly, and in moderation, but they must keep quiet. Blast me, if I can hear my own voice. Away, cook, and deliver my message. Here, take this lantern," snatching one from his sideboard; "now then, go and preach to 'em!"

Sullenly taking the offered lantern, old Fleece limped across the deck to the bulwarks; and then, with one hand dropping his light low over the sea, so as to get a good view of his congregation, with the other hand he solemnly flourished his tongs, and leaning far over the side in a mumbling voice began addressing the sharks, while Stubb, softly crawling behind, overheard all that was said.

"Fellow-critters: I'se ordered here to say dat you must stop dat dam noise dare. You hear? Stop dat dam smackin' ob de lip! Massa Stubb say dat you can fill your dam bellies up to de hatchings, but by Gor! you must stop dat dam racket!"

"Cook," here interposed Stubb, accompanying the word with a sudden slap on the shoulder,—"Cook! why, damn your eyes, you

1 *knee-pans* Kneecaps.

mustn't swear that way when you're preaching. That's no way to convert sinners, cook!"

"Who dat? Den preach to him yourself," sullenly turning to go.

"No, cook; go on, go on."

"Well, den, Belubed fellow-critters:"—

"Right!" exclaimed Stubb, approvingly, "coax 'em to it; try that," and Fleece continued.

"Dough you is all sharks, and by natur wery woracious, yet I zay to you, fellow-critters, dat dat woraciousness—'top dat dam slappin' ob de tail! How you tink to hear, spose you keep up such a dam slappin' and bitin' dare?"

"Cook," cried Stubb, collaring him, "I won't have that swearing. Talk to 'em gentlemanly."

Once more the sermon proceeded.

"Your woraciousness, fellow-critters, I don't blame ye so much for; dat is natur, and can't be helped; but to gobern dat wicked natur, dat is de pint. You is sharks, sartin; but if you gobern de shark in you, why den you be angel; for all angel is not'ing more dan de shark well goberned. Now, look here, bred'ren, just try wonst to be cibil, a helping yourselbs from dat whale. Don't be tearin' de blubber out your neighbour's mout, I say. Is not one shark dood right as toder to dat whale? And, by Gor, none on you has de right to dat whale; dat whale belong to some one else. I know some o' you has berry brig mout, brigger dan oders; but den de brig mouts sometimes has de small bellies; so dat de brig-ness of de mout is not to swaller wid, but to bit off de blubber for de small fry ob sharks, dat can't get into de scrouge[1] to help demselves."

"Well done, old Fleece!" cried Stubb, "that's Christianity; go on."

"No use goin' on; de dam willains will keep a scougin' and slappin' each oder, Massa Stubb; dey don't hear one word; no use a-preachin' to such dam g'uttons as you call 'em, till dare bellies is full, and dare bellies is bottomless; and when dey do get 'em full, dey wont hear you den; for den dey sink in de sea, go fast to sleep on de coral, and can't hear not'ing at all, no more, for eber and eber."

"Upon my soul, I am about of the same opinion; so give the benediction, Fleece, and I'll away to my supper."

---

1 *scrouge* Pushy crowd.

Upon this, Fleece, holding both hands over the fishy mob, raised his shrill voice, and cried—

"Cussed fellow-critters! Kick up de damndest row as ever you can; fill your dam' bellies 'till dey bust—and den die."

"Now, cook," said Stubb, resuming his supper at the capstan; "Stand just where you stood before, there, over against me, and pay particular attention."

"All dention," said Fleece, again stooping over upon his tongs in the desired position.

"Well," said Stubb, helping himself freely meanwhile; "I shall now go back to the subject of this steak. In the first place, how old are you, cook?"

"What dat do wid de 'teak," said the old black, testily.

"Silence! How old are you, cook?"

"'Bout ninety, dey say," he gloomily muttered.

"And you have lived in this world hard upon one hundred years, cook, and don't know yet how to cook a whale-steak?" rapidly bolting another mouthful at the last word, so that morsel seemed a continuation of the question. "Where were you born, cook?"

"'Hind de hatchway, in ferry-boat, goin' ober de Roanoke."[1]

"Born in a ferry-boat! That's queer, too. But I want to know what country you were born in, cook!"

"Didn't I say de Roanoke country?" he cried sharply.

"No, you didn't, cook; but I'll tell you what I'm coming to, cook. You must go home and be born over again; you don't know how to cook a whale-steak yet."

"Bress my soul, if I cook noder one," he growled, angrily, turning round to depart.

"Come back, cook;—here, hand me those tongs;—now take that bit of steak there, and tell me if you think that steak cooked as it should be? Take it, I say"—holding the tongs towards him—"take it, and taste it."

Faintly smacking his withered lips over it for a moment, the old negro muttered, "Best cooked 'teak I eber taste; joosy, berry joosy."

"Cook," said Stubb, squaring himself once more; "do you belong to the church?"

---

1 *Roanoke* River that runs through southern Virginia and northeastern North Carolina.

"Passed one once in Cape-Down," said the old man sullenly.

"And you have once in your life passed a holy church in Cape-Town, where you doubtless overheard a holy parson addressing his hearers as his beloved fellow-creatures, have you, cook! And yet you come here, and tell me such a dreadful lie as you did just now, eh?" said Stubb. "Where do you expect to go to, cook?"

"Go to bed berry soon," he mumbled, half-turning as he spoke.

"Avast! heave to! I mean when you die, cook. It's an awful question. Now what's your answer?"

"When dis old brack man dies," said the negro slowly, changing his whole air and demeanor, "he hisself won't go nowhere; but some bressed angel will come and fetch him."

"Fetch him? How? In a coach and four, as they fetched Elijah?[1] And fetch him where?"

"Up dere," said Fleece, holding his tongs straight over his head, and keeping it there very solemnly.

"So, then, you expect to go up into our main-top, do you, cook, when you are dead? But don't you know the higher you climb, the colder it gets? Main-top, eh?"

"Didn't say dat t'all," said Fleece, again in the sulks.

"You said up there, didn't you? and now look yourself, and see where your tongs are pointing. But, perhaps you expect to get into heaven by crawling through the lubber's hole,[2] cook; but, no, no, cook, you don't get there, except you go the regular way, round by the rigging. It's a ticklish business, but must be done, or else it's no go. But none of us are in heaven yet. Drop your tongs, cook, and hear my orders. Do ye hear? Hold your hat in one hand, and clap t'other a'top of your heart, when I'm giving my orders, cook. What! that your heart, there?—that's your gizzard! Aloft! aloft!—that's it—now you have it. Hold it there now, and pay attention."

"All 'dention," said the old black, with both hands placed as desired, vainly wriggling his grizzled head, as if to get both ears in front at one and the same time.

---

1 *fetched Elijah* The prophet Elijah is taken to heaven in 2 Kings 2.11: "And it came to pass, as they still went on, and talked, that, behold, there appeared a chariot of fire, and horses of fire, and parted them both asunder; and Elijah went up by a whirlwind into heaven."

2 *lubber's hole* Hole in the platform of the masthead that "lubbers" (inexperienced sailors) would climb through; experienced sailors would climb over the outside edge of the platform.

"Well then, cook, you see this whale-steak of yours was so very bad, that I have put it out of sight as soon as possible; you see that, don't you? Well, for the future, when you cook another whale-steak for my private table here, the capstan, I'll tell you what to do so as not to spoil it by overdoing. Hold the steak in one hand, and show a live coal to it with the other; that done, dish it;[1] d'ye hear? And now to-morrow, cook, when we are cutting in the fish, be sure you stand by to get the tips of his fins; have them put in pickle. As for the ends of the flukes, have them soused,[2] cook. There, now ye may go."

But Fleece had hardly got three paces off, when he was recalled.

"Cook, give me cutlets for supper to-morrow night in the mid-watch. D'ye hear? away you sail, then.—Halloa! stop! make a bow before you go.—Avast heaving again! Whale-balls for breakfast—don't forget."

"Wish, by gor! whale eat him, 'stead of him eat whale. I'm bressed if he ain't more of shark dan Massa Shark hisself," muttered the old man, limping away; with which sage ejaculation he went to his hammock.

[In the chapters omitted here, the "cutting in" process is discussed, which begins with stripping the layers of blubber (fat) from the whale.]

Chapter 68. The Blanket

I have given no small attention to that not unvexed subject, the skin of the whale. I have had controversies about it with experienced whalemen afloat, and learned naturalists ashore. My original opinion remains unchanged; but it is only an opinion.

The question is, what and where is the skin of the whale? Already you know what his blubber is. That blubber is something of the consistence of firm, close-grained beef, but tougher, more elastic and compact, and ranges from eight or ten to twelve and fifteen inches in thickness.

Now, however preposterous it may at first seem to talk of any creature's skin as being of that sort of consistence and thickness, yet

1 *dish it* I.e., put it on the plate.
2 *soused* Brined in vinegar or salt.

in point of fact these are no arguments against such a presumption; because you cannot raise any other dense enveloping layer from the whale's body but that same blubber; and the outermost enveloping layer of any animal, if reasonably dense, what can that be but the skin? True, from the unmarred dead body of the whale, you may scrape off with your hand an infinitely thin, transparent substance, somewhat resembling the thinnest shreds of isinglass,[1] only it is almost as flexible and soft as satin; that is, previous to being dried, when it not only contracts and thickens, but becomes rather hard and brittle. I have several such dried bits, which I use for marks in my whale-books. It is transparent, as I said before; and being laid upon the printed page, I have sometimes pleased myself with fancying it exerted a magnifying influence. At any rate, it is pleasant to read about whales through their own spectacles, as you may say. But what I am driving at here is this. That same infinitely thin, isinglass substance, which, I admit, invests the entire body of the whale, is not so much to be regarded as the skin of the creature, as the skin of the skin, so to speak; for it were simply ridiculous to say, that the proper skin of the tremendous whale is thinner and more tender than the skin of a new-born child. But no more of this.

Assuming the blubber to be the skin of the whale; then, when this skin, as in the case of a very large Sperm Whale, will yield the bulk of one hundred barrels of oil; and, when it is considered that, in quantity, or rather weight, that oil, in its expressed state, is only three fourths, and not the entire substance of the coat; some idea may hence be had of the enormousness of that animated mass, a mere part of whose mere integument[2] yields such a lake of liquid as that. Reckoning ten barrels to the ton, you have ten tons for the net weight of only three quarters of the stuff of the whale's skin.

In life, the visible surface of the Sperm Whale is not the least among the many marvels he presents. Almost invariably it is all over obliquely crossed and re-crossed with numberless straight marks in thick array, something like those in the finest Italian line engravings. But these marks do not seem to be impressed upon the isinglass substance above mentioned, but seem to be seen through it, as if they

1 *isinglass* Mica.

2 *integument* Covering, skin.

were engraved upon the body itself. Nor is this all. In some instances, to the quick, observant eye, those linear marks, as in a veritable engraving, but afford the ground for far other delineations. These are hieroglyphical; that is, if you call those mysterious cyphers on the walls of pyramids hieroglyphics, then that is the proper word to use in the present connexion. By my retentive memory of the hieroglyphics upon one Sperm Whale in particular, I was much struck with a plate representing the old Indian characters chiselled on the famous hieroglyphic palisades on the banks of the Upper Mississippi.[1] Like those mystic rocks, too, the mystic-marked whale remains undecipherable. This allusion to the Indian rocks reminds me of another thing. Besides all the other phenomena which the exterior of the Sperm Whale presents, he not seldom displays the back, and more especially his flanks, effaced in great part of the regular linear appearance, by reason of numerous rude scratches, altogether of an irregular, random aspect. I should say that those New England rocks on the sea-coast, which Agassiz[2] imagines to bear the marks of violent scraping contact with vast floating icebergs—I should say, that those rocks must not a little resemble the Sperm Whale in this particular. It also seems to me that such scratches in the whale are probably made by hostile contact with other whales; for I have most remarked them in the large, full-grown bulls of the species.

A word or two more concerning this matter of the skin or blubber of the whale. It has already been said, that it is stript from him in long pieces, called blanket-pieces. Like most sea-terms, this one is very happy[3] and significant. For the whale is indeed wrapt up in his blubber as in a real blanket or counterpane; or, still better, an Indian poncho slipt over his head, and skirting his extremity. It is by reason of this cosy blanketing of his body, that the whale is enabled to keep himself comfortable in all weathers, in all seas, times, and tides. What would become of a Greenland whale, say, in those shuddering, icy

---

1 *famous … Upper Mississippi* Reference is to the Indigenous murals painted before colonization—likely before 1200—on limestone bluffs in present-day Alton, Illinois. One of the murals depicted a Piasa Bird, or dragon. The murals were destroyed when the limestone was mined by the Mississippi Lime Company in the 1870s, but Melville might have seen them intact in 1840.

2 *Agassiz* Louis Agassiz (1807–73) was a Swiss geologist who taught at Harvard University.

3 *happy* Appropriate, fortunate.

seas of the North, if unsupplied with his cosy surtout?[1] True, other fish are found exceedingly brisk in those Hyperborean[2] waters; but these, be it observed, are your cold-blooded, lungless fish, whose very bellies are refrigerators; creatures, that warm themselves under the lee of an iceberg, as a traveller in winter would bask before an inn fire; whereas, like man, the whale has lungs and warm blood. Freeze his blood, and he dies. How wonderful is it then—except after explanation—that this great monster, to whom corporeal warmth is as indispensable as it is to man; how wonderful that he should be found at home, immersed to his lips for life in those Arctic waters! where, when seamen fall overboard, they are sometimes found, months afterwards, perpendicularly frozen into the hearts of fields of ice, as a fly is found glued in amber. But more surprising is it to know, as has been proved by experiment, that the blood of a Polar whale is warmer than that of a Borneo negro[3] in summer.

It does seem to me, that herein we see the rare virtue of a strong individual vitality, and the rare virtue of thick walls, and the rare virtue of interior spaciousness. Oh, man! admire and model thyself after the whale! Do thou, too, remain warm among ice. Do thou, too, live in this world without being of it. Be cool at the equator; keep thy blood fluid at the Pole. Like the great dome of St. Peter's, and like the great whale, retain, O man! in all seasons a temperature of thine own.

But how easy and how hopeless to teach these fine things! Of erections, how few are domed like St. Peter's! of creatures, how few vast as the whale!

Chapter 87. The Grand Armada

The long and narrow peninsula of Malacca, extending south-eastward from the territories of Birmah,[4] forms the most southerly point of all Asia. In a continuous line from that peninsula stretch the long islands of Sumatra, Java, Bally,[5] and Timor; which, with many others, form a

1 *surtout* Overcoat.

2 *Hyperborean* Far northern.

3 *Borneo negro* Indigenous person of Borneo, the largest group of which are the Dayak.

4 *Birmah* Burma, now Myanmar.

5 *Bally* Bali.

vast mole, or rampart, lengthwise connecting Asia with Australia, and dividing the long unbroken Indian ocean from the thickly studded oriental archipelagoes. This rampart is pierced by several sally-ports[1] for the convenience of ships and whales; conspicuous among which are the straits of Sunda and Malacca. By the straits of Sunda, chiefly, vessels bound to China from the west, emerge into the China seas.

Those narrow straits of Sunda divide Sumatra from Java; and standing midway in that vast rampart of islands, buttressed by that bold green promontory, known to seamen as Java Head; they not a little correspond to the central gateway opening into some vast walled empire: and considering the inexhaustible wealth of spices, and silks, and jewels, and gold, and ivory, with which the thousand islands of that oriental sea are enriched, it seems a significant provision of nature, that such treasures, by the very formation of the land, should at least bear the appearance, however ineffectual, of being guarded from the all-grasping western world. The shores of the Straits of Sunda are unsupplied with those domineering fortresses which guard the entrances to the Mediterranean, the Baltic, and the Propontis.[2] Unlike the Danes, these Orientals do not demand the obsequious homage of lowered top-sails from the endless procession of ships before the wind, which for centuries past, by night and by day, have passed between the islands of Sumatra and Java, freighted with the costliest cargoes of the east. But while they freely waive a ceremonial like this, they do by no means renounce their claim to more solid tribute.

Time out of mind the piratical proas[3] of the Malays, lurking among the low shaded coves and islets of Sumatra, have sallied out upon the vessels sailing through the straits, fiercely demanding tribute at the point of their spears. Though by the repeated bloody chastisements they have received at the hands of European cruisers, the audacity of these corsairs has of late been somewhat repressed; yet, even at the present day, we occasionally hear of English and American vessels, which, in those waters, have been remorselessly boarded and pillaged.

1 *sally-ports* Openings (in a fortress, places for troops to exit and make a sudden attack).

2 *Propontis* Classical name for the Sea of Marmara, the body of water that connects the Mediterranean and Black Seas. Its entrances were guarded by the fortress of Gallipoli on the Mediterranean side and by the city of Constantinople (today's Istanbul) on the Black Sea side.

3 *proas* Undecked sailboats with large triangular sails.

With a fair, fresh wind, the Pequod was now drawing nigh to these straits; Ahab purposing to pass through them into the Javan sea, and thence, cruising northwards, over waters known to be frequented here and there by the Sperm Whale, sweep inshore by the Philippine Islands, and gain the far coast of Japan, in time for the great whaling season there. By these means, the circumnavigating Pequod would sweep almost all the known Sperm Whale cruising grounds of the world, previous to descending upon the Line in the Pacific; where Ahab, though everywhere else foiled in his pursuit, firmly counted upon giving battle to Moby Dick, in the sea he was most known to frequent; and at a season when he might most reasonably be presumed to be haunting it.

But how now? in this zoned quest, does Ahab touch no land? does his crew drink air? Surely, he will stop for water. Nay. For a long time, now, the circus-running[1] sun has raced within his fiery ring, and needs no sustenance but what's in himself. So Ahab. Mark this, too, in the whaler. While other hulls are loaded down with alien stuff, to be transferred to foreign wharves; the world-wandering whale-ship carries no cargo but herself and crew, their weapons and their wants. She has a whole lake's contents bottled in her ample hold. She is ballasted with utilities; not altogether with unusable pig-lead and kentledge.[2] She carries years' water in her. Clear old prime Nantucket water; which, when three years afloat, the Nantucketer, in the Pacific, prefers to drink before the brackish fluid, but yesterday rafted off in casks, from the Peruvian or Indian streams. Hence it is, that, while other ships may have gone to China from New York, and back again, touching at a score of ports, the whale-ship, in all that interval, may not have sighted one grain of soil; her crew having seen no man but floating seamen like themselves. So that did you carry them the news that another flood had come; they would only answer—"Well, boys, here's the ark!"

Now, as many Sperm Whales had been captured off the western coast of Java, in the near vicinity of the Straits of Sunda; indeed, as most of the ground, roundabout, was generally recognised by the fishermen as an excellent spot for cruising; therefore, as the Pequod

---

1 *circus-running* Running in a circle. The Roman circus was an oval building in which chariots would race by, going around in laps.

2 *utilities* Useful things; *kentledge* Iron used as weight to steady the ship.

gained more and more upon Java Head, the look-outs were repeatedly hailed, and admonished to keep wide awake. But though the green palmy cliffs of the land soon loomed on the starboard bow, and with delighted nostrils the fresh cinnamon was snuffed in the air, yet not a single jet was descried. Almost renouncing all thought of falling in with any game hereabouts, the ship had well nigh entered the straits, when the customary cheering cry was heard from aloft, and ere long a spectacle of singular magnificence saluted us.

But here be it premised, that owing to the unwearied activity with which of late they have been hunted over all four oceans, the Sperm Whales, instead of almost invariably sailing in small detached companies, as in former times, are now frequently met with in extensive herds, sometimes embracing so great a multitude, that it would almost seem as if numerous nations of them had sworn solemn league and covenant for mutual assistance and protection. To this aggregation of the Sperm Whale into such immense caravans, may be imputed the circumstance that even in the best cruising grounds, you may now sometimes sail for weeks and months together, without being greeted by a single spout; and then be suddenly saluted by what sometimes seems thousands on thousands.

Broad on both bows, at the distance of some two or three miles, and forming a great semicircle, embracing one half of the level horizon, a continuous chain of whale-jets were up-playing and sparkling in the noon-day air. Unlike the straight perpendicular twin-jets of the Right Whale, which, dividing at top, fall over in two branches, like the cleft drooping boughs of a willow, the single forward-slanting spout of the Sperm Whale presents a thick curled bush of white mist, continually rising and falling away to leeward.

Seen from the Pequod's deck, then, as she would rise on a high hill of the sea, this host of vapory spouts, individually curling up into the air, and beheld through a blending atmosphere of bluish haze, showed like the thousand cheerful chimneys of some dense metropolis, descried of a balmy autumnal morning, by some horseman on a height.

As marching armies approaching an unfriendly defile in the mountains, accelerate their march, all eagerness to place that perilous passage in their rear, and once more expand in comparative security upon the plain; even so did this vast fleet of whales now seem hurrying forward through the straits; gradually contracting the wings of their semicircle, and swimming on, in one solid, but still crescentic centre.

Crowding all sail[1] the Pequod pressed after them; the harpooneers handling their weapons, and loudly cheering from the heads of their yet suspended boats. If the wind only held, little doubt had they, that chased through these Straits of Sunda, the vast host would only deploy into the Oriental seas to witness the capture of not a few of their number. And who could tell whether, in that congregated caravan, Moby Dick himself might not temporarily be swimming, like the worshipped white-elephant in the coronation procession of the Siamese! So with stun-sail piled on stun-sail, we sailed along, driving these leviathans before us; when, of a sudden, the voice of Tashtego was heard, loudly directing attention to something in our wake.

Corresponding to the crescent in our van, we beheld another in our rear. It seemed formed of detached white vapors, rising and falling something like the spouts of the whales; only they did not so completely come and go; for they constantly hovered, without finally disappearing. Levelling his glass at this sight, Ahab quickly revolved in his pivot-hole, crying, "Aloft there, and rig whips and buckets to wet the sails;[2]—Malays, sir, and after us!"

As if too long lurking behind the headlands, till the Pequod should fairly have entered the straits, these rascally Asiatics were now in hot pursuit, to make up for their over-cautious delay. But when the swift Pequod, with a fresh leading wind, was herself in hot chase; how very kind of these tawny philanthropists to assist in speeding her on to her own chosen pursuit,—mere riding-whips and rowels[3] to her, that they were. As with glass under arm, Ahab to-and-fro paced the deck; in his forward turn beholding the monsters he chased, and in the after one the bloodthirsty pirates chasing *him*; some such fancy as the above seemed his. And when he glanced upon the green walls of the watery defile in which the ship was then sailing, and bethought him that through that gate lay the route to his vengeance, and beheld, how that through that same gate he was now both chasing and being chased to his deadly end; and not only that, but a herd of remorseless wild

---

1 *Crowding all sail* Hoisting all the ship's sails at once, to increase speed.

2 *wet the sails* Wetting the sails increases their efficacy at catching wind and thus adds speed to the ship.

3 *rowels* Spiked spurs.

pirates and inhuman atheistical devils were infernally cheering him on with their curses;—when all these conceits had passed through his brain, Ahab's brow was left gaunt and ribbed, like the black sand beach after some stormy tide has been gnawing it, without being able to drag the firm thing from its place.

But thoughts like these troubled very few of the reckless crew; and when, after steadily dropping and dropping the pirates astern, the Pequod at last shot by the vivid green Cockatoo Point on the Sumatra side, emerging at last upon the broad waters beyond; then, the harpooneers seemed more to grieve that the swift whales had been gaining upon the ship, than to rejoice that the ship had so victoriously gained upon the Malays. But still driving on in the wake of the whales, at length they seemed abating their speed; gradually the ship neared them; and the wind now dying away, word was passed to spring to the boats. But no sooner did the herd, by some presumed wonderful instinct of the Sperm Whale, become notified of the three keels that were after them,—though as yet a mile in their rear,—than they rallied again, and forming in close ranks and battalions, so that their spouts all looked like flashing lines of stacked bayonets, moved on with redoubled velocity.

Stripped to our shirts and drawers, we sprang to the white-ash, and after several hours' pulling were almost disposed to renounce the chase, when a general pausing commotion among the whales gave animating token that they were now at last under the influence of that strange perplexity of inert irresolution, which, when the fishermen perceive it in the whale, they say he is gallied.[1] The compact martial columns in which they had been hitherto rapidly and steadily

---

1 [Melville's note] To gally, or gallow, is to frighten excessively,—to confound with fright. It is an old Saxon word. It occurs once in Shakspere:— "The wrathful skies

Gallow the very wanderers of the dark,
And make them keep their caves."

Lear, Act III, sc. ii

To common land usages, the word is now completely obsolete. When the polite landsman first hears it from the gaunt Nantucketer, he is apt to set it down as one of the whaleman's self-derived savageries. Much the same is it with many other sinewy Saxonisms [words of early medieval English origin] of this sort, which emigrated to New-England rocks with the noble brawn of the old English emigrants in the time of the Commonwealth [1649–60]. Thus, some of the best and furthest-descended English words—the etymological Howards and Percys [English aristocratic families]—are now democratised, nay, plebeianised—so to speak—in the New World.

swimming, were now broken up in one measureless rout; and like King Porus' elephants in the Indian battle with Alexander,[1] they seemed going mad with consternation. In all directions expanding in vast irregular circles, and aimlessly swimming hither and thither, by their short thick spoutings, they plainly betrayed their distraction of panic. This was still more strangely evinced by those of their number, who, completely paralysed as it were, helplessly floated like water-logged dismantled ships on the sea. Had these Leviathans been but a flock of simple sheep, pursued over the pasture by three fierce wolves, they could not possibly have evinced such excessive dismay. But this occasional timidity is characteristic of almost all herding creatures. Though banding together in tens of thousands, the lion-maned buffaloes of the West have fled before a solitary horseman. Witness, too, all human beings, how when herded together in the sheepfold of a theatre's pit,[2] they will, at the slightest alarm of fire, rush helter-skelter for the outlets, crowding, trampling, jamming, and remorselessly dashing each other to death. Best, therefore, withhold any amazement at the strangely gallied whales before us, for there is no folly of the beasts of the earth which is not infinitely outdone by the madness of men.

Though many of the whales, as has been said, were in violent motion, yet it is to be observed that as a whole the herd neither advanced nor retreated, but collectively remained in one place. As is customary in those cases, the boats at once separated, each making for some one lone whale on the outskirts of the shoal. In about three minutes' time, Queequeg's harpoon was flung; the stricken fish darted blinding spray in our faces, and then running away with us like light, steered straight for the heart of the herd. Though such a movement on the part of the whale struck under such circumstances, is in no wise unprecedented; and indeed is almost always more or less anticipated; yet does it present one of the more perilous vicissitudes

---

1 *King Porus … Alexander* In the Battle of the Hydaspes (326 BCE) Alexander the Great sought to gain territory in northern India but was blocked by King Porus of Paurava. Porus had 200 elephants in the field of battle, many of whom panicked and trampled when their handlers were killed.

2 *theatre's pit* Area before the stage on the first floor. Prior to 1850 or so, this area had no seats and theater-goers would stand; it tended to have more riotous audience members, who would be closely packed together.

of the fishery. For as the swift monster drags you deeper and deeper into the frantic shoal, you bid adieu to circumspect life and only exist in a delirious throb.

As, blind and deaf, the whale plunged forward, as if by sheer power of speed to rid himself of the iron leech that had fastened to him; as we thus tore a white gash in the sea, on all sides menaced as we flew, by the crazed creatures to and fro rushing about us; our beset boat was like a ship mobbed by ice-isles in a tempest, and striving to steer through their complicated channels and straits, knowing not at what moment it may be locked in and crushed.

But not a bit daunted, Queequeg steered us manfully; now sheering off from this monster directly across our route in advance; now edging away from that, whose colossal flukes were suspended overhead, while all the time, Starbuck stood up in the bows, lance in hand, pricking out of our way whatever whales he could reach by short darts, for there was no time to make long ones. Nor were the oarsmen quite idle, though their wonted duty was now altogether dispensed with. They chiefly attended to the shouting part of the business. "Out of the way, Commodore!" cried one, to a great dromedary[1] that of a sudden rose bodily to the surface, and for an instant threatened to swamp us. "Hard down with your tail, there!" cried a second to another, which, close to our gunwale, seemed calmly cooling himself with his own fan-like extremity.

All whaleboats carry certain curious contrivances, originally invented by the Nantucket Indians, called druggs. Two thick squares of wood of equal size are stoutly clenched together, so that they cross each other's grain at right angles; a line of considerable length is then attached to the middle of this block, and the other end of the line being looped, it can in a moment be fastened to a harpoon. It is chiefly among gallied whales that this drugg is used. For then, more whales are close round you than you can possibly chase at one time. But sperm whales are not every day encountered; while you may, then, you must kill all you can. And if you cannot kill them all at once, you must wing them, so that they can be afterwards killed at your leisure. Hence it is, that at times like these the drugg comes into requisition.

---

1 *dromedary* Breed of camel with one hump; here referring to a sperm whale with a particularly large hump.

Our boat was furnished with three of them. The first and second were successfully darted, and we saw the whales staggeringly running off, fettered by the enormous sidelong resistance of the towing drugg. They were cramped like malefactors with the chain and ball. But upon flinging the third, in the act of tossing overboard the clumsy wooden block, it caught under one of the seats of the boat, and in an instant tore it out and carried it away, dropping the oarsman in the boat's bottom as the seat slid from under him. On both sides the sea came in at the wounded planks, but we stuffed two or three drawers and shirts in, and so stopped the leaks for the time.

It had been next to impossible to dart these drugged-harpoons, were it not that as we advanced into the herd, our whale's way greatly diminished; moreover, that as we went still further and further from the circumference of commotion, the direful disorders seemed waning. So that when at last the jerking harpoon drew out, and the towing whale sideways vanished; then, with the tapering force of his parting momentum, we glided between two whales into the innermost heart of the shoal, as if from some mountain torrent we had slid into a serene valley lake. Here the storms in the roaring glens between the outermost whales, were heard but not felt. In this central expanse the sea presented that smooth satin-like surface, called a sleek, produced by the subtle moisture thrown off by the whale in his more quiet moods. Yes, we were now in that enchanted calm which they say lurks at the heart of every commotion. And still in the distracted distance we beheld the tumults of the outer concentric circles, and saw successive pods of whales, eight or ten in each, swiftly going round and round, like multiplied spans of horses in a ring; and so closely shoulder to shoulder, that a Titanic circus-rider might easily have over-arched the middle ones, and so have gone round on their backs. Owing to the density of the crowd of reposing whales, more immediately surrounding the embayed axis of the herd, no possible chance of escape was at present afforded us. We must watch for a breach in the living wall that hemmed us in; the wall that had only admitted us in order to shut us up. Keeping at the centre of the lake, we were occasionally visited by small tame cows and calves; the women and children of this routed host.

Now, inclusive of the occasional wide intervals between the revolving outer circles, and inclusive of the spaces between the various pods in any one of those circles, the entire area at this juncture, embraced by the whole multitude, must have contained at least two or three square miles. At any rate—though indeed such a test at such a time might be deceptive—spoutings might be discovered from our low boat that seemed playing up almost from the rim of the horizon. I mention this circumstance, because, as if the cows and calves had been purposely locked up in this innermost fold; and as if the wide extent of the herd had hitherto prevented them from learning the precise cause of its stopping; or, possibly, being so young, unsophisticated, and every way innocent and inexperienced; however it may have been, these smaller whales—now and then visiting our becalmed boat from the margin of the lake—evinced a wondrous fearlessness and confidence, or else a still becharmed panic which it was impossible not to marvel at. Like household dogs they came snuffling round us, right up to our gunwales, and touching them; till it almost seemed that some spell had suddenly domesticated them. Queequeg patted their foreheads; Starbuck scratched their backs with his lance; but fearful of the consequences, for the time refrained from darting it.

But far beneath this wondrous world upon the surface, another and still stranger world met our eyes as we gazed over the side. For, suspended in those watery vaults, floated the forms of the nursing mothers of the whales, and those that by their enormous girth seemed shortly to become mothers. The lake, as I have hinted, was to a considerable depth exceedingly transparent; and as human infants while suckling will calmly and fixedly gaze away from the breast, as if leading two different lives at the time; and while yet drawing mortal nourishment, be still spiritually feasting upon some unearthly reminiscence;—even so did the young of these whales seem looking up towards us, but not at us, as if we were but a bit of Gulf-weed[1] in their new-born sight. Floating on their sides, the mothers also seemed quietly eyeing us. One of these little infants, that from certain queer tokens seemed hardly a day old, might have measured some fourteen feet in length, and some six feet in girth. He was a little frisky; though as yet his body seemed scarce yet recovered from that irksome position it had so lately occupied in the maternal reticule; where, tail to

1 *Gulf-weed* Also called sargassum, a type of sea-weed found in the Gulf Stream and the Sargasso Sea.

head, and all ready for the final spring, the unborn whale lies bent like a Tartar's[1] bow. The delicate side-fins, and the palms of his flukes, still freshly retained the plaited crumpled appearance of a baby's ears newly arrived from foreign parts.

"Line! line!" cried Queequeg, looking over the gunwale; "him fast! him fast!—Who line him! Who struck?—Two whale; one big, one little!"

"What ails ye, man?" cried Starbuck.

"Look-e here," said Queequeg, pointing down.

As when the stricken whale, that from the tub has reeled out hundreds of fathoms of rope; as, after deep sounding, he floats up again, and shows the slackened curling line buoyantly rising and spiralling towards the air; so now, Starbuck saw long coils of the umbilical cord of Madame Leviathan, by which the young cub seemed still tethered to its dam. Not seldom in the rapid vicissitudes of the chase, this natural line, with the maternal end loose, becomes entangled with the hempen one, so that the cub is thereby trapped. Some of the subtlest secrets of the seas seemed divulged to us in this enchanted pond. We saw young Leviathan amours in the deep.[2]

And thus, though surrounded by circle upon circle of consternations and affrights, did these inscrutable creatures at the centre freely and fearlessly indulge in all peaceful concernments; yea, serenely revelled in dalliance and delight. But even so, amid the tornadoed Atlantic of my being, do I myself still for ever centrally disport in mute calm; and while ponderous planets of unwaning woe revolve round me, deep down and deep inland there I still bathe me in eternal mildness of joy.

---

1 *Tartar's* Belonging to a Tartar, a term that used to be applied to people who lived in Asia and Eastern Europe.

2 [Melville's note] The sperm whale, as with all other species of the Leviathan, but unlike most other fish, breeds indifferently at all seasons; after a gestation which may probably be set down at nine months, producing but one at a time; though in some few known instances giving birth to an Esau and Jacob [twin sons of Isaac and Rebekah, see Genesis 25.19–34]:—a contingency provided for in suckling by two teats, curiously situated, one on each side of the anus; but the breasts themselves extend upwards from that. When by chance these precious parts in a nursing whale are cut by the hunter's lance, the mother's pouring milk and blood rivallingly discolor the sea for rods [unit of measurement, equivalent to 16.5 feet]. The milk is very sweet and rich; it has been tasted by man; it might do well with strawberries. When overflowing with mutual esteem, the whales salute *more hominum* [Latin: as humans do].

Meanwhile, as we thus lay entranced, the occasional sudden frantic spectacles in the distance evinced the activity of the other boats, still engaged in drugging the whales on the frontier of the host; or possibly carrying on the war within the first circle, where abundance of room and some convenient retreats were afforded them. But the sight of the enraged drugged whales now and then blindly darting to and fro across the circles, was nothing to what at last met our eyes. It is sometimes the custom when fast to a whale more than commonly powerful and alert, to seek to hamstring him, as it were, by sundering or maiming his gigantic tail-tendon. It is done by darting a short-handled cutting-spade, to which is attached a rope for hauling it back again. A whale wounded (as we afterwards learned) in this part, but not effectually, as it seemed, had broken away from the boat, carrying along with him half of the harpoon line; and in the extraordinary agony of the wound, he was now dashing among the revolving circles like the lone mounted desperado Arnold, at the battle of Saratoga,[1] carrying dismay wherever he went.

But agonizing as was the wound of this whale, and an appalling spectacle enough, any way; yet the peculiar horror with which he seemed to inspire the rest of the herd, was owing to a cause which at first the intervening distance obscured from us. But at length we perceived that by one of the unimaginable accidents of the fishery, this whale had become entangled in the harpoon-line that he towed; he had also run away with the cutting-spade in him; and while the free end of the rope attached to that weapon, had permanently caught in the coils of the harpoon-line round his tail, the cutting-spade itself had worked loose from his flesh. So that tormented to madness, he was now churning through the water, violently flailing with his flexible tail, and tossing the keen spade about him, wounding and murdering his own comrades.

This terrific object seemed to recall the whole herd from their stationary fright. First, the whales forming the margin of our lake began to crowd a little, and tumble against each other, as if lifted by half spent billows from afar; then the lake itself began faintly to heave and swell;

1 *Arnold ... battle of Saratoga* Benedict Arnold (1741–1801) was a commander in the Continental Army during the American Revolution (he later defected to the British Army). In 1777, while still fighting on the American side, he led key actions in the Battles of Saratoga, a decisive victory over the British.

the submarine bridal-chambers and nurseries vanished; in more and more contracting orbits the whales in the more central circles began to swim in thickening clusters. Yes, the long calm was departing. A low advancing hum was soon heard; and then like to the tumultuous masses of block-ice when the great river Hudson breaks up in Spring, the entire host of whales came tumbling upon their inner centre, as if to pile themselves up in one common mountain. Instantly Starbuck and Queequeg changed places; Starbuck taking the stern.

"Oars! Oars!" he intensely whispered, seizing the helm—"gripe your oars, and clutch your souls, now! My God, men, stand by! Shove him off, you Queequeg—the whale there!—prick him!—hit him! Stand up—stand up, and stay so! Spring, men—pull, men; never mind their backs—scrape them!—scrape away!"

The boat was now all but jammed between two vast black bulks, leaving a narrow Dardanelles[1] between their long lengths. But by desperate endeavor we at last shot into a temporary opening; then giving way rapidly, and at the same time earnestly watching for another outlet. After many similar hair-breadth escapes, we at last swiftly glided into what had just been one of the outer circles, but now crossed by random whales, all violently making for one centre. This lucky salvation was cheaply purchased by the loss of Queequeg's hat, who, while standing in the bows to prick the fugitive whales, had his hat taken clean from his head by the air-eddy made by the sudden tossing of a pair of broad flukes close by.

Riotous and disordered as the universal commotion now was, it soon resolved itself into what seemed a systematic movement; for having clumped together at last in one dense body, they then renewed their onward flight with augmented fleetness. Further pursuit was useless; but the boats still lingered in their wake to pick up what drugged whales might be dropped astern, and likewise to secure one which Flask had killed and waifed.[2] The waif is a pennoned[3] pole,

---

1 *Dardanelles* Also known as the Hellespont, this is the narrow strait that constitutes part of the boundary between Europe and Asia, and that connects the Sea of Marmara with the Mediterranean. In some places, the strait is less than a mile wide.

2 *waifed* Marked with a waif, a flagged pole that the hunters place on the dead whale so they can find it later on; the pole is also used as a means of marking ownership of the whale, should a rival hunter attempt to claim it.

3 *pennoned* Topped with a long, thin flag.

two or three of which are carried by every boat; and which, when additional game is at hand, are inserted upright into the floating body of a dead whale, both to mark its place on the sea, and also as token of prior possession, should the boats of any other ship draw near.

The result of this lowering was somewhat illustrative of that sagacious saying in the Fishery,—the more whales the less fish. Of all the drugged whales only one was captured. The rest contrived to escape for the time, but only to be taken, as will hereafter be seen, by some other craft than the Pequod.

Chapter 89. Fast-Fish and Loose-Fish

The allusion to the waif and waif-poles in the last chapter but one, necessitates some account of the laws and regulations of the whale fishery, of which the waif may be deemed the grand symbol and badge.

It frequently happens that when several ships are cruising in company, a whale may be struck by one vessel, then escape, and be finally killed and captured by another vessel; and herein are indirectly comprised many minor contingencies, all partaking of this one grand feature. For example,—after a weary and perilous chase and capture of a whale, the body may get loose from the ship by reason of a violent storm; and drifting far away to leeward, be retaken by a second whaler, who, in a calm, snugly tows it alongside, without risk of life or line. Thus the most vexatious and violent disputes would often arise between the fishermen, were there not some written or unwritten, universal, undisputed law applicable to all cases.

Perhaps the only formal whaling code authorized by legislative enactment, was that of Holland. It was decreed by the States-General in A.D. 1695. But though no other nation has ever had any written whaling law, yet the American fishermen have been their own legislators and lawyers in this matter. They have provided a system which for terse comprehensiveness surpasses Justinian's Pandects and the By-laws of the Chinese Society for the Suppression of Meddling with other People's Business.[1] Yes; these laws might be engraven on a

1 *Justinian's Pandects* Fifty books of Roman law, codified and compiled by the emperor Justinian I (c. 482–565); *By-laws … Business* An invention of Melville's.

Queen Anne's farthing,[1] or the barb of a harpoon, and worn round the neck, so small are they.

I. A Fast-Fish belongs to the party fast to it.

II. A Loose-Fish is fair game for anybody who can soonest catch it.

But what plays the mischief with this masterly code is the admirable brevity of it, which necessitates a vast volume of commentaries to expound it.

First: What is a Fast-Fish? Alive or dead a fish is technically fast, when it is connected with an occupied ship or boat, by any medium at all controllable by the occupant or occupants,—a mast, an oar, a nine-inch cable, a telegraph wire, or a strand of cobweb, it is all the same. Likewise a fish is technically fast when it bears a waif, or any other recognised symbol of possession; so long as the party waifing it plainly evince their ability at any time to take it alongside, as well as their intention so to do.

These are scientific commentaries; but the commentaries of the whalemen themselves sometimes consist in hard words and harder knocks—the Coke-upon-Littleton[2] of the fist. True, among the more upright and honorable whalemen allowances are always made for peculiar cases, where it would be an outrageous moral injustice for one party to claim possession of a whale previously chased or killed by another party. But others are by no means so scrupulous.

Some fifty years ago there was a curious case of whale-trover[3] litigated in England, wherein the plaintiffs set forth that after a hard chase of a whale in the Northern seas; and when indeed they (the plaintiffs) had succeeded in harpooning the fish; they were at last, through peril of their lives, obliged to forsake not only their lines, but their boat itself. Ultimately the defendants (the crew of another ship) came up with the whale, struck, killed, seized, and finally appropriated it before the very eyes of the plaintiffs. And when those

1 *Queen Anne's farthing* Farthings were small British coins worth a quarter of a penny; in Queen Anne's reign (1701–14), no farthings were minted, as there were too many already in circulation. Only pattern farthings—those made to test the design—were struck in Queen Anne's reign, making them quite rare.

2 *Coke-upon-Littleton* First volume (of four) of Sir Edward Coke's *Institutes of the Lawes of England* (1628). This first volume covers tenures of property (as well as other areas of law). The work was influential on the founders of the United States and on American jurisprudence.

3 *whale-trover* Law action to recover a stolen whale.

defendants were remonstrated with, their captain snapped his fingers in the plaintiffs' teeth, and assured them that by way of doxology[1] to the deed he had done, he would now retain their line, harpoons, and boat, which had remained attached to the whale at the time of the seizure. Wherefore the plaintiffs now sued for the recovery of the value of their whale, line, harpoons, and boat.

Mr. Erskine was counsel for the defendants; Lord Ellenborough was the judge. In the course of the defence, the witty Erskine went on to illustrate his position, by alluding to a recent crim. con. case,[2] wherein a gentleman, after in vain trying to bridle his wife's viciousness, had at last abandoned her upon the seas of life; but in the course of years, repenting of that step, he instituted an action to recover possession of her. Erskine was on the other side; and he then supported it by saying, that though the gentleman had originally harpooned the lady, and had once had her fast, and only by reason of the great stress of her plunging viciousness, had at last abandoned her; yet abandon her he did, so that she became a loose-fish; and therefore when a subsequent gentleman re-harpooned her, the lady then became that subsequent gentleman's property, along with whatever harpoon might have been found sticking in her.

Now in the present case Erskine contended that the examples of the whale and the lady were reciprocally illustrative of each other.

These pleadings, and the counter pleadings, being duly heard, the very learned judge in set terms decided, to wit,—That as for the boat, he awarded it to the plaintiffs, because they had merely abandoned it to save their lives; but that with regard to the controverted whale, harpoons, and line, they belonged to the defendants; the whale, because it was a Loose-Fish at the time of the final capture; and the harpoons and line because when the fish made off with them, it (the fish) acquired a property in those articles; and hence anybody who afterwards took the fish had a right to them. Now the defendants afterwards took the fish; ergo, the aforesaid articles were theirs.

A common man looking at this decision of the very learned Judge, might possibly object to it. But ploughed up to the primary rock of

---

1 *doxology* Song of praise that concludes the collection of the offering during a church service; the captain is here sealing (confirming the rightness of) his case.

2 *crim. con. case* "Criminal conversation" case (abbreviated "crim. con."), i.e., an adultery case ("conversation" was a common euphemism for sexual intercourse).

the matter, the two great principles laid down in the twin whaling laws previously quoted, and applied and elucidated by Lord Ellenborough in the above cited case; these two laws touching Fast-Fish and Loose-Fish, I say, will, on reflection, be found the fundamentals of all human jurisprudence; for notwithstanding its complicated tracery of sculpture, the Temple of the Law, like the Temple of the Philistines, has but two props to stand on.[1]

Is it not a saying in every one's mouth, Possession is half of the law: that is, regardless of how the thing came into possession? But often possession is the whole of the law. What are the sinews and souls of Russian serfs and Republican slaves[2] but Fast-Fish, whereof possession is the whole of the law? What to the rapacious landlord is the widow's last mite[3] but a Fast-Fish? What is yonder undetected villain's marble mansion with a door-plate for a waif; what is that but a Fast-Fish? What is the ruinous discount which Mordecai, the broker, gets from poor Woebegone, the bankrupt, on a loan to keep Woebegone's family from starvation;[4] what is that ruinous discount but a Fast-Fish? What is the Archbishop of Savesoul's income of £100,000 seized from the scant bread and cheese of hundreds of thousands of broken-backed laborers (all sure of heaven without any of Savesoul's help) what is that globular £100,000 but a Fast-Fish? What are the Duke of Dunder's[5] hereditary towns and hamlets but Fast-Fish? What to that redoubted harpooneer, John Bull,[6] is poor Ireland, but a Fast-Fish? What to that apostolic lancer, Brother

---

1 *Temple of the Philistines ... stand on* In the biblical story of the Israelite hero Samson, the Philistines display Samson in their temple after capturing and blinding him, but Samson uses his God-given strength to break the two pillars supporting the temple's roof, thereby collapsing it and killing all the Philistines as well as himself. See Judges 16.23–30.

2 *Republican slaves* Slaves in a Republic—specifically, the United States.

3 *widow's last mite* See Luke 21.1–4, where Christ teaches that when the poor widow offers her two mites—the small sum of money that is all she can afford—to God, such charity is worth more than all the donations of the rich.

4 *discount* Loan percentage; *Mordecai ... starvation* Melville here employs the anti-Semitic stereotype of the Jewish moneylender who extorts high percentages of interest on a loan of money.

5 *Archbishop of Savesoul ... Duke of Dunder* Inventions of Melville's. "Dunder" refers to the dregs left behind when fermenting molasses to make rum.

6 *John Bull* Traditional personification of England (much like Uncle Sam is in the United States).

Jonathan, is Texas[1] but a Fast-Fish? And concerning all these, is not Possession the whole of the law?

But if the doctrine of Fast-Fish be pretty generally applicable, the kindred doctrine of Loose-Fish is still more widely so. That is internationally and universally applicable.

What was America in 1492 but a Loose-Fish, in which Columbus struck the Spanish standard by way of waifing it for his royal master and mistress? What was Poland to the Czar? What Greece to the Turk? What India to England? What at last will Mexico be to the United States? All Loose-Fish.

What are the Rights of Man and the Liberties of the World but Loose-Fish? What all men's minds and opinions but Loose-Fish? What is the principle of religious belief in them but a Loose-Fish? What to the ostentatious smuggling verbalists are the thoughts of thinkers but Loose-Fish? What is the great globe itself[2] but a Loose-Fish? And what are you, reader, but a Loose-Fish and a Fast-Fish, too?

> [In the chapters omitted here, the *Pequod* meets a French ship, the *Bouton Rose* (the *Rose-bud*) which had hoisted alongside it two "blasted whales"—dead whales found at sea. The *Rose-bud* was thus enveloped in an intolerable stench. One of the whales was dried up, and thus known by Stubb to contain a rare and valuable substance: ambergris, a waxy aromatic substance widely used in the perfume industry. Ambergris is found only in the bodies of sperm whales that have died of a digestive ailment. The captain and crew of the *Rose-bud* were unaware of the potential treasure, and Stubb convinces them to let him tow away the dried up whale, thus securing a substantial amount of money.]

Chapter 93. The Castaway

It was but some few days after encountering the Frenchman, that a most significant event befell the most insignificant of the Pequod's crew; an event most lamentable; and which ended in providing the

1 *Brother Jonathan ... Texas* Reference to President John Tyler (1790–1862), who was determined to annex the Republic of Texas and add another slave state to the South; the annexation was ratified in 1845.

2 *great globe itself* See Shakespeare's *The Tempest* (1610–11), 4.1.141–44: "And like the baseless fabric of this vision, / The cloud-capped towers, the gorgeous palaces, / The solemn temples, the great globe itself— / Yea, all which it inherit—shall dissolve."

sometimes madly merry and predestinated craft with a living and ever accompanying prophecy of whatever shattered sequel might prove her own.

Now, in the whale ship, it is not every one that goes in the boats. Some few hands are reserved called ship-keepers, whose province it is to work the vessel while the boats are pursuing the whale. As a general thing, these ship-keepers are as hardy fellows as the men comprising the boats' crews. But if there happen to be an unduly slender, clumsy, or timorous wight[1] in the ship, that wight is certain to be made a ship-keeper. It was so in the Pequod with the little negro Pippin by nick-name, Pip by abbreviation. Poor Pip! ye have heard of him before; ye must remember his tambourine on that dramatic midnight, so gloomy-jolly.[2]

In outer aspect, Pip and Dough-Boy made a match, like a black pony and a white one, of equal developments, though of dissimilar colour, driven in one eccentric span.[3] But while hapless Dough-Boy was by nature dull and torpid in his intellects, Pip, though over tender-hearted, was at bottom very bright, with that pleasant, genial, jolly brightness peculiar to his tribe; a tribe, which ever enjoy all holidays and festivities with finer, freer relish than any other race. For blacks, the year's calendar should show naught but three hundred and sixty-five Fourth of Julys and New Year's Days. Nor smile so, while I write that this little black was brilliant, for even blackness has its brilliancy; behold yon lustrous ebony, panelled in king's cabinets. But Pip loved life, and all life's peaceable securities; so that the panic-striking business in which he had somehow unaccountably become entrapped, had most sadly blurred his brightness; though, as ere long will be seen, what was thus temporarily subdued in him, in the end was destined to be luridly illumined by strange wild fires, that fictitiously showed him off to ten times the natural lustre with which in his native Tolland County in Connecticut, he had once enlivened

1 *wight* Person.

2 *Poor Pip! ... gloomy-jolly* The incident referred to here takes place in Chapter 40, "Midnight. Forecastle," a chapter structured like a play and consisting solely of dialogue. It records the ships' watch singing and talking together. Pip is forced to play the tambourine, and the chapter ends with Pip's soliloquy, expressing his fears of the white whale. Pip, as a young black person of low rank on the *Pequod*, has good reason to fear whiteness, both of the whale and human variety.

3 *span* Two horses harnessed together. Usually both horses are of similar size and color.

many a fiddler's frolic on the green; and at melodious even-tide, with his gay ha-ha! had turned the round horizon into one star-belled tambourine. So, though in the clear air of day, suspended against a blue-veined neck, the pure-watered diamond drop will healthful glow; yet, when the cunning jeweller would show you the diamond in its most impressive lustre, he lays it against a gloomy ground, and then lights it up, not by the sun, but by some unnatural gases. Then come out those fiery effulgences, infernally superb; then the evil-blazing diamond, once the divinest symbol of the crystal skies, looks like some crown-jewel stolen from the King of Hell. But let us to the story.

It came to pass, that in the ambergris affair Stubb's after-oarsman chanced so to sprain his hand, as for a time to become quite maimed; and, temporarily, Pip was put into his place.

The first time Stubb lowered with him, Pip evinced much nervousness; but happily, for that time, escaped close contact with the whale; and therefore came off not altogether discreditably; though Stubb observing him, took care, afterwards, to exhort him to cherish his courageousness to the utmost, for he might often find it needful.

Now upon the second lowering, the boat paddled upon the whale; and as the fish received the darted iron, it gave its customary rap, which happened, in this instance, to be right under poor Pip's seat. The involuntary consternation of the moment caused him to leap, paddle in hand, out of the boat; and in such a way, that part of the slack whale line coming against his chest, he breasted it overboard with him, so as to become entangled in it, when at last plumping into the water. That instant the stricken whale started on a fierce run, the line swiftly straightened; and presto! poor Pip came all foaming up to the chocks[1] of the boat, remorselessly dragged there by the line, which had taken several turns around his chest and neck.

Tashtego stood in the bows. He was full of the fire of the hunt. He hated Pip for a poltroon.[2] Snatching the boat-knife from its sheath, he suspended its sharp edge over the line, and turning towards Stubb, exclaimed interrogatively, "Cut?" Meantime Pip's blue, choked face plainly looked, Do, for God's sake! All passed in a flash. In less than half a minute, this entire thing happened.

---

1 *chocks* Wooden fittings placed on the boat's railings to guide the whale line.

2 *poltroon* Wretched coward.

"Damn him, cut!" roared Stubb; and so the whale was lost and Pip was saved.

So soon as he recovered himself, the poor little negro was assailed by yells and execrations from the crew. Tranquilly permitting these irregular cursings to evaporate, Stubb then in a plain, business-like, but still half humorous manner, cursed Pip officially; and that done, unofficially gave him much wholesome advice. The substance was, Never jump from a boat, Pip, except—but all the rest was indefinite, as the soundest advice ever is. Now, in general, *Stick to the boat*, is your true motto in whaling; but cases will sometimes happen when *Leap from the boat*, is still better. Moreover, as if perceiving at last that if he should give undiluted conscientious advice to Pip, he would be leaving him too wide a margin to jump in for the future; Stubb suddenly dropped all advice, and concluded with a peremptory command, "Stick to the boat, Pip, or by the Lord, I won't pick you up if you jump; mind that. We can't afford to lose whales by the likes of you; a whale would sell for thirty times what you would, Pip, in Alabama.[1] Bear that in mind, and don't jump any more." Hereby perhaps Stubb indirectly hinted, that though man loved his fellow, yet man is a money-making animal, which propensity too often interferes with his benevolence.

But we are all in the hands of the Gods; and Pip jumped again. It was under very similar circumstances to the first performance; but this time he did not breast out the line; and hence, when the whale started to run, Pip was left behind on the sea, like a hurried traveller's trunk. Alas! Stubb was but too true to his word. It was a beautiful, bounteous, blue day; the spangled sea calm and cool, and flatly stretching away, all round, to the horizon, like gold-beater's skin[2] hammered out to the extremest. Bobbing up and down in that sea, Pip's ebon[3] head showed like a head of cloves. No boat-knife was lifted when he fell so rapidly astern. Stubb's inexorable back was turned upon him; and the whale was winged. In three minutes, a whole mile of shoreless ocean was between Pip and Stubb. Out from the centre of the sea, poor

---

1 *a whale … Alabama* Stubb is comparing the whale's monetary value to that of Pip if he were sold into slavery in Alabama.

2 *gold-beater's skin* Metalsmiths used membranes from ox or calf intestines to separate sheets of gold when beating them thin to create gold leaf.

3 *ebon* I.e., ebony, black.

Pip turned his crisp, curling, black head to the sun, another lonely castaway, though the loftiest and the brightest.

Now, in calm weather, to swim in the open ocean is as easy to the practised swimmer as to ride in a spring-carriage[1] ashore. But the awful lonesomeness is intolerable. The intense concentration of self in the middle of such a heartless immensity, my God! who can tell it? Mark, how when sailors in a dead calm bathe in the open sea—mark how closely they hug their ship and only coast along her sides.

But had Stubb really abandoned the poor little negro to his fate? No; he did not mean to, at least. Because there were two boats in his wake, and he supposed, no doubt, that they would of course come up to Pip very quickly, and pick him up; though, indeed, such considerations towards oarsmen jeopardized through their own timidity, is not always manifested by the hunters in all similar instances; and such instances not unfrequently occur; almost invariably in the fishery, a coward, so called, is marked with the same ruthless detestation peculiar to military navies and armies.

But it so happened, that those boats, without seeing Pip, suddenly spying whales close to them on one side, turned, and gave chase; and Stubb's boat was now so far away, and he and all his crew so intent upon his fish, that Pip's ringed horizon began to expand around him miserably. By the merest chance the ship itself at last rescued him; but from that hour the little negro went about the deck an idiot; such, at least, they said he was. The sea had jeeringly kept his finite body up, but drowned the infinite of his soul. Not drowned entirely, though. Rather carried down alive to wondrous depths, where strange shapes of the unwarped primal world glided to and fro before his passive eyes; and the miser-merman, Wisdom, revealed his hoarded heaps; and among the joyous, heartless, ever-juvenile eternities, Pip saw the multitudinous, God-omnipresent, coral insects, that out of the firmament of waters heaved the colossal orbs. He saw God's foot upon the treadle[2] of the loom, and spoke it; and therefore his shipmates called him mad. So man's insanity is heaven's sense; and wandering from all mortal reason, man comes at last to that celestial thought, which, to reason, is absurd and frantic; and weal[3] or woe, feels then uncompromised, indifferent as his God.

---

1 *spring-carriage* Carriage mounted on springs to absorb shocks from uneven roads.

2 *treadle* Lever worked with the foot to power the loom.

3 *weal* Riches, prosperity.

For the rest, blame not Stubb too hardly. The thing is common in that fishery; and in the sequel of the narrative, it will then be seen what like abandonment befell myself.

Chapter 94. A Squeeze of the Hand

That whale of Stubb's, so dearly purchased, was duly brought to the Pequod's side, where all those cutting and hoisting operations previously detailed, were regularly gone through, even to the baling of the Heidelburgh Tun, or Case.[1]

While some were occupied with this latter duty, others were employed in dragging away the larger tubs, so soon as filled with the sperm; and when the proper time arrived, this same sperm was carefully manipulated ere going to the try-works,[2] of which anon.

It had cooled and crystallized to such a degree, that when, with several others, I sat down before a large Constantine's bath[3] of it, I found it strangely concreted into lumps, here and there rolling about in the liquid part. It was our business to squeeze these lumps back into fluid. A sweet and unctuous duty! No wonder that in old times this sperm was such a favorite cosmetic. Such a clearer! such a sweetener! such a softener! such a delicious mollifier! After having my hands in it for only a few minutes, my fingers felt like eels, and began, as it were, to serpentine and spiralize.

As I sat there at my ease, cross-legged on the deck; after the bitter exertion at the windlass;[4] under a blue tranquil sky; the ship under

1 *Heidelburgh Tun, or Case* A Heidelburgh tun is a huge wine vat located in the castle of Heidelberg, Germany. The current one in the cellar at Heidelberg can hold 57,854 gallons of wine. In Chapter 77, "The Great Heidelburgh Tun," Melville describes the section of the sperm whale's head—the forehead—as a similarly vast container, "one immense honeycomb of oil," which is emptied by the use of buckets lowered into the head on a pole by one of the seamen (Tashtego is the baler in Chapter 78, "Cistern and Buckets").

2 *try-works* System used to boil the oil out of blubber (known as "trying"oil).

3 *Constantine's bath* The complex of thermal baths built by the emperor Constantine I (c. 272–337) was located on Quirinal Hill in Rome; Melville could also be referring to the bath in Helenopolis that Constantine visited near the end of his life in an attempt to revitalize his health (he died shortly afterwards).

4 *bitter exertion at the windlass* The windlass is an instrument used on board a ship to haul an anchor up and down, and also to haul a bucket up and down. Ishmael is likely referring to the work of the sailors who anchored Tashtego while he bailed out the head of the sperm whale.

indolent sail, and gliding so serenely along; as I bathed my hands among those soft, gentle globules of infiltrated tissues, woven almost within the hour; as they richly broke to my fingers, and discharged all their opulence, like fully ripe grapes their wine; as I snuffed up that uncontaminated aroma,—literally and truly, like the smell of spring violets; I declare to you, that for the time I lived as in a musky meadow; I forgot all about our horrible oath; in that inexpressible sperm, I washed my hands and my heart of it; I almost began to credit the old Paracelsan superstition that sperm is of rare virtue in allaying the heat of anger;[1] while bathing in that bath, I felt divinely free from all ill-will, or petulance, or malice, of any sort whatsoever.

Squeeze! squeeze! squeeze! all the morning long; I squeezed that sperm till I myself almost melted into it; I squeezed that sperm till a strange sort of insanity came over me; and I found myself unwittingly squeezing my co-laborers' hands in it, mistaking their hands for the gentle globules. Such an abounding, affectionate, friendly, loving feeling did this avocation beget; that at last I was continually squeezing their hands, and looking up into their eyes sentimentally; as much as to say,—Oh! my dear fellow beings, why should we longer cherish any social acerbities, or know the slightest ill-humor or envy! Come; let us squeeze hands all round; nay, let us all squeeze ourselves into each other; let us squeeze ourselves universally into the very milk and sperm of kindness.

Would that I could keep squeezing that sperm for ever! For now, since by many prolonged, repeated experiences, I have perceived that in all cases man must eventually lower, or at least shift, his conceit of attainable felicity; not placing it anywhere in the intellect or the fancy; but in the wife, the heart, the bed, the table, the saddle, the fire-side, the country; now that I have perceived all this, I am ready to squeeze case eternally. In thoughts of the visions of the night,[2] I

---

1 *Paracelsan ... anger* Paracelsus (c. 1493–1541) was a Swiss alchemist and philosopher. He believed that an emotion such as anger was held not only in the "mind and fist" but would be present in all the organs of the body. Releasing sperm would be, then, a release of anger.

2 *In thoughts ... night* See Job 4.13–17: "In thoughts from the visions of the night, when deep sleep falleth on men, / Fear came upon me, and trembling, which made all my bones to shake. / Then a spirit passed before my face; the hair of my flesh stood up: / It stood still, but I could not discern the form thereof: an image was before mine eyes, there was silence, and I heard a voice saying, / Shall mortal man be more just than God? shall a man be more pure than his maker?"

saw long rows of angels in paradise, each with his hands in a jar of spermaceti.

* * * * * *

Now, while discoursing of sperm, it behooves to speak of other things akin to it, in the business of preparing the sperm whale for the try-works.

First comes white-horse, so called, which is obtained from the tapering part of the fish, and also from the thicker portions of his flukes. It is tough with congealed tendons—a wad of muscle—but still contains some oil. After being severed from the whale, the white-horse is first cut into portable oblongs ere going to the mincer. They look much like blocks of Berkshire marble.[1]

Plum-pudding is the term bestowed upon certain fragmentary parts of the whale's flesh, here and there adhering to the blanket of blubber, and often participating to a considerable degree in its unctuousness. It is a most refreshing, convivial, beautiful object to behold. As its name imports, it is of an exceedingly rich, mottled tint, with a bestreaked snowy and golden ground, dotted with spots of the deepest crimson and purple. It is plums of rubies, in pictures of citron. Spite of reason, it is hard to keep yourself from eating it. I confess, that once I stole behind the foremast to try it. It tasted something as I should conceive a royal cutlet from the thigh of Louis le Gros[2] might have tasted, supposing him to have been killed the first day after the venison season, and that particular venison season contemporary with an unusually fine vintage of the vineyards of Champagne.

There is another substance, and a very singular one, which turns up in the course of this business, but which I feel it to be very puzzling adequately to describe. It is called slobgollion; an appellation original with the whalemen, and even so is the nature of the substance. It is an ineffably oozy, stringy affair, most frequently found in the tubs of sperm, after a prolonged squeezing, and subsequent decanting. I hold it to be the wondrously thin, ruptured membranes of the case, coalescing.

Gurry, so called, is a term properly belonging to right whalemen, but sometimes incidentally used by the sperm fishermen. It desig-

---

1 *Berkshire marble* Marble quarried from the valleys of the Hoosic and Housatonic rivers in the Berkshire mountains of Massachusetts.

2 *Louis le Gros* Louis VI (1081–1137) of France, also known as "Louis the Fat."

nates the dark, glutinous substance which is scraped off the back of the Greenland or right whale, and much of which covers the decks of those inferior souls who hunt that ignoble Leviathan.

Nippers. Strictly this word is not indigenous to the whale's vocabulary. But as applied by whalemen, it becomes so. A whaleman's nipper is a short firm strip of tendinous stuff cut from the tapering part of Leviathan's tail: it averages an inch in thickness, and for the rest, is about the size of the iron part of a hoe. Edgewise moved along the oily deck, it operates like a leathern squilgee; and by nameless blandishments, as of magic, allures along with it all impurities.

But to learn all about these recondite matters, your best way is at once to descend into the blubber-room, and have a long talk with its inmates. This place has previously been mentioned as the receptacle for the blanket-pieces, when stript and hoisted from the whale. When the proper time arrives for cutting up its contents, this apartment is a scene of terror to all tyros, especially by night. On one side, lit by a dull lantern, a space has been left clear for the workmen. They generally go in pairs,—a pike-and-gaff-man and a spade-man. The whaling-pike is similar to a frigate's boarding-weapon of the same name. The gaff is something like a boat-hook. With his gaff, the gaffman hooks on to a sheet of blubber, and strives to hold it from slipping, as the ship pitches and lurches about. Meanwhile, the spade-man stands on the sheet itself, perpendicularly chopping it into the portable horse-pieces.[1] This spade is sharp as hone can make it; the spademan's feet are shoeless; the thing he stands on will sometimes irresistibly slide away from him, like a sledge.[2] If he cuts off one of his own toes, or one of his assistants', would you be very much astonished? Toes are scarce among veteran blubber-room men.

Chapter 95. The Cassock

Had you stepped on board the Pequod at a certain juncture of this post-mortemizing of the whale; and had you strolled forward nigh the windlass, pretty sure am I that you would have scanned with no small curiosity a very strange, enigmatical object, which you would

1 *horse-pieces* Term for large pieces of whale blubber.

2 *sledge* Sleigh.

have seen there, lying along lengthwise in the lee scuppers.[1] Not the wondrous cistern in the whale's huge head; not the prodigy of his unhinged lower jaw; not the miracle of his symmetrical tail; none of these would so surprise you, as half a glimpse of that unaccountable cone,[2]—longer than a Kentuckian is tall, nigh a foot in diameter at the base, and jet-black as Yojo, the ebony idol of Queequeg. And an idol, indeed, it is; or, rather, in old times, its likeness was. Such an idol as that found in the secret groves of Queen Maachah in Judea; and for worshipping which, King Asa, her son, did depose her, and destroyed the idol, and burnt it for an abomination at the brook Kedron, as darkly set forth in the 15th chapter of the First Book of Kings.[3]

Look at the sailor, called the mincer, who now comes along, and assisted by two allies, heavily backs the grandissimus,[4] as the mariners call it, and with bowed shoulders, staggers off with it as if he were a grenadier carrying a dead comrade from the field. Extending it upon the forecastle deck, he now proceeds cylindrically to remove its dark pelt, as an African hunter the pelt of a boa. This done he turns the pelt inside out, like a pantaloon leg; gives it a good stretching, so as almost to double its diameter; and at last hangs it, well spread, in the rigging, to dry. Ere long, it is taken down; when removing some three feet of it, towards the pointed extremity, and then cutting two slits for arm-holes at the other end, he lengthwise slips himself bodily into it. The mincer now stands before you invested in the full canonicals[5] of his calling. Immemorial to all his order, this investiture alone will adequately protect him, while employed in the peculiar functions of his office.

That office consists in mincing the horse-pieces of blubber for the pots; an operation which is conducted at a curious wooden horse,[6]

---

1 *scuppers* Gaps in the ship's side that are level with the deck so water may run off the deck to the sea.

2 *enigmatical object ... unaccountable cone* Ishmael is discussing the penis of the whale.

3 *Queen Maachah ... Kings* See 1 Kings 15.11–13: "And Asa did that which was right in the eyes of the Lord, as did David his father. / And he took away the sodomites out of the land, and removed all the idols that his fathers had made. / And also Maachah his mother, even her he removed from being queen, because she had made an idol in a grove; and Asa destroyed her idol, and burnt it by the brook Kidron."

4 *grandissimus* Latin: most tall, greatest.

5 *canonicals* Items of dress worn by the clergy.

6 *wooden horse* Work bench or work board.

planted endwise against the bulwarks, and with a capacious tub beneath it, into which the minced pieces drop, fast as the sheets from a rapt orator's desk. Arrayed in decent black; occupying a conspicuous pulpit; intent on bible leaves; what a candidate for an archbishoprick,[1] what a lad for a Pope were this mincer![2]

Chapter 99. The Doubloon

Ere now it has been related how Ahab was wont to pace his quarter-deck, taking regular turns at either limit, the binnacle and mainmast; but in the multiplicity of other things requiring narration it has not been added how that sometimes in these walks, when most plunged in his mood, he was wont to pause in turn at each spot, and stand there strangely eyeing the particular object before him. When he halted before the binnacle, with his glance fastened on the pointed needle in the compass, that glance shot like a javelin with the pointed intensity of his purpose; and when resuming his walk he again paused before the mainmast, then, as the same riveted glance fastened upon the riveted gold coin there, he still wore the same aspect of nailed firmness, only dashed with a certain wild longing, if not hopefulness.

But one morning, turning to pass the doubloon, he seemed to be newly attracted by the strange figures and inscriptions stamped on it, as though now for the first time beginning to interpret for himself in some monomaniac way whatever significance might lurk in them. And some certain significance lurks in all things, else all things are little worth, and the round world itself but an empty cipher, except to sell by the cartload, as they do hills about Boston,[3] to fill up some morass in the Milky Way.

---

1 *leaves* Pages; *archbishoprick* An excellent example of the "dick" jokes that suffuse the novel; Melville's idiosyncratic spelling here emphasizes the pun (an "archbishopric" is the land over which an archbishop would be responsible).

2 [Melville's note] Bible leaves! Bible leaves! This is the invariable cry from the mates to the mincer. It enjoins him to be careful, and cut his work into as thin slices as possible, inasmuch as by so doing the business of boiling out the oil is much accelerated, and its quantity considerably increased, besides perhaps improving it in quality.

3 *sell by the cartload ... hills about Boston* The city of Boston expanded its territory through landfill projects (for example the 1856 filling of Back Bay, a tidal marsh that was filled with land carted in from Needham, a hilly town 25 miles outside the city).

Now this doubloon was of purest, virgin gold, raked somewhere out of the heart of gorgeous hills, whence, east and west, over golden sands, the head-waters of many a Pactolus[1] flows. And though now nailed amidst all the rustiness of iron bolts and the verdigris[2] of copper spikes, yet, untouchable and immaculate to any foulness, it still preserved its Quito[3] glow. Nor, though placed amongst a ruthless crew and every hour passed by ruthless hands, and through the livelong nights shrouded with thick darkness which might cover any pilfering approach, nevertheless every sunrise found the doubloon where the sunset left it last. For it was set apart and sanctified to one awe-striking end; and however wanton in their sailor ways, one and all, the mariners revered it as the white whale's talisman. Sometimes they talked it over in the weary watch by night, wondering whose it was to be at last, and whether he would ever live to spend it.

Now those noble golden coins of South America are as medals of the sun and tropic token-pieces. Here palms, alpacas, and volcanoes; sun's disks and stars; ecliptics,[4] horns-of-plenty, and rich banners waving, are in luxuriant profusion stamped; so that the precious gold seems almost to derive an added preciousness and enhancing glories, by passing through those fancy mints, so Spanishly poetic.

It so chanced that the doubloon of the Pequod was a most wealthy example of these things. On its round border it bore the letters, REPUBLICA DEL ECUADOR: QUITO. So this bright coin came from a country planted in the middle of the world, and beneath the great equator, and named after it; and it had been cast midway up the Andes, in the unwaning clime that knows no autumn. Zoned by those letters you saw the likeness of three Andes' summits; from one a flame; a tower on another; on the third a crowing cock; while arching over all was a segment of the partitioned zodiac, the signs all marked with their usual cabalistics, and the keystone[5] sun entering the equinoctial point at Libra.

---

1 *Pactolus* River in Turkey that contained electrum, an alloy of gold and silver, which was used for making coins for the ancient civilization of Lydia.

2 *verdigris* The greenish-blue rust that forms naturally on copper.

3 *Quito* Capital of Ecuador, where the coin was minted.

4 *ecliptics* Conjunctions of the moon and sun when eclipses take place.

5 *cabalistics* Mystical symbols; *keystone* Central, vital.

Before this equatorial coin, Ahab, not unobserved by others, was now pausing.

"There's something ever egotistical in mountain-tops and towers, and all other grand and lofty things; look here,—three peaks as proud as Lucifer. The firm tower, that is Ahab; the volcano, that is Ahab; the courageous, the undaunted, and victorious fowl, that, too, is Ahab; all are Ahab; and this round gold is but the image of the rounder globe, which, like a magician's glass, to each and every man in turn but mirrors back his own mysterious self. Great pains, small gains for those who ask the world to solve them; it cannot solve itself. Methinks now this coined sun wears a ruddy face; but see! aye, he enters the sign of storms,[1] the equinox! and but six months before he wheeled out of a former equinox at Aries! From storm to storm! So be it, then. Born in throes, 'tis fit that man should live in pains and die in pangs! So be it, then! Here's stout stuff for woe to work on. So be it, then."

"No fairy fingers can have pressed the gold, but devil's claws must have left their mouldings there since yesterday," murmured Starbuck to himself, leaning against the bulwarks. "The old man seems to read Belshazzar's awful writing.[2] I have never marked the coin inspectingly. He goes below; let me read. A dark valley between three mighty, heaven-abiding peaks, that almost seem the Trinity, in some faint earthly symbol. So in this vale of Death, God girds us round; and over all our gloom, the sun of Righteousness still shines a beacon and a hope. If we bend down our eyes, the dark vale shows her mouldy soil; but if we lift them, the bright sun meets our glance half way, to cheer. Yet, oh, the great sun is no fixture; and if, at midnight, we would fain snatch some sweet solace from him, we gaze for him in vain! This coin speaks wisely, mildly, truly, but still sadly to me. I will quit it, lest Truth shake me falsely."

---

1 *sign of storms* I.e., Libra. The fall equinox falls in Libra and the spring equinox in Aries; both equinoctial times of year are associated with stormy weather.

2 *Belshazzar's awful writing* In Daniel 5, a disembodied hand writes King Belshazzar's fate on the wall; no astrologer or fortuneteller in the land could decipher it, but the prophet Daniel is called, and he tells Belshazzar that his ungodly ways have been weighed in the balance and found wanting, and that his kingdom will fall. Belshazzar dies that night, and the Median leader Darius takes over the kingdom.

"There now's the old Mogul,"[1] soliloquized Stubb by the try-works, "he's been twigging[2] it; and there goes Starbuck from the same, and both with faces which I should say might be somewhere within nine fathoms long. And all from looking at a piece of gold, which did I have it now on Negro Hill or in Corlaer's Hook,[3] I'd not look at it very long ere spending it. Humph! in my poor, insignificant opinion, I regard this as queer. I have seen doubloons before now in my voyagings; your doubloons of old Spain, your doubloons of Peru, your doubloons of Chili, your doubloons of Bolivia, your doubloons of Popayan;[4] with plenty of gold moidores and pistoles, and joes, and half joes, and quarter joes.[5] What then should there be in this doubloon of the Equator that is so killing wonderful? By Golconda![6] let me read it once. Halloa! here's signs and wonders truly! That, now, is what old Bowditch in his Epitome[7] calls the zodiac, and what my almanac below calls ditto. I'll get the almanac and as I have heard devils can be raised with Daboll's arithmetic, I'll try my hand at raising a meaning out of these queer curvicues here with the Massachusetts calendar.[8] Here's the book. Let's see now. Signs and wonders; and the sun, he's always among 'em. Hem, hem, hem; here they are—here they go—all alive:—Aries, or the Ram; Taurus, or the Bull and Jimimi! here's Gemini himself, or the Twins. Well; the sun he wheels among 'em. Aye, here on the coin he's just crossing the threshold between two

1 *Mogul* The Mughals (or Moguls, as their name was usually rendered in the nineteenth century) were autocratic rulers of a Muslim empire in South Asia that existed from the sixteenth century through to the nineteenth.

2 *twigging* Inspecting.

3 *Negro Hill* Name applied in the nineteenth century to the north slope of Beacon Hill, where sixty-one per cent of the black population of Boston lived. The area was also known for prostitution; *Corlaer's Hook* Neighborhood on the Lower East Side of Manhattan. Known as the Hook to sailors, this area was notorious as a wild place with a large number of prostitutes (it is where the word "hooker" originated).

4 *Popayan* City in Colombia, known for its coin mint.

5 *moidores … quarter joes* These are all names for various types and sizes of gold coins.

6 *Golconda* Place containing riches, such as the famous Indian Golconda diamonds.

7 *Bowditch in his Epitome* Nathaniel Bowditch (1773–1838) was an American mathematician, who wrote a book on navigation known as the *Epitome*.

8 *Daboll's arithmetic* Nathan Daboll's *Complete Schoolmaster's Assistant* (1799) was a common math textbook in America; *curvicues* I.e., curlicues; *Massachusetts calendar* Almanac for Massachusetts, containing a calendar-year of important dates, as well as daily astrological and weather forecasts.

of twelve sitting-rooms[1] all in a ring. Book! you lie there; the fact is, you books must know your places. You'll do to give us the bare words and facts, but we come in to supply the thoughts. That's my small experience, so far as the Massachusetts calendar, and Bowditch's navigator, and Daboll's arithmetic go. Signs and wonders, eh? Pity if there is nothing wonderful in signs, and significant in wonders! There's a clue somewhere; wait a bit; hist—hark! By Jove, I have it! Look you, Doubloon, your zodiac here is the life of man in one round chapter; and now I'll read it off, straight out of the book. Come, Almanack! To begin: there's Aries, or the Ram—lecherous dog,[2] he begets us; then, Taurus, or the Bull—he bumps us the first thing; then Gemini, or the Twins—that is, Virtue and Vice; we try to reach Virtue, when lo! comes Cancer the Crab, and drags us back; and here, going from Virtue, Leo, a roaring Lion, lies in the path—he gives a few fierce bites and surly dabs with his paw; we escape, and hail Virgo, the Virgin! that's our first love; we marry and think to be happy for aye,[3] when pop comes Libra, or the Scales—happiness weighed and found wanting; and while we are very sad about that, Lord! how we suddenly jump, as Scorpio, or the Scorpion, stings us in the rear; we are curing the wound, when whang come the arrows all round; Sagittarius, or the Archer, is amusing himself. As we pluck out the shafts, stand aside! here's the battering-ram, Capricornus, or the Goat; full tilt, he comes rushing, and headlong we are tossed; when Aquarius, or the Water-bearer, pours out his whole deluge and drowns us; and to wind up with Pisces, or the Fishes, we sleep. There's a sermon now, writ in high heaven, and the sun goes through it every year, and yet comes out of it all alive and hearty. Jollily he, aloft there, wheels through toil and trouble; and so, alow here, does jolly Stubb. Oh, jolly's the word for aye! Adieu, Doubloon! But stop; here comes little King-Post; dodge round the try-works, now, and let's hear what he'll have to say. There; he's before it; he'll out with something presently. So, so; he's beginning."

"I see nothing here, but a round thing made of gold, and whoever raises a certain whale, this round thing belongs to him. So, what's all

---

1 *twelve sitting-rooms* Twelve signs of the zodiac.

2 *Aries ... lecherous dog* In Greek and Egyptian mythology (and elsewhere), the ram was associated with sexual prowess.

3 *aye* Ever.

this staring been about? It is worth sixteen dollars, that's true; and at two cents the cigar, that's nine hundred and sixty cigars. I wont smoke dirty pipes like Stubb, but I like cigars, and here's nine hundred and sixty of them; so here goes Flask aloft to spy 'em out."

"Shall I call that wise or foolish, now; if it be really wise it has a foolish look to it; yet, if it be really foolish, then has it a sort of wiseish look to it. But, avast; here comes our old Manxman—the old hearse-driver, he must have been, that is, before he took to the sea. He luffs[1] up before the doubloon; halloa, and goes round on the other side of the mast; why, there's a horse-shoe nailed on that side; and now he's back again; what does that mean? Hark! he's muttering—voice like an old worn-out coffee-mill. Prick ears, and listen!"

"If the White Whale be raised, it must be in a month and a day, when the sun stands in some one of these signs. I've studied signs, and know their marks; they were taught me two score years ago, by the old witch in Copenhagen. Now, in what sign will the sun then be? The horse-shoe sign; for there it is, right opposite the gold. And what's the horse-shoe sign? The lion is the horse-shoe sign—the roaring and devouring lion.[2] Ship, old ship! my old head shakes to think of thee."

"There's another rendering now; but still one text. All sorts of men in one kind of world, you see. Dodge again! here comes Queequeg—all tattooing—looks like the signs of the Zodiac himself. What says the Cannibal? As I live he's comparing notes; looking at his thigh bone; thinks the sun is in the thigh, or in the calf, or in the bowels, I suppose, as the old women talk Surgeon's Astronomy[3] in the back country. And by Jove, he's found something there in the vicinity of his thigh—I guess it's Sagittarius, or the Archer. No: he don't know what to make of the doubloon; he takes it for an old button off some king's trowsers. But, aside again! here comes that ghost-devil, Fedallah; tail coiled out of sight as usual, oakum in the toes of his pumps[4] as usual. What does he say, with that look of his? Ah, only makes a sign to the

---

1 *luffs* Steers into the wind.

2 *devouring lion* I.e., the sign of Leo.

3 *Surgeon's Astronomy* Perhaps a malapropism for James Ferguson's *Astronomical Tables* (1763), more widely known as "Ferguson's Astronomy," a popular introductory book.

4 *oakum* Loose fibers from hemp ropes that have been unwound and separated, often used as a caulking material; *pumps* Shoes.

sign and bows himself; there is a sun on the coin—fire worshipper, depend upon it. Ho! more and more. This way comes Pip—poor boy! would he had died, or I; he's half horrible to me. He too has been watching all of these interpreters—myself included—and look now, he comes to read, with that unearthly idiot face. Stand away again and hear him. Hark!"

"I look, you look, he looks; we look, ye look, they look."

"Upon my soul, he's been studying Murray's Grammar![1] Improving his mind, poor fellow! But what's that he says now—hist!"

"I look, you look, he looks; we look, ye look, they look."

"Why, he's getting it by heart—hist! again."

"I look, you look, he looks; we look, ye look, they look."

"Well, that's funny."

"And I, you, and he; and we, ye, and they, are all bats; and I'm a crow, especially when I stand a'top of this pine tree here. Caw! caw! caw! caw! caw! caw![2] Ain't I a crow? And where's the scare-crow? There he stands; two bones stuck into a pair of old trowsers, and two more poked into the sleeves of an old jacket."

"Wonder if he means me?—complimentary!—poor lad!—I could go hang myself. Any way, for the present, I'll quit Pip's vicinity. I can stand the rest, for they have plain wits; but he's too crazy-witty for my sanity. So, so, I leave him muttering."

"Here's the ship's navel, this doubloon here, and they are all on fire to unscrew it. But, unscrew your navel, and what's the consequence?[3] Then again, if it stays here, that is ugly, too, for when aught's nailed to the mast it's a sign that things grow desperate. Ha, ha! old Ahab! the White Whale; he'll nail ye! This is a pine tree. My father, in old Tolland county, cut down a pine tree once, and found a silver ring grown over in it; some old darkey's wedding ring. How did it get there? And so they'll say in the resurrection, when they come to fish up this old mast, and find a doubloon lodged in it, with bedded oysters for the shaggy

---

1 *I look ... Murray's Grammar* Pip is conjugating the verb "to look"; Lindley Murray's *The English Grammar* (1793) was a commonly used school textbook in America.

2 *Caw! ... caw!* Line from the minstrel song "Old King Crow."

3 *unscrew ... consequence* According to folk legend, if you unscrew your navel your bum falls off.

bark. Oh, the gold! the precious, precious, gold! the green miser'll[1] hoard ye soon! Hish! hish! God goes 'mong the worlds blackberrying. Cook! ho, cook! and cook us! Jenny! hey, hey, hey, hey, hey, Jenny, Jenny! and get your hoe-cake done!"[2]

[In chapters omitted here, the *Pequod* meets a British ship, the *Samuel Enderby*, and Ahab gains news of Moby Dick. The captain of the *Enderby* had lost both an arm and a leg to the white whale the season before and is shocked by Ahab's desire to hunt down Moby Dick.]

Chapter 102. A Bower in the Arsacides[3]

Hitherto, in descriptively treating of the Sperm Whale, I have chiefly dwelt upon the marvels of his outer aspect; or separately and in detail upon some few interior structural features. But to a large and thorough sweeping comprehension of him, it behooves me now to unbutton him still further, and untagging the points of his hose,[4] unbuckling his garters, and casting loose the hooks and the eyes of the joints of his innermost bones, set him before you in his ultimatum;[5] that is to say, in his unconditional skeleton.

But how now, Ishmael? How is it, that you, a mere oarsman in the fishery, pretend to know aught about the subterranean parts of the whale? Did erudite Stubb, mounted upon your capstan, deliver lectures on the anatomy of the Cetacea; and by help of the windlass, hold up a specimen rib for exhibition? Explain thyself, Ishmael. Can you land a full-grown whale on your deck for examination, as a cook dishes a roast-pig? Surely not. A veritable witness have you hitherto been, Ishmael; but have a care how you seize the privilege of Jonah alone; the privilege of discoursing upon the joists and beams; the rafters, ridge-pole, sleepers,[6] and under-pinnings, making up the

---

1 *green miser'll* Davy Jones, the sailors' devil. To drown or be shipwrecked is to be sent to "Davy Jones's locker."

2 *Jenny ... hoe-cake done* Another line from "Old King Crow." A hoecake is a thin cornbread, so named because it was originally baked on the blade of a cotton-field hoe.

3 *Arsacides* Solomon Islands, located northeast of Australia.

4 *untagging ... hose* Untying the laces of his trousers.

5 *ultimatum* Fundamentals.

6 *ridge-pole* Beam running along the roof ridge, to which the rafters are attached; *sleepers* Horizontal support beams used in the floors and walls of buildings.

frame-work of leviathan; and belike of the tallow-vats, dairy-rooms, butteries, and cheeseries in his bowels.

I confess, that since Jonah, few whalemen have penetrated very far beneath the skin of the adult whale; nevertheless, I have been blessed with an opportunity to dissect him in miniature. In a ship I belonged to, a small cub Sperm Whale was once bodily hoisted to the deck for his poke or bag, to make sheaths for the barbs of the harpoons, and for the heads of the lances. Think you I let that chance go, without using my boat-hatchet and jack-knife, and breaking the seal and reading all the contents of that young cub?

And as for my exact knowledge of the bones of the leviathan in their gigantic, full grown development, for that rare knowledge I am indebted to my late royal friend Tranquo, king of Tranque, one of the Arsacides. For being at Tranque, years ago, when attached to the trading-ship Dey of Algiers, I was invited to spend part of the Arsacidean holidays with the lord of Tranque, at his retired palm villa at Pupella; a sea-side glen not very far distant from what our sailors called Bamboo-Town, his capital.

Among many other fine qualities, my royal friend Tranquo, being gifted with a devout love for all matters of barbaric vertù,[1] had brought together in Pupella whatever rare things the more ingenious of his people could invent; chiefly carved woods of wonderful devices, chiselled shells, inlaid spears, costly paddles, aromatic canoes; and all these distributed among whatever natural wonders, the wonder-freighted, tribute-rendering waves had cast upon his shores.

Chief among these latter was a great Sperm Whale, which, after an unusually long raging gale, had been found dead and stranded, with his head against a cocoa-nut tree, whose plumage-like, tufted droopings seemed his verdant jet. When the vast body had at last been stripped of its fathom-deep enfoldings, and the bones become dust dry in the sun, then the skeleton was carefully transported up the Pupella glen, where a grand temple of lordly palms now sheltered it.

The ribs were hung with trophies; the vertebræ were carved with Arsacidean annals, in strange hieroglyphics; in the skull, the priests kept up an unextinguished aromatic flame, so that the mystic head

1 *vertù* Art and rarities.

again sent forth its vapory spout; while, suspended from a bough, the terrific lower jaw vibrated over all the devotees, like the hair-hung sword that so affrighted Damocles.[1]

It was a wondrous sight. The wood was green as mosses of the Icy Glen;[2] the trees stood high and haughty, feeling their living sap; the industrious earth beneath was as a weaver's loom, with a gorgeous carpet on it, whereof the ground-vine tendrils formed the warp and woof, and the living flowers the figures.[3] All the trees, with all their laden branches; all the shrubs, and ferns, and grasses; the message-carrying air; all these unceasingly were active. Through the lacings of the leaves, the great sun seemed a flying shuttle weaving the unwearied verdure. Oh, busy weaver! unseen weaver!—pause!—one word!—whither flows the fabric? what palace may it deck? wherefore all these ceaseless toilings? Speak, weaver!—stay thy hand!—but one single word with thee! Nay—the shuttle flies—the figures float from forth the loom; the freshet-rushing carpet for ever slides away. The weaver-god, he weaves; and by that weaving is he deafened,[4] that he hears no mortal voice; and by that humming, we, too, who look on the loom are deafened; and only when we escape it shall we hear the thousand voices that speak through it. For even so it is in all material factories. The spoken words that are inaudible among the flying spindles; those same words are plainly heard without the walls, bursting from the opened casements. Thereby have villainies been detected. Ah, mortal! then, be heedful; for so, in all this din of the great world's loom, thy subtlest thinkings may be overheard afar.

---

1 *hair-hung sword … Damocles* According to an ancient Greek story, Damocles, an admiring courtier to Dionysius II of Syracuse (c. 397–343 BCE), was so enamored with the power of the king that Dionysius allowed him to take his place for one day. While enjoying the luxuries of wealth, Damocles noticed a sword hung above the throne by a single horsehair. This reminder of the perils of power was enough for Damocles to wish to return to his own status and avoid the dangers of kingship.

2 *Icy Glen* Park near Stockbridge, Massachusetts, known for its rock fissures and deep mosses, and for the persistence of ice in its rocks through to summer. Melville's home, Arrowhead, where he wrote most of *Moby-Dick*, was not far from the park, which is now known as Ice Glen.

3 *figures* Embroidered images.

4 *by that weaving … deafened* The clatter of the loom makes it hard for the weaver to hear what is said to him or her, and it can also, particularly in industrial factories with many looms working at once, eventually cause more permanent deafness. As Melville points out below, the need to speak loudly to each other in a weaving factory means that someone outside a window could hear everything the weavers say to one another.

Now, amid the green, life-restless loom of that Arsacidean wood, the great, white, worshipped skeleton lay lounging—a gigantic idler! Yet, as the ever-woven verdant warp and woof intermixed and hummed around him, the mighty idler seemed the cunning weaver; himself all woven over with the vines; every month assuming greener, fresher verdure; but himself a skeleton. Life folded Death; Death trellised Life; the grim god wived with youthful Life, and begat him curly-headed glories.

Now, when with royal Tranquo I visited this wondrous whale, and saw the skull an altar, and the artificial smoke ascending from where the real jet had issued, I marvelled that the king should regard a chapel as an object of vertù. He laughed. But more I marvelled that the priests should swear that smoky jet of his was genuine. To and fro I paced before this skeleton—brushed the vines aside—broke through the ribs—and with a ball of Arsacidean twine, wandered, eddied long amid its many winding, shaded colonnades and arbors. But soon my line was out; and following it back, I emerged from the opening where I entered. I saw no living thing within; naught was there but bones.

Cutting me a green measuring-rod, I once more dived within the skeleton. From their arrow-slit in the skull, the priests perceived me taking the altitude of the final rib, "How now!" they shouted; "Dar'st thou measure this our god! That's for us." "Aye, priests—well, how long do ye make him, then?" But hereupon a fierce contest rose among them, concerning feet and inches; they cracked each other's sconces with their yard-sticks—the great skull echoed—and seizing that lucky chance, I quickly concluded my own admeasurements.

These admeasurements I now propose to set before you. But first, be it recorded, that, in this matter, I am not free to utter any fancied measurement I please. Because there are skeleton authorities you can refer to, to test my accuracy. There is a Leviathanic Museum, they tell me, in Hull, England, one of the whaling ports of that country, where they have some fine specimens of fin-backs and other whales. Likewise, I have heard that in the museum of Manchester, in New Hampshire, they have what the proprietors call "the only perfect specimen of a Greenland or River Whale in the United States." Moreover, at a place in Yorkshire, England, Burton Constable by name, a certain Sir Clifford Constable has in his possession the skeleton of a

Sperm Whale, but of moderate size, by no means of the full-grown magnitude of my friend King Tranquo's.

In both cases, the stranded whales to which these two skeletons belonged, were originally claimed by their proprietors upon similar grounds. King Tranquo seizing his because he wanted it; and Sir Clifford, because he was lord of the seignories[1] of those parts. Sir Clifford's whale has been articulated[2] throughout; so that, like a great chest of drawers, you can open and shut him, in all his bony cavities—spread out his ribs like a gigantic fan—and swing all day upon his lower jaw. Locks are to be put upon some of his trap-doors and shutters; and a footman will show round future visitors with a bunch of keys at his side. Sir Clifford thinks of charging twopence for a peep at the whispering gallery in the spinal column; threepence to hear the echo in the hollow of his cerebellum; and sixpence for the unrivalled view from his forehead.

The skeleton dimensions I shall now proceed to set down are copied verbatim from my right arm, where I had them tattooed; as in my wild wanderings at that period, there was no other secure way of preserving such valuable statistics. But as I was crowded for space, and wished the other parts of my body to remain a blank page for a poem I was then composing—at least, what untattooed parts might remain—I did not trouble myself with the odd inches; nor, indeed, should inches at all enter into a congenial admeasurement of the whale.

[Ishmael sets out his measurements of the skeleton in the next chapter (omitted here), entitled "Measurement of the Whale's Skeleton," which in length was seventy-two feet long, denoting a whale that in life would have been about ninety feet long.

In following chapters, Starbuck reports to Ahab that there is a leak of the oil stowed in the ship's hold, and the *Pequod* needs to pause on its mission while they find the leak and stop it. Queequeg then falls ill and asks the carpenter to build him a canoe that can serve as his coffin; he then recovers from his illness. The ship encounters a typhoon and survives the storm.]

---

1 *seignories* Lordships, manors. Sir Clifford held rank over the lesser titled landowners in the area.

2 *articulated* Linked by joints and screws.

Chapter 128. The Pequod Meets the Rachel[1]

Next day, a large ship, the Rachel, was descried, bearing directly down upon the Pequod, all her spars thickly clustering with men. At the time the Pequod was making good speed through the water; but as the broad-winged windward stranger shot nigh to her, the boastful sails all fell together as blank bladders that are burst, and all life fled from the smitten hull.

"Bad news; she brings bad news," muttered the old Manxman. But ere her commander, who, with trumpet to mouth, stood up in his boat; ere he could hopefully hail, Ahab's voice was heard.

"Hast seen the White Whale?"

"Aye, yesterday. Have ye seen a whale-boat adrift?"

Throttling his joy, Ahab negatively answered this unexpected question; and would then have fain boarded the stranger, when the stranger captain himself, having stopped his vessel's way, was seen descending her side. A few keen pulls, and his boat-hook soon clinched the Pequod's main-chains, and he sprang to the deck. Immediately he was recognised by Ahab for a Nantucketer he knew. But no formal salutation was exchanged.

"Where was he?—not killed!—not killed!" cried Ahab, closely advancing. "How was it?"

It seemed that somewhat late on the afternoon of the day previous, while three of the stranger's boats were engaged with a shoal of whales, which had led them some four or five miles from the ship; and while they were yet in swift chase to windward, the white hump and head of Moby Dick had suddenly loomed up out of the water, not very far to leeward; whereupon, the fourth rigged boat—a reserved one—had been instantly lowered in chase. After a keen sail before the wind, this fourth boat—the swiftest keeled of all—seemed to have succeeded in fastening—at least, as well as the man at the mast-head could tell anything about it. In the distance he saw the diminished dotted boat; and then a swift gleam of bubbling white water; and after that nothing more; whence it was concluded that the stricken whale must have indefinitely run away with his pursuers, as often happens. There was

1 *The Rachel* See Jeremiah 31.15: "Thus saith the Lord; A voice was heard in Ramah, lamentation, and bitter weeping; Rahel [Rachel] weeping for her children refused to be comforted for her children, because they were not."

some apprehension, but no positive alarm, as yet. The recall signals were placed in the rigging; darkness came on; and forced to pick up her three far to windward boats—ere going in quest of the fourth one in the precisely opposite direction—the ship had not only been necessitated to leave that boat to its fate till near midnight, but, for the time, to increase her distance from it. But the rest of her crew being at last safe aboard, she crowded all sail—stunsail on stunsail—after the missing boat; kindling a fire in her try-pots for a beacon; and every other man aloft on the look-out. But though when she had thus sailed a sufficient distance to gain the presumed place of the absent ones when last seen; though she then paused to lower her spare boats to pull all around her; and not finding anything, had again dashed on; again paused, and lowered her boats; and though she had thus continued doing till daylight; yet not the least glimpse of the missing keel had been seen.

The story told, the stranger Captain immediately went on to reveal his object in boarding the Pequod. He desired that ship to unite with his own in the search; by sailing over the sea some four or five miles apart, on parallel lines, and so sweeping a double horizon, as it were.

"I will wager something now," whispered Stubb to Flask, "that some one in that missing boat wore off that Captain's best coat; mayhap, his watch—he's so cursed anxious to get it back. Who ever heard of two pious whale-ships cruising after one missing whale-boat in the height of the whaling season? See, Flask, only see how pale he looks—pale in the very buttons of his eyes—look—it wasn't the coat—it must have been the—"

"My boy, my own boy is among them. For God's sake—I beg, I conjure"—here exclaimed the stranger Captain to Ahab, who thus far had but icily received his petition. "For eight-and-forty hours let me charter your ship—I will gladly pay for it, and roundly pay for it—if there be no other way—for eight-and-forty hours only—only that—you must, oh, you must, and you *shall* do this thing."

"His son!" cried Stubb, "oh, it's his son he's lost! I take back the coat and watch—what says Ahab? We must save that boy."

"He's drowned with the rest on 'em, last night," said the old Manx sailor standing behind them; "I heard; all of ye heard their spirits."

Now, as it shortly turned out, what made this incident of the Rachel's the more melancholy, was the circumstance, that not only was one of the Captain's sons among the number of the missing boat's crew; but among the number of the other boat's crews, at the same time, but on the other hand, separated from the ship during the dark vicissitudes of the chase, there had been still another son; as that for a time, the wretched father was plunged to the bottom of the cruellest perplexity; which was only solved for him by his chief mate's instinctively adopting the ordinary procedure of a whale-ship in such emergencies, that is, when placed between jeopardized but divided boats, always to pick up the majority first. But the captain, for some unknown constitutional reason, had refrained from mentioning all this, and not till forced to it by Ahab's iciness did he allude to his one yet missing boy; a little lad, but twelve years old, whose father with the earnest but unmisgiving hardihood of a Nantucketer's paternal love, had thus early sought to initiate him in the perils and wonders of a vocation almost immemorially the destiny of all his race. Nor does it unfrequently occur, that Nantucket captains will send a son of such tender age away from them, for a protracted three or four years' voyage in some other ship than their own; so that their first knowledge of a whaleman's career shall be unenervated by any chance display of a father's natural but untimely partiality, or undue apprehensiveness and concern.

Meantime, now the stranger was still beseeching his poor boon of Ahab; and Ahab still stood like an anvil, receiving every shock, but without the least quivering of his own.

"I will not go," said the stranger, "till you say aye to me. Do to me as you would have me do to you[1] in the like case. For you too have a boy, Captain Ahab—though but a child, and nestling safely at home now—a child of your old age[2] too—Yes, yes, you relent; I see it—run, run, men, now, and stand by to square in the yards."

"Avast," cried Ahab—"touch not a rope-yarn"; then in a voice that prolongingly moulded every word—"Captain Gardiner, I will not do it. Even now I lose time. Good-bye, good-bye. God bless ye, man, and may I forgive myself, but I must go. Mr. Starbuck, look at the binnacle watch, and in three minutes from this present instant warn

---

1 *Do to me ... to you* See Matthew 7.12: "Therefore all things whatsoever ye would that men should do to you, do ye even so to them: for this is the law and the prophets."

2 *child of your old age* See Genesis 37.3: "Now Israel loved Joseph more than all his children, because he was the son of his old age: and he made him a coat of many colours."

off all strangers: then brace forward again, and let the ship sail as before."

Hurriedly turning, with averted face, he descended into his cabin, leaving the strange captain transfixed at this unconditional and utter rejection of his so earnest suit. But starting from his enchantment, Gardiner silently hurried to the side; more fell than stepped into his boat, and returned to his ship.

Soon the two ships diverged their wakes; and long as the strange vessel was in view, she was seen to yaw hither and thither at every dark spot, however small, on the sea. This way and that her yards were swung round; starboard and larboard, she continued to tack; now she beat against a head sea; and again it pushed her before it; while all the while, her masts and yards were thickly clustered with men, as three tall cherry trees, when the boys are cherrying among the boughs.

But by her still halting course and winding, woeful way, you plainly saw that this ship that so wept with spray, still remained without comfort. She was Rachel, weeping for her children, because they were not.

Chapter 132. The Symphony

It was a clear steel-blue day. The firmaments of air and sea were hardly separable in that all-pervading azure; only, the pensive air was transparently pure and soft, with a woman's look, and the robust and man-like sea heaved with long, strong, lingering swells, as Samson's chest in his sleep.[1]

Hither, and thither, on high, glided the snow-white wings of small, unspeckled birds; these were the gentle thoughts of the feminine air; but to and fro in the deeps, far down in the bottomless blue, rushed mighty leviathans, sword-fish, and sharks; and these were the strong, troubled, murderous thinkings of the masculine sea.

But though thus contrasting within, the contrast was only in shades and shadows without; those two seemed one; it was only the sex, as it were, that distinguished them.

---

1 *Samson's ... sleep* Samson was one of the Israelite judges in the Book of Judges (see Chapters 13–16), who had superhuman strength. His lover Delilah betrays him for 1,100 silver coins, cutting his hair in his sleep, which was the source of his power. He is then delivered over to the Philistines, who gouge out his eyes and imprison him.

Aloft, like a royal czar and king, the sun seemed giving this gentle air to this bold and rolling sea; even as bride to groom. And at the girdling line of the horizon, a soft and tremulous motion—most seen here at the equator—denoted the fond, throbbing trust, the loving alarms, with which the poor bride gave her bosom away.

Tied up and twisted; gnarled and knotted with wrinkles; haggardly firm and unyielding; his eyes glowing like coals, that still glow in the ashes of ruin; untottering Ahab stood forth in the clearness of the morn; lifting his splintered helmet of a brow to the fair girl's forehead of heaven.

Oh, immortal infancy, and innocency of the azure! Invisible winged creatures that frolic all round us! Sweet childhood of air and sky! how oblivious were ye of old Ahab's close-coiled woe! But so have I seen little Miriam and Martha, laughing-eyed elves, heedlessly gambol around their old sire; sporting with the circle of singed locks which grew on the marge[1] of that burnt-out crater of his brain.

Slowly crossing the deck from the scuttle,[2] Ahab leaned over the side and watched how his shadow in the water sank and sank to his gaze, the more and the more that he strove to pierce the profundity. But the lovely aromas in that enchanted air did at last seem to dispel, for a moment, the cankerous thing in his soul. That glad, happy air, that winsome sky, did at last stroke and caress him; the step-mother world, so long cruel—forbidding—now threw affectionate arms round his stubborn neck, and did seem to joyously sob over him, as if over one, that however wilful and erring, she could yet find it in her heart to save and to bless. From beneath his slouched hat Ahab dropped a tear into the sea; nor did all the Pacific contain such wealth as that one wee drop.

Starbuck saw the old man; saw him, how he heavily leaned over the side; and he seemed to hear in his own true heart the measureless sobbing that stole out of the centre of the serenity around. Careful not to touch him, or be noticed by him, he yet drew near to him, and stood there.

Ahab turned.

"Starbuck!"

---

1 *marge* I.e., margin.

2 *scuttle* Covered square hole that is a means of moving between decks.

"Sir."

"Oh, Starbuck! it is a mild, mild wind, and a mild looking sky. On such a day—very much such a sweetness as this—I struck my first whale—a boy-harpooneer of eighteen! Forty—forty—forty years ago!—ago! Forty years of continual whaling! forty years of privation, and peril, and storm-time! forty years on the pitiless sea! for forty years has Ahab forsaken the peaceful land, for forty years to make war on the horrors of the deep! Aye and yes, Starbuck, out of those forty years I have not spent three ashore. When I think of this life I have led; the desolation of solitude it has been; the masoned, walled-town of a Captain's exclusiveness, which admits but small entrance to any sympathy from the green country without—oh, weariness! heaviness! Guinea-coast slavery[1] of solitary command!—when I think of all this; only half-suspected, not so keenly known to me before—and how for forty years I have fed upon dry salted fare—fit emblem of the dry nourishment of my soul!—when the poorest landsman has had fresh fruit to his daily hand, and broken the world's fresh bread to my mouldy crusts—away, whole oceans away, from that young girl-wife I wedded past fifty, and sailed for Cape Horn the next day, leaving but one dent in my marriage pillow—wife? wife?—rather a widow with her husband alive! Aye, I widowed that poor girl when I married her, Starbuck; and then, the madness, the frenzy, the boiling blood and the smoking brow, with which, for a thousand lowerings old Ahab has furiously, foamingly chased his prey—more a demon than a man!—aye, aye! what a forty years' fool—fool—old fool, has old Ahab been! Why this strife of the chase? why weary, and palsy the arm at the oar, and the iron, and the lance? how the richer or better is Ahab now? Behold. Oh, Starbuck! is it not hard, that with this weary load I bear, one poor leg should have been snatched from under me? Here, brush this old hair aside; it blinds me, that I seem to weep. Locks so grey did never grow but from out some ashes! But do I look very old, so very, very old, Starbuck? I feel deadly faint, bowed, and humped, as though I were Adam, staggering beneath the piled

1 *Guinea-coast slavery* The Bay of Guinea on the West Coast of Africa was where many enslaved West Africans were shipped from to the Americas.

centuries since Paradise.[1] God! God! God!—crack my heart!—stave my brain!—mockery! mockery! bitter, biting mockery of grey hairs, have I lived enough joy to wear ye; and seem and feel thus intolerably old? Close! stand close to me, Starbuck; let me look into a human eye; it is better than to gaze into sea or sky; better than to gaze upon God. By the green land; by the bright hearth-stone! this is the magic glass, man; I see my wife and my child in thine eye. No, no; stay on board, on board!—lower not when I do; when branded Ahab gives chase to Moby Dick. That hazard shall not be thine. No, no! not with the far away home I see in that eye!"

"Oh, my Captain! my Captain! noble soul! grand old heart, after all! why should any one give chase to that hated fish! Away with me! let us fly these deadly waters! let us home! Wife and child, too, are Starbuck's—wife and child of his brotherly, sisterly, play-fellow youth; even as thine, sir, are the wife and child of thy loving, longing, paternal old age! Away! let us away!—this instant let me alter the course! How cheerily, how hilariously, O my Captain, would we bowl on our way to see old Nantucket again! I think, sir, they have some such mild blue days, even as this, in Nantucket."

"They have, they have. I have seen them—some summer days in the morning. About this time—yes, it is his noon nap now—the boy vivaciously wakes; sits up in bed; and his mother tells him of me, of cannibal old me; how I am abroad upon the deep, but will yet come back to dance him again."

"'Tis my Mary, my Mary herself! She promised that my boy, every morning, should be carried to the hill to catch the first glimpse of his father's sail! Yes, yes! no more! it is done! we head for Nantucket! Come, my Captain, study out the course, and let us away! See, see! the boy's face from the window! the boy's hand on the hill!"

But Ahab's glance was averted; like a blighted fruit tree he shook, and cast his last, cindered apple to the soil.

"What is it, what nameless, inscrutable, unearthly thing is it; what cozzening,[2] hidden lord and master, and cruel, remorseless emperor

---

1 *Adam … Paradise* I.e., Ahab feels as Adam did centuries after the Fall from Eden, having suffered and toiled and faced the inevitability of death, while also remembering what it was like to be immortal and innocent. Adam lived to be 930 years old after the Fall. See Genesis 2–5.

2 *cozzening* Deceptive, cheating.

commands me; that against all natural lovings and longings, I so keep pushing, and crowding, and jamming myself on all the time; recklessly making me ready to do what in my own proper, natural heart, I durst not so much as dare? Is Ahab, Ahab? Is it I, God, or who, that lifts this arm? But if the great sun move not of himself; but is as an errand-boy in heaven; nor one single star can revolve, but by some invisible power; how then can this one small heart beat; this one small brain think thoughts; unless God does that beating, does that thinking, does that living, and not I. By heaven, man, we are turned round and round in this world, like yonder windlass, and Fate is the handspike.[1] And all the time, lo! that smiling sky, and this unsounded sea! Look! see yon Albicore![2] who put it into him to chase and fang that flying-fish? Where do murderers go, man! Who's to doom,[3] when the judge himself is dragged to the bar? But it is a mild, mild wind, and a mild looking sky; and the air smells now, as if it blew from a far-away meadow; they have been making hay somewhere under the slopes of the Andes, Starbuck, and the mowers are sleeping among the new-mown hay. Sleeping? Aye, toil we how we may, we all sleep at last on the field. Sleep? Aye, and rust amid greenness; as last year's scythes flung down, and left in the half-cut swaths—Starbuck!"

But blanched to a corpse's hue with despair, the Mate had stolen away.

Ahab crossed the deck to gaze over on the other side; but started at two reflected, fixed eyes in the water there. Fedallah was motionlessly leaning over the same rail.

[In the chapters omitted here, Moby Dick is seen and the boats—excepting Starbuck's—give chase. On the first day of the chase, Moby Dick bites Ahab's boat in two. The crews survive, but Moby Dick's fierce attack is seen as an ill omen. On the second day, all three boats are wrecked by Moby Dick, and Fedallah is entangled in the whale lines and dragged under the sea. Ahab remembers Fedallah's prophecy that he, Fedallah, would be killed first, "but still would be seen again ere I [Ahab] could perish."]

---

1 *handspike* Nautical tool, much like a crowbar, used to help move and shift heavy items, particularly artillery.

2 *Albicore* I.e., the albacore tuna.

3 *doom* Judge.

Chapter 135. The Chase.—Third Day

The morning of the third day dawned fair and fresh, and once more the solitary night-man at the fore-mast-head was relieved by crowds of the daylight look-outs, who dotted every mast and almost every spar.

"D'ye see him?" cried Ahab; but the whale was not yet in sight.

"In his infallible wake, though; but follow that wake, that's all. Helm there; steady, as thou goest, and hast been going. What a lovely day again! were it a new-made world, and made for a summer-house to the angels, and this morning the first of its throwing open to them, a fairer day could not dawn upon that world. Here's food for thought, had Ahab time to think; but Ahab never thinks; he only feels, feels, feels; *that's* tingling enough for mortal man! to think's audacity. God only has that right and privilege. Thinking is, or ought to be, a coolness and a calmness; and our poor hearts throb, and our poor brains beat too much for that. And yet, I've sometimes thought my brain was very calm—frozen calm, this old skull cracks so, like a glass in which the contents turned to ice, and shiver it. And still this hair is growing now; this moment growing, and heat must breed it; but no, it's like that sort of common grass that will grow anywhere, between the earthy clefts of Greenland ice or in Vesuvius lava. How the wild winds blow it; they whip it about me as the torn shreds of split sails lash the tossed ship they cling to. A vile wind that has no doubt blown ere this through prison corridors and cells, and wards of hospitals, and ventilated them, and now comes blowing hither as innocent as fleeces. Out upon it!—it's tainted. Were I the wind, I'd blow no more on such a wicked, miserable world. I'd crawl somewhere to a cave, and slink there. And yet, 'tis a noble and heroic thing, the wind! who ever conquered it? In every fight it has the last and bitterest blow. Run tilting[1] at it, and you but run through it. Ha! a coward wind that strikes stark naked men, but will not stand to receive a single blow. Even Ahab is a braver thing—a nobler thing than *that*. Would now the wind but had a body; but all the things that most exasperate and outrage mortal man, all these things are bodiless, but only bodiless as objects, not as agents. There's a

---

1 *tilting* Charging on horseback with a lance (as in a joust).

most special, a most cunning, oh, a most malicious difference! And yet, I say again, and swear it now, that there's something all glorious and gracious in the wind. These warm Trade Winds, at least, that in the clear heavens blow straight on, in strong and steadfast, vigorous mildness; and veer not from their mark, however the baser currents of the sea may turn and tack, and mightiest Mississippies of the land swift and swerve about, uncertain where to go at last. And by the eternal Poles! these same Trades that so directly blow my good ship on; these Trades, or something like them—something so unchangeable, and full as strong, blow my keeled soul along! To it! Aloft there! What d'ye see?"

"Nothing, sir."

"Nothing! and noon at hand! The doubloon goes a-begging! See the sun! Aye, aye, it must be so. I've oversailed him. How, got the start? Aye, he's chasing *me* now; not I, *him*—that's bad; I might have known it, too. Fool! the lines—the harpoons he's towing. Aye, aye, I have run him by last night. About! about! Come down, all of ye, but the regular look outs! Man the braces!"[1]

Steering as she had done, the wind had been somewhat on the Pequod's quarter, so that now being pointed in the reverse direction, the braced ship sailed hard upon the breeze as she rechurned the cream in her own white wake.

"Against the wind he now steers for the open jaw," murmured Starbuck to himself, as he coiled the new-hauled main-brace upon the rail. "God keep us, but already my bones feel damp within me, and from the inside wet my flesh. I misdoubt me that I disobey my God in obeying him!"

"Stand by to sway me up!" cried Ahab, advancing to the hempen basket.[2] "We should meet him soon."

"Aye, aye, sir," and straightway Starbuck did Ahab's bidding, and once more Ahab swung on high.

A whole hour now passed; gold-beaten out to ages. Time itself now held long breaths with keen suspense. But at last, some three points off the weather bow, Ahab descried the spout again, and instantly

1 *braces* Ropes used for trimming the sails.

2 *basket* Starting in Chapter 130, Ahab began to look out for Moby Dick himself. Unable to climb to the mast-head on account of his leg, he climbs into a basket that is then hauled up by Starbuck to the mast-head and secured.

from the three mast-heads three shrieks went up as if the tongues of fire[1] had voiced it.

"Forehead to forehead I meet thee, this third time, Moby Dick! On deck there!—brace sharper up; crowd her into the wind's eye. He's too far off to lower yet, Mr. Starbuck. The sails shake! Stand over that helmsman with a top-maul! So, so; he travels fast, and I must down. But let me have one more good round look aloft here at the sea; there's time for that. An old, old sight, and yet somehow so young; aye, and not changed a wink since I first saw it, a boy, from the sand-hills of Nantucket! The same!—the same!—the same to Noah as to me. There's a soft shower to leeward. Such lovely leewardings! They must lead somewhere—to something else than common land, more palmy than the palms. Leeward! the white whale goes that way; look to windward, then; the better if the bitterer quarter. But good bye, good bye, old mast-head! What's this?—green? aye, tiny mosses in these warped cracks. No such green weather stains on Ahab's head! There's the difference now between man's old age and matter's. But aye, old mast, we both grow old together; sound in our hulls, though, are we not, my ship? Aye, minus a leg, that's all. By heaven this dead wood has the better of my live flesh every way. I can't compare with it; and I've known some ships made of dead trees outlast the lives of men made of the most vital stuff of vital fathers. What's that he[2] said? he should still go before me, my pilot; and yet to be seen again? But where? Will I have eyes at the bottom of the sea, supposing I descend those endless stairs? and all night I've been sailing from him, wherever he did sink to. Aye, aye, like many more thou told'st direful truth as touching thyself, O Parsee; but, Ahab, there thy shot fell short. Good-bye, mast-head—keep a good eye upon the whale, the while I'm gone. We'll talk to-morrow, nay, to-night, when the white whale lies down there, tied by head and tail."

1 *the tongues of fire* When the Holy Ghost descends on the Apostles at Pentecost and gives them the power of speech, it appears as tongues of fire. See Acts 2.2–4: "And suddenly there came a sound from heaven as of a rushing mighty wind, and it filled all the house where they were sitting. / And there appeared unto them cloven tongues like as of fire, and it sat upon each of them. / And they were all filled with the Holy Ghost, and began to speak with other tongues, as the Spirit gave them utterance."

2 *he* I.e., Fedallah.

He gave the word; and still gazing round him, was steadily lowered through the cloven blue air to the deck.

In due time the boats were lowered; but as standing in his shallop's stern, Ahab just hovered upon the point of the descent, he waved to the mate,—who held one of the tackle-ropes on deck—and bade him pause.

"Starbuck!"

"Sir?"

"For the third time my soul's ship starts upon this voyage, Starbuck."

"Aye, sir, thou wilt have it so."

"Some ships sail from their ports, and ever afterwards are missing, Starbuck!"

"Truth, sir: saddest truth."

"Some men die at ebb tide; some at low water; some at the full of the flood;—and I feel now like a billow that's all one crested comb,[1] Starbuck. I am old;—shake hands with me, man."

Their hands met; their eyes fastened; Starbuck's tears the glue.

"Oh, my captain, my captain!—noble heart—go not—go not!—see, it's a brave man that weeps; how great the agony of the persuasion then!"

"Lower away!"—cried Ahab, tossing the mate's arm from him. "Stand by the crew!"

In an instant the boat was pulling round close under the stern.

"The sharks! the sharks!" cried a voice from the low cabin-window there; "O master, my master, come back!"

But Ahab heard nothing; for his own voice was high-lifted then; and the boat leaped on.

Yet the voice spake true; for scarce had he pushed from the ship, when numbers of sharks, seemingly rising from out the dark waters beneath the hull, maliciously snapped at the blades of the oars, every time they dipped in the water; and in this way accompanied the boat with their bites. It is a thing not uncommonly happening to the whale-boats in those swarming seas; the sharks at times apparently following them in the same prescient way that vultures hover over the

1 *billow … comb* I.e., like a wave that has crested and is about to crash down into the trough.

banners of marching regiments in the east. But these were the first sharks that had been observed by the Pequod since the White Whale had been first descried; and whether it was that Ahab's crew were all such tiger-yellow barbarians, and therefore their flesh more musky to the senses of the sharks—a matter sometimes well known to affect them,—however it was, they seemed to follow that one boat without molesting the others.

"Heart of wrought steel!" murmured Starbuck gazing over the side, and following with his eyes the receding boat—"canst thou yet ring boldly to that sight?—lowering thy keel among ravening sharks, and followed by them, open-mouthed to the chase; and this the critical third day?—For when three days flow together in one continuous intense pursuit; be sure the first is the morning, the second the noon, and the third the evening and the end of that thing—be that end what it may. Oh! my God! what is this that shoots through me, and leaves me so deadly calm, yet expectant,—fixed at the top of a shudder! Future things swim before me, as in empty outlines and skeletons; all the past is somehow grown dim. Mary, girl! thou fadest in pale glories behind me; boy! I seem to see but thy eyes grown wondrous blue. Strangest problems of life seem clearing; but clouds sweep between—Is my journey's end coming? My legs feel faint; like his who has footed it all day. Feel thy heart,—beats it yet? Stir thyself, Starbuck!—stave it off—move, move! speak aloud!—Mast-head there! See ye my boy's hand on the hill?—Crazed;—aloft there!—keep thy keenest eye upon the boats:—mark well the whale!—Ho! again!—drive off that hawk! see! he pecks—he tears the vane"—pointing to the red flag flying at the main-truck[1]—"Ha! he soars away with it!—Where's the old man now? see'st thou that sight, oh Ahab!—shudder, shudder!"

The boats had not gone very far, when by a signal from the mast-heads—a downward pointed arm, Ahab knew that the whale had sounded; but intending to be near him at the next rising, he held on his way a little sideways from the vessel; the becharmed crew maintaining the profoundest silence, as the head-beat waves hammered and hammered against the opposing bow.

1 *main-truck* Cap of wood on the top of the main mast.

"Drive, drive in your nails, oh ye waves! to their uttermost heads drive them in! ye but strike a thing without a lid; and no coffin and no hearse can be mine:—and hemp only can kill me![1] Ha! ha!"

Suddenly the waters around them slowly swelled in broad circles; then quickly upheaved, as if sideways sliding from a submerged berg of ice, swiftly rising to the surface. A low rumbling sound was heard; a subterraneous hum; and then all held their breaths; as bedraggled with trailing ropes, and harpoons, and lances, a vast form shot lengthwise, but obliquely from the sea. Shrouded in a thin drooping veil of mist, it hovered for a moment in the rainbowed air; and then fell swamping back into the deep. Crushed thirty feet upwards, the waters flashed for an instant like heaps of fountains, then brokenly sank in a shower of flakes, leaving the circling surface creamed like new milk round the marble trunk of the whale.

"Give way!" cried Ahab to the oarsmen, and the boats darted forward to the attack; but maddened by yesterday's fresh irons that corroded in him, Moby Dick seemed combinedly possessed by all the angels that fell from heaven. The wide tiers of welded tendons overspreading his broad white forehead, beneath the transparent skin, looked knitted together; as head on, he came churning his tail among the boats; and once more flailed them apart; spilling out the irons and lances from the two mates' boats, and dashing in one side of the upper part of their bows, but leaving Ahab's almost without a scar.

While Daggoo and Queequeg were stopping the strained planks; and as the whale swimming out from them, turned, and showed one entire flank as he shot by them again; at that moment a quick cry went up. Lashed round and round to the fish's back; pinioned in the turns upon turns in which, during the past night, the whale had reeled the involutions of the lines around him, the half torn body of the Parsee was seen; his sable raiment frayed to shreds; his distended eyes turned full upon old Ahab.

The harpoon dropped from his hand.

"Befooled, befooled!"—drawing in a long lean breath—"Aye, Parsee! I see thee again.—Aye, and thou goest before; and this, *this* then is the hearse that thou didst promise. But I hold thee to the last

---

1 *hemp ... me* Another of Fedallah's prophesies. See Chapter 117, "The Whale Watch." Ahab interpreted Fedallah's prophecy to mean he would die on the gallows, and that he was otherwise "immortal on land and on sea."

letter of thy word. Where is the second hearse?[1] Away, mates, to the ship! those boats are useless now; repair them if ye can in time, and return to me; if not, Ahab is enough to die—Down, men! the first thing that but offers to jump from this boat I stand in, that thing I harpoon. Ye are not other men, but my arms and my legs; and so obey me.—Where's the whale? gone down again?"

But he looked too nigh the boat; for as if bent upon escaping with the corpse he bore, and as if the particular place of the last encounter had been but a stage in his leeward voyage, Moby Dick was now again steadily swimming forward; and had almost passed the ship,—which thus far had been sailing in the contrary direction to him, though for the present her headway had been stopped. He seemed swimming with his utmost velocity, and now only intent upon pursuing his own straight path in the sea.

"Oh! Ahab," cried Starbuck, "not too late is it, even now, the third day, to desist. See! Moby Dick seeks thee not. It is thou, thou, that madly seekest him!"

Setting sail to the rising wind, the lonely boat was swiftly impelled to leeward, by both oars and canvas. And at last when Ahab was sliding by the vessel, so near as plainly to distinguish Starbuck's face as he leaned over the rail, he hailed him to turn the vessel about, and follow him, not too swiftly, at a judicious interval. Glancing upwards, he saw Tashtego, Queequeg, and Daggoo, eagerly mounting to the three mast-heads; while the oarsmen were rocking in the two staved boats which had but just been hoisted to the side, and were busily at work in repairing them. One after the other, through the port-holes, as he sped, he also caught flying glimpses of Stubb and Flask, busying themselves on deck among bundles of new irons and lances. As he saw all this; as he heard the hammers in the broken boats; far other hammers seemed driving a nail into his heart. But he rallied. And now marking that the vane or flag was gone from the main-mast-head, he shouted to Tashtego, who had just gained that perch, to descend again for another flag, and a hammer and nails, and so nail it to the mast.

---

1 *hearse that thou didst promise ... second hearse* In Chapter 117, "The Whale Watch," Fedallah gave another prophecy: "I said, old man, that ere thou couldst die on this voyage, two hearses must verily be seen by thee on the sea; the first not made by mortal hands; and the visible wood of the last one must be grown in America."

Whether fagged by the three days' running chase, and the resistance to his swimming in the knotted hamper he bore; or whether it was some latent deceitfulness and malice in him: whichever was true, the White Whale's way now began to abate, as it seemed, from the boat so rapidly nearing him once more; though indeed the whale's last start had not been so long a one as before. And still as Ahab glided over the waves the unpitying sharks accompanied him; and so pertinaciously stuck to the boat; and so continually bit at the plying oars, that the blades became jagged and crunched, and left small splinters in the sea, at almost every dip.

"Heed them not! those teeth but give new rowlocks to your oars. Pull on! 'tis the better rest, the shark's jaw than the yielding water."

"But at every bite, sir, the thin blades grow smaller and smaller!"

"They will last long enough! pull on!—But who can tell"—he muttered—"whether these sharks swim to feast on the whale or on Ahab?—But pull on! Aye, all alive, now—we near him. The helm! take the helm! let me pass,"—and so saying two of the oarsmen helped him forward to the bows of the still flying boat.

At length as the craft was cast to one side, and ran ranging along with the White Whale's flank, he seemed strangely oblivious of its advance—as the whale sometimes will—and Ahab was fairly within the smoky mountain mist, which, thrown off from the whale's spout, curled round his great, Monadnock[1] hump; he was even thus close to him; when, with body arched back, and both arms lengthwise highlifted to the poise, he darted his fierce iron, and his far fiercer curse into the hated whale. As both steel and curse sank to the socket, as if sucked into a morass, Moby Dick sideways writhed; spasmodically rolled his nigh flank against the bow, and, without staving a hole in it, so suddenly canted the boat over, that had it not been for the elevated part of the gunwale to which he then clung, Ahab would once more have been tossed into the sea. As it was, three of the oarsmen—who foreknew not the precise instant of the dart, and were therefore unprepared for its effects—these were flung out; but so fell, that, in an instant two of them clutched the gunwale again, and rising to its level on a combing wave, hurled themselves bodily inboard again; the

---

1 *Monadnock* Mountain in New Hampshire that rises high above all the land surrounding it.

third man helplessly dropping astern, but still afloat and swimming.

Almost simultaneously, with a mighty volition of ungraduated, instantaneous swiftness, the White Whale darted through the weltering sea. But when Ahab cried out to the steersman to take new turns with the line, and hold it so; and commanded the crew to turn round on their seats, and tow the boat up to the mark; the moment the treacherous line felt that double strain and tug, it snapped in the empty air!

"What breaks in me? Some sinew cracks!—'tis whole again; oars! oars! Burst in upon him!"

Hearing the tremendous rush of the sea-crashing boat, the whale wheeled round to present his blank forehead at bay; but in that evolution, catching sight of the nearing black hull of the ship; seemingly seeing in it the source of all his persecutions; bethinking it—it may be—a larger and nobler foe; of a sudden, he bore down upon its advancing prow, smiting his jaws amid fiery showers of foam.

Ahab staggered; his hand smote his forehead. "I grow blind; hands! stretch out before me that I may yet grope my way. Is't night?"

"The whale! The ship!" cried the cringing oarsmen.

"Oars! oars! Slope downwards to thy depths, O sea, that ere it be for ever too late, Ahab may slide this last, last time upon his mark! I see: the ship! the ship! Dash on, my men! Will ye not save my ship?"

But as the oarsmen violently forced their boat through the sledge-hammering seas, the before whale-smitten bow-ends of two planks burst through, and in an instant almost, the temporarily disabled boat lay nearly level with the waves; its half-wading, splashing crew, trying hard to stop the gap and bale out the pouring water.

Meantime, for that one beholding instant, Tashtego's mast-head hammer remained suspended in his hand; and the red flag, half-wrapping him as with a plaid, then streamed itself straight out from him, as his own forward-flowing heart; while Starbuck and Stubb, standing upon the bowsprit beneath, caught sight of the down-coming monster just as soon as he.

"The whale, the whale! Up helm, up helm! Oh, all ye sweet powers of air, now hug me close! Let not Starbuck die, if die he must, in a woman's fainting fit. Up helm, I say—ye fools, the jaw! the jaw! Is this the end of all my bursting prayers? all my life-long fidelities? Oh, Ahab, Ahab, lo, thy work. Steady! helmsman, steady. Nay, nay! Up helm again! He turns to meet us! Oh, his unappeasable brow drives on towards one, whose duty tells him he cannot depart. My God, stand by me now!"

"Stand not by me, but stand under me, whoever you are that will now help Stubb; for Stubb, too, sticks here. I grin at thee, thou grinning whale! Who ever helped Stubb, or kept Stubb awake, but Stubb's own unwinking eye? And now poor Stubb goes to bed upon a mattrass that is all too soft; would it were stuffed with brushwood! I grin at thee, thou grinning whale! Look ye, sun, moon, and stars! I call ye assassins of as good a fellow as ever spouted up his ghost. For all that, I would yet ring glasses with ye, would ye but hand the cup! Oh, oh! oh, oh! thou grinning whale, but there'll be plenty of gulping soon! Why fly ye not, O Ahab! For me, off shoes and jacket to it; let Stubb die in his drawers! A most mouldy and over salted death, though;—cherries! cherries! cherries! Oh, Flask, for one red cherry ere we die!"

"Cherries? I only wish that we were where they grow. Oh, Stubb, I hope my poor mother's drawn my part-pay ere this; if not, few coppers will now come to her, for the voyage is up."

From the ship's bows, nearly all the seamen now hung inactive; hammers, bits of plank, lances, and harpoons, mechanically retained in their hands, just as they had darted from their various employments; all their enchanted eyes intent upon the whale, which from side to side strangely vibrating his predestinating head, sent a broad band of overspreading semicircular foam before him as he rushed. Retribution, swift vengeance, eternal malice were in his whole aspect, and spite of all that mortal man could do, the solid white buttress of his forehead smote the ship's starboard bow, till men and timbers reeled. Some fell flat upon their faces. Like dislodged trucks, the heads of the harpooneers aloft shook on their bull-like necks. Through the breach, they heard the waters pour, as mountain torrents down a flume.[1]

"The ship! The hearse!—the second hearse!" cried Ahab from the boat; "its wood could only be American!"

Diving beneath the settling ship, the whale ran quivering along its keel; but turning under water, swiftly shot to the surface again, far off the other bow, but within a few yards of Ahab's boat, where, for a time, he lay quiescent.

---

1 *flume* Stream.

"I turn my body from the sun. What ho, Tashtego! let me hear thy hammer. Oh! ye three unsurrendered spires of mine; thou uncracked keel; and only god-bullied hull; thou firm deck, and haughty helm, and Pole-pointed prow,—death-glorious ship! must ye then perish, and without me? Am I cut off from the last fond pride of meanest shipwrecked captains? Oh, lonely death on lonely life! Oh, now I feel my topmost greatness lies in my topmost grief. Ho, ho! from all your furthest bounds, pour ye now in, ye bold billows of my whole foregone life, and top this one piled comber[1] of my death! Towards thee I roll, thou all-destroying but unconquering whale; to the last I grapple with thee; from hell's heart I stab at thee; for hate's sake I spit my last breath at thee. Sink all coffins and all hearses to one common pool! and since neither can be mine, let me then tow to pieces, while still chasing thee, though tied to thee, thou damned whale! *Thus*, I give up the spear!"

The harpoon was darted; the stricken whale flew forward; with igniting velocity the line ran through the groove;—ran foul. Ahab stooped to clear it; he did clear it; but the flying turn caught him round the neck, and voicelessly as Turkish mutes bowstring their victim,[2] he was shot out of the boat, ere the crew knew he was gone. Next instant, the heavy eye-splice[3] in the rope's final end flew out of the stark-empty tub, knocked down an oarsman, and smiting the sea, disappeared in its depths.

For an instant, the tranced boat's crew stood still; then turned. "The ship? Great God, where is the ship?" Soon they through dim, bewildering mediums saw her sidelong fading phantom, as in the gaseous Fata Morgana;[4] only the uppermost masts out of water; while fixed by infatuation, or fidelity, or fate, to their once lofty perches, the pagan harpooneers still maintained their sinking lookouts on the sea. And now, concentric circles seized the lone boat itself, and all its crew, and each floating oar, and every lance-pole, and spinning,

---

1 *piled comber* Cresting wave.

2 *Turkish mutes … victim* In the Ottoman Empire, mutes were employed as court assassins, and they used bow-strings to strangle their victims.

3 *eye-splice* Looped end of a rope.

4 *Fata Morgana* Mirage seen above the horizon line; this type of mirage is named after the sorceress Morgan le Fay from Arthurian legend.

animate and inanimate, all round and round in one vortex, carried the smallest chip of the Pequod out of sight.

But as the last whelmings intermixingly poured themselves over the sunken head of the Indian at the mainmast, leaving a few inches of the erect spar yet visible, together with long streaming yards of the flag, which calmly undulated, with ironical coincidings, over the destroying billows they almost touched;—at that instant, a red arm and a hammer hovered backwardly uplifted in the open air, in the act of nailing the flag faster and yet faster to the subsiding spar. A sky-hawk that tauntingly had followed the main-truck downwards from its natural home among the stars, pecking at the flag, and incommoding Tashtego there; this bird now chanced to intercept its broad fluttering wing between the hammer and the wood; and simultaneously feeling that etherial thrill, the submerged savage beneath, in his death-gasp, kept his hammer frozen there; and so the bird of heaven, with archangelic shrieks, and his imperial beak thrust upwards, and his whole captive form folded in the flag of Ahab, went down with his ship, which, like Satan, would not sink to hell till she had dragged a living part of heaven along with her, and helmeted herself with it.

Now small fowls flew screaming over the yet yawning gulf; a sullen white surf beat against its steep sides; then all collapsed, and the great shroud of the sea rolled on as it rolled five thousand years ago.

Epilogue

"And I only am escaped alone to tell thee." Job.[1]

The drama's done. Why then here does any one step forth?—Because one did survive the wreck.

It so chanced, that after the Parsee's disappearance, I was he whom the Fates ordained to take the place of Ahab's bowsman, when that bowsman assumed the vacant post; the same, who, when on the last day the three men were tossed from out of the rocking boat, was dropped astern. So, floating on the margin of the ensuing scene, and in full sight of it, when the half-spent suction of the sunk ship reached me, I was then, but slowly, drawn towards the closing vortex. When I reached it,

1 *And I only … Job* See Job 1.14–19, when four separate messengers come to tell Job about the deaths of all his family and the loss of all his property.

it had subsided to a creamy pool. Round and round, then, and ever contracting towards the button-like black bubble at the axis of that slowly wheeling circle, like another Ixion[1] *I did revolve. Till, gaining that vital centre, the black bubble upward burst; and now, liberated by reason of its cunning spring, and, owing to its great buoyancy, rising with great force, the coffin life-buoy*[2] *shot lengthwise from the sea, fell over, and floated by my side. Buoyed up by that coffin, for almost one whole day and night, I floated on a soft and dirgelike main. The unharming sharks, they glided by as if with padlocks on their mouths; the savage sea-hawks sailed with sheathed beaks. On the second day, a sail drew near, nearer, and picked me up at last. It was the devious-cruising*[3] *Rachel, that in her retracing search after her missing children, only found another orphan.*

—1851

1 *Ixion* After murdering his father-in-law, Ixion was punished by being bound to a fiery wheel that would spin eternally.

2 *coffin life-buoy* The canoe-coffin that Queequeg had built when he was ill. In Chapter 126, "The Life-Buoy," the canoe is made water-tight and replaces the ship's life-buoy (which had been lost).

3 *devious-cruising* Sailing a winding, circuitous course.

In Context

Nineteenth-Century Images of Whales and Whaling

The Essex Struck by a Whale, engraving from *The Mariner's Chronicle*, New Haven: A.B. Wilcox, 1834. Courtesy of the New Bedford Whaling Museum. www.whalingmuseum.org. This is one of the earliest images depicting the *Essex* disaster to be printed in the United States.

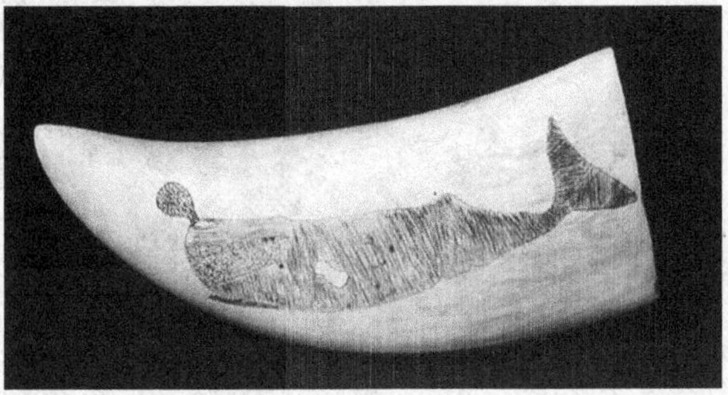

Unknown artist, engraved sperm whale tooth (skrimshander), depicting large sperm whale spouting blood, c. mid-nineteenth century. Accession no. 1977.0127.001. Image courtesy of the Nantucket Historical Association.

William James Linton, 1812–98, *Boats Attacking Whales*, 1830–39. Ref: A-109-046. Alexander Turnbull Library, Wellington, New Zealand. https://natlib.govt.nz/records/22859435. Reproduced with permission.

In the Whale's Jaw, frontispiece from William S. Davis, *Nimrod of the Sea: or, The American Whaleman*, 1874.

There She Blows, illustration from William S. Davis, *Nimrod of the Sea: or, The American Whaleman*, 1874.

Cutting In, illustration from William S. Davis, *Nimrod of the Sea: or, The American Whaleman*, 1874.

The Story of the *Essex*

from Owen Chase, *Narrative of the Most Extraordinary and Distressing Shipwreck of the Whale-Ship* Essex, *of Nantucket; Which Was Attacked and Finally Destroyed by a Large Spermaceti-Whale, in the Pacific Ocean; With an Account of the Unparalleled Sufferings of the Captain and Crew During a Space of Ninety-three Days at Sea, in Open Boats in the Years 1819 & 1820* (1821)[1]

When Melville was cruising for whales on the *Acushnet* in 1841, he met a young man named William Chase, who lent Melville a copy of his father Owen Chase's *Narrative*. The book recounts the wrecking of the whaling ship *Essex*, on which Owen Chase was first mate, by a large sperm whale. Melville was profoundly affected by the book: "The reading of this wondrous story upon the landless sea, and so close to the very latitude of the shipwreck had a surprising effect." Scholars agree that the story of the *Essex* was a key source for the climax of *Moby-Dick*. Melville also mentions the disaster earlier in *Moby-Dick*, in the chapter "The Affidavit," where he cites the *Essex* story as an example of the destructive capacity of sperm whales.

from Chapter 1

The ship Essex, commanded by captain George Pollard, junior, was fitted out at Nantucket, and sailed on the 12th day of August, 1819, for the Pacific Ocean, on a whaling voyage. Of this ship I was first mate. She had lately undergone a thorough repair in her upper works, and was at that time, in all respects, a sound, substantial vessel: she had a crew of twenty-one men, and was victualled[2] and provided for two years and a half. We left the coast of America with a fine breeze, and steered for the Western Islands.[3] … In latitude 1° 0' S. longitude 118° W.[4] on the 16th of November, in

1 Text is based on the first 1821 edition.

2 *victualled* Stored with food and water.

3 *Western Islands* The Azores, an island group 870 miles off the coast of Portugal.

4 *latitude 1° 0' S. longitude 118° W.* In the South Pacific Ocean, about 1,800 miles west of the Galapagos Islands.

the afternoon, we lost a boat during our work in a shoal of whales. I was in the boat myself, with five others, and was standing in the fore part, with the harpoon in my hand, well braced, expecting every instant to catch sight of one of the shoal which we were in, that I might strike; but judge of my astonishment and dismay, at finding myself suddenly thrown up in the air, my companions scattered about me, and the boat fast filling with water. A whale had come up directly under her, and with one dash of his tail, had stove her bottom in, and strewed us in every direction around her. We, however, with little difficulty, got safely on the wreck, and clung there until one of the other boats which had been engaged in the shoal, came to our assistance, and took us off. Strange to tell, not a man was injured by this accident. Thus it happens very frequently in the whaling business, that boats are stove; oars, harpoons, and lines broken; ankles and wrists sprained; boats upset, and whole crews left for hours in the water, without any of these accidents extending to the loss of life. …

from Chapter 2

I have not been able to recur to the scenes which are now to become the subject of description, although a considerable time has elapsed, without feeling a mingled emotion of horror and astonishment at the almost incredible destiny that has preserved me and my surviving companions from a terrible death. Frequently, in my reflections on the subject, even after this lapse of time, I find myself shedding tears of gratitude for our deliverance, and blessing God, by whose divine aid and protection we were conducted through a series of unparalleled suffering and distress, and restored to the bosoms of our families and friends. There is no knowing what a stretch of pain and misery the human mind is capable of contemplating, when it is wrought upon by the anxieties of preservation; nor what pangs and weaknesses the body is able to endure, until they are visited upon it; and when at last deliverance comes, when the dream of hope is realized, unspeakable gratitude takes possession of the soul, and tears of joy choke the utterance. … But I proceed to the recital. On the 20th of November, (cruising in latitude 0° 40' S. longitude 119° 0' W.[1]) a shoal of whales was discovered off the lee-bow.[2] The weather at this time was extremely fine and clear, and it was about 8 o'clock in the morning, that the man at the mast-head[3] gave the usual cry of, "there she blows." The ship was immediately put away,[4] and we ran down in the direction for them. When we had got within half a mile of the place where they were observed, all our boats were lowered down, manned, and we started in pursuit of them. The ship, in the meantime, was brought to the wind, and the main-top-sail hove aback,[5] to wait for us. I had the harpoon in the second boat; the captain preceded me in the first. When I arrived at the spot where we calculated they were, nothing was at first to be seen. We lay on our oars in anxious expectation of discovering them come up somewhere near us. Presently one rose, and spouted a short distance ahead of my boat; I made all speed towards it, came up with, and struck it; feeling the harpoon in him, he threw himself, in an agony, over towards the boat, (which at that time was up alongside of him,) and giving a severe blow with his tail, struck the boat near the edge of the water, amidships, and stove a hole in her. I immediately took up the boat hatchet, and cut the line, to disengage the boat from the whale, which by this time was running off with great velocity. I succeeded in getting clear of him, with the loss of the harpoon and line; and finding the water to pour fast in the boat, I hastily stuffed three or four of our jackets in the hole, ordered one man to keep constantly bailing, and the rest to pull immediately for the ship; we succeeded in keeping the boat free, and shortly gained the ship. The captain and the second mate, in the other two boats, kept up the pursuit, and soon struck another whale. They being at this time a considerable distance to leeward, I went forward, braced around the mainyard,[6] and put the ship off in a direction for them; the boat which had been stove was immediately hoisted in, and after

1 *latitude 0° 40' S. longitude 119° 0' W.* Also in the South Pacific, not far from the previously footnoted location.

2 *lee-bow* Side of the ship's bow that is turned away from the wind.

3 *mast-head* Highest part of the mast, often supplied with a small platform for observation.

4 *put away* Redirected.

5 *main-top-sail hove aback* The sail above the main sail was hauled back, so that the wind would stop propelling the ship.

6 *leeward* The side of a ship facing away from the wind; *mainyard* Wooden support for the ship's biggest sail.

examining the hole, I found that I could, by nailing a piece of canvas over it, get her ready to join in a fresh pursuit, sooner than by lowering down the other remaining boat which belonged to the ship. I accordingly turned her over upon the quarter,[1] and was in the act of nailing on the canvas, when I observed a very large spermaceti whale, as well as I could judge, about eighty-five feet in length; he broke water about twenty rods off our weather-bow,[2] and was lying quietly, with his head in a direction for the ship. He spouted two or three times, and then disappeared. In less than two or three seconds he came up again, about the length of the ship off, and made directly for us, at the rate of about three knots. The ship was then going with about the same velocity. His appearance and attitude gave us at first no alarm; but while I stood watching his movements, and observing him but a ship's length off, coming down for us with great celerity, I involuntarily ordered the boy at the helm to put it hard up; intending to sheer off and avoid him. The words were scarcely out of my mouth, before he came down upon us with full speed, and struck the ship with his head, just forward of the fore-chains;[3] he gave us such an appalling and tremendous jar, as nearly threw us all on our faces. The ship brought up as suddenly and violently as if she had struck a rock, and trembled for a few seconds like a leaf. We looked at each other with perfect amazement, deprived almost of the power of speech. Many minutes elapsed before we were able to realize the dreadful accident; during which time he passed under the ship, grazing her keel as he went along, came up alongside of her to leeward, and lay on the top of the water, (apparently stunned with the violence of the blow,) for the space of a minute; he then suddenly started off, in a direction to leeward. After a few moments' reflection, and recovering, in some measure, from the sudden consternation that had seized us, I of course concluded that he had stove a hole in the ship, and that it would be necessary to set the pumps going. Accordingly they were rigged, but had not been in operation more than one minute, before I perceived the head of the ship to be gradually settling down in the water; I then ordered the signal to be set for the other boats, which,

---

1 *quarter* Upper side of the boat.

2 *rods* A rod is a unit of measurement equivalent to 16.5 feet; *weather-bow* Side of the ship's bow facing the wind.

3 *fore-chains* Tackle that is either near or attached to the mainmast.

scarcely had I dispatched, before I again discovered the whale, apparently in convulsions, on the top of the water, about one hundred rods to leeward. He was enveloped in the foam of the sea, that his continual and violent thrashing about in the water had created around him, and I could distinctly see him smite his jaws together, as if distracted with rage and fury. He remained a short time in this situation, and then started off with great velocity, across the bows of the ship, to windward. By this time the ship had settled down a considerable distance in the water, and I gave her up as lost. I however, ordered the pumps to be kept constantly going, and endeavoured to collect my thoughts for the occasion. I turned to the boats, two of which we then had with the ship, with an intention of clearing them away, and getting all things ready to embark in them, if there should be no other resource left; and while my attention was thus engaged for a moment, I was aroused with the cry of a man at the hatchway, "here he is—he is making for us again." I turned around, and saw him about one hundred rods directly ahead of us, coming down apparently with twice his ordinary speed, and to me at that moment, it appeared with tenfold fury and vengeance in his aspect. The surf flew in all directions about him, and his course towards us was marked by a white foam of a rod in width, which he made with the continual violent thrashing of his tail; his head was about half out of water, and in that way he came upon, and again struck the ship. I was in hopes when I descried him making for us, that by a dexterous movement of putting the ship away immediately, I should be able to cross the line of his approach, before he could get up to us, and thus avoid, what I knew, if he should strike us again, would prove our inevitable destruction. I bawled out to the helmsman, "hard up!" but she had not fallen off more than a point,[1] before we took the second shock. I should judge the speed of the ship to have been at this time about three knots, and that of the whale about six. He struck her to windward, directly under the cathead,[2] and completely stove in her bows. He passed under the ship again, went off to leeward, and we saw no more of him. Our situation at this juncture can be more readily imagined than described. The shock to our feelings was such, as I am sure none can have an

1 *fallen off … point* Shifted more than one interval of navigational direction.

2 *cathead* Beam that stretches horizontally from both sides of a ship's bow.

adequate conception of, that were not there: the misfortune befell us at a moment when we least dreamt of any accident; and from the pleasing anticipations we had formed, of realizing the certain profits of our labour, we were dejected by a sudden, most mysterious, and overwhelming calamity. Not a moment, however, was to be lost in endeavouring to provide for the extremity to which it was now certain we were reduced. We were more than a thousand miles from the nearest land, and with nothing but a light open boat, as the resource of safety for myself and companions. I ordered the men to cease pumping, and everyone to provide for himself; seizing a hatchet at the same time, I cut away the lashings of the spare boat, which lay bottom up, across two spars directly over the quarter deck, and cried out to those near me, to take her as she came down. They did so accordingly, and bore her on their shoulders as far as the waist of the ship. The steward had in the meantime gone down into the cabin twice, and saved two quadrants, two practical navigators,[1] and the captain's trunk and mine; all which were hastily thrown into the boat, as she lay on the deck, with the two compasses which I snatched from the binnacle.[2] He attempted to descend again; but the water by this time had rushed in, and he returned without being able to effect his purpose. By the time we had got the boat to the waist, the ship had filled with water, and was going down on her beam-ends:[3] we shoved our boat as quickly as possible from the plank-shear[4] into the water, all hands jumping in her at the same time, and launched off clear of the ship. We were scarcely two boat's lengths distant from her, when she fell over to windward, and settled down in the water.

Amazement and despair now wholly took possession of us. We contemplated the frightful situation the ship lay in, and thought with horror upon the sudden and dreadful calamity that had overtaken us. We looked upon each other, as if to gather some consolatory sensa-

1 *quadrants* Instruments for taking measurements of angles up to 90 degrees; *practical navigators* Copies of Nathaniel Bowditch's *American Practical Navigator* (1802), a popular navigational text, written so that even those who were untrained could figure out how to plot the course of a ship. The text is continually updated in new editions and continues to be published by the U.S. Government.

2 *binnacle* Box near the helm of a boat where the compasses are kept.

3 *on her beam-ends* I.e., with its deck at a right angle to the water (the ship having heeled over on its side).

4 *plank-shear* Planks covering the gunwale or outer edge of the ship.

tion from an interchange of sentiments, but every countenance was marked with the paleness of despair. Not a word was spoken for several minutes by any of us; all appeared to be bound in a spell of stupid[1] consternation; and from the time we were first attacked by the whale, to the period of the fall of the ship, and of our leaving her in the boat, more than ten minutes could not certainly have elapsed! God only knows in what way, or by what means, we were enabled to accomplish in that short time what we did; the cutting away and transporting the boat from where she was deposited would of itself, in ordinary circumstances, have consumed as much time as that, if the whole ship's crew had been employed in it. My companions had not saved a single article but what they had on their backs; but to me it was a source of infinite satisfaction, if any such could be gathered from the horrors of our gloomy situation, that we had been fortunate enough to have preserved our compasses, navigators, and quadrants. After the first shock of my feelings was over, I enthusiastically contemplated them as the probable instruments of our salvation; without them all would have been dark and hopeless. Gracious God! what a picture of distress and suffering now presented itself to my imagination. The crew of the ship were saved, consisting of twenty human souls. All that remained to conduct these twenty beings through the stormy terrors of the ocean, perhaps many thousand miles, were three open light boats. The prospect of obtaining any provisions or water from the ship, to subsist upon during the time, was at least now doubtful. How many long and watchful nights, thought I, are to be passed? How many tedious days of partial starvation are to be endured, before the least relief or mitigation of our sufferings can be reasonably anticipated? We lay at this time in our boat, about two ship's lengths off from the wreck, in perfect silence, calmly contemplating her situation, and absorbed in our own melancholy reflections, when the other boats were discovered rowing up to us. They had but shortly before discovered that some accident had befallen us, but of the nature of which they were entirely ignorant. The sudden and mysterious disappearance of the ship was first discovered by the boat-steerer in the captain's boat, and with a horror-struck countenance and voice, he suddenly exclaimed, "Oh, my God! where is the ship?" Their operations upon

---

1 *stupid* Insensible, numb.

this were instantly suspended, and a general cry of horror and despair burst from the lips of every man, as their looks were directed for her, in vain, over every part of the ocean. They immediately made all haste towards us. The captain's boat was the first that reached us. He stopped about a boat's length off, but had no power to utter a single syllable: he was so completely overpowered with the spectacle before him, that he sat down in his boat, pale and speechless. I could scarcely recognise his countenance, he appeared to be so much altered, awed, and overcome, with the oppression of his feelings, and the dreadful reality that lay before him. He was in a short time however enabled to address the inquiry to me, "My God, Mr. Chase, what is the matter?" I answered, "We have been stove by a whale." ...

After several hours of idle sorrow and repining I began to reflect upon the accident, and endeavoured to realize by what unaccountable destiny or design, (which I could not at first determine,) this sudden and most deadly attack had been made upon us: by an animal, too, never before suspected of premeditated violence, and proverbial for its insensibility[1] and inoffensiveness. Every fact seemed to warrant me in concluding that it was anything but chance which directed his operations; he made two several[2] attacks upon the ship, at a short interval between them, both of which, according to their direction, were calculated to do us the most injury, by being made ahead, and thereby combining the speed of the two objects for the shock; to effect[3] which, the exact manoeuvres which he made were necessary. His aspect was most horrible, and such as indicated resentment and fury. He came directly from the shoal which we had just before entered, and in which we had struck three of his companions, as if fired with revenge for their sufferings. But to this it may be observed, that the mode of fighting which they always adopt is either with repeated strokes of their tails, or snapping of their jaws together; and that a case, precisely similar to this one, has never been heard of amongst the oldest and most experienced whalers. To this I would answer, that the structure and strength of the whale's head is admirably designed for this mode of attack; the most prominent part of which is almost as hard and as tough as iron; indeed, I can compare it to nothing else but the inside

1 *insensibility* Inability to feel emotion or pain.

2 *several* Distinct.

3 *effect* Accomplish.

of a horse's hoof, upon which a lance or harpoon would not make the slightest impression. The eyes and ears are removed nearly one-third the length of the whole fish, from the front part of the head, and are not in the least degree endangered in this mode of attack. At all events, the whole circumstances taken together, all happening before my own eyes, and producing, at the time, impressions in my mind of decided, calculating mischief, on the part of the whale, (many of which impressions I cannot now recall,) induce me to be satisfied that I am correct in my opinion. It is certainly, in all its bearings, a hitherto unheard of circumstance, and constitutes, perhaps, the most extraordinary one in the annals of the fishery.

Selection of Melville's Letters to Hawthorne, 1851[1]

To Nathaniel Hawthorne, Early May 1851
Pittsfield[2]

My Dear Hawthorne,—I should have been rumbling down to you in my pine-board chariot a long time ago, were it not that for some weeks past I have been more busy than you can well imagine,—out of doors,—building and patching and tinkering away in all directions. Besides, I had my crops to get in,—corn and potatoes (I hope to show you some famous ones by and by),—and many other things to attend to, all accumulating upon this one particular season. I work myself; and at night my bodily sensations are akin to those I have so often felt before, when a hired man, doing my day's work from sun to sun. But I mean to continue visiting you until you tell me that my visits are both supererogatory[3] and superfluous. With no son of man do I stand upon any etiquette or ceremony, except the Christian ones of charity and honesty. I am told, my fellow-man, that there is an aristocracy of the brain. Some men have boldly advocated and asserted it. Schiller[4] seems to have done so, though I don't know much about him. At any rate, it is true that there have been those who, while earnest in behalf of political equality, will accept the intellectual estates.[5] And I can well perceive, I think, how a man of superior mind can, by its intense cultivation, bring himself, as it were, into a certain spontaneous aristocracy of feeling,—exceedingly nice[6] and

1 The texts presented here have been prepared while consulting *The Letters of Herman Melville* (1960), edited by Merrell R. Davis and William H. Gilman, and the Northwestern-Newberry volume, *Correspondence* (1993), edited by Lynn Horth.

2 *Pittsfield* In the Berkshire mountains in western Massachusetts.

3 *supererogatory* More often than is desired.

4 *Schiller* Friedrich Schiller (1759–1805) was an influential German poet, playwright, and philosopher.

5 *those who … intellectual estates* I.e., some people who are staunch advocates of political equality still accept a hierarchy of intellectual capacity. The "estates" were the Estates-General, the hierarchical social order of pre-Revolutionary France (the clergy were the First Estate, the nobility the Second, and the rest of the people the Third).

6 *nice* Refined.

fastidious,—similar to that which, in an English Howard, conveys a torpedo-fish[1] thrill at the slightest contact with a social plebian. So, when you see or hear of my ruthless democracy on all sides, you may possibly feel a touch of a shrink, or something of that sort. It is but nature to be shy of a mortal who boldly declares that a thief in jail is as honorable a personage as Gen. George Washington. This is ludicrous. But Truth is the silliest thing under the sun. Try to get a living by the Truth—and go to the Soup Societies.[2] Heavens! Let any clergyman try to preach the Truth from its very stronghold, the pulpit, and they would ride him out of his church on his own pulpit bannister. It can hardly be doubted that all Reformers are bottomed upon[3] the truth, more or less; and to the world at large are not reformers almost universally laughingstocks? Why so? Truth is ridiculous to men. Thus easily in my room here do I, conceited and garrulous, reverse the test of my Lord Shaftesbury.[4]

It seems an inconsistency to assert unconditional democracy in all things, and yet confess a dislike to all mankind—in the mass. But not so.—But it's an endless sermon,—no more of it. I began by saying that the reason I have not been to Lenox[5] is this,—in the evening I feel completely done up, as the phrase is, and incapable of the long jolting to get to your house and back. In a week or so, I go to New York, to bury myself in a third-story room, and work and slave on my "Whale" while it is driving through the press. *That* is the only way I can finish it now,—I am so pulled hither and thither by circumstances. The calm, the coolness, the silent grass-growing mood in which a man *ought* always to compose,—that, I fear, can seldom be mine. Dollars damn me; and the malicious Devil[6] is forever grinning in upon me, holding the door ajar. My dear Sir, a presentiment is on

---

1 *English Howard* Member of the aristocratic Howard family in England; *torpedo-fish* Another name for an electric ray, which uses an electric discharge to numb prey and defend itself against predators.

2 *Soup Societies* I.e., soup kitchens.

3 *bottomed upon* Founded upon.

4 *test of my Lord Shaftesbury* Anthony Ashley Cooper, the 3rd Earl of Shaftesbury (1671–1713), was a prominent philosopher. In his *Sensus Communis: An Essay on the Freedom of Wit and Humour* (1709), he wrote that one test of truth is that it can survive ridicule.

5 *Lenox* The Hawthorne family lived in Lenox, Massachusetts for eighteen months in 1850–51. Melville's farm in Pittsfield was six miles away.

6 *Devil* Beside its usual meaning, this term can also refer to a printer's young assistant or apprentice.

me,—I shall at last be worn out and perish, like an old nutmeg-grater, grated to pieces by the constant attrition of the wood, that is, the nutmeg. What I feel most moved to write, that is banned,—it will not pay. Yet, altogether, write the *other* way I cannot. So the product is a final hash, and all my books are botches. I'm rather sore, perhaps, in this letter, but see my hand!—four blisters on this palm, made by hoes and hammers within the last few days. It is a rainy morning; so I am indoors, and all work suspended. I feel cheerfully disposed, and therefore I write a little bluely. Would the Gin were here! If ever, my dear Hawthorne, in the eternal times that are to come, you and I shall sit down in Paradise, in some little shady corner by ourselves; and if we shall by any means be able to smuggle a basket of champagne there (I won't believe in a Temperance Heaven[1]), and if we shall then cross our celestial legs in the celestial grass that is forever tropical, and strike our glasses and our heads together, till both musically ring in concert,—then, O my dear fellow-mortal, how shall we pleasantly discourse of all the things manifold which now so distress us,—when all the earth shall be but a reminiscence, yea, its final dissolution an antiquity. Then shall songs be composed as when wars are over; humorous, comic songs,—"Oh, when I lived in that queer little hole called the world," or, "Oh, when I toiled and sweated below," or, "Oh, when I knocked and was knocked in the fight"—yes, let us look forward to such things. Let us swear that, though now we sweat, yet it is because of the dry heat which is indispensable to the nourishment of the vine which is to bear the grapes that are to give us the champagne hereafter.

But I was talking about the "Whale." As the fishermen say, "he's in his flurry"[2] when I left him some three weeks ago. I'm going to take him by his jaw, however, before long, and finish him up in some fashion or other. What's the use of elaborating what, in its very essence, is so short-lived as a modern book? Though I wrote the Gospels in this century, I should die in the gutter.—I talk all about myself, and this is selfishness and egotism. Granted. But how help it? I am writing to you; I know little about you, but something about myself so I write

---

1 *Temperance Heaven* I.e., a heaven that doesn't allow alcohol (the Temperance Movement sought to limit or outlaw the consumption of alcohol).

2 *in his flurry* When applied to whales, this expression means that the whale is in the last burst of agitation before death.

about myself,—at least, to you. Don't trouble yourself, though, about writing; and don't trouble yourself about visiting; and when you *do* visit, don't trouble yourself about talking. I will do all the writing and visiting and talking myself.—By the way, in the last "Dollar Magazine" I read "The Unpardonable Sin."[1] He was a sad fellow, that Ethan Brand. I have no doubt you are by this time responsible for many a shake and tremor of the tribe of "general readers." It is a frightful poetical creed that the cultivation of the brain eats out the heart. But it's my *prose* opinion that in most cases, in those men who have fine brains and work them well, the heart extends down to hams.[2] And though you smoke them with the fire of tribulation, yet, like veritable hams, the head only gives the richer and the better flavor. I stand for the heart. To the dogs with the head! I had rather be a fool with a heart, than Jupiter Olympus[3] with his head. The reason the mass of men fear God, and *at bottom dislike* Him, is because they rather distrust His heart, and fancy Him all brain like a watch. (You perceive I employ a capital initial in the pronoun referring to the Deity; don't you think there is a slight dash of flunkeyism[4] in that usage?) Another thing. I was in New York for four-and-twenty hours the other day, and saw a portrait of N.H. And I have seen and heard many flattering (in a publisher's point of view) allusions to the "Seven Gables."[5] And I have seen "Tales," and "A New Volume" announced,[6] by N.H. So upon the whole, I say to myself, this N.H. is in the ascendant. My dear Sir, they begin to patronize. All Fame is patronage. Let me be infamous: there is no patronage in *that*. What "reputation" H.M. has is horrible. Think of it! To go down to posterity is bad enough, anyway;

---

1 *last ... "The Unpardonable Sin"* Hawthorne's story "The Unpardonable Sin" was published in *Holden's Dollar Magazine* in May 1851.

2 *hams* Backs of the thighs.

3 *Jupiter Olympus* In Roman mythology, Jupiter is the king of the gods, and Mount Olympus is where he dwells.

4 *flunkeyism* Acting like a flunkey, a person who flatters those in higher positions to gain favor.

5 *Seven Gables* Hawthorne's novel *The House of Seven Gables: A Romance* was published in April 1851.

6 *Tales ... announced* Melville is referring to advertisements for upcoming publications; from 17 May to 9 August the publisher Ticknor, Reed & Fields advertised in *Literary World* that they had "in Press ... [a] New Volume of Stories by Hawthorne" and "a new volume by Hawthorne."

but to go down as a "man who lived among the cannibals"![1] When I speak of posterity, in reference to myself, I only mean the babies who will probably be born in the moment immediately ensuing upon my giving up the ghost. I shall go down to some of them, in all likelihood. Typee will be given to them, perhaps, with their gingerbread. I have come to regard this matter of Fame as the most transparent of all vanities. I read Solomon[2] more and more, and every time see deeper and deeper and unspeakable meanings in him. I did not think of Fame, a year ago, as I do now. My development has been all within a few years past. I am like one of those seeds taken out of the Egyptian Pyramids, which, after being three thousand years a seed and nothing but a seed, being planted in English soil, it developed itself, grew to greenness, and then fell to mould.[3] So I. Until I was twenty-five, I had no development at all. From my twenty-fifth year I date my life. Three weeks have scarcely passed, at any time between then and now, that I have not unfolded within myself. But I feel that I am now come to the inmost leaf of the bulb, and that shortly the flower must fall to the mould. It seems to me now that Solomon was the truest man who ever spoke, and yet that he a little *managed* the truth with a view to popular conservatism; or else there have been many corruptions and interpolations of the text.—In reading some of Goethe's sayings, so worshipped by his votaries, I came across this, "*Live in the all.*"[4] That is to say, your separate identity is but a wretched one,—good; but get out of yourself, spread and expand yourself, and bring to yourself the

---

1 *man who lived among the cannibals* Melville is reflecting on his own reputation, which at this time was based on the popularity of his first book, *Typee* (1846), an account of his time living among the Marquesas islanders in 1842. The work made him famous as the "man who lived among the cannibals."

2 *Solomon* King of Israel in the Hebrew Bible (the Old Testament) who was renowned for his wisdom; he is traditionally considered the author of three biblical books: Proverbs, Ecclesiastes, and the Song of Songs. Melville alludes in the previous sentence to a passage in Ecclesiastes 1: "Vanity of vanities, saith the Preacher, vanity of vanities; all is vanity. / What profit hath a man of all his labour which he taketh under the sun?" (2–3).

3 *seeds … mould* Earlier in 1851 the English novelist G.P.R. James (1799–1860) had taken a house in Stockbridge, Massachusetts, where he experimented with farming. He planted some seeds of Egyptian wheat taken from a mummy casket, but while the seeds initially sprouted, they did not thrive.

4 *Goethe* Johann Wolfgang von Goethe (1749–1832) was a German writer and scientist whose works had a profound influence on nineteenth-century European, British, and American literatures; *Live in the all* A partial translation from Goethe's poem "Generalbeichte" (1801), lines 24–25.

tinglings of life that are felt in the flowers and the woods, that are felt in the planets Saturn and Venus, and the Fixed Stars. What nonsense! Here is a fellow with a raging toothache. "My dear boy," Goethe says to him, "you are sorely afflicted with that tooth; but you must *live in the all*, and then you will be happy!" As with all great genius, there is an immense deal of flummery in Goethe, and in proportion to my own contact with him, a monstrous deal of it in me.

H. Melville.

P.S. "Amen!" saith Hawthorne.

N.B. This "all" feeling, though, there is some truth in. You must often have felt it, lying on the grass on a warm summer's day. Your legs seem to send out shoots into the earth. Your hair feels like leaves upon your head. This is the *all* feeling. But what plays the mischief with the truth is that men will insist upon the universal application of a temporary feeling or opinion.

P.S. You must not fail to admire my discretion in paying the postage on this letter.

To Nathaniel Hawthorne, 29 June 1851
Pittsfield

My dear Hawthorne—The clear air and open window invite me to write to you. For some time past I have been so busy with a thousand things that I have almost forgotten when I wrote you last, and whether I received an answer. This most persuasive season has now for weeks recalled me from certain crotchetty and over doleful chimeras,[1] the like of which men like you and me and some others, forming a chain of God's posts round the world, must be content to encounter now and then, and fight them the best way we can. But come they will,—for, in the boundless, trackless, but still glorious wild wilderness through which these outposts run, the Indians do sorely abound, as well as the insignificant but still stinging mosquitoes. Since you have been here, I have been building some shanties of houses (connected with the old one) and likewise some shanties of chapters

1 *chimeras* Imaginary monsters. In Greek mythology, chimeras were fire-breathing creatures with a lion's head, a goat's body, and a serpent's tail.

and essays. I have been plowing and sowing and raising and painting and printing and praying,—and now begin to come out upon a less bustling time, and to enjoy the calm prospect of things from a fair piazza at the north of the old farm house here.

Not entirely yet, though, am I without something to be urgent with. The "Whale" is only half through the press; for, wearied with the long delay of the printers, and disgusted with the heat and dust of the babylonish[1] brick-kiln of New York, I came back to the country to feel the grass—and end the book reclining on it, if I may.—I am sure you will pardon this speaking all about myself, for if I *say* so much on that head, be sure all the rest of the world are thinking about themselves ten times as much. Let us speak, although we show all our faults and weaknesses,—for it is a sign of strength to be weak, to know it, and out with it,—not in set way and ostentatiously, though, but incidentally and without premeditation.—But I am falling into my old foible—preaching. I am busy, but shall not be very long. Come and spend a day here, if you can and want to; if not, stay in Lenox, and God give you long life. When I am quite free of my present engagements, I am going to treat myself to a ride and a visit to you. Have ready a bottle of brandy, because I always feel like drinking that heroic drink when we talk ontological heroics together. This is rather a crazy letter in some respects, I apprehend. If so, ascribe it to the intoxicating effects of the latter end of June operating upon a very susceptible and peradventure feeble temperament.

Shall I send you a fin of the *Whale* by way of a specimen mouthful? The tail is not yet cooked—though the hell-fire in which the whole book is broiled might not unreasonably have cooked it all ere this. This is the book's motto (the secret one),—Ego non baptiso te in nomine[2]—but make out the rest yourself.

H.M.

---

1 *babylonish* Like the city of Babylon, which Christians have long associated with sensuality and evil; the city is personified as the "Whore of Babylon" in the biblical book of Revelation.

2 *Ego ... nomine* Latin: I do not baptize thee in the name [of the father]. In *Moby-Dick*, Ahab asks the three harpooners to join him in a corrupted version of a baptism, dipping the barbs of their harpoons in their own blood, while Ahab utters an altered version of the sacrament in Latin: "Ego non baptize te in nominee patris, sed in nominee diaboli" (I do not baptize you in the name of the father, but in the name of the devil").

To Nathaniel Hawthorne, 17 November 1851
Pittsfield

My Dear Hawthorne,—People think that if a man has undergone any hardship, he should have a reward; but for my part, if I have done the hardest possible day's work, and then come to sit down in a corner and eat my supper comfortably—why, then I don't think I deserve any reward for my hard day's work—for am I not now at peace? Is not my supper good? My peace and my supper are my reward, my dear Hawthorne. So your joy-giving and exultation-breeding letter is not my reward for my ditcher's work[1] with that book, but is the good goddess's bonus over and above what was stipulated—for not one man in five cycles, who is wise, will expect appreciative recognition from his fellows, or any one of them. Appreciation! Recognition! Is love appreciated? Why, ever since Adam,[2] who has got to the meaning of this great allegory—the world? Then we pygmies must be content to have our paper allegories but ill comprehended. I say your appreciation is my glorious gratuity. In my proud, humble way,—a shepherd-king,[3]—I was lord of a little vale in the solitary Crimea; but you have now given me the crown of India. But on trying it on my head, I found it fell down on my ears, notwithstanding their asinine[4] length—for it's only such ears that sustain such crowns.

Your letter was handed me last night on the road going to Mr. Morewood's,[5] and I read it there. Had I been at home, I would have sat down at once and answered it. In me divine magnanimities are spontaneous and instantaneous—catch them while you can. The

---

1 *ditcher's work* I.e., hard, exhausting labor.

2 *ever since Adam* I.e., ever since the beginning of humankind (in the biblical book of Genesis, Adam is the first human created by God).

3 *shepherd-king* Perhaps a reference to the biblical King David, who begins life as a shepherd; perhaps also a reference to the title character in Christopher Marlowe's *Tamburlaine the Great* (1587), who starts off as a shepherd and then conquers a great swath of Asia.

4 *asinine* Donkey-like. Likely also a reference to the character of Bottom in Shakespeare's *A Midsummer Night's Dream* (c. 1595–96). Bottom is a humble artisan who, through fairy magic, is given the head and ears of an ass; the fairy queen, Titania, becomes enraptured by him, and, while the spell lasts, Bottom is treated like a king consort.

5 *Mr. Morewood* John Rowland Morewood (1821–1903) was Melville's neighbor in Pittsfield. Melville was close to John Morewood's wife, Sarah Morewood (1823–63); some have speculated that the two were lovers and that Sarah was one of Melville's motivations for his move to Pittsfield.

world goes round, and the other side comes up. So now I can't write what I felt. But I felt pantheistic then—your heart beat in my ribs and mine in yours, and both in God's. A sense of unspeakable security is in me this moment, on account of your having understood the book. I have written a wicked book, and feel spotless as the lamb. Ineffable socialities are in me. I would sit down and dine with you and all the gods in old Rome's Pantheon.[1] It is a strange feeling—no hopefulness is in it, no despair. Content—that is it; and irresponsibility; but without licentious inclination. I speak now of my profoundest sense of being, not of an incidental feeling.

Whence come you, Hawthorne? By what right do you drink from my flagon of life? And when I put it to my lips—lo, they are yours and not mine. I feel that the Godhead is broken up like the bread at the Supper, and that we are the pieces.[2] Hence this infinite fraternity of feeling. Now, sympathizing with the paper, my angel turns over another page. You did not care a penny for the book. But, now and then as you read, you understood the pervading thought that impelled the book—and that you praised. Was it not so? You were archangel enough to despise the imperfect body, and embrace the soul. Once you hugged the ugly Socrates because you saw the flame in the mouth, and heard the rushing of the demon,—the familiar,[3]—and recognized the sound; for you have heard it in your own solitudes.

My dear Hawthorne, the atmospheric skepticisms steal into me now, and make me doubtful of my sanity in writing you thus. But, believe me, I am not mad, most noble Festus![4] But truth is ever

---

1 *Rome's Pantheon* Ancient Roman temple built c. 113–125 CE; "pantheon" means "common to the gods" or "sacred to the gods"; the temple was surrounded by statues of Roman deities.

2 *Godhead is broken ... pieces* See Matthew 26.26: "And as they were eating, Jesus took bread, and blessed it, and brake it, and gave it to the disciples, and said, Take, eat; this is my body."

3 *hugged the ugly Socrates* The Greek philosopher Socrates (469–399 BCE) was notoriously ugly. In Plato's dialogue *The Symposium* (c. 385–370 BCE), a beautiful young man named Alcibiades relates his failed attempt to seduce Socrates; *demon,—the familiar* In Plato's dialogue *The Apology* (c. 399 BCE), Socrates claims to follow the dictates of his "daimonion" (his "divine something"), a voice that warns him against behaving in immoral ways. Socrates' faith in his "daimonion" resulted in one of the charges for which he was eventually sentenced to death by the state. A "familiar" is a spirit or creature that helps a person, often associated with witches.

4 *I am not mad ... Festus* Porcius Festus was the Roman procurator of Judea from 59 to 62 CE. The Apostle Paul was brought before Festus for trial, which is described in Acts 25–26. Melville here cites Acts 26.24–25: "And as he thus spake for himself, Festus said with a loud voice, Paul, thou art beside thyself; much learning doth make thee mad. / But he

incoherent, and when the big hearts strike together, the concussion is a little stunning. Farewell. Don't write a word about the book. That would be robbing me of my miserly delight. I am heartily sorry I ever wrote anything about you[1]—it was paltry. Lord, when shall we be done growing? As long as we have anything more to do, we have done nothing. So, now, let us add Moby Dick to our blessing, and step from that. Leviathan is not the biggest fish;—I have heard of Krakens.[2]

This is a long letter, but you are not at all bound to answer it. Possibly, if you do answer it, and direct it to Herman Melville, you will missend it—for the very fingers that now guide this pen are not precisely the same that just took it up and put it on this paper. Lord, when shall we be done changing? Ah! it's a long stage, and no inn in sight, and night coming, and the body cold. But with you for a passenger, I am content and can be happy. I shall leave the world, I feel, with more satisfaction for having come to know you. Knowing you persuades me more than the Bible of our immortality.

What a pity, that, for your plain, bluff letter, you should get such gibberish! Mention me to Mrs. Hawthorne and to the children, and so, good-by to you, with my blessing.

Herman.

P.S. I can't stop yet. If the world was entirely made up of Magians,[3] I'll tell you what I should do. I should have a paper-mill established at one end of the house, and so have an endless riband of foolscap[4] rolling in upon my desk; and upon that endless riband I should write a thousand—a million—billion thoughts, all under the form of a letter to you. The divine magnet is on you, and my magnet responds. Which is the biggest? A foolish question—they are *One*.

H.

---

said, I am not mad, most noble Festus; but speak forth the words of truth and soberness."

1 *wrote anything about you* Melville is referring here to his review "Hawthorne and His Mosses" (1850).

2 *Krakens* Enormous sea monsters with a squid- or octopus-like appearance.

3 *Magians* Magicians.

4 *riband of foolscap* Large roll of writing paper.

P.P.S. Don't think that by writing me a letter, you shall always be bored with an immediate reply to it—and so keep both of us delving over a writing-desk eternally. No such thing! I sh'n't always answer your letters, and you may do just as you please.